Songs of Christmas

The Cape Light Novels

CAPE LIGHT

HOME SONG

A GATHERING PLACE

A NEW LEAF

A CHRISTMAS PROMISE

THE CHRISTMAS ANGEL

A CHRISTMAS TO REMEMBER

A CHRISTMAS VISITOR

A CHRISTMAS STAR

A WISH FOR CHRISTMAS

ON CHRISTMAS EVE

CHRISTMAS TREASURES

A SEASON OF ANGELS

SONGS OF CHRISTMAS

The Angel Island Novels

THE INN AT ANGEL ISLAND

THE WEDDING PROMISE

A WANDERING HEART

THE WAY HOME

Thomas Kinkade's Cape Light

Songs of Christmas

KATHERINE SPENCER

B

BERKLEY BOOKS, NEW YORK

THE BERKLEY PUBLISHING GROUP
Published by the Penguin Group
Penguin Group (USA) LLC
375 Hudson Street, New York, New York 10014, USA

USA I Canada I UK I Ireland I Australia I New Zealand I India I South Africa I China

Penguin Books Ltd., Registered Offices: 80 Strand, London WC2R 0RL, England
For more information about the Penguin Group, visit penguin.com.

This book is an original publication of The Berkley Publishing Group.

Library of Congress Cataloging-in-Publication Data

Spencer, Katherine, (date–)
Thomas Kinkade's Cape Light : Songs of Christmas / Katherine Spencer.
pages cm. — (Cape light ; 2)
ISBN 978-0-425-25569-8 (hardback)
1. Cape Light (Imaginary place)—Fiction.   2. Christmas stories.   3. Christian fiction.
I. Kinkade, Thomas, 1958–2012.   II. Title.   III. Title: Cape light.   IV. Title: Songs of Christmas.
PS3553.A489115T46 2013
813'.54—dc23
2013017985

FIRST EDITION: November 2013

PRINTED IN THE UNITED STATES OF AMERICA

10 9 8 7 6 5 4 3 2 1

Cover image: *Victorian Christmas* by Thomas Kinkade copyright © 1991 Thomas Kinkade.
Cover design by Lesley Worrell.

To singers and musicians everywhere—
many in my own life—
who so generously share their gifts
and bring so much joy to others

DEAR READER

Christmas Eve was a magical time for me as child. My parents always hosted a huge Christmas Eve party for our entire family. We had many traditions, including a very long dinner, with many courses, served at a very long table.

Of course, the constant question from the children was: When can we open the presents? Finally, when it seemed no one could stand it anymore—or eat any more—all the guests would be herded into the living room to sit near the Christmas tree, which by then was surrounded with so many gifts, all beautifully wrapped and labeled, that you had to step around the packages to find a chair.

The kids held their breath and tried to sit still and be good. Someone—my grandfather usually—was going to step up and play Santa, calling out the names now, right?

Wrong. First we had to sing Christmas carols. Little booklets were passed around by my mother, who seemed to take special pleasure in the delay.

It is very interesting that now I hardly remember the annual flurry of tearing off wrapping paper and bows that followed the singing. I do remember the songs, all of them, and how our family had a special way of shouting out the "Ho-ho-ho!" in "Jingle Bells." And sang "O Come All Ye Faithful" with such slow, sweet sincerity—although quite off-key.

My mother saved those Christmas carol booklets, and though not all have survived, with the aid of copying machines, we still have a full set, which we take out every Christmas and pass around to our guests . . . to the delight of the adults and the frustration of the younger set.

But I trust that someday they, too, will cherish the memory of singing along with their family, songs of faith and good cheer, the essence and ever-lasting spirit of Christmas that cannot be ordered online or bought in any store.

I hope this story will remind you of the songs and traditions you and yours enjoy at this season and your own cherished Christmas memories.

Katherine Spencer

CHAPTER ONE

THE SCENT OF ROASTING TURKEY AND ALL THE TRIMMINGS filled every corner of the crowded kitchen behind Willough-by's Fine Foods & Catering. It filled Amanda's head, too, like a heavy, rich perfume.

Amanda loved the smell, which announced the holiday as nothing else could. But on this particular Thanksgiving morning, she wasn't roused by the lovely aroma while cuddling under a quilt or two. She was already hard at work in her stepmother's catering shop, and had been there since very early that morning.

Even here, the delicious smell conjured up so many memories—family and friends gathered around a big table, dishes passing from hand to hand. Her father carefully carving. Her sisters and cousins all vying for a chance to break the wishbone, until a concerned adult inevitably stepped in to pick the two lucky opponents. Amanda could still remember the excitement of being chosen.

A mountain of wishes would be inspired by all the turkeys cooked in the big commercial ovens here today, now being packed for delivery. Amanda knew what she would wish for—just a chance to make a living playing her cello.

She had tried hard to do just that for the past few months in New York City, sharing an apartment with friends after finishing a graduate degree at the prestigious Juilliard School. But things had not worked out as she had hoped.

So here she was, back in Cape Light, living at home with her parents and her little sister, Betty. Working in her stepmother's shop, packing about a million pies to go out with the dinner orders.

Amanda was happy to do her task in a quiet corner while the rest of the shop's staff dashed around in a frantic but strangely coordinated ballet, putting finishing touches on the many side dishes, packing containers, and assembling each order. Her stepmother, Molly, in her usual firm but cheerful way, sailed right in, orchestrating the chaos.

"We're doing great, guys. Do we need to make more gravy? I thought that second pot would do it . . ."

Amanda focused on her job as the staff debated the gravy question, as well as a few others.

Finally, Molly flung open the back door, and a gust of cold air swept through the small, hot space. Everyone paused to take a deep, refreshing breath.

Molly glanced at her watch. "Nine fifty a.m., right on schedule. You're the best, all of you." She checked a clipboard as she looked over the packed orders that now stood side by side on the long steel table, the countertops, and even the floor. "Let's load the first van. Sonia can leave with Brian. The route is near your house, Sonia. You can drop off Brian and take the van home when you're done."

"Sounds good. I should get there just in time to take my own bird out of the oven." Sonia, the most senior worker in the shop, grabbed a large box and carried it out to the nearest of the two vans that were parked by the back door. Brian, a kitchen helper who was just out of high school, followed with another box.

"I can help." Amanda came forward and grabbed another box.

"Pink tickets go with Sonia, yellow tickets with us," Molly instructed.

Amanda nodded and checked the ticket on the box she was holding. She also hid her reaction to the news that she and Molly were going to drive around town making deliveries, too. They had arrived at the shop in pitch darkness, and Amanda was still half-asleep now. It had been hard getting out of bed at such an early hour, especially since she had stayed up way past midnight with her stepsisters, Lauren and Jill, who had just gotten home for the holiday. The three sisters hadn't seen one another for months and had tons of catching up to do.

But Molly needed her here this morning, no question. Molly's catering partner, Betty Bowman, was in Chicago, visiting her son and daughter-in-law and her new granddaughter. Molly had been all in favor of Betty's trip, nearly pushing her best friend out the door last weekend. But she had also told Amanda they would have to pick up the slack. That's what it took when you ran your own business.

These past few weeks, Amanda had become reacquainted with her stepmother's steadfast "whatever it takes" attitude, a trait she had come to admire, even envy. Though when Amanda had first met Molly, over ten years ago, she had found many things about her personality more than a little intimidating. Amanda had never met anyone like her.

Amanda's mother had died when she was only eleven; she and her father had moved to Cape Light from Worcester three years later. She had always been shy, and the deep loss caused her to withdraw even more. Even her father had trouble reaching her. But Molly—and her two daughters, Lauren and Jill—had swept into their lives like a force of nature, surrounding both of them with hope and love. Amanda was just coming to see what a gift that had been.

While Molly could be impatient and overly blunt at times, she was also amazingly warm, funny, and forgiving. Amanda knew she would always be pretty much the opposite of her stepmother, but she wouldn't change a thing about her.

She wasn't sure when it had happened, but at some point in her adolescence—not too long after Molly and her father had married—Amanda stopped thinking of Molly as a "step" anything and just called her "Mom" . . . and had made a special place in her heart for her, too.

If only she had inherited some of Molly's genetic material.

Maybe with a bit more of Molly's grit, she wouldn't have been so easily chewed up and spit out by city life and the fierce competition in her field. She would have managed to stick it out until she made a breakthrough. She wouldn't have been so easily defeated.

But I can't look at it that way, she reminded herself. *Listening to these doubting voices in my head won't get me anywhere.* Molly and her father kept reminding her of that. It was her father who finally persuaded her to come home.

"You just need to get a second wind, honey, to regroup and make a new plan. Come home for the holidays. You can still go to auditions and interviews. And you'll have more time to practice without all the pressure of paying the rent for a few months. Come back and let us help you. That's what we're here for."

Amanda knew her father meant well, but coming home to a small town in Massachusetts did feel like a big step backward. She had loved living in New York, having her own apartment, and supporting herself. Even if it meant taking lots of jobs that had nothing to do with music, like temping in an office or waiting tables. But when both of her roommates suddenly needed to move out and Amanda was stuck with the entire rent and utility bills, and a good job she'd been counting on—as a musical accompanist for a well-known dance troupe—failed to come through, she knew it was time to take her parents' advice, give notice on the lease, pack up, and go home.

"One down, one to go." Molly waved cheerfully at Sonia as she drove the first van out of the lot. Amanda waved, too, then followed Molly back into the kitchen.

"We must have made half the turkeys in town today, Mom."

Molly laughed. "If not half, then very close. Hope we can fit the rest in our van." Molly surveyed the boxes that were left. "I really don't want to come back for a second load."

Amanda didn't want to either, but she always tried to do whatever was asked without complaint, just like any other employee. It wasn't easy being the boss's daughter.

They had just started loading the second van when Amanda heard knocking on the front door of the shop. The sound stopped for a moment, then started up again, even louder.

Molly heard it, too. "Can't they see we're closed today? I taped a big sign right in the middle of the door last night. Would someone please tell that person to come back tomorrow?"

"I'll go." Amanda quickly walked through the kitchen and the swinging door that opened into the shop.

She saw a man outside, peering through the panes of glass on the shop door. His hands cupped his eyes for a better view. When he spotted her coming to his rescue, he stepped backed and smiled.

Whoa, cute one, she thought. He was about her age, maybe a few years older. Despite the cold, he wore just a thick sweater and a tweed blazer with a pair of worn jeans. He smiled even wider when she unlocked the door, and the words "We're closed" got stuck in her throat. A breeze tossed his wavy brown hair. His sparkling blue eyes and charming smile were more than distracting.

Amanda was suddenly conscious of her unflattering uniform, lopsided ponytail, and the fact that she had rolled out of bed before dawn and had barely washed her face.

Great. First good-looking guy I've seen around here in weeks, and I look like I've been slaving in a medieval kitchen . . . And I must smell like a roast turkey.

She ducked her head and opened the door a crack. "I'm sorry, the shop is closed today. We're only here to fill the catering orders. There's a sign . . ." She checked the door but realized the sign was missing. Then she noticed it had fluttered to the ground. "Oh, here it is . . . See?" She picked up the sheet of paper and held it out for him to read.

"Oh, right. Sorry to bother you. But all I need is a pie. A pumpkin pie? Or maybe apple? A small pecan? There must be one spare, leftover pie back there . . . somewhere?"

He peered over her shoulder as if he suspected piles of pies were stashed behind the kitchen door. Amanda didn't know what to say. She actually knew that this was true. There were piles of pies back there, and probably at least one spare.

She also knew Molly had told her to shoo him away. But his imploring expression was now as distracting as his smile had been moments before.

Before she could answer, the door to the kitchen opened and Molly appeared. "Amanda? Are you all right out here?"

Amanda turned to her stepmother. "This customer just needs a pie. There are a few extra, aren't there?"

"Any kind would do," he jumped in. "I promised I'd get it here. Otherwise, my mother would have baked it herself." Amanda wasn't surprised. A lot of people said that about Molly's food, especially the bakery items. The shop made everything from scratch with the same recipes and ingredients Molly used at home. "She had so much to do to make dinner, I didn't want her to have to bake, too."

Thoughtful and considerate of his mother, as well? That did seem too good to be true. Amanda wondered if he was making all this up. She glanced at Molly to gauge her reaction. Her stepmother had an infallible baloney detector and could smell a story a mile off.

Molly squinted at him, then finally waved her hand. "Oh, get him a pie, Amanda. For goodness' sake. How about pumpkin? I'm sure we have a few extra in that category."

"Pumpkin would be perfect."

"Okay. I'll be right back." Amanda followed Molly to the kitchen and found a pumpkin pie that was already boxed. "It's twelve dollars, right?"

Molly was flipping through a thick sheaf of orders. "The register is closed. Just give it to him. After that sweet story about his mom and all . . ." She looked up and rolled her eyes, but Amanda could tell she'd been won over. "It *is* Thanksgiving."

"Whatever you say." Molly was so generous. She never missed a chance to share the shop's abundance and her own good fortune.

Amanda pushed through the swinging door again and spotted her customer standing just where she had left him. He met her glance as she walked over, smiling mostly with his eyes.

Amanda presented the box. "Here you are. One pumpkin pie."

"I appreciate this very much. What do I owe you?" He balanced the box in one hand and reached for his wallet with the other.

"No charge. My step . . . I mean, the owner," she quickly corrected herself, "said not to worry about it."

"Are you sure? I'd be happy to pay you double," he added with another disarming smile. "Honestly."

Amanda shook her head. "It's fine. Happy Thanksgiving."

"Thanks. Same to you. You already made my day happy."

He looked down at her a moment as if he wanted to say something more. Then he just smiled, pulled open the door, and walked out.

For goodness' sake . . . it was only a pie. But Amanda couldn't help feeling a little glow. She latched the door, then watched him walk quickly across the street, holding the box with both hands. She was in the kitchen mostly, rarely working out in the shop. Did attractive guys swoop in here all the time? She would have to ask Molly to be assigned to the counter more often.

When Amanda returned to the kitchen, it was much quieter and practically empty. Most of the staff had pulled off their aprons and headed home. The few left were busily cleaning, eager to take off after this last task was done.

The second van stood by the back door, every inch filled with boxes. Molly held the clipboard of orders, along with her keys. "Grab your things, honey. Time to go."

After calling out a few final instructions and good wishes to the lingering crew, Molly jumped behind the steering wheel and started the van. Amanda sat on the passenger's side and quickly fastened her belt. Molly was a good driver, but she was in a hurry, and Amanda knew this could be a wild ride.

A few minutes later, they were navigating the winding streets of Cape Light. Amanda held the list of orders in her lap and kept track of their deliveries, checking off each one. The streets seemed so quiet, with few people out besides dedicated joggers and dog walkers.

After living in the city, the town looked different to her. Even more charming. A perfect New England village, like something out of a travel guide or picture book. She hadn't appreciated it as much while growing up. While she definitely didn't want to be stuck here forever, there was something comforting about the maze of treelined back streets—the rows of old homes, many true Victorians or vintage cottages—so quaint and impervious to change.

Molly had held many jobs before starting the catering business, including driving a taxi and a school bus. She knew every street and crooked, curving lane, and she practically knew all the house numbers of her customers by heart.

When they finally reached the bottom of the list, there were a few boxes left in the van. But those were for their own Thanksgiving dinner.

Molly was making the turkey at home. They had so many people coming, they needed two. But all the side dishes and desserts were coming from the shop.

"If I sell it to other people, it should be good enough for us to eat, too, don't you think?" she had said to the family.

Of course, many of their guests, like her aunt Jessica and Grandma Marie, would bring their own special dishes to the dinner. There was never any lack of food at their family parties, that was for sure.

"Mission accomplished," Molly announced, taking a turn out of the village center toward the development of newer homes where they lived. "Right on schedule, too. I bet you didn't believe me when I said we'd be done by noon, did you?"

"To tell you the truth, when we were all up to our ears in cranberry sauce . . . I did have a few doubts."

Molly laughed and patted her shoulder. "Thanks for helping me today. I love this business most of the time, but the holidays get too crazy. Or I'm getting too old for it, especially with Betty away. I do love having you at the shop right now, sweetie, even though it's just a lily pad for you."

"A lily pad?" Amanda laughed and glanced down at herself. "Did I turn into a toad or something? I know I need a shower."

"You know what I mean. You've been a good sport. But I know working for me is just a temporary thing, a resting spot before you take another leap. Even if you don't find an opening with an orchestra right away, there must be some job around here that suits you better. More related to music, I mean."

"I hope so." Amanda didn't mind icing cakes and making gourmet sandwiches, but she didn't expect to stay at the shop forever either. A job in music, even a temporary one, would be an improvement. Though she had no idea what that job could be. She had studied performance and didn't have a teaching certificate. She'd considered going back to school to get one but dreaded the thought of more classes, papers, and exams. She wasn't even sure she wanted to be a teacher. She wanted to play her cello. She didn't want to just fall into some career path accidentally—or out of desperation. Not yet, anyway.

"Don't worry. Something will turn up." Molly's words cut into her rambling thoughts, as if her stepmother had read her mind. "We want you to just relax and enjoy the family time. I love having all my girls home. Your father does, too. I shouldn't have even brought it up. Me and my big mouth, right?"

Amanda smiled at her. Restraint had never been Molly's strong suit. "It's okay, Mom. I know what you're trying to say."

"Do you, honey? I guess what I really want to say is that I understand that this is a hard time for you. We know how dedicated you are to your music, and we know you feel discouraged right now. But it will all work out. You're so very talented. Anyone can see that. You just need a break. Just one good opportunity. You'll see."

Amanda appreciated her stepmother's words, though she secretly wondered if they were true. She had always believed she had the talent, skill, dedication, and discipline needed to be a professional musician. Lately, though, she'd begun to doubt herself. She always seemed to get so close only to learn that some other cellist had beaten her out for a good job opportunity.

When Amanda didn't answer, Molly glanced at her. "'If a candle will doubt, it will go out.' Someone really famous said that. I just can't remember who it was right now. You don't want to go out, do you?" she asked, her tone half-serious, half-teasing.

Amanda shook her head. "No, that doesn't sound like fun."

"Of course not. You're just getting started." They had reached the house, and Molly steered the van into the driveway. "I had some bleak times before I met your father. I'd been through a horrendous divorce and was supporting Jill and Lauren all on my own. Working two or three jobs at a time, trying to pay the bills *and* be a good mom *and* make something of myself. When I look back, I can see I was usually my own worst enemy."

"But you always tried so hard to get ahead. How were you your own worst enemy?"

"My attitude, sweetheart. I acted very brash, but deep down, I was terrified. My flame was always sputtering."

Amanda laughed at the way Molly described herself. "So don't sputter? Is that what you're trying to tell me?"

"That's right." Molly nodded. "You have all the right stuff, kiddo. No question. Shine on . . . Now, let's get all this food in the house. We'll be over twenty with the neighbors and all the Warwicks coming . . ."

Molly paused and rolled her eyes at the mention of her sister-in-law Jessica's side of the family. Aunt Jessica's sister, Emily Warwick, wasn't the problem. Amanda thought Emily was smart and fun, even though being the mayor of Cape Light all these years gave her a certain air of authority.

It was Jessica and Emily's mother, Lillian Warwick Elliot, who got under Molly's skin. Amanda knew that Molly had once worked as a house cleaner for Lillian. She hadn't won her approval then and barely did now. But it was gracious of her mom to entertain the snobbish old woman and her husband, Dr. Elliot. It was her father's connection to Dr. Elliot that had brought them to Cape Light in the first place. Her father specialized in family medicine and had moved to Cape Light to take over Dr. Elliot's practice when he had retired, which was over ten years ago now.

Amanda well remembered that fateful day when she and her father had driven from Worcester to Cape Light. Molly had been hired to clean the house they were renting and had been a one-woman welcoming committee to the town, along with her two daughters.

That was the day Amanda had met Lauren, who became her best friend, and Jillian, who became her little sister. That was the lucky day for everyone, the day their new family had come together for the first time under one roof . . . though they had no way of knowing all that was to come.

Dr. Elliot was then, and remained, as friendly and obliging as his wife was snobbish and critical. Somehow they balanced each other, and Lillian wasn't too hard to take at a big party. Amanda knew Molly could handle her.

"I see your sisters at the window. Tell them to come out and help carry."

Amanda waved to her stepsisters, Lauren and Jill. Lauren was her own age and was working in a Boston art gallery after finishing her degree in art history, and Jillian was in her second year of college in Philadelphia, still trying to figure out a major.

"I hope they set the table and basted the turkeys, like I told them." Molly jumped out of the van and pulled open the sliding side door. "And I hope they kept an eye on Betty," she added, mentioning her youngest daughter. "I never know what that child is going to get into."

Amanda laughed. Betty was a sweetheart but very mischievous. Named after Molly's best friend and business partner, Betty Bowman, Betty was six years old and in the first grade. That had been the best thing about moving back home, the chance to spend more time with her. And her other sisters, too, who were just home until Sunday but would be coming back soon for Christmas.

"So, how's it going? Any disasters to report?" Molly asked when Lauren and Jill hurried toward them.

"Everything's under control, Mom. No worries." Lauren stepped up and took a box, then turned to Amanda. "Hmm . . . Is that a new perfume you're wearing—Eau de Giblets?"

Amanda couldn't help laughing. "You're wasted at the art gallery, Lauren. You should try stand-up."

"Sorry, Manda Bear, I couldn't resist. But you do you look cute in your uniform," her sister teased.

"Thanks. You can borrow it anytime. But it might be a little tight on you." Amanda knew that last part wasn't true. Lauren had a great figure. But she did love the reaction on Lauren's face. The score was even now.

"We had a little smoke in the kitchen," Jill confessed, grabbing the last box and a bag of bread. "But we put the oven fan on. It's fine now."

"Smoke? That doesn't sound good." Molly stopped in her tracks, looking alarmed.

"We let Betty try the basting thing, and she shot turkey juice all over the place. I told Jill that would happen," Lauren explained.

Molly sighed. "As long as nothing is burned . . . Okay, troops, follow me. Let the games begin."

Amanda fell in line behind her mother and sisters. She had been tired in the van but now felt a burst of energy. Being around her sisters was like downing a double espresso.

There are lots of good things about moving back home, Amanda decided as she carried the box of aromatic food into the house. She would try to take her parents' advice and enjoy being here for the holidays. And not worry so much about finding her dream job.

At least, not today, Amanda promised herself. Though she did plan to make a grab for one end of that wishbone.

"WHAT DO YOU THINK, LILLIAN? RED POLKA DOT, OR THIS YELLOW number with the fleur-de-lis?" Dr. Ezra Elliot lifted his chin, waiting for his wife's opinion on his choice of bow tie.

Lillian was seated at her dressing table, putting on her earrings. She glanced at him. "The red looks like Christmas, and the yellow one is positively blinding. It's Thanksgiving, Ezra, not the Fourth of July."

Ezra laughed. "I can always count on you for an honest critique, dear. I must say that."

"If you don't want my opinion, why ask at all?"

Ezra had expected that reply. He heard it at least once a day. "Point taken. So, I'm zero for two. What do you suggest?"

"The brown or burgundy. Either would match your shirt and vest much better than those two." She flipped her hand at his closet, then turned back to her reflection in the glass.

He walked over to his wardrobe, where his ample collection of bow ties hung from a rack. "I can't find the brown . . . Maybe Mrs. Fallon removed it. I think it had a stain."

Their devoted housekeeper, Mrs. Fallon, who cooked, cleaned, and took care of just about everything in Lillian's huge house, had left a few days ago to visit her family in Connecticut. Her daughter had recently given birth to triplets, and this was the first big family holiday since the babies were born.

He and Lillian had to muddle along on their own for a few days. They managed, but just barely. Ezra, for one, looked forward to Mrs. Fallon's return on Sunday night.

"Well . . . the burgundy one, then. Something more subdued," Lillian suggested, working on her second earring. She put on her reading glasses in order to undo the clasp. "Where did you get that polka-dot number? At a street fair?"

Ezra nearly laughed aloud. Calling anything a purchase from a street fair was Lillian's idea of a very low blow.

"I think you gave it to me, dear. For Christmas one year." He knew that wasn't true, but just said it to rile her a bit. It was really so easy. He had to purse his lips to keep from laughing as he watched her reaction in the dressing table mirror.

"You are very much mistaken. I would never buy such a thing." She shook her head, a hairpin at the back of her French twist coming loose.

She quickly reached up to fix it. "I've never purchased a polka-dot item of clothing in my life. Swiss dot . . . maybe. It was very much in style at one time. But that was long ago."

He finally laughed, looking over his bow ties again. "I am joking, Lily. I bought it for myself. In a daring mood. I'll wear the burgundy today, though. It will do just as well."

"Don't wear it on my account," she returned, opening a velvet neck-lace case. "I wouldn't dream of squelching your spirit."

He yanked off the offending neckwear, flipped his collar up, and replaced it with the burgundy. "You never squelch my spirit, Lily. You keep me at the top of my game. Top of my game," he repeated, winking at her.

Lillian met his glance and shook her head. But he could see the color rise a shade in her pale complexion. He still got her blushing. And at their age. That was something. A bit of sweetness in his cup, to be sure.

"Are you done fooling with that knot yet?" She turned as he twisted the silk into a taut, smooth bow, then flattened it with his hand. "Come here, please. Help me do this necklace. I can't find the catch. My fingers are so stiff today."

"Don't trouble yourself. I can get it." He walked over and took the necklace of amethyst beads that matched her earrings and comple-mented her white hair, blue eyes, and lavender sweater set—cashmere, of course. A silk scarf with a pattern of lavender and pink hues sat on the dressing table, waiting to be draped around her shoulders.

Lillian had always dressed with taste and elegance. Regally, in fact. She sailed through life the same way. That was one of the qualities that had first attracted him, so very long ago.

"There you are; all set." He stepped back once the necklace was fas-tened.

She rearranged the beads a moment before drawing her mouth into a frown as she applied her lipstick. Then she slowly rose and checked their reflection as they stood side by side. "Well, here we are. Take it or leave it."

"I'll take it," he said decisively. Ezra took her arm and draped it through his own. "You look especially lovely in that color. It suits you."

"Really? I think it makes me look a bit anemic. But what can you do? You look smart. *Sans* polka dots."

He turned and smiled at her. "What would I do without you? I could barely dress myself."

"You know that's not true." She withdrew her arm and picked up her purse from the dressing table. "At our stage in life, we do need to pool our resources. What's left of them."

A harsh observation, perhaps, but Ezra knew what she was saying. They were married late in life and they did rely on each other. More and more as time went on.

"I think we do surprisingly well together. That's the main thing I'm thankful for today, Lillian. Having you beside me, as my wife."

Lillian met his loving glance a moment and blinked, a sudden glassy sheen in her gaze and a twitch at the corner of her mouth the only clues that gave her away. But Ezra was adept at reading even these small signs. Her heart had been moved by his declaration. He was sure of that.

She grabbed his hand and squeezed it just a moment. "Enough chatter. We don't want to be late to the Hardings'. Though there's always such a crowd at their parties, no one will notice if we're missing."

Holiday parties at Molly and Matt Harding's house were inevitably large, boisterous affairs. Ezra enjoyed them for the most part, though Lillian found them tiring. He would undoubtedly hear the usual critique later this evening.

But he was pleased to be heading there on Thanksgiving. At his age, every day was a holiday of gratitude. He was thankful just to wake up in the morning, alive and well, and find he'd been blessed with the gift of another day. This day, out of all the rest, was the perfect opportunity to focus and meditate on those sentiments.

THE GATHERING AT THE HARDING HOME WAS JUST AS LILLIAN HAD expected. Too many people, too much food, and far too much noise. She was dismayed to find that the Hardings had acquired an even larger—and louder—TV. Most of the guests were gathered in the great room, off the spacious modern kitchen, watching a football game.

Including her husband, who had parted from her soon after they arrived. When had he become such a big sports fan? She couldn't imagine how that had happened. Unless there was something in the drink he had in hand. It looked like ginger ale, but you never knew. He did seem to be competing for the "Life of the Party" prize this afternoon.

Lillian headed for the living room, hobbling along on her cane. She narrowly missed being knocked over by a pack of overstimulated children, led by that little wildcat, Betty. She looked like an angel with those blond curls, but she was a hellion. Took after her mother, no doubt.

Lillian settled herself in an armchair tucked into a corner. She had barely gotten comfortable when her own daughter Emily appeared.

"Are you all right, Mother? Can I get you anything to eat? The appetizers are delicious."

Emily offered to share her plate. Lillian waved her hand as if chasing off an annoying insect. "Oh, I can't eat any of that. I'd be up all night."

Emily shrugged and smiled. "I'll be in the gym all week. But it will be worth it."

"What about dinner? When will the real meal be served? I'm ravenous."

"In a little while. I think Molly is nearly ready."

"A professional cook and she takes this long to get the meal out? I'm sure she doesn't keep her customers waiting this way. She would never stay in business."

Emily took a bite of a canapé before she answered. It looked like some sort of toasted cheese on a cracker. It did smell appetizing, Lillian had to admit. But she didn't dare chance it.

"I'm sure dinner will be worth waiting for, Mother. It always is."

"I might debate that," Lillian replied, lowering her tone. "But it would hardly be polite."

"Hardly," Emily agreed, seeming amused. Lillian resented that look, which was a bit smug. Why did her children find her so awfully entertaining?

Emily was suddenly called away by her husband, Dan Forbes, and Lillian had no chance to ask her.

Lillian contented herself with glancing around at the tall windows, strung with garlands of autumn leaves, and the huge fireplace, its mantel decked with white chrysanthemums and golden candles. Molly Willoughby Harding had done very well for herself, now that she was the most famous cook in town, with a thriving business. This was a fine house, even though it was not to Lillian's taste. A mini-mansion, she supposed you'd have to call it. Molly had married well the second time around, nabbing herself a doctor, even though she had barely finished high school. But she was smart, no doubt about that. She didn't start her business on his money either—she did it all on her own.

Who would have imagined she'd get this far way back when? Lillian certainly had not. She knew Molly when she was a cleaning girl . . . her own cleaning girl, in fact.

People can change. Rarely. But some managed it. Still, Lillian was not that impressed. Some might rave about Molly's cooking, like her daughters and their husbands. But Molly's recipes were not for anyone dieting or prone to digestive upset. She, for one, would eat sparingly today, and with care. She hoped Ezra would, too, though she doubted that.

She caught her husband's eye as he rounded the appetizer table, drawing him to her side with a glance.

"Enjoying yourself?" she asked him.

"Yes, I am. At least one of us has to. What are you doing hiding in the corner, Lily? Do you feel all right?"

"I might ask you the same. When did you develop such a passion for football?"

"They call it socializing, dear. You should try it sometime."

She shrugged and smoothed her skirt. "I'm too old to learn new tricks. You know that. Do you think they'll shut off that infernal TV during dinner?"

"One of the guests has a son playing on a college team, starting lineup. The game is over. The boy's team won by one point, with a forty-yard field goal. Very exciting."

"How interesting . . . rah, rah." She picked a bit of lint off her sweater.

Ezra laughed and shook his head, then offered her his hand. "Come along. I think you just need some attention. Did you see the place cards? We've been seated next to Sara and Luke," he added, mentioning her oldest granddaughter, who had once lived with Lillian and maintained a close relationship with her. Sara was married now and lived in Boston, where she worked as a reporter for the *Boston Globe*. Sara's visits home were a rare treat, for both of them. "That was very thoughtful of Molly."

"Yes," Lillian had to agree. *Molly probably thought Sara and Luke were the only couple who could tolerate my company,* she added silently. But it would be nice to visit with her granddaughter. She and Sara loved to talk books and debate politics.

Lillian took her husband's arm and allowed him to help her to the table. She actually needed her cane to get around, but hated to be seen using it anywhere outside of her home. Ezra knew that and always obliged without her asking. A true gentleman.

Dinner was ready, and the other guests were seeking their places as well. Ezra found their seats and pulled out her chair.

"Thank you, Ezra," she said as she sat.

"Not at all." He pulled out his own chair and sat beside her, gazing around the table with total contentment. "What a lovely table setting, and what a pretty centerpiece. Don't you think? Everything smells so good. It's going to be a wonderful dinner."

She didn't reply, but she really didn't have to. Ezra was pleased enough for the both of them. Pleased as punch. She had once thought him a bit of a fool. Well, more than a bit, to be perfectly truthful. But she had long since revised—and even reversed—that opinion. Now she actually envied his ever-sunny disposition. You could drop him in the middle of the Sahara, and he'd praise the sand dunes and sunshine.

Lillian opened her napkin and spread it on her lap. It was going to be a long and trying day for her, but she would put a good face on it. For Ezra's sake and for her family's. After all, it was a holiday. She knew she should be thankful just to be celebrating another one, even if she didn't feel particularly grateful right now. She would be happy when it was over and they were home again, just the two of them, in the quiet sanctuary of their own home. For which she was most sincerely thankful.

Dear God, thank you for my mobility, the invitation to join this party— noisy and confused as it is—and sharing this meal today. Thank you for dear Ezra. I don't know how he puts up with me. No one else will. And thank you most of all for our home and independence. I pray that we may spend the rest of our days there together.

LILLIAN WASN'T SURE WHY SHE HAD WOKEN UP. A DREAM, PERHAPS, that she couldn't remember even as she opened her eyes and got her bearings. She soon realized Ezra was not beside her . . . and not in the bathroom either. She put on her robe and slippers and slowly made her way to the staircase. From the landing, she saw the lights on downstairs and heard the sound of newspapers rattling.

She carefully made her way down and found him in the living room, sitting in a wing chair, working on a crossword puzzle.

"Why are you up, Ezra? Don't you feel well?"

Ezra shook his head. "A little heartburn, that's all."

"I'm not surprised." She gave him a knowing look, but he ignored her.

"Neither am I. I can't possibly be the only man in America who's up right now, feeling as if he ate too well."

"If you'd passed on that stuffing, like I told you—"

"I wouldn't be human," he finished for her. "No stuffing on Thanksgiving? That's positively unpatriotic, Lillian."

"It was loaded with sausage and those strange mushrooms she uses."

"It was delicious, every bite. And so was the second slice of pie. There, I've saved you the trouble of scolding me for that, too."

She sat on the sofa, across from him. "Well, now you're paying for it. Something's disagreed with you—maybe just the general mayhem over there. I like a quiet day, the kind I used to host here. Not a big hullabaloo."

Ezra put his glasses back on and picked up the crossword puzzle. "A little hullabaloo now and again isn't the worst thing. Gets your blood up."

"Your blood pressure, you mean." She sighed and shook her head. "How are we related to Matt and Molly Harding anyway? My son-in-law's sister? That's stretching it a bit, don't you think?"

"You know full well that Jessica's husband, Sam Morgan, is Molly's brother. Besides, Matt Harding is a good man and a fine doctor. I trusted him to take over my practice, you may recall. I think that counts for something."

"A tenuous connection, at best. I, for one, resent the way we're just dragged along like baggage if we want to spend the day with our real family. Matt may be an excellent physician, but why does he need such a big TV? Shouldn't the TV screen be smaller than the actual football field?"

Ezra finally looked up from his newspaper, laughing. "Good one, my dear. I'm sorry you didn't enjoy yourself, but I had a wonderful time. It's good for us to get out and socialize. I just read the other day that social connections are vital for a long, healthy life. And to keep the gray matter healthy." He tapped his temple with his pencil.

"So I should regard these events as a necessary evil, like eating my vegetables? Isn't my conversation stimulating enough to keep your mind keen? You were buzzing around me like an amorous bee for years before we married, for just that reason."

"I am still buzzing around you, dear. You're still my queen bee; never doubt it. I've been thinking we ought to have a big party for our wedding anniversary this year. It will be four years this coming Valentine's Day. Did you realize that?"

"Is it that many already? How quickly time passes."

"When you're having fun. Don't forget that part," he said, catching her eye with a twinkling glance.

Lillian didn't reply but also could not suppress a small smile. She and Ezra did have fun. A type uniquely their own, which would probably not even seem amusing to anyone else. But they did enjoy their life together. They were so perfectly suited to each other.

She could never understand now why it had taken her so long—so many decades, in fact—to see that. Who else had known her and loved her as long? Or loved her as well? Who else truly understood her or could put up with her many moods the way Ezra did? Not even her own daughters. She and Ezra Elliot had traveled a long road together, and she could still finish the crossword questions he left blank. And he could do the same for her.

"Are you stuck on that puzzle?" she asked suddenly, backing away from her sentimental turn of mind. "Give it here."

She reached for the folded sheet of newspaper, but he pulled it back, teasing her. "Not so fast. I'm just getting warmed up."

She sat back, feeling frustrated. He peered at her. "All right, I guess I can use some help. Chatty. Nine letters, ends in *S*."

She thought about it for only a moment. "Oh, that's easy. Garrulous."

He checked the spaces. "Right on target . . . All right, you take over. I'm going to make some ginger tea. That should settle what ails me." He rose and rubbed his stomach. "Want some?"

Lillian eagerly took the newspaper and pencil from him, feeling victorious. "I would like some, thank you. With a drop of honey. I bet I can finish this before you come back."

"Really? I'll take that bet. Loser cooks breakfast—and washes up."

"You're on." She nodded and focused on the puzzle, knowing that no matter which of them actually won, Ezra would probably make breakfast anyway. He was a far better cook. She had been known to burn water.

With Mrs. Fallon gone these past few days, they had to share the housework. They were quite spoiled, Lillian knew. She looked forward to Mrs. Fallon's return—was counting the hours, if the truth be told. The house just didn't seem right without her.

Lillian's thoughts wandered as she examined the puzzle's empty spaces. She could see where Ezra had gotten stuck. Thirty-four down. The clue was "steeple," five letters. The answer had to be "spire." But it didn't fit because he had put the wrong answer in thirty-one across.

"I see where you've gone off track," she shouted to the kitchen. "Thirty-one across. It's 'poisonous.' Not 'pernicious.' And you've spelled it wrong. Otherwise it never would have fit," she mumbled to herself.

"Are you sure?" He poked his head out the door a moment, then went back into the kitchen. "No wonder I was in a—"

Ezra abruptly stopped talking midsentence.

Lillian sat up alertly, listening. "Ezra . . . what did you say?"

When he didn't answer, she turned and stared at the doorway, which was now empty.

Then she heard a low gasping sound and a horrendous clatter. It sounded as if a metal pot and even some dishes had crashed to the floor . . . and as though Ezra had fallen, too.

She dropped the newspaper and used both hands to lift herself up off her seat as fast as she was able, not so silently cursing her age and infirmities and the stiffness in her legs that kept her from running to him.

"Ezra? What's happened? Did you fall?"

She stumbled across the living room, her cane swinging wildly, ignoring a searing pain in her hip and knee, listening for his answer beyond her heaving breath.

All she heard was a long, low moan.

"Dear God! You've hurt yourself . . . I'm coming, Ezra . . . I'm right here . . . don't move a muscle . . ."

Finally, she saw him—sprawled out on the floor, curled on his side, his arm twisted at an odd, painful-looking angle. Blood oozed from a cut on his head where he had struck the edge of something sharp. She tossed the cane aside and kneeled down as best she could next to him. His eyes were closed. She prayed to God he was conscious.

"Ezra . . . ?" She patted his cheek. "Can you hear me? Open your eyes, Ezra, please."

His eyelids fluttered a moment, then finally opened. "Lily . . . I blacked out. A pain in my chest . . . So sharp . . . it came on me so . . ."

"Don't try to speak. Save your strength. Just try to stay awake. I'm calling an ambulance. Don't close your eyes, Ezra. Try to stay awake," she implored him.

She could see him swallow back another groan as he nodded. Lillian clung to a kitchen chair and then to the edge of the table, slowly levering herself off the floor. She stumbled to the phone and quickly dialed 911.

"I need an ambulance right away. My husband has fallen and I can't get him up. He may have had a heart attack," she quickly told the operator.

The dispatcher asked a few questions, and Lillian tried to answer calmly, without losing her temper. "Yes, please. Thirty-three Providence Street. Come to the back door. We're in the kitchen."

"The ambulance is on the way, ma'am," the operator said, and finally Lillian was able to hang up. She walked to the back door and unlatched it, then returned to Ezra.

"They're coming. It'll be just a few minutes. Please don't close your eyes like that." She walked over to him and, this time, sat in a chair beside his prone body. She would have gotten closer but she was afraid she wouldn't be able to get up and open the door when the ambulance came. She knew she should call someone else, her daughter Emily probably. But she didn't want to leave Ezra again. She leaned down and took his hand. His ice-cold touch gave her gooseflesh.

"Can you hear me?" she whispered. "Can't you open your eyes just a little and look at me?"

He blinked, trying to respond. But finally, his eyes didn't open.

"Oh, Ezra . . . don't leave me. Not yet . . . I couldn't bear it."

CHAPTER TWO

⌒

A s you already know, Ezra, your injuries and the
trauma from the fall are one issue," Dr. Newton explained.
"The heart attack is another—"

"*Mild* heart attack," Lillian clarified. "No need to exaggerate the
situation."

"Mother, please. Just let Dr. Newton finish." Emily gave her a look.

"Go on, Doctor. You were saying?" Ezra prodded him.

"Yes, thankfully, it was a mild heart attack, but it was not the first
one, which, as you know, makes any cardiac event more significant. Still,
you're coming along nicely, Ezra. You'll probably be ready for release on
Tuesday. But I strongly advise that you move from here to a rehab center
for your recovery."

Ezra looked surprised by this suggestion.

Lillian was, too. "Do you mean a nursing home?"

"Not a nursing home, no," Dr. Newton replied carefully. "Though many facilities that provide rehabilitation also have sections that care for permanent residents."

"Permanent residents, hah!" Lillian nearly spat the term back at him. "Inmates," she mumbled under her breath.

Emily gave her another look. "Why do you suggest the rehabilitation facility, Doctor? Can you please explain?"

"And how long would I be there?" Ezra asked.

Lillian glanced at him. *You're not going anywhere,* she telegraphed with her eyes. She sat back in a chair next to Ezra's bed. He was sitting up against the tilted mattress. Only one tube extended from his arm today. That was a good sign. He had more color in his cheeks, and his voice sounded stronger, too. Pretty good progress for only two days after the fall. And at his age. She had nearly had a heart attack herself when it happened. But here they were, back to fight another day.

Ezra's grip felt stronger, too, as he took her hand in his and gently squeezed.

"About six to eight weeks," Dr. Newton replied, "depending on how quickly you heal. From what you and your wife told the home care counselor, it sounds as if there isn't adequate support at home to fully facilitate your recovery."

"Oh, fiddlesticks. Speak English," Lillian snapped. "Aren't you just trying to say we're two decrepit codgers who can barely take care of ourselves when we're healthy, much less when dealing with a setback? Is that it?"

Dr. Newton wasn't cowed. "Mrs. Elliot, I need to be sure your husband will have the care he needs, which will include daily physical therapy once those casts come off. There's no question he can get all that in a skilled-nursing facility. I'm not at all sure he can get it at home."

"That's true, Mother. Please try to think of what's best for Ezra," Emily advised.

Lillian sat back and pursed her lips. Ezra wouldn't be happy apart from her. That would slow down his recovery as much as anything. Didn't Emily and this doctor realize that?

"There's a very good facility in Beverly that may have an opening," Dr. Newton continued.

"Beverly? How am I supposed to get down there every day—fly on my broomstick?"

Ezra laughed and patted her hand. The doctor looked like he wanted to laugh, too. Emily looked annoyed. "Jessica and I can drive you," she said. "And I'm sure Sam and Dan will pitch in. We'll all help."

"You say that now, but when the time comes, there's always something more important. Some emergency with the garbage pickup in town or the parking meters. Your sister is the same with her priorities. I know how that goes."

"Calm down, dear. We'll figure it out."

Lillian turned to her husband. "Why can't you just come home? We're not alone. We have Mrs. Fallon, and we can bring people in—as needed," she qualified. She didn't want a parade of paraprofessionals marching through her home, of course. That wasn't going to happen. But they would need a visiting nurse or aide during the day—and a physical therapist, once Ezra was well enough for that.

"Who is Mrs. Fallon?" The doctor rifled through his papers.

"Our live-in housekeeper," Lillian informed him. "She's completely devoted to Ezra. She's been with him for years."

"She's a lovely woman, very capable," Ezra agreed. "But we can't expect to turn her into a nurse, too."

Lillian could see both the doctor and Emily about to reply but she beat them to it. "Nonsense. She adores you. She would hate the idea of you being sent away as much as I do. She'll be happy to help me care for you. We'll give her some extra pay."

Ezra shook his head. "She'd probably do it anyway."

"Yes, she would. I don't want you shipped off to Beverly or some-place where I can't see you. I don't want you shipped off at all."

The doctor heaved a loud sigh. Lillian had almost forgotten he was there. A beeper clipped to his belt sounded, and he quickly checked the message.

"I'm sorry, I have to go. If you are determined to keep your husband at home, Mrs. Elliot, we'll need to work out an adequate plan for his care. Twenty-four-hour care," he repeated, his tone sounding like a warning. "Mrs. Cole, the social worker assigned to your case, can help you with that."

Lillian had already met Mrs. Cole. She would be easier to get around than Dr. Newton, and he was already in retreat mode. She wasn't worried. "Thank you, Doctor. We'll speak to her right away," she promised.

"I'll look in on you tomorrow, Ezra. Keep up the good work."

Ezra smiled. "Thank you, Doctor. Same to you."

Emily rose from her seat and picked up her purse. "I can see you're determined, Mother. I'll go find Mrs. Cole and start working on this. We'll need to rent a hospital bed and bring in a nurse or home health aide during the day, and at night, too. I hope you realize that it won't just be business as usual. This is going to change your routine."

"A small price to pay compared to shipping Ezra off to goodness knows where."

"Thank you for arranging all this, Emily. I appreciate it. I suppose I would prefer to be at home, if that can be worked out," Ezra said honestly.

Emily's gaze softened as she looked over at him. He wasn't just her stepfather; she had known Ezra all her life. He had been her father's oldest friend and practically the only person in town who had stood by her family when they were weathering some very bad times. She felt protective toward him, as she would toward her own father, had he lived this long.

"I'm happy to help, Ezra. Let me see what I can do." She slung her purse strap over her shoulder, then hurried off.

Once Emily had gone, Ezra said, "I know you have your heart set on my coming home, Lily. But it might not work out. I've got a broken leg and a broken arm, and I'm recovering from a heart attack. I'm going to need a lot of help, and it's not going to be easy on anyone. So prepare yourself."

"I'll prepare the bedroom on the first floor for you to sleep in. That's the only thing I'll prepare. I won't see you carried off. I know about those places. Next thing you know, they'll want to keep you there."

"Don't be silly. That's not true at all. I'm sure it's just as the doctor described: a skilled-nursing facility. Though I will admit, I'd rather not spend two or three months away from home. Away from you."

"My point exactly. We'll do fine with Mrs. Fallon and some medical people coming in a few hours here and there. You'll spring back much faster in your own home, I guarantee it."

Ezra reached over and patted her hand. "All right, dear. If you feel so strongly about it."

"I do feel strongly about it, and I'm right. You'll see."

AMANDA HAD BEEN BACK FOR NEARLY A MONTH BUT HAD NOT YET attended church. At this time of year, Molly often had to work in the shop or cater a party on weekends, and Amanda worked with her. This weekend, with her sisters home, her parents decided that the family would attend the Sunday service together. Their announcement Saturday night was greeted by a chorus of groans.

"Yes, I'm sure you'd all rather sleep late and spend the rest of the morning eating a big breakfast and giving each other manicures," Molly had replied. "But I need to show off my beautiful daughters once in a while. This is the perfect opportunity. You'll have to indulge me."

"And we all have a lot to be thankful for," Amanda's father added. "Thanksgiving isn't just one day of the year."

Amanda and her sisters responded with a few more halfhearted grumbles but knew it was pointless to argue. Amanda didn't mind going to church with her family now and again. She always did when she came home from school. But she had gotten out of the habit of attending on her own ever since she started college. She hadn't even looked for a church in New York.

The old stone church on the green had not changed one bit, she noticed as they drove toward it. *Though maybe there's more ivy climbing its walls,* she thought as her father searched for a parking space.

The big arched wooden doors still stood open, even though her family was among the last to arrive. With the help of Tucker Tulley, one of the deacons, they soon found seats toward the back of the sanctuary. Amanda was surprised to see nearly every seat filled. She didn't recognize many faces, though she did see Molly's brother—her uncle Sam— sitting with her aunt Jessica and her cousins. And Emily Warwick, her husband, Dan, and their daughter, Janie.

Of course, Lillian Warwick and her husband Dr. Elliot were not there. He had fallen down on Thanksgiving night and was still in the hospital. Her family had heard the news through her aunt Jessica. Her father and mother planned to visit him in the hospital that afternoon.

Sophie Potter, another familiar face from her childhood, also sat nearby, and she greeted the Hardings with a nod and a fond glance.

Amanda smiled back. She couldn't look at Sophie without thinking of apples. Sophie even looked a bit like an apple now, with her round face and pink cheeks. Amanda knew that she still lived on Potter Orchard and wondered if the old woman worked outdoors any longer. It seemed impossible, unless you knew Sophie.

Reverend Ben Lewis was still their minister. She had always liked

Reverend Ben. He had a wonderful gift for showing how spiritual ideas worked in everyday life. Even so, her mind wandered during the opening announcements and call to worship, her attention called back only when it was time to sing the first hymn.

The choir wasn't large like ones she had seen in some bigger churches. Even so, they could have had a richer, more energetic sound, she decided. She wondered if she was being overly critical, returning here after years of studying and playing with professional musicians. Still, she had once stood on those risers herself and sung in that choir, and she was pretty sure it had sounded better than the group here this morning. The choice of music seemed a little predictable as well.

Why don't you relax and stop being such a big critic, she told herself. *It's tough to get any sort of quality performance from amateur singers. The church is lucky to have people giving their time and effort up there every Sunday, no matter what they sound like.*

The hymn they were singing, "All Things Bright and Beautiful," was one of Amanda's favorites. She sang the final verse wholeheartedly and was pleased to hear that the choir picked up with a strong finish.

"All things bright and beautiful, All creatures great and small, All things wise and wonderful, The Lord God made them all . . ."

The theme of the service was gratitude, as she had expected it would be this weekend. Reverend Ben gathered the children around for his "Time with Children" talk and showed them how the pilgrims set five kernels of corn on each dish at the first Thanksgiving. He even had a dinner plate with bits of corn as a prop.

"I bet most of you have learned that the first Thanksgiving was a big feast, celebrating the harvest and the end of the harsh times the settlers had endured during their first year in America. Why put measly little corn kernels on their dish first, when there was all that delicious food they had cooked? Does anybody know why they did that?"

Amanda watched the children respond. A few hands went up, rather tentatively. Her little sister Betty, however, waved her hand wildly and jumped to her feet when Reverend Ben called on her.

"Look, it's Betty," her mom whispered excitedly.

"Shhh. I want to hear what she says," her dad said.

Betty raised her voice to be heard. "The pilgrims put corn kernels out to make them remember that they only had a little food when they came here . . . and they should be happy to have a lot."

"That's right, Betty. Very good." Reverend Ben nodded his head and smiled. "They put the corn kernels on their plate every Thanksgiving Day after that, and many families still follow that tradition. We do it at our house. For each of the five kernels," he added, holding one up for the children to see, "we tell everyone else at the table about a blessing in our life, something we're thankful for. Here's a bit of corn," he said, handing one down to Janie Forbes. "What would you give thanks for?"

Janie seemed shy for a moment. She looked down and shrugged. "I'd say thanks for my new dog, Pearl. She sleeps on my bed at night."

Everyone looked over at Emily and Dan, Amanda included. Emily smiled and shook her head. She didn't seem the type of mother who would let a dog sleep on a bed. But it just went to show, you never could tell. Amanda liked her even more after hearing that.

After a few more real-life examples, the children were herded out of the sanctuary by their Sunday school teachers. The scriptures were read and the adult sermon soon began, with the same theme.

"An attitude of gratitude is not just for Thanksgiving Day, but can be a daily practice. It's a way of looking at the world and appreciating the precious gifts in each of our lives that we take for granted.

"No one's life is perfect, despite the images we see on television and in the movies. And when we visit our Facebook friends," Reverend Ben added with a grin. "Everyone is always celebrating or going on vacation. We compare and despair, don't we?

"But happiness and a sense of abundance are not about how much you own, or how big your bank account might be. Or how successful you are in your career. One merely needs to glance at a newspaper or magazine to find a story about some successful, wealthy person who seems to have everything but is unhappy or unfulfilled."

Amanda listened while gazing at the stained-glass windows. They were still beautiful, filtering the sunlight with jewel-toned hues. But here and there, they were marred with random patches of black plastic and duct tape, covering broken spots, she assumed. She wondered how that had happened and if the windows would be repaired.

Reverend Ben's voice drew her back to the sermon. ". . . that sense of fulfillment is something that happens deep inside," he was saying. "It's something that has little, or nothing, to do with those external measures."

Had she been comparing herself to other people too much? Did she take her advantages for granted and focus too much on things that were missing in her life right now? At least she had wonderful parents who believed in her and were happy to help in any way they could. Not everyone she knew could say that.

And she had great sisters, who were as close as best friends. She did have a lot to be thankful for. More than a list of five things, that was for sure.

Right after the sermon, the choir sang a hymn. Amanda rose with the rest of congregation and sang along. A few people turned to look at her, though she didn't understand why.

"You're a diva out here," Lauren whispered. "You'd better watch out. The choir director might kidnap you."

Amanda poked her sister with her elbow, while looking straight ahead and keeping a perfectly straight face as she finished singing the hymn.

As the service ended, Amanda's mind was on the rest of the day. She and her family were heading to a restaurant in Newburyport for lunch. After that they were going shopping, if there was enough time. Jill had her bags in the car and had to be dropped off at the train station in the afternoon. Amanda would be sad to see her younger sister go, but at least Lauren didn't need to leave until tomorrow morning. Amanda knew they would stay up late again, talking.

Then Lauren will be gone, too, and I'll be back at the food shop. That realization brought her down, but Amanda didn't want to dwell on that now. Her sisters would be home again soon, for Christmas, and would stay even longer then.

Amanda hoped her family would make a quick exit out a side door, but Molly had other intentions and managed to steer her family into Reverend Ben's direction. Luckily, they didn't have to wait long in the line of congregants who wanted to greet him.

"I really enjoyed the service, Reverend Ben. Especially your sermon," Molly said. "I love that story about the corn. I've never heard it before."

"Your Betty was a big help," Reverend Ben said with a smile. "We have to give her some credit, too."

Betty had just come out of Sunday school and ran up to Molly, clinging to her coat.

"I'm just grateful to have my girls together for a few days. That counts a few times on my list," her father said.

"I believe it does," Reverend Ben agreed, smiling at the older sisters. "But I guess you'll all be leaving tonight. Except for Betty."

"Oh, Amanda's is home with us right now," her father explained.

"She's been working with me," Molly chimed in. "Just temporarily. Until she finds something more . . . musical."

Amanda wouldn't have minded explaining her situation to Reverend Ben, but her parents wouldn't let her get a word in. They forgot some-times that she was twenty-five and capable of speaking for herself.

Reverend Ben quickly turned to Amanda. His blue eyes grew wide behind his gold-rimmed glasses. "I just happen to know of a job that is definitely more musical than working for your mother. And I'm sure you would qualify."

"Really? What sort of job?"

"Right here at the church. Our music director, Mrs. Wilmott, just gave me notice on Friday. Her husband has been promoted and his firm wants him to start immediately, at a different branch, on Long Island. They're leaving town this weekend and staying with relatives down there until they find a new home. I wish them all the luck in the world, of course. But, frankly, I don't know how we're going to get through the holidays without a music director." Reverend Ben seemed as flustered as she had ever seen him. "Even if you helped out for just a few weeks, Amanda, I'd consider it a gift from heaven above . . . and a great favor."

Amanda wasn't sure what to say. The job was certainly more suited to her background than working at the catering shop. But she didn't even know what a church music director did, besides rehearse and conduct the choir.

She glanced over at her parents. Molly looked like she was about to burst but was bravely holding back, knowing it was Amanda's place to answer. Meanwhile, her father was making one of his blank faces that clearly said *I don't want to influence you, but I really think this is great!* Amanda knew she had to say something. Everyone was staring at her.

"I would be very interested to hear more, Reverend," Amanda said finally. "Can I come and speak to you about it?"

"Yes, of course. That's exactly what we should do. Can you come to my office tomorrow? Eleven or so? I'll tell you everything you need to know."

Amanda nodded in agreement. Reverend Ben was so kind, and had known her such a long time. This would be the most relaxed interview she had ever had.

Of course her family started talking about the job as soon as they stepped outside. Lauren patted her on the back, with premature congratulations. "Good work. I think Reverend Ben would have hired you on the spot if you had let him."

Amanda was about to answer when her mother chimed in. "What did I tell you? I knew it was a good idea to come to church today. I knew something good would come along for you, honey."

Before Amanda could respond, her father weighed in. "We know it's not exactly what you want, Amanda, but it would be very good experience, and will look good on your résumé. I'm sure Reverend Ben would give you a great reference when something better comes along."

Her father already had her hired and moving on to a better job. Amanda found that speed-dial scenario amusing.

"Even if you just work there for the holidays," Molly added. "Think of it as just a little—"

"Yes, I know, a lily pad," Amanda said quickly.

Molly paused then nodded. "That's right. That's all I meant to say."

"I bet the hours are flexible," her father mused. "There will probably be plenty of time to practice your cello or go to auditions. I'm sure Reverend Ben would understand."

"It all sounds great, I agree . . . except that I have no idea what a church music director does. But I'm willing to find out," Amanda added quickly, not wanting to sound negative. "No offense, Mom. But I probably would like working at the church better than in your shop."

"No offense taken," Molly replied with a grin, knowing that if Amanda didn't see another turkey or pie until next Thanksgiving, it would be too soon.

THAT NIGHT, AS EXPECTED, AMANDA AND LAUREN STAYED UP VERY late, hanging out in the bedroom they had once shared, trying on the new nail polish and makeup they had bought in Newburyport and talking about everything: relationships with guys, the latest movies and music, life ambitions. That was one thing Amanda missed about living at home—all the closeness with Lauren and Jill.

"I miss you, Snorie," Amanda had confessed, using Lauren's old nickname, which was a variation of Laurie and had been inspired in the days when Lauren and Amanda shared a bedroom, though Lauren had never actually snored, as Amanda recalled. Well, maybe once or twice, when she had a cold.

"I miss you, too, Manda Bear. Why don't we move to the same city and get an apartment together?" Lauren suggested. They were trying out some dark blue polish Lauren had found. "It worked in New York."

"I know," Amanda said, with longing in her voice. When they were both in school in New York, they had shared an apartment in Brooklyn. But then Lauren had taken a job in Boston, and Amanda had moved into Manhattan to share an apartment with friends.

"It would be so much fun," Lauren said.

"It would be fun. Except that we would need jobs in the same city. I just need a job, period."

"I think this church thing will work out. You don't have to stay there forever. But it will get you out of Mom's shop and back into music."

"Does that mean you're going to move back to Cape Light and get a job here, too? We can get an apartment in the village. In some cute Victorian with a turret room. Like sisters in a Jane Austen novel."

At a certain point in high school, she and Lauren had devoured the complete works of Jane Austen, starting with *Pride and Prejudice* and working their way through the rest of the novels with ease. And they watched all the movie versions so many times over that they sometimes started talking to each other as if they were the Bennet sisters.

Amanda was teasing, of course. It was bad enough that she had to give up her dream of living in a big city. She would never want Lauren to meet the same fate.

"The sisters in Jane Austen novels would never be allowed to live in town on their own, Amanda. They would have to live with a chaperone, a maiden aunt, or a widowed friend of the family," Lauren reminded her. "Besides, Mom and Dad would have a fit if we lived in town and rented instead of staying here. Maybe they would let us make an apartment in the basement. Remember when we put up all those posters and Christmas lights and turned it into a dance studio?"

"That was total genius." Amanda smiled at the fond memories, especially of the dance routines they'd made up. "Okay, so if our jobs don't pan out, you move back home and we'll open a dance studio in the basement. Deal?"

Lauren laughed and shook Amanda's hand. "Deal. Oh, sorry . . . I smudged your polish."

They both checked Amanda's manicure. There was a tiny smudge on her thumb, but Amanda didn't mind. "No worries. This color is a little intense for me." She knew Lauren loved it. She had always had a bolder fashion sense. But it reminded Amanda of model paint she had once used for a school project. "I think Sapphire Midnight nails would be pushing it a bit for my interview, don't you?"

Lauren laughed. "Right. Not the best choice for the new church music director. We must have Celestial Pink or Heavenly Clouds around here somewhere . . ."

While Lauren searched the plastic bin where the girls stored manicure supplies, Amanda began removing the dark polish. "New church music director"? The words were a little jarring. It was not a title she had ever aspired to. But Amanda pushed her doubts aside. She would meet with Reverend Ben and hear more. One step at a time.

THE NEXT MORNING, SHE WOKE BEFORE THE ALARM, AND DRESSED quickly in a dark blue sweater, gray skirt, and black boots. She pulled her hair back in a low ponytail, and grabbed a few copies of her résumé.

Molly drove both her and Lauren to town, dropping Lauren at the train station first. Amanda was sorry to see her go and knew she would be counting the days until Lauren came back for Christmas. "Chin up, Manda Bear. Text me after, right away. I have to hear what happened."

Amanda agreed and hugged her sister good-bye. A few minutes later, Molly dropped her off at the green, in front of the old stone church. "Good luck, honey. Come over to the shop when you're done. I'm dying to hear how it goes." Her mom waved and pulled away.

Amanda felt a little like she'd been left off for her first day of school as she walked up the stone path toward the church. She lingered, taking in the view. A deep blue sky stretched out over the village green and harbor, reflected in the gently rocking waves, which were calm for this time of year.

The church had been built in such an illogical place, so close to the water, exposed to the harshest weather and the winds coming off the sea. But it was certainly one of the prettiest spots in town and probably proved that the early settlers had an aesthetic side and were not merely practical.

It would be nice to walk along the harbor every day if she worked here, or to be able to go into the village anytime she wanted. She hadn't thought about that before.

Amanda entered the church through a side door near Reverend Ben's office and suddenly felt a little nervous. Her family had been talking about the job so much, she doubted they would understand if she didn't take it. What if she didn't even get it? What if Reverend Ben decided he had overestimated her credentials, or the church council got involved? Amanda hadn't even considered that.

All you have to do is listen. You don't have to decide today, she reminded herself.

The door to the church office was open, and Amanda walked in. The church secretary, Mrs. Honeyfield, was typing on her computer, but quickly looked up and smiled. "Good morning, Amanda. Reverend Ben is in the sanctuary. He told me to send you in when you arrived."

"Thanks." Amanda left the office and headed for the sanctuary. Perhaps Reverend Ben wanted to hear her play the piano or organ? Keyboards were not her main instrument, though she played well enough for the typical hymns and miscellaneous church music. If he asked her to play something, a few pieces she knew by heart came to mind. Besides, there was plenty of sheet music in the church. Amanda was sure she could find at least one piece she knew.

Just relax and take a breath. This is going to work out fine, one way or another, she reminded herself.

Amanda was so caught up in silently coaching herself that she walked straight into a ladder set up near the sanctuary's side aisle.

There was a momentary clatter as her shoulder hit the metal frame.

"Whoa there!" a deep voice called out from above, echoing in the empty sanctuary.

Startled, she looked up and saw a man struggling to get his balance. He reached out and clung to the metal handle of a window, waiting for the ladder to settle. Amanda felt her heart jump into her throat. She grabbed the ladder and held it firmly, trying to steady it.

"I'm so sorry. Are you all right?" she called up.

He glanced down over one broad shoulder. His face was shaded by a baseball cap, and she could hardly see his expression. "I'm still up here, not down there with you. So I guess that's a good sign . . . Don't you know it's bad luck to walk into a ladder?"

Amanda squinted, taken aback by his tone. "I think the problem is walking *under* a ladder, not into one. Why did you set it up so close to the door? You should have put a sign outside or something."

He glanced down, taking in her complaint. She had a feeling he was smiling, though she couldn't quite see his face. He didn't seem remorseful at all; rather, he seemed amused at her comeback.

"I did put a sign up; it must have fallen down. Take a look around the floor. Wait, I'll come down and find it."

Amanda stepped back, feeling confused. She rarely lost it like that and scolded total strangers. Now she felt silly about her reaction. She was just wound up about this interview—and had taken it out on him.

I really should apologize, she thought, while another part of her wished she could just find Reverend Ben. She sighed and looked around for the reverend. Couldn't he rescue her from this silly confrontation?

The workman descended the ladder quickly, moving with the kind of agile grace that she associated with athletes. Then he bent over and scooped up a sheet of paper from the floor.

"Here it is . . . See? I wasn't making that up."

"I didn't think you were." Amanda looked at the handwritten sign that read, *Caution—Use Other Door.*

She was about to say more when she finally looked at the man's face and was startled to see the sparkling blue eyes and disarming smile she so clearly remembered.

"Oh . . . it's you . . . the pie guy."

The pie guy? Where had that come from? How lame could you get?

If the term bothered him, he didn't show it. He smiled at her. "Yes, Bakery Girl. It is I, Pie Guy." He dipped his head in a mock formal greeting. "How was your Thanksgiving?"

"It was fine. How was yours? How did the pie work out?"

"Oh, it was a big hit. I was a real hero. I owe you one."

Amanda didn't know what to say to that. "Let's call it even, then. I think I just used up my favor, nearly launching you off that ladder."

He laughed, looking even cuter. "Come to think of it, I think you did."

Before she could answer, she heard sounds from up near the altar. A door opened, and Reverend Ben came out of the sacristy, the small storeroom where the sacred vessels, linens, and candles for the service were kept. The reverend was carrying a small, flat box.

"I did find it, finally," he called out in a cheerful voice. "Sorry to keep you waiting." He looked pleased as he noticed Amanda there. "Thanks for coming, dear," he said to her. "I'll be with you in a moment. We're trying to get these windows fixed." He turned to the young man. "I saved a few pieces of the broken glass," he explained, handing him the box.

The pie guy—Amanda didn't know how else to think of him— opened it and looked inside with interest but didn't touch anything, as if the contents were very fragile and precious.

So the pie guy worked with stained glass. He was sort of an artist, then, wasn't he? That made sense to her, even though she had only exchanged a few words with him.

"I don't know if it will help you, but we saved whatever we could find," the minister said.

"It does help, thank you, Reverend. I have to make new templates for the broken pieces. These fragments will help me gauge the color and thickness." He put the cover back on the box and set it next to a large canvas tool bag. "I'm going to look at all the windows and make some notes. Then I'll call you about the repairs."

Reverend Ben nodded. "Sounds like a plan. Just be careful on that ladder."

The pie guy glanced over at Amanda. "I'll try. I already had one close call today . . . Some pretty girl sailed in here and nearly knocked me off my feet."

Reverend Ben laughed. Amanda felt herself blush. She looked down at her boots. What a flirt. Did those corny lines really work for him? She would have asked him that point-blank if Reverend Ben weren't standing there.

He's caught your attention, a little voice inside her pointed out. *Corny lines and all.*

Seconds later, Reverend Ben led her out of the sanctuary. Amanda felt relieved. The pie guy was up on the ladder again, and she could feel him watching her go. She was tempted to say good-bye but decided not to.

Though as she walked away, she wondered about his name. She still didn't know it, and it felt too awkward to ask Reverend Ben. *Time to get focused on this interview, Amanda, and put that awfully handsome, flirtatious guy out of your mind.*

REVEREND BEN SHOWED AMANDA INTO HIS OFFICE AND TOOK A SEAT behind his desk. She made herself comfortable in an armchair. "Here's a copy of my résumé," she said, handing it to him. "I thought you might want to see it."

"Thank you. I do." The reverend glanced down at the sheet, peering over the edge of his gold-rimmed glasses.

As he studied her credentials, she studied him. She had known the minister ever since she was a little girl, and he never seemed to change. Well, a little, but not very much. He had always been bald on top, making up for that with a thick beard, which was a dark reddish-brown color now flecked with silver strands, as was the band of curly dark hair around his head. His face showed few wrinkles, mostly at the corners of his eyes. His cheeks were still round and rosy, his blue eyes bright behind his glasses.

She recalled that he'd had a heart problem a few years ago and had almost retired. She had come back from school for Christmas and there had been a female minister in his place. Amanda was glad that Reverend Ben had stayed on. Even though she didn't attend church much, she liked knowing he was here. This church wouldn't be the same without him.

He looked up suddenly and leaned back in his chair. "Very impressive. I've heard about your studies and awards from your parents, of course. And I recall your beautiful voice from when you sang with the choir." Amanda had been in the church choir when she was in high school. In college, her entire focus was on the cello. She had not sung in public for a long time. "It's very impressive to see it all on paper," he continued. "No question that you're qualified. More than qualified, I'd say."

Amanda felt a bit self-conscious at all the compliments. "Thank you, Reverend. Maybe you should tell me more about the job. What exactly does the music director do? Besides rehearse the choir, I mean. I'm pretty sure I can handle that part of the job, but there must be more to it."

"Oh, there is, believe me. But not all that much," he hurried to add. "I have an official job description here somewhere. Let me read it to you."

He found the sheet of paper on his desk and ran down the key responsibilities of the position—planning the hymns and any special music for each service, managing and rehearsing the choir. On Sundays, conducting the choir, playing the piano and the organ, and, once a month, teaching a music class to the Sunday school students.

"You would need to be at the church about fifteen to twenty hours a week. So I suppose it's not a truly full-time job. The hours are fairly flexible. Except for Sundays," he added.

"That sounds perfect," she said. It would give her time to practice for her auditions.

"The salary is competitive for this sort of position," he went on, then quoted a figure that sounded very generous. "Do you have any questions?"

Most of the job description consisted of self-explanatory tasks that Amanda had expected. There was one part, however, that she didn't quite understand. "About the meetings to plan the worship service. Do you mean I would pick out the hymns?"

"More or less. You would meet with me at least once a week. We try to plan a few weeks ahead. The season of Advent, for instance, that's a distinct part of the church calendar, and we would plan it as one block. There are a lot of favorite hymns and incidental music we draw from. I'll have certain themes worked out for my sermons, and we try to choose hymns that resonate with those ideas. Or we think of interesting musical events—soloists or duets—playing related pieces. It's usually someone from the congregation. We have many talented musicians here." He paused and met her gaze. "Is this making any sense to you?"

Amanda nodded. "Yes, I think so. Like last Sunday, because it was Thanksgiving weekend, we sang hymns that focused on gratitude."

"That's right." He nodded. "That takes some figuring out, and we don't want to always be repeating the same old, same old. It's very important to keep the worship service fresh and interesting. The music is an essential component of worship. It expresses a spiritual dimension that touches people in a certain way, beyond the liturgy and prayers . . . or even my wise and witty sermons," he added, with his characteristic self-effacing humor.

Amanda nodded but didn't reply. From her music history classes, she knew that church music was meant to bring people closer to God. But somehow she hadn't thought about this job that way, as having a spiritual dimension.

"A music director's ideas and inspirations contribute to the entire worship experience," Reverend Ben went on. "It's a very important job, really, and I'm guessing you'll be very good at it."

"But I don't attend church much," she reminded him. "I mean, not since I left for college."

"Yes, I know. That part isn't important. If you take the job, you would have to be here every Sunday, so that glitch will solve itself," he added with a small smile. "You have a great gift, Amanda. Expressing that gift, sharing it . . . that helps us all to be in touch with something greater, something divine. That's what music is, you know. It unites us in one feeling and puts us in touch with another realm. Which is why beautiful, uplifting music is part of most any worship service in any culture or period of history, especially in our tradition. 'Make a joyful noise unto the Lord' the Psalms say.

"You know, when I was in seminary," he continued, "I had a wonderful professor who used to start every class by having us sing a hymn. He used to say that some of the best theology could be found in a hymnal . . . and some of the worst, I'm sure," he added with a smile. "But I think you get my meaning. Music in church is more than just a pleasant listening experience. Anyone taking this job will need to understand that . . . even if the notion is new to you."

Amanda knew that music took you places, out of day-to-day reality in some way. She always knew she was having a good practice session or performance when she felt carried away. When she lost track of everything—where she was and even how long she had been playing.

But she had never given much thought to music as some sort of bridge between the earthly realm and the divine, as Reverend Ben suggested. He was so sure of his perspective that he didn't even seem to think she had to agree with him.

Otherwise, the job seemed interesting to her, much more interesting than working in the catering shop. And it paid a lot better, too.

"I hope I've covered everything. Any other questions?" he asked.

"I think I have a good idea of what's expected," Amanda said.

"If you're interested, we'd love to have you here. As I told you, Mrs. Wilmott had to leave town immediately, so you can start tomorrow if you'd like." He cleared his throat. "There is one more thing. I under-

stand from your folks that your stay here is—what did Molly call it?—
something to do with frogs . . ."

"A lily pad," Amanda said with a laugh.

"Exactly," Reverend Ben agreed. "I know that your goal is to play in
an orchestra, not direct a small church choir. So this may well be a temporary position for you. All I ask is that you stay through Christmas. We
do need someone to get the choir through all the holiday services. And
you don't need to give me your answer now. You can think about it. Talk
to your parents tonight," he suggested.

"I don't need to think it over, Reverend Ben. I'd be happy to work
here," she replied. "And yes, I can start tomorrow, and I'll stay through
Christmas."

He looked very pleased, and relieved, by her answer. "That's wonderful. I can't wait to tell the council we've filled this position, and with
such a qualified young woman, so well known to us."

He jumped up from his chair, remembering that she needed to fill
out some forms to make it official. They found what was needed with the
help of the Mrs. Honeyfield. "You can just fill these in at home and
bring them back tomorrow. Most of the music for the next service is
already set. I can give you a list and find the sheet music for you if you
want to start familiarizing yourself."

"That would be great. Thanks."

After receiving the schedule, Amanda followed Reverend Ben back
to the sanctuary, where he hoped to find the sheet music at the piano.
Amanda braced herself, preparing to encounter the pie guy again.

But the sanctuary was empty, his ladder and tool bag gone. Maybe
his work was done here. She wasn't sure if she was relieved or disappointed. Then she felt annoyed at herself for even noticing.

"Here we are." Reverend Ben handed her a black binder full of
music. "I think you'll find everything there. If not, we can look for the

rest tomorrow. Choir practice is on Thursday nights at seven. You have some time to review the hymns for Sunday."

"Thanks again for hiring me," Amanda said as she buttoned her coat.

"We're very fortunate to have you here, Amanda. I feel God's hand in this. It's an answer to my prayers, you coming along just in time to help us."

No one had ever called Amanda an answer to their prayers before. It seemed a great compliment—and a large order to fill.

"I'll do my best, Reverend," she promised.

He replied with his gentle smile. "I'm sure you will."

CHAPTER THREE

UCKILY IT WAS MY LEFT ARM. I CAN STILL DO THE CROSS-
word puzzle." Emily came into the room just as Ezra was
holding up his broken left arm for Mrs. Fallon to see. Leave it to Ezra to
find an upside to this calamity.

Mrs. Fallon seemed suitably impressed. She had rushed back from
her holiday weekend and had only had Monday to prepare the house for
Ezra's return. But, as always, she had done a wonderful job.

"Look at the cast they gave me. All cushy, with Velcro straps," he
continued. "In my day it was pure plaster, all the way. Of course, the one
on my leg is an old-fashioned model." He peered over the blanket at his
right leg, which was covered with a plaster cast that stretched from above
his knee, his toes poking out the bottom.

"You poor thing!" Mrs. Fallon said. "Are you in any pain?"

"Oh, not much. A little at night, when I'm sleeping."

"And when he's showing off," Emily's mother cut in. "Best not to
encourage him."

Lillian turned to her husband, who just that morning had been sent home in an ambulance and carried into the house on a gurney, then settled gently on a rented hospital bed that was set up in a spare bedroom on the first floor.

"So, how would you feel now if you looked around and found yourself in some strange room, in some dingy, sterile-looking rehab center?" Lillian asked.

Emily was holding a vase of flowers and a pile of magazines. She set the vase on the dresser where Ezra could see it. "I doubt the places Dr. Newton recommended were that horrible, Mother."

"I, for one, am relieved that we'll never find out," Lillian replied. "I'm sure Ezra is glad, too, to be in his own home, with me and Mrs. Fallon."

"I know, dear. I have only you to thank," he said graciously.

"There's nothing like your own home when you're not feeling well, Emily," Lillian continued. "When you get to our age, you'll understand."

"I already understand," Emily assured her. She was just concerned about how the seniors would manage, even with loyal Mrs. Fallon there to help. It was hard to tell Mrs. Fallon's age—somewhere in her early sixties? She was strong and capable, and Emily trusted her judgment, but she couldn't be everywhere at once.

Emily walked over to Ezra's bed and left the magazines on the nightstand. "How do you feel, Ezra? Did the ride in the ambulance bother you?"

He shrugged a bony shoulder. "It was interesting. I like seeing all the new equipment they carry. Those young men are strong. Lifted me right up. I felt like an emperor being paraded through the streets of Rome."

Emily smiled. He did watch a lot of the History Channel. "I guess you could have used the wheelchair. But it was faster that way," she said.

"We've rented a very nice chair for you. Top of the line," Lillian told him. "We can try it out later and make sure it works right."

"You may have to move some furniture so that Ezra can get around," Emily realized. "Do you want me to help you?"

Mrs. Fallon looked as if she would have welcomed the help, but her mother quickly brushed the offer aside. "That's all right, Emily. We can manage. Can't we, Martha?"

"Of course we can, Mrs. Elliot. Would you like anything, sir? Some hot tea?" she asked Ezra.

"Some tea would be nice. I'm feeling a little tired out," Ezra admitted, his eyes starting to droop.

"You need to rest," Lillian agreed. "That's what will do you the most good." She yanked the curtains closed, shutting out the bright sunlight. "You take a nap and we'll have lunch together later."

"I've made some nice chicken soup for you, Dr. Elliot," Mrs. Fallon said.

"With dumplings?"

Emily smiled at the hopeful note in his tone.

"Of course there are dumplings, Dr. Elliot. I couldn't serve soup to you without them."

"I could," her mother murmured. "All that pasty dough. It will lie very heavy in his stomach."

But Emily could see that even Lillian did not have the heart to deprive Ezra of his favorite comfort food on his homecoming day.

Ezra smiled, visions of dumplings dancing in his head, as he drifted off to sleep. Lillian let Emily and Mrs. Fallon pass in front of her, then walked out herself, shutting the door.

"Rest is the best thing for him," Lillian announced.

"Yes, it is. But the doctor said he has to be out of bed and sitting in a chair for a few hours a day also. So he doesn't catch pneumonia," Emily reminded her.

"Ezra is a doctor. He knows that," Lillian snapped.

Emily ignored her peckish tone. "You shouldn't shut the door all the way," she noted, opening it up. "You might not hear if he tries to call you. You should have a monitor in there. I'll pick one up and bring it by later."

"Good idea, Mayor Warwick," Mrs. Fallon said. "It's hard to hear Dr. Elliot's voice sometimes when he calls, even when he's well."

Emily saw her mother purse her lips. Obviously, she had not thought of that. "All right, get a monitor." Lillian shrugged, as if the device would comfort Emily but was not really needed. "Until then, we'll keep an ear out. No need to worry."

Emily was about to remark that she did worry. Her mother's hearing was quite compromised—since she refused to wear her hearing aids out of vanity—and Mrs. Fallon was always in the kitchen with some noisy appliance going, as well as the tiny TV she had there so she could watch her talk shows as she worked.

Though none of this boded well, Emily knew she had no choice but to sit back and see how it played out.

"I called the visiting nurse service. Someone is coming this afternoon."

"So soon? He's barely gotten out of the hospital," Lillian protested.

Emily could have predicted that reaction. "Yes, this afternoon. They need to check his vital signs several times a day. In addition to his broken limbs, Ezra had also had a heart attack. You know we have to take that seriously. As we discussed, you are going to need some help here, Mother. Otherwise this won't work out," Emily warned in an even tone.

"Yes, yes, I know. We'll figure it out as we go along," Lillian promised. "Thank you for helping fetch Ezra. Now I'm sure you have pressing business back at the Village Hall."

That was her mother's way of dismissing her. Emily was ready to go anyway. She picked up her coat and handbag. "I'll be back later. Call me if you need anything."

"We will," her mother added with her tight "Will you *please* go away now?" smile. "Don't worry. We'll be just dandy."

Emily left her settled in her favorite wingback chair, surveying her small but precious kingdom with an air of regal composure.

"AFTER YOU PULL OPEN THIS SECTION, YOU PUSH BACK THE ROLLER and then use these little wooden tongs to pull the paper out. You have to be careful. The metal parts get hot . . ."

Mrs. Honeyfield, the church secretary, was trying to explain how to remove a jammed piece of paper from the copy machine. Amanda was only half-listening. She held the binder of hymns close to her body, wondering if she was in over her head here.

Not just with the copier, which seemed to hate her at first sight. But with the whole job of church music director.

Just chill. It's your first day, she reminded herself. *It's not even lunchtime yet. You can't learn everything in one morning.*

"It's much easier if you don't tear it. Try to just gently tug . . . see?" Mrs. Honeyfield demonstrated, slowly slipping out the offending sheet that had brought the big machine to a grinding halt.

"Thanks." Amanda nodded and stepped back as the older woman snapped all the parts back together again.

Amanda knew she would never remember this magic routine. She had battled plenty of copiers in college libraries and the offices of music departments, and each had its own peculiarities. Amanda rarely had luck with any of them.

"I don't think it likes me. Machines never do," she told the secretary.

Mrs. Honeyfield stared at her. Amanda could see she didn't get the joke and didn't think the machine had any feelings one way or the other.

"If you have a problem with it, the instruction guide is right here, dear." She smiled politely and patted a laminated booklet that hung on the side of the big, ugly machine.

Mrs. Honeyfield returned to her desk to answer the phone, and

Amanda turned back to the copier and tried again. She needed copies of the worship plan she and Reverend Ben had just worked out. The meeting had lasted over an hour. She didn't think it would always go on that long, but it was her first day, and there was a lot to explain, especially with Christmas coming.

Worship services were planned on Tuesday, with a short review on Thursday or Friday. So today had been a good day of the week to start the job.

Thursday night choir rehearsals were most important, and Amanda expected that role to be the most challenging. Then there was the service on Sundays, of course. The tip of iceberg, actually, though it was the part that was most visible and significant to the congregation.

At least she had her own little office, in a cozy corner of the choir room. She was eager to get back there and go through the desk and examine the bulletin board. Maybe her predecessor had left some helpful hints and reminders. But first she had to review Sunday's hymns. Since she wasn't that familiar with the hymnal yet, Reverend Ben had given her some leeway and suggested she go over the hymns they had selected to make sure she felt comfortable reviewing them with the choir and playing them on the piano and organ. Amanda had appreciated that.

With a binder of sheet music under her arm, Amanda headed into the sanctuary. She had been in there briefly that morning when Reverend Ben showed her the piano and organ. A few lights were still on, shining down on the altar area. Amanda didn't bother turning on the rest.

She sat at the piano and opened the cover. Her fingers glided along the smooth, cool keys in an easy, rippling scale. She hadn't played keyboards much in the last few years, devoting herself entirely to the cello. But she had practiced at home last night and felt her touch returning. It was amazing how the body remembered some skills before, or even without, the conscious mind. Like riding a bike, for instance, or playing an instrument.

The choir was scheduled to sing "We Wait in Hope for the Lord" as

Sunday's opening hymn. Amanda played a few bars and then began to sing along. She didn't do a very good job with the first few bars, she thought. She paused and tried it again, finally hitting a high note that had been out of reach on her first try.

She sang to the end of the next bar and stopped to make a note on the music. A sharp, slow clap suddenly broke the silence. She lifted her head and turned, peering into the shadowy sanctuary. Was Reverend Ben listening to her? Amanda had been surprised when he hadn't asked her to play the piano or organ during their interview. Maybe now he was checking out her skills.

A figure stepped forward, down the center aisle, out of the darkness. Definitely a man, and definitely not the reverend. It was the pie guy again. Amanda felt her breath catch and quickly looked back at the piano. *I should call him the spy guy now,* Amanda thought, feeling both excited to see him again and very self-conscious.

"You have a lovely voice," he said. "You don't even need a microphone."

"The acoustics are good in here. This church is known for that." Amanda fussed with the sheet music, trying to ignore him as he came closer.

"Are you going to sing on Sunday?"

"No, but I'll be conducting the choir." She looked up at him quickly. He was standing near the piano now, just a few steps away. "I'm the new music director."

"Really? So you work here. How about Willoughby's; do you work there, too?"

Amanda looked down at the piano and closed the cover. "My mothe—stepmother, actually—owns the shop. I was just helping out for a while."

"Oh. Very interesting." She couldn't tell from his tone if he was sincere or mocking her. Or flirting with her. Maybe a mixture of all three?

Before she could reply, he added, "So you're not a bakery girl after all. You're a musician?"

"Yes, I'm a musician." *Or trying to be,* she amended silently. She started to gather the sheets of music and put them back in the binder, but it was suddenly a mess, with pages springing out all over the place. She wanted to make a fast getaway but feared she would leave a trail of music in her wake.

She felt him studying her and glanced up. He was tall and had broad shoulders, which looked even wider as he crossed his arms over his chest and stared down at her.

She was sorry now that she had dressed in such a hurry this morning, pulling on a cream-colored turtleneck and a tweedy brown skirt. Her long hair was brushed back in a ponytail and she wore no makeup, just a dab of lip gloss. She usually dressed with more flair but thought she should look conservative for a job in a church. And it never occurred to her that there would be anyone here to dress up for. *Well, wrong about that one,* she realized. She would definitely do better tomorrow.

Though his outfit wasn't unremarkable, he looked fairly remarkable in it. He wore a dark blue pullover today that was stained with paint and maybe varnish. The spots matched the marks on his faded jeans and boots. Despite the worn wardrobe, or maybe because of it, he looked as if he had just stepped off the cover of *GQ* or out of some glossy advertisement for male magnetism and charisma.

He caught her gaze and smiled at her in a way that was totally unnerving. As if he had just guessed everything she had been thinking about him.

"So, are you going to sing some more?" The light in his blue eyes was so encouraging, Amanda was tempted to comply.

Instead, she rose from the bench and grabbed the binder. "Uh, no. I'm not. Time to go," she replied. "See you."

"Really? I was hoping to hear the rest of the song."

Amanda quickly escaped up the center aisle and dared a glance back at him. "Sorry, show's over. Next performance is Sunday. No tickets required," she added with a wry grin.

"Yes, I remember." He nodded, as if acknowledging that he didn't attend church much. "Wait. You never told me your name. Or should I just call you Music Girl?"

Amanda couldn't help but smile at that twist. She turned at the top of the aisle. "It's Amanda . . . Amanda Harding." She paused. "So . . . should I just call you Window Guy now?"

He laughed, a warm, deep sound. "It's Gabriel . . . Gabriel Bailey. I thought you'd never ask."

She left the sanctuary and headed to her office. And couldn't stop smiling. Gabriel Bailey . . . Pie Guy, Spy Guy . . . and Window Guy . . . was extremely cute and clever.

And even though dating was low on her list right now, Amanda knew she would happily agree to go out with him . . . if he asked her.

She ducked into the choir room with a surprisingly happy feeling. Who would have thought she would meet a guy like that at this job? Would he be around a lot, working on the windows? Or was this just a random thing? Maybe she could find out somehow.

At least you know his name now, she told herself. *And he knows yours. That's a start.*

"Emily? Is that you?"

"Yes, it's me, Mother. I have the monitor."

Emily had returned to her mother's house on Tuesday after work, bringing the baby monitor and some other items she thought they might need. She let herself in with her own key, since she knew that the task of answering the door was a long and sometimes painful one for her mother and that Mrs. Fallon might be helping Ezra.

Her mother had called from the living room but appeared in the foyer with surprising speed. "Thank goodness you're here. Something terrible has happened."

"What is it?" Emily's heart jumped. "Is it Ezra?"

What a fool I was to leave them alone. They didn't even get through his first day home. I knew this was a recipe for disaster. Even with Mrs. Fallon here—

"Ezra is fine. Comfortable as a clam." Her mother waved a thin, bony hand, heavy with antique rings. "It's Mrs. Fallon. Her daughter, rather. We just had a call. There's been an accident. Holly is in the hospital. Yale Medical Center, so that's good. Not critical, thank goodness, but very serious. An injury to her back. They're not sure yet if she'll need surgery."

Emily gasped out loud. "The poor woman . . . what about the babies?"

"The children are home with their father, safe and sound," Lillian cut in, dispelling her fears about the triplets. She turned and walked back into the living room, leaning heavily on her cane with each step.

"Martha wants to go down there right away," Lillian added. "At least until they can get some help in."

Emily nodded. She knew how devoted Mrs. Fallon was to her only child, Holly, and her husband—and now her three, practically newborn, grandchildren.

She doubted Mrs. Fallon would return to Massachusetts any time soon, even if Holly and her husband did bring in more help. Her mother was fooling herself to think otherwise. Mrs. Fallon was a dedicated employee, no question, but her family needed her now.

"Where is she?" Emily asked.

"Upstairs in her room, packing." Her mother balanced on her cane a second, then dropped heavily onto the sofa. "She's driving to New Haven tonight. The sensible thing would be to wait until the morning, but she won't listen to reason."

Emily didn't reply. Lillian had always been a very reasonable parent, never swept away by emotions, rarely rushing anywhere on her daughters' behalf. Emily had harbored her share of disappointments about Lillian's mothering. But she had learned to forgive and let go, to accept her mother for who she was.

"This accident leaves us in the lurch, doesn't it?" Lillian admitted. "At least for a few days."

"I think Mrs. Fallon needs to be with her family, Mother. Probably for a few weeks."

Lillian looked surprised at that prediction. "A few weeks? Do you really think so? That doesn't work out for us at all . . ."

"Mother, it's her daughter, with three infants. Even if Holly doesn't need surgery, she'll definitely need a lot of help right now—and the peace of mind of having her mother there."

Her mother's mouth twisted, as if she were struggling to swallow something very sour. "I suppose . . . Oh, here she is." Lillian hoisted herself up on her cane as Mrs. Fallon came down the stairs. Emily heard an odd bumping sound, then saw the housekeeper carrying two large suitcases, one in each hand. She set them down in the foyer, near the front door.

Well, that was a clue right there. She planned on staying in Connecticut as long as she needed to, no question.

Mrs. Fallon came into the living room, and Emily greeted her. "I'm so sorry to hear about Holly. Have you heard anything more?"

The older woman looked as if she had been crying. "Thank you, Emily. No, David hasn't called back yet. I just want to get down there to see her. Especially if she's going to have an operation tonight."

"Yes, of course. We'll all be thinking of your family and praying for them. Especially for Holly." Emily gently touched Mrs. Fallon's shoulder.

"Thank you, Emily. I'm sorry to leave you all in the lurch like this, with Dr. Elliot so sick—"

"Don't worry about that now. We'll be all right. You need to be with Holly and David, and your grandchildren," Emily assured her. She glanced at her mother. "Isn't that right, Mother?"

Lillian paused a moment, then nodded quickly. "Yes, of course. Such sad news. We wish you all the best. You'd better get on the road, Martha. It's a long drive."

Emily knew that in her mother's mind, Mrs. Fallon was abandoning them. Her farewell barely masked her annoyance.

Mrs. Fallon didn't seem to notice. Or maybe she was used to Lillian by now and just ignored her slights.

"Yes, I should get going. I just want to say good-bye to Dr. Elliot," she added. She turned and headed for his room, with Emily and Lillian behind her.

Ezra was sitting up in bed, reading a book. He quickly put it aside when he saw Mrs. Fallon.

"Any more news?" he asked with concern.

Mrs. Fallon shook her head. "Just the same that I told you before. I'm going now, Dr. Elliot. I'm sorry to leave you like this, but—"

"Now, now. Don't you be apologizing to me. Don't give it a thought. It will help Holly enormously to see you by her bedside. Best medicine in the world, I guarantee it. Godspeed, Martha. Give us an update on Holly when you can. We'll be praying for you all," he promised.

He took her hand in his, and Mrs. Fallon leaned down and gave him a quick hug.

"Good-bye now. I'll be in touch," Mrs. Fallon promised.

Lillian and Ezra said good-bye again, and Emily walked her to the front door. "Do you need any help with your bags?" she asked.

"Oh, I can do it. Never pack more than you can carry. That's my rule for traveling." She leaned over and grabbed her bags; luckily, she was quite strong.

Emily opened the door for her. Mrs. Fallon paused before she walked through. "I hope it works out here with your parents. I know how important it is to your mother to have Dr. Elliot at home while he recovers."

"I'm going to stay over here tonight, and we'll figure it out tomorrow." Emily had already made that decision, though she'd had no time to call home and tell her husband, Dan. "I'm sure we can get some help in here quickly. No need to give it another thought. You have a safe trip."

The door closed behind Mrs. Fallon, and Emily wondered if her assurances were true. She braced herself for a royal battle with her mother about bringing help in. They would need someone here around the clock. *Total strangers,* her mother would complain.

But what was the alternative? Send Ezra to a rehabilitation center, as his doctor had first suggested. She already knew what her mother thought about that. And she also knew her mother would do her best to sabotage every health care helper that stepped through the door.

Then what?

Emily dreaded the answer to that question.

Chapter Four

As Emily expected, lining up qualified help from a home nursing service was not a problem. How long those helpers would last at her mother's house was the question. They had been through this before, when her mother had fallen and broken her hip. Emily and her sister, Jessica, both dreaded dealing with the situation again. There was no reason to think it would go any more smoothly. Their mother was already boiling oil to toss over the castle walls at the invaders.

Emily had called Jessica the night before, filling her in on Mrs. Fallon's sudden, game-changing departure. Jessica, always willing to help, had arrived bright and early Wednesday morning so Emily could run back home and change for work. But from the moment she opened her eyes, Lillian debated the need for twenty-four-hour help, insisting to her daughters that it wasn't necessary. Emily, fearing Lillian would never let the new hire past the door, decided to put on her clothes from the day before and stay, at least until the aide arrived. Sometimes it took both of them to handle their mother.

Alice Briggs seemed promising. She greeted Emily with a calm, confident smile and an attitude to match. Lillian tried to intimidate her as soon she set foot in the house, questioning her credentials and experience. Alice was unflustered, easily fending off this first attack.

Emily and Jessica glanced at each other. Round one, Alice—a hopeful sign. But there was no guarantee Nurse Briggs would last until lunch.

While Alice hovered over Ezra, taking his vital signs, and Lillian hovered over Alice, the sisters slipped into the kitchen.

"She's the brassy type. I like that. I think she'll give Mother a fair fight," Emily predicted in a low tone.

"Let's hope so," Jessica agreed. "You go, Em. I'll stay a little longer, see how it goes. I don't have to be in until eleven; I have late hours today."

Jessica worked at a bank in town. She had been there many years, off and on, as her three children were growing up, and was now a senior manager. Even though they both worked on Main Street, the sisters rarely had the chance to meet, for lunch or even coffee. It was usually some family gathering or problem with their mother that brought them together. Emily wished she had more time with her sister. Even though Jess was nine years younger, she was still Emily's best friend.

"If you have the time to spare, I'm going to run home and change. I hope I don't need to start leaving things here."

"Don't even say it," Jessica warned. Years ago, after Lillian had taken a fall, Emily had practically been living there until her older daughter, Sara, actually did move in to help her grandmother.

"Good point; I won't. But even if Mother tolerates Alice, there are two more aides coming, one at five o'clock and one at eleven. They really need round-the-clock care right now."

"We'll just have to see how the rest of the helpers add up. So far, so good?" Jessica offered optimistically.

"I guess so. But even if these nurses work out, we've still just solved half the problem. If only we could find one person, who would live in and also do some light cooking and housework. Like Mrs. Fallon." Those chores were not really covered by the aides they had hired.

"Mrs. Fallon is one in a million," Jessica said.

"She gets along with Mother, so I'd guess she's one in a trillion," Emily corrected her before giving her sister a quick hug and heading on her way. She could hear her mother and Alice Briggs conversing in an animated tone.

". . . but he always has a shower in the evening," Lillian was saying.

"It's healthier in the morning," Alice countered.

Oh dear, they're at it already, Emily thought as she slunk out of the house. Her mother was a tireless opponent and relished a battle of wits . . . or of "nitwits," as she was likely to call it.

Alice Briggs had no idea what she was up against.

EMILY FINISHED WORK EARLIER THAN USUAL. IT WAS JUST FOUR o'clock, but she was dragging after not sleeping well at her mother's the night before, and she decided to head home. But first she swung by Providence Street to see how things were going.

As Emily walked up the path to the front door, she braced herself. Lillian had called twice and left long messages. No emergencies, thank goodness, just petty problems with Ms. Briggs. Emily was sure Lillian had a laundry list of complaints by now.

Instead of using her key, she rang the bell. Her finger had barely lifted off the button when the front door flew open. Emily expected to see her mother. But it was Alice Briggs, coat on and medical bag clamped beneath her arm.

"You're here. Good. I was just going to call . . . I can't wait for the evening nurse. I have to go." Ms. Briggs swept past her, practically knocking Emily out of the way as she left the house.

"But . . . wait . . . you're supposed to stay until five. Until the next nurse gets here."

Alice Briggs turned at the bottom of the steps. "I'm sorry. Mrs. Elliot is impossible. I can't work under these conditions. I'm a qualified professional. I don't have to take that sort of abuse."

"I'm sorry. She can be very difficult, I know." Emily followed her down the steps, trying explain. "I'll talk to her. She's just scared. She can't stand losing her autonomy."

Ms. Briggs shook her head. "I won't be back tomorrow. I quit." She adjusted the strap on her medical bag. "The agency will find someone. Call tonight. It's not too late."

Emily sighed and nodded. "I'll do that."

"Good night then, and good luck," Ms. Briggs added in a tart tone. As if to say, "With your mother, you'll need it."

Emily already knew that. Well, the evening shift nurse would be around very shortly, she thought, checking her watch. Then the overnight nurse.

Her mother would probably run through all three of them and need replacements for tomorrow. She would call the agency right away and get to work on it. But she didn't think this system would last very long, not more than another day or so. Then where would they be—back to square one?

LILLIAN HAD SEEN EMILY'S CAR PULL UP AND HAD PEEKED OUT THE window, watching her daughter and that horrid health aide converse.

She was greatly relieved when Emily had not been able to persuade that Briggs person to stay. Once she was sure the annoying woman was gone for good, Lillian hobbled back to Ezra's room and sat in a chair by his bed, her cross-stitch project in hand.

"Mother, what is going on here?" Emily turned to Ezra, remembering her manners. "Hello, Ezra. How are you feeling?"

"I'm coming along, Emily, coming along."

"No thanks to that Briggs woman. He'd be dead by now if I let her have her way."

Emily's eyes narrowed. "Really? And how is that? Did she contradict you on something? Suggest you serve prune juice instead of orange?"

Lillian shook her head, pulling the thread through the taut fabric with care. "No need to be sarcastic, Emily. The buck stops here with Ezra's health. I have to oversee his care. Anyone can put on a uniform and pump up a blood pressure kit. That doesn't make you a genius in my book."

"Oh, Lily, she was perfectly competent," Ezra said. "So she disagreed with you a few times. She was doing her job. You were much too hard on her. I hope you find some manners and apologize tomorrow."

"Ha!" Lillian replied, not even looking up.

"Well, that boat has sailed, Mother. Ms. Briggs will not be returning. She just quit. But I think you already knew that."

Lillian glanced over her reading glasses at Ezra. "See? What did I tell you? Totally unprofessional."

"For goodness' sake, you show no mercy, Lily," Ezra chided her.

"It's all right, Ezra," Emily said. "I'll call the agency. They'll send someone else tomorrow morning."

"My, what a drama. You'd think I chased off Florence Nightingale and Clara Barton rolled into one. Nurse Briggs talked a good game, but she was quite incompetent . . . and cocky. I saved Ezra from a medical catastrophe, and this is the thanks I get."

Emily wondered if she should bother asking for details. Of course that line of questioning was futile. Her mother could not be trusted to relay the truth; she would make up anything at this point.

The door chimes sounded then. The second-shift nurse, right on time.

Lillian looked up and dropped her stitching into her lap. "Did you call your sister already?"

"It's the second-shift nurse, Mother. Don't you remember? You need help around the clock. Nine, five, and midnight. We discussed this." Emily sighed as she headed to the door.

"Oh, bother," Lillian said with vehemence. "I just get my house back, and another stranger comes barging in."

Emily let in the new health aide, a woman in her midfifties with a round, pleasant face and a warm smile.

"How do you do? I'm Nancy Ames, from the agency."

"Nice to meet you, Nancy. I'm Emily Warwick, Mrs. Elliot's daughter and Dr. Elliot's stepdaughter. He's the patient."

"Yes, I know. I read the medical report before I came."

She had removed her coat and hung it on the rack in the foyer. Just like Alice Briggs, she wore a neat uniform and carried a medical bag. "May I meet the patient?"

"Of course. Come right this way." Emily led her through the house. "Dr. Elliot is a very easy patient. My mother, however, can be very demanding," she said honestly. "She's suspicious of anyone coming into the house."

"Many seniors are like that. I understand," she said calmly.

Nancy Ames seemed the opposite of Alice Briggs; soft-spoken, no hard edges or brassy confidence. Though she also seemed a solid, centered person, one who could stand her ground.

Emily introduced her to her mother and Ezra and, a short time later, left for home. Ms. Ames was looking over the records Ms. Briggs had left and asking Ezra questions. Lillian was interrupting, answering for him, but Ms. Ames remained calm, practically blending in with the woodwork. How could her mother find fault with that? Maybe this nurse had a better temperament for the household and her mother had been right to let the morning nurse go.

Emily was fast asleep that night when her cell phone rang, buzzing loudly on the nightstand. As the town's mayor, she was often called in the middle of the night to be informed about emergencies. She sat up in bed and snapped on a light. The number was unfamiliar—not the police or fire chief or even the sanitation department.

"Emily Warwick," she answered quickly.

"I'm sorry to wake you. This is Nancy Ames. There's a problem at your mother's house. I think we need your help."

"What sort of problem? Is everyone all right?" Emily jumped out of bed and grabbed her robe.

"Your mother and Dr. Elliot are fine. But it's the end of my shift. The night nurse is here. She's outside. Your mother is refusing to let her in. She says she doesn't want anyone else here tonight, and she wouldn't be able to sleep with a stranger roaming around and—"

"Yes, yes, I understand," Emily cut in.

"I offered to stay," Nancy Ames added, "but she didn't want that either."

"That was good of you, thank you," Emily said sincerely. "I'm sorry for your trouble. Where are you now?"

Emily could hear her mother in the background, talking in a harsh tone, though she couldn't discern her words.

"I'm in the mudroom. Your mother wants me to go, but I told her I wouldn't leave until I called you."

Cornered in the mudroom. Standing her ground, unwilling to abandon her post, poor woman. Emily could just picture it.

"Thank you so much. Could you possibly wait a few minutes? I'll be there right away."

Nancy assured Emily that she would do that. Emily was both relieved and totally incensed at her mother. She pulled sweats on over her pajamas, knowing she would be sleeping at her mother's house for the rest of the night.

Dan had managed to sleep through the phone call, but now rolled over groggily. "Something going on at Lillian's? Are they all right?"

"They're fine, but my mother's driving everyone else crazy. As usual."

Emily yanked on some socks and her sneakers. "She won't let the night nurse in and is kicking out the evening shift. I have to sleep there again." Emily pulled out a pantsuit and a sweater from her closet and some other items she would need in the morning, packing everything in a nylon tote bag. "You'll have to drive Janie to school tomorrow. Make sure she takes her lunch. Have her call me when she gets up, okay?"

"Okay, honey. Will do. We'll be fine." Dan worked at home and had always taken a big interest in caring for Janie, much more than other fathers Emily knew. Which worked out well, since her job was so demanding. As the former owner and editor-in-chief of the village newspaper, he had put in his share of office hours. But that was behind him now. His second career was writing about local history and sailing his boat.

"Do you want me to go? You still have to get to the office tomorrow."

Emily sighed. He was sweet to offer, but she was afraid her mother wouldn't let him in either.

"Thanks, honey. I'd better do it. But this can't go on for the next two months. Jess and I have to figure something else out. I just don't know what."

EMILY HAD SET HER PHONE ALARM THE NIGHT BEFORE AND WOKE AT the usual time, seven a.m. It took her a few moments to realize that she wasn't at home, but in the guest room at her mother's house.

Lillian had been very blasé last night when Emily had arrived, acting as if she didn't understand what all the fuss was about. As if this middle-of-the-night visit had been Emily overreacting and she'd had nothing to do with it at all.

Emily had expected that, too.

One in the morning had not been the moment to bring her sister into the situation. But Emily knew Jessica was up at seven, too, and she dialed her number before she even got out of bed.

"I'm at Mother's again," Emily reported. "She kicked out the evening nurse, who was very pleasant and easygoing, and she wouldn't let the night shift in. I came over so they wouldn't be alone."

"I'm sorry, Em. Why didn't you call me? Isn't it my turn to sleep on that awful old mattress?"

"That's all right. No reason for both of us to have a bad back this week."

"Why are you talking so quietly? I can hardly hear you."

"I think Mother's still sleeping, and I don't want to wake her up," Emily said. Her mother's room was next door. Lillian's hearing could be awful—or sharper than radar, depending on the situation. Emily didn't want her up until she and her sister had devised their next move.

"We need a new plan, Jess. The agency won't send an endless stream of aides."

"I have some news. I was talking to Molly last night, and she gave me the name of a woman who sounds perfect. Someone who worked in her shop while getting a home health aide certificate. She's actually a professional nurse with a specialty in cardiac care in her own country. She's moved here from El Salvador and needs to be recertified before she can work in a hospital again. Molly says she's terrific and can get along with anyone. And she would be willing to live in and do the cooking and cleaning."

Emily felt suddenly awake, a jolt of hope coursing through her like a cup of hot coffee. "That sounds too good to be true. What's her name?"

"Estrella Salazar. Molly couldn't say enough good things about her, and you know how tough my sister-in-law can be."

That was true. Molly was no pushover. Her recommendation went far with Emily.

"Is she available? When can we meet her?" Emily sat up, searching for something to write on.

"I sent her an email last night, and she just sent a note back. She can come to Mother's house this morning for an interview. I told her ten o'clock. What do you think?"

"Perfect, Jess." Emily felt like giving her sister a huge hug. "I don't want to get my hopes up."

"I know what you mean, but let's be optimistic. Seek and ye shall find, right?"

Emily smiled. That was one of her favorite verses, too. "Right. And the person for this job will have to be heaven-sent. I don't know how else they would manage it."

"ESTRELLA? WHAT SORT OF NAME IS THAT?" LILLIAN FACED HER TWO daughters, her back up like a cat's.

"She's from El Salvador. She's trained as a cardiac care nurse but can't work in a hospital here yet. She needs to get recertified," Jessica explained.

"Right, and I'm actually a brain surgeon in my native land. Didn't I ever tell you that?"

Emily smiled tightly, forcing herself to remain calm. "She's bringing her references, Mother. We'll check everything. She is certified in home health care in Massachusetts. There's no question of that."

Lillian sighed and sipped her coffee. Though Emily and Jessica had warned her that Estrella was coming at ten, she had made no effort to get dressed. And it was nearly ten.

"And she'll take care of the housework, as well?" Ezra asked. Emily had fixed him breakfast on a tray, and they were all in his room while he ate. "That would be a help."

"She'll live in and take care of everything, just like Mrs. Fallon. It would be best to have one person here around the clock. Not three," Emily added.

"How about zero?" Lillian countered. "Annoying busybodies. They hardly give him a moment's peace, justifying their own existence."

"Come now, Lily. Look at me. I can't even get out of this bed without a crane. We definitely need some help. But I vote for just one. One good person whom we can get to know. Three is a little overwhelming," Ezra confessed.

"Then I hope you like her, Ezra," Emily replied sincerely.

Before they could ask any more questions, the doorbell chimed. Jessica jumped up. "Right on time. I'll bring her back so we can all talk together."

"I can't meet anyone. I'm not dressed." Lillian tightened the belt on her silk robe for effect. "Ask her if she'll come back later. If she's unemployed, she must have all day free."

"We made the appointment for ten, Mother, and we're going to have the interview as planned," Emily said firmly.

"Just freshen up and throw something on, Lily. We'll chat a little until you come down," Ezra suggested.

Lillian stood up from her chair, looking miffed. "I can't just *throw something on*. And I won't entertain in this state of *déshabille* . . ."

"Oh, brother, she's talking French. Watch out, ladies." Ezra rubbed his cheek, looking distressed. He was an expert at reading the signs of Lillian's temper by now.

"Suit yourself, Mother," Emily stated flatly.

"Fine. I'll be in my room. I can see I have no say any longer about what goes on under my own roof. You two have reduced me to the state of a powerless child. With the help of that turncoat." Lillian swung her cane in Ezra's direction, balancing herself with the other hand on the back of her chair.

"Lily, don't flounce off like that," Ezra said, clearly not offended. "Stay and meet this new helper. What do we have to lose?"

But her mother was already at the door and didn't even turn to glance back. "If you don't know the answer to that question, Ezra, you don't deserve to know."

What is the answer? Emily wondered. Her mother feared losing her independence, her autonomy—and believed Ezra should fear it and fight it, too. That had to be it.

Ezra sat back against his pillows, looking a bit frustrated but not all that put out by Lillian's dramatic exit. "She needs some time alone," he said. "The last few days have been difficult for her, with me getting sick like this. And she knows she can't care for me on her own. It's been a lot of stress for your mother. I worry about her."

That was just like Ezra, too, to worry about her mother when he was the one who really needed care.

"All the more reason to get some good, live-in help here," Emily replied.

Ezra nodded. "No argument here, Emily. Believe me."

Before Emily could answer, Jessica appeared with a woman who had to be Estrella. She was very pretty, Emily thought, guessing her to be in her midthirties. She had fine features, high cheekbones, and dark eyes. Dimples showed in each cheek as she smiled hello. Her thick, dark hair was pulled back in a bun, and she wore small gold earrings and a gold wedding band.

She had already taken off her coat but carried a large handbag with a manila folder tucked in the outside pocket. Her résumé and references, Emily hoped. She wasn't wearing a uniform, but a blue sweater set and black pants. Tasteful and conservative.

Even her mother would have approved, Emily thought, if she had troubled herself to be in the room.

"It's very nice to meet you, Estrella," Ezra said. "Thank you for coming over on such short notice."

"Thank you for getting in touch with me. I'm happy to help if I can," she replied politely, deep dimples appearing in her cheeks.

Ezra was totally charmed, Emily could tell. He sat up a little higher and smiled back, looking over Estrella's résumé. "Let's see . . . so you came to the US seven years ago, and have mainly been working in health care," he began.

"I take other types of jobs in between, if I can't find a home-health position. But that's what I'm trained to do. I was a nurse in a cardiac care unit at a hospital in El Salvador for almost ten years, before coming here. But I haven't been able to get certified in nursing again. It's complicated. My English wasn't good at first. It's been . . . frustrating," she admitted.

"Yes, I imagine it must be," Jessica said sympathetically.

"Where did you work last? Here in town?"

Estrella described her last position. She had worked in the home of a family Emily knew, the Gilmores. George Gilmore, who was about her mother's age, had recently passed away from heart failure and other complications. George had been living with his son Tom's family, and Estrella moved in to care for him during his final days.

It would be easy to get a frank, detailed reference from the Gilmores, Emily thought. She could call Mary or Tom this morning. Estrella spoke with a slight accent, Emily noticed, but was very fluent in English. Her mother wouldn't be able to complain about any communication problem, though she'd probably try.

"So you're able to live in. That will work out for you?" Emily asked, wanting to make sure.

"It's not a problem. I've been asked to do that before. My mother lives with us, so she will care for my children."

"Oh, you have a family. I didn't realize that." Ezra looked concerned. "How many children do you have, Estrella?"

"Two, a boy and a girl. Marta is six and Jorge is eight," she said proudly. "They're good children. They mind their *abuela*. I do whatever the job requires."

Estrella hadn't mentioned a husband, though she wore a ring. Emily didn't think it was polite to ask. It did sound as if she might be the sole breadwinner for her children and mother.

"You can have at least one evening and one day off a week," Jessica offered. "My sister and I will come and help out. That won't be a problem."

"Our housekeeper, Mrs. Fallon, always had a day off," Ezra explained. "She's down in Connecticut, helping her daughter."

Estrella nodded. "Yes, Mrs. Morgan told me that in her email."

They each had a few more questions for Estrella, and she had a few of her own about Ezra's condition and medical needs. She seemed satisfied with the salary they were offering as well.

"It's been delightful to meet you," Ezra said when it was finally time for her to go. She stood by his bed and shook his hand. *"Mucho gusto,"* he added, testing out his Spanish.

Estrella's face lit with a smile. *"Gracias.* It was very nice to meet you as well, Dr. Elliot."

"Is this interview being conducted in a foreign language? Then I haven't missed much." Lillian came through the door, leaning heavily on her cane. "When did you learn to speak Spanish?" she asked Ezra. "I had no idea."

"There are many things you still don't know about me, dear," Ezra said calmly. "Estrella, this is my wife, Mrs. Elliot. Lillian, this is Estrella Salazar. We've had a very good chat."

"Isn't that delightful." Lillian's tone was dry as she looked Estrella up and down—searching for some fault she could fix on, Emily had no doubt.

Estrella smiled at Lillian politely. "I can stay longer if there's anything you would like to ask me, Mrs. Elliot."

Lillian considered the offer a moment. "I'm sure my husband and daughters have asked enough. Don't mind me. My opinion counts very little around here," she added with a shrug. "I just do whatever they tell me. You know how it is when you get old."

Emily met Jessica's wide-eyed gaze, and it was hard not to laugh out loud.

"Oh, Lily, come on. No need to get that way," Ezra urged her.

He looked over again at their visitor. "Thank you again for coming. We'll be in touch very soon, I'm sure."

"Either Jessica or I will give you a call later today," Emily promised. She was already in favor of hiring her, but they did have to check her references.

"Thank you, Ms. Warwick. I look forward to it."

Jessica showed Estrella out, and the others waited a few moments before they started to talk about her.

"I think she's perfect," Emily stated. "I hope her references check out. She worked for Tom and Mary Gilmore. I'm sure they can tell us all we need to know." Emily took out her phone. "I'm going to call them right now."

"Yes, call them, Emily. I'd like to hear what they say," Ezra said eagerly.

Lillian sat down in the chair beside Ezra's bed. "I can already tell you're smitten," she said to him. "But what about communicating clearly? That could be a problem. It could be dangerous for you."

"Her communication skills are excellent. I understood her perfectly and vice versa," Ezra countered. "I just said a few words in Spanish to break the ice."

"What ice was that, Ezra? It seemed positively tropical in here when I came in."

Ezra ignored her. "If her references check out, she can start tomorrow if she likes."

"Tomorrow? I've barely said two words to the woman." Lillian sounded shocked and upset. "'Hello and good-bye' was the extent of it. I think she should come back, have a second visit with us. After all, she'll be living here, day and night. It's important to get to know her better before she moves in."

Jessica had returned and cast Emily a worried look. "That's true, Mother. But we may lose her if we drag this out too long."

"Oh, piddle-paddle. What's meant to be is meant to be," Lillian said.

"And 'actions speak louder than words,' my dear," Ezra countered. "Anyone can talk a good game at an interview. You said so yourself. Let's hire her, see her in action. Then you be the judge."

Clever Ezra, he was the only one who could outsmart their mother. Emily loved to see him in action.

"All well and good," Lillian retorted. "But if it doesn't work out, one of us will have to fire her. Have you thought of that?"

Ezra cocked his head to one side. "True, dear. But I would leave that job to you. You're quite good at it and have the most experience. Though you can jump the gun at times; even the best candidates need a learning curve."

Emily exchanged looks with Jessica again. She felt as if they were watching a championship tennis match. Their mother was nimble, no question. But Ezra had the edge and seemed ready to close it out—game, set, and match.

"A probationary period?" Lillian returned in a huffy tone. "Is that what you're suggesting?"

"If you want to call it that, fine with me," he agreed.

"All right, have it your way. If her references check out and that résumé isn't a work of fiction, I suppose we could give this Estelle person a try."

"*Estrella,*" Ezra corrected her. "The word means *star* in Spanish."

Lillian rolled her eyes. "Heaven help me. I don't even like films with subtitles. Do you really think this can work?" she asked her husband.

"I believe she'll work out just fine," he assured her.

Emily waited for further debate from her mother. But finally, Lillian just levered herself up from her chair with her cane and swung out of the room. "Do what you like. Don't mind me. I only own this house, that's all," she said tartly.

Jessica cast a worried glance at Ezra.

"Don't worry. I know how to handle your mother," Ezra promised.

Emily certainly hoped so. If not, they were running out of solutions.

AMANDA DIDN'T SEE GABRIEL AT CHURCH ON WEDNESDAY AND DIDN'T notice his truck in the parking lot on Thursday morning either. Even after chatting a bit with Mrs. Honeyfield about the window repairs, it was hard to tell when she might run into him again . . . and she didn't want to seem too obvious in her questions.

She had chosen her outfit for the day with much more care—a dark blue sweaterdress that complemented her blue eyes, with high black boots and arty, hanging earrings Lauren had given her. She had also gotten up earlier to blow out her hair, telling herself that all this primping was not because of Gabriel. The choir was meeting that night for rehearsal, and she knew that feeling confident about her appearance would give her a bit of an edge in managing the choir members for the first time. She was a little nervous about the rehearsal and wanted to be totally prepared, completely acquainted with the music and the various parts of each song, especially the sections that might trip them up and need extra coaching.

She was in the sanctuary, working on the well-known Advent hymn they would sing on Sunday, "O Come, O Come, Emmanuel," when she heard the distinct sound of a ladder rattling just outside the big doors. She turned to see Gabriel walking into the sanctuary, toting the long ladder and his canvas tool bag.

He was taking care not to scratch the varnished wood moldings around the doorway, so it took him a moment to notice her. He smiled, looking surprised and pleased. "Am I interrupting you again? I can come back later."

"It's okay. I'm just about done here." She was, too, and just about to leave for lunch, though she did suddenly consider staying a little longer to talk to him.

"If I'm making too much noise, just let me know. It shouldn't take me that long."

Amanda was sorry to hear that but kept her voice bright as she replied, "No problem." She turned back to the piano, made a few more notes near the end of the hymn, then gathered up her music.

Gabriel had set up the ladder nearby and climbed up about halfway. There was a light tapping sound as he began to work on a section of a window. Amanda closed the piano and walked over to watch him. It looked as if he was stripping away the thick, dark frame around a section of glass. He gently pried and tapped with a sharp tool until fragments of glass broke apart into his hand. "Watch out! Some of this might fall near you."

Amanda stepped back, but he seemed to catch the pieces easily.

"I know, it looks like I'm making it worse, right?"

"Well, yes," Amanda admitted with a smile.

"'If you want to make an omelet, you have to break some eggs,'" he said. "Same with fixing stained glass. This piece was cracked and was going to fall out soon anyway. I'll take these fragments back to my shop to match the color as closely as possible, then make a new piece to replace it."

"How do you manage to knock out just the one section?"

"That part is a little tricky. The answer is: Very carefully." He glanced down at her and grinned. "I just want to make sure the church doesn't get any feathered visitors before I patch this up." He was quickly covering the hole in the window with a bit of plastic and duct tape. Amanda was mesmerized by how quickly and smoothly his hands moved as he worked. "I'll have this one fixed before Sunday. The rest shouldn't take too much longer."

Amanda wondered what he meant by that. Would he be around until Christmas, or be done before then?

There were three arched windows on each side of the sanctuary and a round window at the base of the steeple, visible behind the balcony. Quite a few of the windows were patched together with duct tape and plastic, and she secretly hoped they would take longer than he predicted.

"That's my favorite window," she said after a moment. "Maybe because it's so Christmassy."

The window he was working on depicted the manger on Christmas night, with Mary and Joseph on either side of the crèche and the holy infant swaddled in white, the stable animals looking on at the humble scene. The sky above the manger was a mosaic of dark blue glass, with a large, golden star hovering above.

Gabriel nodded. "I love this one, too." He leaned back a bit to look up at the window. "I love the placement of the figures, the way their bodies bend toward the cradle. The colors blend perfectly, and there's so much expression . . . It's really amazing work."

"Yes, it is amazing. I could never have explained it quite that way," she admitted. "But that is why I like it so much."

He climbed down from the ladder and was suddenly quite close to her. "Which is your next favorite?" he asked curiously.

"I'm not sure," she said honestly, gazing at the other, beautiful choices. "I like the one with the dove," she said, pointing to the first window on the other side of the sanctuary. "It's a little different from the others, a lot brighter . . . How old are these windows? Are they as old as the church?"

"Not quite. The church was originally built in the Colonial era. But the early settlers didn't use stained glass in their churches, even though they had the technology and it's a tradition that goes back to the Middle Ages."

"That makes sense. They were Protestants, so I guess they were trying to break away from those traditions of adornment," she said.

"That was it exactly. But there was a fire in this church in the early 1800s. Everything burned down except for the stone walls. When it was rebuilt, which took years, a wealthy church member donated the windows. Cyrus Krupp, I think his name was. Anyway, by that time the taste and style of church decor had loosened up a bit, and the congregation was very happy to have the more colorful windows installed."

"I can see why. They're very beautiful, and the light coming through them makes the sanctuary look . . . well, even more sacred."

"Yes, the colors are perfect. I think the artists who created these scenes did a wonderful job. Though there's no real record of who they were," he added, gazing around. "These are probably the nicest windows of any church in the area . . . and I've seen all of them," he added with a grin. She smiled back, but before she could reply, he said, "I'm sorry, I didn't mean to go on like that. You asked me a simple question and you got an art history lesson."

"It was interesting," Amanda assured him. "I've looked at these windows for years and never really appreciated them. It's sad, though, that the artists don't get any credit for their beautiful work."

"In some ways," he agreed. "But maybe they didn't want any. I think that designing these windows had to take a deep spiritual commitment and inspiration. Maybe they felt the usual recognition was not appropriate, the way some people feel about an act of charity. Sometimes it's more satisfying to do work like that anonymously."

Amanda nodded. She understood what he meant. The scenes were very evocative and did inspire a feeling of contemplation, very much like the right music during the service. Something about both the music and the light pouring through the stained-glass windows seemed to lift her heart.

She turned and looked back at Gabriel. He was not only attractive but thoughtful. She had expected just a quick, casual chat and instead he had changed the way she saw the church—or at least its windows.

She was about to walk into town for a bite to eat and thought she might ask if he wanted to join her. It wasn't usually her style to ask a guy out, but Gabriel was so easy to talk to, she felt as if she had already known him a long time, though it had only been a few days.

But before she could summon up the nerve, Reverend Ben appeared at the back of the sanctuary. "Amanda, there you are. I'm glad I caught you. Mrs. Honeyfield is just typing up the program, and I wondered if you could give it a quick proofread."

"Yes, of course, Reverend. I'll be right there," Amanda told him. The reverend smiled and nodded, then disappeared.

"Well, duty calls," Gabriel said lightly. "I did enjoy our talk, Amanda."

"So did I," she said, feeling suddenly shy. "It was very . . . informative."

"Really? Any time you need to know more about windows, I'm your man."

He caught her gaze and held it. Amanda felt her breath catch but tried hard to hide it. "I'll keep that in mind. Thanks."

Hugging the binder of music, she turned and headed out of the sanctuary.

One window down, but several to go, she told herself. There would be plenty of chances to ask Gabriel to have lunch . . . if he didn't ask her first.

AMANDA SCANNED THE ROSTER MRS. WILMOTT HAD LEFT. THERE were twenty-one singers in the choir. Glancing up, she did a quick head count and was relieved to see that practically all of them had shown up for rehearsal. Small groups were gathering and warming up, going over their parts. She could immediately tell that there were some strong voices, which was definitely a plus, and also some that were weaker. She knew there had been no auditions for the choir; anyone in the congregation was welcome to join. Which was as it should be in a church, and part of the joy of it, Amanda thought. But it was also a challenge to her now.

At seven sharp she called the group to order and asked them to take their places on the risers. They were not required to stand during the entire service, so there were chairs set on the risers for them.

Amanda took her seat at the piano and turned to them. "I'm glad to see that you're all here tonight. That shows real commitment." It might have also meant that they were curious to check out their new director, but Amanda ignored that possibility. "I'm sure it's hard to switch music directors like this right before Christmas. A little like getting a new coach just as you're ready to go into the World Series."

"Well, maybe it's not quite *that* hard," drawled Jack Sawyer, who owned the Christmas tree farm outside of town, drawing a round of laughter from the group.

"I heard you all sing on Sunday, and I think there's a lot of talent here," Amanda went on with a smile. "I think that you're a very good choir," she added, stretching her opinion a bit. "But I know that with a little more work, you can be a great choir. I really mean that."

She paused to see how they were taking this. It was hard to tell. Everyone was older than she was, some by many decades. Her aunt Jessica sat in the soprano section and gave her an encouraging smile. So did Sophie Potter.

"Mrs. Wilmott left some notes about the hymns you've been working on, and I'm not going to make any changes."

They all looked relieved to hear that. Reverend Ben and the former music director had picked out a list of familiar holiday hymns and carols. Amanda imagined that the group had sung many of them before, so that was a plus. How well they sang them was the question. And could they improve at this late date?

"As we all know, Christmas Day is the high point of the church calendar, and the worship music is so important. Reverend Ben says it's part of what helps us be in touch with the divine. So let's work hard to sing these beautiful hymns in a way that no one in this congregation will ever forget."

She asked them to stand and started them off with a few minutes of warm-up exercises for their lips and tongues. These were mainly non-sense sounds, sung to tunes that went up and down the scales. Some had lyrics, like "Many mumbling mice are making midnight music in the moonlight, mighty nice." But the exercises were also a good way to break the ice and get everyone to relax, which was important for a good sound from the group as well.

While they ran through their drills, Amanda assessed the singers. The bass and tenor sections were predictably all male, with the exception of Olga Ingram, a retired schoolteacher fairly new to the church, who had a very low voice for a woman and sang tenor. Frank Borge, who sang bass, stood on the highest tier at the back of the room and was probably the strongest and most polished in the group. He had toured in light opera and musical theater and still performed with local acting groups. Amanda already sensed that he took himself very seriously and was a bit of a male diva, if there was such a thing. But the others seemed to respect him, so it wouldn't be hard to give him the solos he might feel were his due.

Claire North, who lived on Angel Island and helped run the inn there, sang soprano. She had a surprisingly strong, clear voice for a woman her age and a wonderful range, Amanda noted. She was a perfect candidate for solos. Sophie Potter had another lovely soprano voice, and so did her aunt Jessica.

They warmed up next with some scales, and finally, Amanda was ready to start rehearsing the anthem, introit, and hymns they would sing on Sunday. She wanted to run through some of the other carols that were scheduled for Christmas Day, as well, and hoped they would have enough time.

The choral introit was the first piece of music in the service and sung before the reverend's call to worship. This week, Reverend Ben had chosen "We Wait in Hope for the Lord," in keeping with the Advent theme of waiting for the birth of the Messiah. The lyrics were based on Psalm 33 and were both comforting and inspiring.

The short piece was familiar to the group and they performed it fairly well, though not as smoothly as Amanda would have liked. She worked with them on their energy and diction, noting when to pause for a breath and when not to.

The next run-through was an improvement, and the last and final, even better yet. She was encouraged and turned next to the most important hymn, which the choir would perform for the congregation, "O Come, O Come, Emmanuel."

"I've sung this many times without ever really thinking of the words or their meaning," Amanda admitted. "But Reverend Ben explained to me that the hymn was a favorite for Advent, dating back to at least the twelfth century, originally composed in Latin for Advent vespers. It's based on a passage from the Book of Isaiah in the Old Testament—a prophecy that God would send a sign to the people of Israel, called Emmanuel—and a passage from the gospel of Matthew in the New Testament that states the fulfillment of the prophecy in the birth of Jesus of Nazareth."

"It's a beautiful hymn," Sophie Potter said, "and a classic."

Amanda ran through the piece once with them, eager to see how well they knew it. *Not very well at all,* she thought. The tempo was slow and it was always a challenge, even for a professional choir, to keep the song from dragging, as if they were each tugging along a sack of bricks.

There was also some mumbling, with lyrics not crisply pronounced. Amanda decided to work with the bass section first. She coached them after they ran through the first few measures, then had an idea.

"I'd like to do something a little different with this piece. Nothing too radical, but it should make the performance a little more dramatic." All eyes turned toward her curiously. She had them now, Amanda realized.

"Frank, I'd like you to sing the opening measures, solo, a cappella. Like a lone voice in the desert, calling up to heaven . . . 'Come, savior. Come to us. God promised you were coming and we need you. We're suffering,'" she added, paraphrasing the lyrics.

Amanda next turned to Claire North. "After Frank sings the first measure . . . and to the middle of the second," she said, checking the music again, "I want you to sing solo, the next two measures, until the refrain. As if you were an answering voice. Then I'll start playing the accompaniment, and everyone will join together in the refrain," she added. "You'll all sing in unison for the next three verses. Then at the very end, we'll close with Frank and Claire singing solo again . . . How does that sound?"

The group looked pleased. Something new and different took them out of their comfort zone a bit but also made things more interesting. Frank was eager to show what he could do with this. He stood a little taller and held out his sheet music. Claire sat up a little higher as well, getting ready for her part.

Amanda practiced with Frank and Claire first, while the others waited. Their solos were relatively brief, but sounded quite beautiful, she thought.

Next, she rehearsed the sopranos and altos, then the basses and tenors, and then they put it all together. The hymn had seven verses, but there were only four measures of music for each verse. Still, it was long enough, Amanda thought.

They had to sing it several times and work on the harmonies, especially the rising moments, which called for more energy and expression.

Finally, they seemed to have it down. They all looked a bit tired, and Amanda realized that over an hour had passed; she wondered if maybe Mrs. Wilmott hadn't worked them quite as hard in rehearsals.

"Good job. It sounds great," she praised them. Now if they could only remember the nuances on Sunday. "Let's go over the second hymn quickly. I promise I won't keep you much longer."

No one groaned out loud, though there were a few questioning glances. But they dutifully turned to another piece in their binders, "Watchers, Tell Us of the Night," which they would sing on Sunday with the congregation.

The hymn was short, only three verses, and once they had it down fairly well, Amanda was satisfied. She didn't want to risk a mutiny at her first meeting with them.

"Thanks, everyone. Please be at church by nine on Sunday morning so we can warm up and rehearse a bit."

They all looked quite relieved to be released; a few of the members on the higher risers practically jumped down. Others, like her aunt and Sophie, took their time.

"That was very invigorating, Amanda." Sophie tugged on her big coat and fastened the buttons. "Sometimes I feel like I could sing all night."

Amanda smiled. What spirit she had. "I almost did make you sing all night, Sophie. I sort of lost track of the time," she confessed.

"It was a longer practice than we're used to," her aunt Jessica admitted. "But I think we needed it. We need to get into better shape for Christmas."

"I agree," Claire North said. "It's like exercising. No sweat, no gain. I'm going to practice my solo at home," she promised Amanda. "I'll be well prepared for Sunday. Thank you for picking me out."

"Thank you, Claire." Amanda stood and cleared the sheet music from the piano. "I'm sure you'll be wonderful."

A few more members bid her good night, then Amanda was alone in the sanctuary again. She sat on the piano bench, feeling suddenly quite drained. She had worked hard, even though she hadn't been singing. It was like coaching a team from the sidelines. It was almost easier to just get out there and play, she realized.

She thought they had improved tonight, but she was still a little nervous about Sunday's service and positively panicked when she thought about Christmas. She had assumed this job would be easy. But the Christmas service, she could now tell, was going to take everything that she and the choir had to give. And Christmas was less than three weeks away.

CHAPTER FIVE

*A*MANDA WOKE UP ON SUNDAY MORNING TO FIND THE
world covered in a soft blanket of snow. It was hard to leave
her warm, cozy bed, but she forced herself out from under the covers.
She had to get to church well before the service began, snow or no snow,
and she rushed to get ready. She grabbed a travel mug of coffee and a
muffin, then dashed out to clean off her car.

As she drove toward the village, a few flakes still drifted down from
lavender-gray clouds that hung low in the sky. Even a light snow like this
would keep many people home this morning, and she didn't expect the
pews to be filled. Which was a good thing, from her point of view, today
being her big debut as music director.

She should have practiced the organ piece she was going to play during the offering. She had hoped to run through it a few times before the
service began, but could see that wasn't going to happen now. It was
more important to warm up the choir and have them practice their songs

a few times. She was curious to see if they remembered the points she had tried to drill into them during the rehearsal.

Amanda didn't expect anyone in her family to be at church today. Molly had to work this morning. The wave of Christmas parties her company catered was just starting. Her father had wanted to come, but Betty had a cold and he thought she should stay in all day so she wouldn't miss school on Monday.

Her aunt Jessica and uncle Sam were there, of course, since Sam was the head deacon and Aunt Jess was in the chorus. They would provide more than enough cheerleading, Amanda was sure. She felt nervous and wasn't sure why. She had played for much tougher audiences. She wasn't even really in the spotlight, just a supporting player. But members of the congregation would be watching to see how well she did her new job, that was for sure.

Most of the choir members had arrived by the time Amanda got there. She herded them into the sanctuary and managed to squeeze in a quick rehearsal. Then it was time for them to put on their robes and prepare for their entrance.

She saw Reverend Ben greeting members of the congregation as they came in. "Good morning, Amanda. Ready for your first service?"

Amanda forced a smile. "I think so."

He patted her shoulder. "Don't worry, it will be fine. I've made the biggest gaffes in church history up there. No one seems to notice."

Amanda had a feeling he was just saying that to make her feel better. Funny thing was, it worked.

Reverend Ben peered into the sanctuary, then checked his watch. "I think we can start. I'll collect the choir. You settle in and play the opening music, then let me know when you're ready to start the entrance hymn."

Amanda nodded, feeling suddenly nervous again. She walked into the sanctuary and headed up the side aisle. The pews were not filled, but there were many more in attendance this morning than she had expected.

She had to check the organ first and purposely kept her head down as she adjusted the stool and arranged her music. She knew that everyone wished her well—all the people who were sitting out there and had watched her grow up in this church. But looking at any of them would be distracting right now. And she felt distracted enough.

Then she went over to the piano, where she had to play the introit, "We Wait and Hope for the Lord." She would be switching back and forth between the piano and organ several times during the service, and hoped she wouldn't forget any of her cues.

She started with some incidental music, a classical piece to set the mood for spiritual contemplation. It was a good way for her to warm up at the instrument, too. She was glad to be starting at the piano, where she had more confidence. She wasn't very comfortable at the organ. She barely knew how to work all the knobs and pedals and pretty much dreaded moving over there later.

When she had finished the mood-setting piece, she turned and glanced over her shoulder, looking for Reverend Ben. Her gaze never quite reached the spot, snagged instead by the sight of Gabriel Bailey, who sat in one of the rear pews. He looked straight at her and smiled, then nodded encouragingly.

She met his gaze a moment and couldn't help smiling back.

Did he usually come to church, or had he come because he knew it was her first Sunday?

She noticed a teenage boy sitting next to him, looking like a lankier, gawkier version of Gabriel. A younger brother? Had to be, she thought. She liked the mature version better, but it was fun to see what Gabriel must have looked like in high school. Still pretty cute, she thought.

She quickly looked for Reverend Ben again and saw him at the sanctuary doors. The choir stood behind him, lined up in two neat rows. He lifted his hand and she turned back to the keyboard. She sat up straight, took a breath, and said a silent prayer: *Please help me do a good job up here, God, and let the music touch everyone who's come to church today and help them feel closer to You.*

She struck down hard on the opening chords and felt, rather than saw, the congregation sit up and take notice, their scattered attention fully focused on the music and the procession of the choir to the altar.

The sanctuary filled with sound as the choir began to sing, moving in a stately procession down the center aisle, their red robes rustling, followed by Reverend Ben in his white cassock and bright blue vestment.

He sang, too, his strong tenor voice filling out the blend of voices nicely. He took his place in front of the altar as the choir climbed into the risers and completed the piece. *They did a good job,* Amanda thought, feeling encouraged.

The service began with the call to worship and opening prayers. It was soon time for the choir to sing "O Come, O Come, Emmanuel."

Amanda was a little nervous. The brief rehearsal before the service had not assured her that this more complicated arrangement was going to work. She wondered now if she should have left well enough alone and not tried to challenge them.

But when the moment came to start the hymn, she met Frank's gaze with a confident nod and conducted with one hand while her other rested on the silent piano keys. His deep, unaccompanied voice seemed to fill the sanctuary, stilling every other sound as he sang the opening lyrics.

Her glance flew next to Claire, who was standing and ready for her part. She came in right on cue, her voice exceptionally clear and strong. She had practiced and it showed, and Amanda was grateful for that effort.

Amanda signaled, and the rest of the group rose, singing the chorus in unison as she struck the chords on the piano. They moved through the rest of the verses with a flub or two, but did manage to keep up the energy.

Amanda had sung the hymn herself many times without ever really thinking about the words or their meaning. Now, as the voices blended and lifted, she felt something inside of her lift, too. The choir seemed imbued with a special energy. It wasn't just their colorful robes or Sunday smiles. It was something inside them, coming through, in their expressions, in their eyes. Something in their hearts shining through. It was real spirit, Reverend Ben might say. When the final notes of the song sounded, with only Frank and Claire ending the hymn with their unaccompanied voices, Amanda sat back with a small but amazed smile.

The congregation was silent a moment, then broke into applause. Which Reverend Ben did not normally encourage, but did permit on special occasions, and from his broad smile, Amanda could tell this was one of them.

"Fine job, choir. Thank you very, very much," he said heartily.

Amanda kept her gaze down on the piano keys and music. Then she stole a glance at the choir members, who beamed with pride. *They did a wonderful job and moved the congregation,* she realized. *And I helped them.*

That was the high point of the service for her. The rest went by in a blur and with a few missteps. Finding herself at the piano when she should have been at the organ and losing her place a moment in one of the hymns. But the seasoned choir members picked up her slack. Sophie Potter, who sat close to the piano, cast her more than one encouraging look. Most other members were understanding, too. Vera Plante did seem disgruntled at one point, but you can't win them all, Amanda reflected.

She was greatly relieved when the congregation rose with their hymnals in hand, ready to start the closing song, "Watchers, Tell Us of the Night." Reverend Ben sang along for a while, then walked to the back of the sanctuary to give his closing blessing.

Amanda played a few bars of incidental music, and the service was over. "Amen," she sighed quietly as she finally stood up from the piano.

As the sanctuary quickly emptied, Amanda accepted a few words of congratulations from choir members. Sophie, of course, was the first. "Good job, Amanda. You play so well. It's a pleasure to sing along."

Amanda thanked her, thinking how good-hearted Sophie was, always lifting others up with a kind word or compliment.

"Lovely solo, Frank," Amanda said as their bass star walked by.

"Thank you for asking me, Amanda. I think your idea worked out very well. Very creative," he added. "I hope we can do more interesting arrangements."

"I hope so, too," Amanda replied.

Her aunt Jessica bounded down from the risers and gave her a hug.

"Your mom told me to text her right away," she admitted. "I'm sending a great review."

"Thanks, Aunt Jess." Considering how close her family was, and how all of them belonged to this church, Amanda had no doubts that a full report would reach her parents before she even got home.

Her uncle Sam waved from the other side of the sanctuary and managed to give her a thumbs-up, though his arms were full of pine boughs. The deacons were staying after the service today and decorating the church. Jessica walked over to join him and gather up Amanda's three cousins.

Amanda picked up her music and headed for the choir room. Reverend Ben was still at the back of the sanctuary, speaking to a group of church members. She glanced around at the back pews, hoping to see Gabriel still there, but he was already gone. *Oh well, no big deal,* she told herself. But she did feel a little let down.

"Nicely done, Amanda," Reverend Ben said as she walked by.

Amanda smiled and thanked him, then quickened her pace toward the choir room. She put her things away quickly and grabbed her coat.

A few of the singers were still there, slipping out of their robes before they headed off for the rest of their day. They offered their congratulations, and their words of praise made Amanda feel good, even though she knew there was room for improvement. At least she had her first service under her belt. The rest had to be easier.

As she passed through the big sanctuary doors, the chilly air felt refreshing. The clouds had cleared, and bright sunlight sparkled on the pure white snow that covered the village green. Amanda decided to walk across the green and stop in at her mother's shop. She was sure Molly would appreciate a full, firsthand report of the service, if she was there. If she was already out working at a party, Amanda decided she could at least get something good to eat for lunch.

She had barely walked a few steps down the path when she felt a big wet splat on her back. A snowball? She turned and looked around but couldn't spot the culprit.

"Whoops . . . sorry, lady!" a male voice shouted out.

Before she could catch sight of him, a more familiar face popped out from behind a nearby tree.

"Amanda! . . . That was meant for me." Gabriel was suddenly standing beside her, brushing snow off her coat.

"Oh, it's all right. It's just snow." She turned toward him, and their faces were very close. His cheeks were red from the frosty air, and his eyes looked very bright.

He was starting to answer when another snowball—flying at lightning speed—hit him on the back and pushed him toward her. He had to grip her arm to keep from falling over.

Loud laughter sounded from across the green. "Got you that time!"

"Cheap shot!" Gabriel shouted back. Now Amanda could see their nemesis, who was also hiding behind a tree. Gabriel's brother, of course, whom she had seen earlier in church. He had scooped up more snow and was already packing another missile.

"Uh-oh . . . Quick, get behind the tree again." Gabriel tugged her arm and pulled her behind a nearby tree. Just in time, too, as big snow-balls pelted the other side of the trunk.

"Looks like we're under attack," Amanda said quietly.

"I think so. Time to reload and defend ourselves." Gabriel scooped up some snow and began making a snowball.

"Two against one? That's not fair," Amanda objected.

"Don't worry. He's got a friend over there," Gabriel replied, squint-ing toward their opponents. "Here's the plan. You sneak up that path and get closer. I'll walk out, as the decoy. When they show themselves, hurl your snowballs with all you've got."

Amanda nodded and began making some snowballs of her own. She wasn't that athletic and hadn't been in a snowball fight for years, but she hoped she could complete this simple assignment.

She pulled up the hood on her coat and quickly trotted up the side path. When she was closer to Gabriel's brother, she turned and looked back.

Gabriel nodded and then, somewhat theatrically, stepped out from cover and ran to the middle of the green. "Okay, guys, I'm coming for you," he called out. "Come out and fight like real men . . ."

Gabriel's brother and his friend suddenly jumped out from their hid-ing places, too. Before they could bombard Gabriel, Amanda tossed snowballs with both hands and managed to hit her target both times. Then she jumped behind a tree again.

The teenagers stared around in surprise, looking for her, and then Gabriel got them, too.

Then they realized they'd been tricked and pelted him. He tried to get away, but he was laughing so hard, his feet slipping in the snow, he could barely run to her tree and hide with her. But he finally made it, just in time. He stood very close beside her as the other side of the tree trunk was bombarded with snowballs.

"Good job. You should have seen my brother's face. I'm glad you're on my side."

"Just a lucky shot," she admitted. She wanted to look out from behind the tree but didn't dare. "How long do you think they're going to keep that up?"

The snowballs were still flying, but quite a few missed the tree and landed near their feet, or even behind them.

"Knowing my brother . . . they could be out there until spring." He slowly leaned over and waved a gloved hand. "Okay . . . truce?" The snowballs kept coming. Gabriel reached into his jacket pocket and pulled out his key ring, then waved it.

"You can borrow the truck," he called out.

The snowballs suddenly stopped. "Really?"

Gabriel put his head around the tree. "For an hour. And don't do anything stupid."

Amanda felt safe enough now to finally step out from behind the tree, too.

"That's pretty generous of you. Or desperate," she added.

"We were supposed to go over to some sports store for a new basketball. He can go with his buddy. A small price to pay," he added.

"Very clever," she replied.

"I thought so," he said with a smug but charming smile.

The two boys had run toward them through the snow. Now Gabriel's brother grabbed the keys and shot him a victorious grin. "An hour isn't very long," he pointed out.

"If I tell you an hour, you'll come back in two," Gabriel said. "Just keep your cell phone on."

"Okay, will do. See you later." The boys dashed off, and Gabriel turned to her.

"Well, that's settled," Amanda said, amused. "But what are you going to do without your truck? Do you need a ride?"

"I might need a ride," he answered with a thoughtful expression. "But first, I thought I'd take you to lunch. Unless you have plans?"

Amanda was surprised by the invitation, and very pleased.

"Sure. Lunch sounds great."

"Where would you like to go?"

"I don't know. Anywhere is fine." She shrugged. "Anywhere that serves hot chocolate," she amended.

"Good point. Hot chocolate is definitely required after a snowball battle. I think it's a state law now." His serious tone made her laugh again. "Let's see . . . How about the Clam Box? They definitely serve hot chocolate . . . and it's definitely anywhere. Or even nowhere, some people would say."

She found herself laughing again. A light wind off the harbor blew a few strands of her hair across her eyes. She swiped them away with her hand.

"My parents always took us there right after church when we were in school," she said. "They used to serve pancakes all day on Sundays, all you can eat."

"Same here. That's what made me think of it. You can't go wrong with their pancakes."

"As opposed to the rest of the menu?" she asked.

"Exactly." He nodded and smiled, then met her gaze. His eyes were so blue, as blue as the sky or the water in the harbor. She felt herself blush and hoped he would think it was just the cold air.

He was dressed for church and looked very different than he did in his work clothes. Though he was more than attractive in either style, she thought.

"So you belong to this church?" she asked curiously as they began to walk across the green toward town. "I've never seen you here."

"My family has belonged for a long time, but we were never that regular about attending. On holidays, mostly." He stuck his hands in his pockets, and their steps fell into sync. "But I've been coming more since my dad died. Reverend Ben was a big help to our family when my father passed away. He's great to talk to, and I like to hear his sermons."

Amanda nodded, feeling sad about his loss, though she hardly knew him. "I like his sermons, too. He manages to take spiritual ideas that I never really understood and makes you understand how they apply to your everyday life. It's hard to explain," she added, wondering if she had managed it at all. "But I usually get something helpful out of what he says."

"I know what you mean. I do, too."

They walked along a little farther without talking. They had taken the path that wound along the harbor, and Amanda enjoyed the view. The harbor was empty this time of year, with only a few hardy boats tied up on their moorings—fishing and clamming boats mainly.

"That's too bad about your father. Did he pass away recently?" she asked.

"It's been about two years now. Sometimes, it still feels like yesterday," he admitted. "My mom's had a rough time. He was pretty young and it was very sudden. He left for work one day and didn't come back."

"Oh, how awful," Amanda said sincerely.

"It was a heart attack. He worked too hard and never took care of himself."

"What did he do for a living?"

"Stained-glass artist." He glanced at her and smiled. "I was at RISD," he added, referring to the Rhode Island School of Design. "But I came home and decided to stay, take over the business. My mother works, but she doesn't make enough to take care of herself and my brother—he's a junior in high school now, but he was only thirteen then. So I took over the shop. I used to work with my dad when I was in high school, so I already knew the business. It won't be forever. I mean, if I don't want it to be. My mom went back to school last year, part-time. She's studying to be a teacher. She'll be certified soon."

"Oh, that's great," Amanda said.

It was noble of him to have put aside his own plans to help his family, she thought. Not too many guys her age—well, he was a few years older, but still—would have made that sacrifice and sounded so comfortable with it. The admission made her see him in a different light.

The Clam Box wasn't too crowded, considering it was a Sunday at noon. A waitress with dark red hair seated them at a table near the window and handed them two menus. "The specials are on the board," she said as she filled their water glasses.

Gabriel folded his menu and put it aside. "I already know what I want. But you take a minute," he said to Amanda.

"I know, too," she said, closing her menu.

The waitress pulled out her pad. "Shoot," she said, looking at Amanda.

"I'll have the three-stack hot cakes, with a fruit cup, and hot chocolate, please."

"I'll have the same," Gabriel said.

"You got it. Be right back with the hot chocolate."

"I was going to order a side of bacon, but the fruit cup is much healthier," he said as their waitress hurried off. "See, you're a good influence on me."

Amanda laughed. "Don't worry, I won't hold it against you if you want to have some totally unhealthy breakfast meat."

"That's okay." He shook his head, looking fine with his decision. Then his hand suddenly popped up. "Waitress?" he called, making Amanda laugh.

Their waitress didn't hear him; she was nowhere to be seen.

"I was only kidding. I fooled you, right?"

Amanda nodded. "Yes, you did. What did you study at RISD, stand-up comedy?"

"Exactly. A double major in stand-up comedy and fine art. I was planning to be a post-Impressionist comedian. I still might try for it," he added.

"That act would be original." Amanda guessed he was only half-joking now. "Do you still paint?" she asked, eager to know more about him.

"It's funny—not so much anymore. Now that I'm working with glass all the time, I find that my ideas for my own artwork come to mind in that medium. A lot of the work I do nine-to-five is repair and renovation, like at the church. Interesting but not that creative. That's why I enjoy making my own pieces, which are more original."

She knew that there were great works of art in stained glass—the windows in many of the medieval and Renaissance churches, or those of the artists Louis Tiffany and Marc Chagall. But she understood what Gabriel was trying to say. It was the difference between practicing your craft and being truly creative.

"I feel that way about some jobs I've had playing the piano or cello. They're sort of routine, not too much creativity involved. But when I have the time to play music I really love, it's much more satisfying . . . and it makes up for the rest."

"You play the cello, too? What are you, a one-woman orchestra?"

"Hardly," she said, feeling her cheeks get warm again under his admiring gaze. "Most professional musicians have some knowledge of keyboards. But the cello is my main instrument. I'm hoping to play professionally in an orchestra somewhere."

Their waitress returned with their orders, setting down the food and adding a pitcher of syrup and a bowl of butter pats. "Anything else?" she asked.

Amanda liked cinnamon on her pancakes and French toast . . . on a lot of things, actually, but before she had the chance to ask, Gabriel said, "Could you please bring some cinnamon when you have a chance?"

She disappeared again and he sat back, looking at his pancakes. "You go ahead. I can't eat them without cinnamon."

She leaned back, too, placing her fork on the side of her dish. "I can wait . . . I like cinnamon, too," she admitted, feeling a strange, secret bond with him.

This was so silly, she almost wanted to laugh. She would have to call Lauren later. She had already told Lauren about the super cute guy who got the free pumpkin pie on Thanksgiving.

"He sounds like a total hottie. I think you ought to follow a trail of pie crumbs or something and find out where he lives," her sister had advised. Amanda hadn't spoken to Lauren all week; she was going to love hearing there was more to the Pie Guy story.

"You have a funny smile on your face, Amanda. Is it the cinnamon pancakes?" Gabriel's question broke into her rambling thoughts.

She shook her head. "I was thinking about my sister, Lauren. My stepsister, actually. But we're super close. We were best friends in middle school when our parents got married," she explained.

"Really? That must have been fun." Their waitress had returned with the cinnamon, and he politely offered it to Amanda first.

"It was like having a sleepover with your best pal every night. It still is," she admitted, thinking about their all-night gabfests. "I was just thinking of something funny," she explained. *About you,* she secretly added as she handed him the spice.

"Sounds like you miss her." He shook some cinnamon onto his pancakes and took a bite.

"I do," she replied. "I have two other sisters, Jillian and Betty," she added. "Jill is away, too. She's still in college. Betty is six. She's growing up like an only child, since the rest of us are living away."

"Yeah, that can happen. But . . . you still live here, don't you?" He looked puzzled, as if wondering if he had missed something.

"Good point. I was just trying to make sure you were paying attention," she joked.

"Oh, I haven't missed a word, Amanda. Don't worry." He looked up and caught her gaze for a moment. His blue eyes were pretty amazing, like diving into the deep end of a swimming pool on a very hot day.

She almost forgot what she was about to say.

"I was living in New York City," she explained. "I moved there after grad school and had an apartment with a few friends. But it didn't work out, and I moved back to Cape Light a few weeks ago."

She practically swallowed the last few sentences. It was hard to admit. She knew it wasn't really a failure—just a temporary setback—but it still stung. It still felt hard to say the words out loud, especially when Gabriel Bailey seemed so . . . so impressed with her or something.

He didn't say anything at first, and she wondered if he thought less of her now. "New York's loss, Cape Light's gain, I'd say. So, what were you doing in New York? You weren't a church music director down there, were you?"

Amanda laughed. "Everything but. I took a lot of different jobs, some musical and some not. I worked as an accompanist at a dance studio, played evenings in a restaurant, and waited tables at the same restaurant other nights, too," she admitted. "I was really trying to find a place in an orchestra with my cello and was auditioning a lot."

"I see. So you're a serious musician. You want to play at Carnegie Hall, or Lincoln Center, something like that?"

"Something like that." Right now she would settle for the most unknown orchestra in the most obscure city in the country. But she didn't tell him that.

"I took the job at church because it's better than working in my mom's shop, but I'm still sending out my tapes and waiting to hear about auditions." She wondered if this would dampen his interest in her. She suddenly hoped not.

Gabriel nodded. "That's good," he said. "It's important to set your sights high. Anyone can see that you're very talented."

"Thanks . . . We'll see." She rarely talked about herself this much, and she was curious about him. "So what are your stained-glass works like? Are they in any special style?"

He looked pleased at her interest, but there was a teasing light in his eyes, too. "Let's see . . . how can I describe them? They're sort of . . . flat and square . . . though some are curved around the edges," he added in a perfectly serious tone. "And colorful," he added thoughtfully.

She played along. "And made out of glass?"

He looked pleased by that response. "Yes, exactly."

She couldn't keep a straight face any longer and started laughing. "Seriously, is your work abstract? Realistic? Somewhere in between? . . . Or maybe you don't want to tell me? That's all right, I understand. Sometimes it's hard to describe an artistic style. I was just wondering."

Gabriel shook his head. "I didn't mean to be facetious. It's nice of you to ask. I guess you could say the style is sort of abstract, but not just mosaic designs. You can tell what you're looking at, most of the time . . . Does that help?"

She nodded. "It helps a lot. Do you enter any exhibits or show your work in any galleries?"

She wondered then if she was asking too many questions. He looked a little put off by that line of inquiry.

"I sell a few pieces in my shop. But mainly, I just enjoy making it," he explained.

Amanda decided not to press him. "Maybe I could see your work sometime," she said finally.

He smiled again. "Yes, I hope you can . . . Hey, I almost forgot, you did a great job today at the service. Were you nervous?"

"A little," she admitted. "Did it show? I know I hit a few bad notes."

"No one noticed," he assured her. "It's a lot to coordinate. I'm not even sure when I should stand up with the hymnal or sit down," he added, making her laugh.

Amanda knew that accepting compliments was not easy for her, but his words made her feel good. "Thanks. I'll be better next week."

"More hot chocolate over here? More pancakes? Some coffee, maybe? It's all you can eat." Their waitress appeared, slinging two glass coffee canisters like a cowboy with six guns.

"I'm fine, thank you," Amanda replied. "This hit the spot."

"No more for me, thanks." Gabriel's phone buzzed, and he picked it up off the table. "Sorry, I have to check this."

Amanda nodded. It usually didn't bother her if someone she was with checked their phone. As long they weren't staring at it all through the meal. And Gabriel had certainly given her plenty of attention—more than she was used to.

She wondered if a girlfriend was getting in touch with him. He was probably involved with someone. He had to have girls falling all over him.

"My brother, Taylor." He slipped the phone in his jacket pocket. "He is actually getting in touch on time. Feeling a little guilty about nearly killing us with those snowballs, I guess."

So it wasn't a girlfriend, she thought, feeling relieved and a little silly. Well, that didn't mean there wasn't a girl someplace.

"He went over to a sports store and is coming back to town. I guess I'd better get going so he can pick me up."

"That's all right. I have to go, too." Amanda was surprised to see the time. They'd been sitting there talking for over an hour.

The waitress had left the check and Gabe picked it up. "Why don't we split it?" Amanda offered, reaching for her wallet. "We both ate the same thing."

Gabe shook his head. "I invited you to lunch. It's my treat . . . even though it was only pancakes."

His tone implied the meal should have been much grander . . . or would be the next time. Would there be a next time? She hoped so. He was so attractive and so easy to talk to. Maybe she wouldn't be in town that long, but it would be fun to hang out with him while she was. She hoped that confiding her plans hadn't made him think twice about getting to know her better. Still, she didn't regret being honest. She didn't really know how to be anything else. Only time would tell if the admission had put him off.

They left the diner and stood on the sidewalk a moment. Gabriel spotted his truck a little farther down Main Street and waved to his brother.

"Well, it's coming back in one piece, so I guess I should be thankful." He turned to Amanda. "This was fun. I hope you'll get caught in the cross fire of one of our snowball fights again sometime."

"Well, I'm going to practice my aim, just in case."

"As long as you're on my team, that's fine with me." He laughed at her, then leaned over and quickly kissed her cheek. "See you," he said as the truck pulled up.

She felt surprised by his quick, casual kiss, and practically lightheaded. "Good-bye, Gabriel," she said finally.

He was already climbing into the truck, making his brother move over so he could drive. He turned and waved to her, then pulled away.

Amanda stood in front of the diner a moment, getting her bearings. Of all the things she had anticipated happening today, this impromptu date was not one of them. Her mother sometimes said the surprises in life usually turn out better than anything you plan. That was certainly true this morning.

Amanda wondered when she would see Gabriel again. He might not be back in church on Monday. But she knew she would see him soon, and that thought made her smile as she walked back toward the harbor. Everything looked so fresh and new today, covered with the glistening snow. This had turned out to be a good day, that was for sure. Better than she'd ever expected.

*   *   *

"ARE YOU PURPOSELY TRYING TO DRIVE ME CRAZY?" LILLIAN SWEPT into Ezra's room just as Estrella was leaving. She practically knocked the nurse down, but didn't bother to apologize. Or even make eye contact. Ezra wasn't surprised. She had barely said a civil word to the poor woman since Estrella had arrived. It had been four days now.

Ezra was waiting for Lillian to get tired of this battle and gracefully retreat. But she showed no signs of backing down.

"Drive you crazy? What did I do now?" he asked innocently, though he knew he was not the target of her ire—not really. "It's amazing how much trouble a man can get into, lying sick in bed all day. I positively amaze myself."

Her eyes narrowed as she stood at the end of his bed. "Don't be cute, Ezra. It doesn't suit you."

"Point taken. But I still don't understand the problem."

"You know very well what I mean," she insisted. She walked across the room and sat down heavily in the armchair. "I heard the both of you in here, chattering away. Couldn't understand a word of it. Probably complaining about me, right?" She didn't bother to wait for his answer. "You might as well have been planning a bank robbery for all I know. I've told you before, it's very rude. And how am I supposed to oversee your care if I can't understand what she's doing to you? Can you answer me that? Why, these helpers could kill you, give you the wrong dose of medication or something. The buck stops here, Ezra," she insisted, tapping her chest. "I can't make sure she's doing her job correctly if I need an interpreter."

Ezra tilted his head back. He had been talking with Estrella in Spanish. That was it. Lillian didn't like it. She felt left out. He understood that and had taken care not to do it when she was in the room. That was not polite, as she pointed out.

"I understand, dear . . . but when was this exactly? I didn't see you in the room a few minutes ago. Are my eyes going on me, too?" he asked innocently. "Or were you standing by the doorway . . . eavesdropping?"

The color rose in her cheeks, and she sat up straight, looking quite offended.

"If you had made yourself known, we would have stopped speaking Spanish at once," Ezra went on in a reasonable tone. "Estrella has offered to help me brush up on my Spanish, and I've offered to help her improve her English," he explained.

"Really? Well, so far, it looks as if you're getting the better end of that bargain. And I was not eavesdropping. How dare you accuse me of such a thing? I was about to come in and check on you when I heard you both in here, yammering away. I wanted to watch her, candidly. She's still on probation, you know."

So she was spying on Estrella, trying to gather some evidence to make a case against the young woman. That made sense. But he didn't want to accuse Lillian of that. Not quite yet.

"Yes, I know. She's been here almost a week. I have absolutely no complaints."

"It's hardly a week. She started Friday and it's only Tuesday . . . that's not even five full days. I'm not sure this is working out, Ezra. I'm not sure at all."

Ezra sighed. They had agreed Estrella would work for a week before they decided if she would stay on. Ezra thought Lillian would have come around by now. The clock was ticking down.

There was just something she didn't like about Estrella. Maybe because she couldn't find anything precisely *not* to like about her, and couldn't catch her doing anything wrong? That's what was driving his wife crazy, he thought.

"Look, Lily," he said, "I understand that all of this is terrible for you. I am so sorry to have gotten sick and put you in this position where you have to take care of me, where we need additional help in the house. I'm just glad we have someone here who can help, who has the medical training that I'm afraid I need right now."

"Yes, well . . ." Lillian began, but before she could say more, Estrella returned with a tray of covered dishes and her medical kit.

"Time to check your vital signs, Dr. Ezra." She took his wrist in one hand, found his pulse, and focused on her watch.

Lillian sat silently, watching. After a moment, Estrella marked his heart rate on her chart. "Eighty-five," she said.

"A little fast," he noted.

"Yes, it is," Estrella agreed.

It had been lower in the morning, Ezra recalled. He would bet his pressure was higher, too, he thought as Estrella put the cuff around his arm. He had Lillian to thank for that—Lillian and her mood.

"What's the pressure?" Lillian asked curtly as Estrella completed the test.

"One hundred forty over eighty," she reported.

"That's too high," Lillian said. "You're putting too much salt in his food. Maybe he needs a water pill . . . or some change in his medication."

"I've been cooking salt-free for Dr. Ezra, Mrs. Elliot," Estrella said politely. "And preparing only foods that are naturally low in sodium. I don't think it could be that . . . and I don't think he needs a medication change right now. But I will tell Dr. Newton what you said this afternoon when he calls."

Dr. Newton called every day to check on Ezra's condition and was due to visit at the end of the week. All of the visiting nurses had spoken to him, reporting Ezra's pulse and blood pressure and other vital signs. Ezra knew that Estrella wasn't trying to overstep her authority, but he could tell Lillian didn't see it that way.

"I'll speak to Dr. Newton myself," Lillian insisted.

"Yes, of course you will," Ezra chimed in. "I want to talk to him, too.

But Estrella has to report her chart. You know that, Lily. They all do it," he added.

Lillian pursed her lips, her eyes focused on Estrella, who had taken out an electronic thermometer and slipped a fresh cover on it.

"What are you doing with that thing?" Lillian asked.

"Taking his temperature," Estrella said.

"He doesn't have a fever," Lillian huffed.

"The incision is still healing. It's important to check and make sure there's no infection," Estrella said calmly. She had stuck the end of the instrument into Ezra's ear a moment, and when it made a beeping sound, drew it out.

Ezra wasn't used to the gadget and rubbed his ear. "Did that hurt your ear?" Lillian asked quickly, her tone laced with concern.

"No, dear, but it did tickle," he replied honestly. He glanced at Estrella, trying not to smile, and could see she was doing the same. If they shared a laugh at Lillian's expense, it would be like tossing oil on a flame.

Estrella concentrated on the thermometer. "Your temperature is ninety-seven point five. A little low, but nothing to be concerned about."

"No fever, you mean. See, I told you. I can tell when he has a fever. I can just see it in his eyes," Lillian insisted.

Estrella didn't reply. She didn't even react as she put her instruments away, Ezra noticed. She had a remarkable temperament. She was so centered, she didn't let anyone throw her off balance, not even Lillian. Not so far, anyway.

She looked up and smiled at both of them. "It's time for your show, Dr. Ezra. Would you like me to turn on the TV?"

Ezra was following a show on the History Channel about the US presidents. Lillian had been watching it with him. "I think it's Ulysses S. Grant today, dear. Care to watch with me? It should be a good one."

"In here? How utterly depressing. We'll watch in the living room, like the healthy, able-bodied adults that we are. This TV is just for drifting off," she insisted. "Has she been encouraging you to lie abed like a couch potato all day and watch TV?"

"No, not at all," Ezra insisted. "What a thing to say."

"Really?" Lillian looked as if she didn't believe him. "The next thing you know, she'll be feeding you through a straw," she grumbled.

Ezra was about to argue that he was not particularly healthy, nor able-bodied. Having broken weight-bearing bones, he couldn't be hopping up and down from the bed all day. Even in that infernal chair his wife had rented for him.

But I could be in a lot worse shape, he reflected, and getting out of bed for a while was necessary for his recovery. Especially to keep his lungs clear and keep his metabolism moving. He knew that well enough. It was just the way Lillian put it that irked him.

Before he could say a word to counter her, she turned to Estrella. "Are you trying to weaken him even further?"

"Of course not, Mrs. Elliot. Dr. Ezra always watches his show in here," Estrella replied.

"Since you've arrived, you mean. He needs to get out of bed and sit in his chair. You should know that better than I," Lillian insisted.

Ezra had been out of his bed that morning while Lillian was upstairs doing her hair. That's why he was tired now.

Estrella cast a questioning glance his way, but he waved his hand. "I think I will join Mrs. Elliot in the living room for a while, if you'll be so kind as to fetch my crutches," he said. "Maybe we'll have a hand of gin rummy afterward, eh, Lily?"

He tried to catch his wife's eye, hoping to soften her up. She was feeling displaced by this new helper and just needed some attention.

Lillian deigned to glance his way. "Maybe . . . if you're not too tired and weak to hold up the cards," she added in a sardonic tone.

"I shall gather my strength," Ezra promised, but his wife did not smile at the jest. It was, Ezra realized, going to be an even more difficult recovery than he had expected.

THAT EVENING, EZRA WAS ALONE WHEN ESTRELLA CAME IN TO GIVE him his nightly medications. Lillian had just left him, heading upstairs to bed. Flaring up all afternoon had worn her out, and she was ready to turn in a little earlier than usual.

"Here are your pills, Dr. Ezra. I spoke to Dr. Newton about your blood pressure spiking up today. He doesn't want to change the medication dosage until he sees you tonight."

"That makes sense." Ezra held the three pills on his palm then tossed them back. Estrella quickly gave him a glass of water. "I think it was just a fluke," he said after he had swallowed them down. *A fluke named Lillian Warwick Elliot,* he might have added.

Estrella nodded. "Yes, sir. Could be. But we need to watch it. I want to take your pressure again, if you don't mind."

Ezra offered his good arm. "Be my guest. I'm sure it's gone down."

Estrella wrapped the cuff and pumped it up, then watched the gauge.

"Estrella," he began, not sure of what the right words might be. "Please don't be upset by Mrs. Elliot's comments. She's very glad to have your help. It's just that this is a hard time for her, with my injury and convalescence. And it's difficult for her to allow anyone she doesn't know well to come in here."

Estrella nodded, then marked a notation on her chart. "I understand, Dr. Elliot. I am not taking this personally. She's frightened," she said simply. "That why she acts angry, no?"

"Yes, that's it exactly." He was relieved that she was so perceptive and understanding.

"My little girl, Marta, sometimes acts like that," she said quietly.

"Really? How old is she again?" He knew she had children, but realized that so far he had never really asked about them.

"She's six years old, in the first grade. She can read very well," Estrella said proudly. "Sometimes corrects my English."

"Keep her reading, that's important. And how about your boy, how old is he?"

"Jorge is eight. He's a good student, too, but had some trouble in school last year."

"Oh, why was that? Too interested in sports or video games?"

Estrella shook her head and looked down at the chart again. "When my husband died. A hard loss for both of them. He still doesn't really understand why his *papi* is gone."

Ezra felt as if he had been punched in the stomach. *She's a widow?* He had not imagined that. "I am so sorry. I had no idea. You didn't mention your husband. But you wear a ring," he added.

She nodded, her pretty smile now a tight, thin line. "Yes, I wear my ring. I am not ready to take it off." She paused and took a breath, composing herself. "It's not your fault, Dr. Ezra. I didn't tell you."

"I know, but—"

She shook her head. "I didn't tell you or Mrs. Elliot or your daughters on purpose. I want to be hired for my skills. Not out of your sympathy."

"Of course." Ezra nodded. He understood perfectly. "That's why we did hire you . . . and we have not been disappointed," he insisted. He paused, wondering if he should say more. Now he was curious about her home life. "So, can you tell me a little more about your family? You said you were from El Salvador. Is that where your husband was from, too?"

Estrella smiled and shook her head. "No, my husband was American. But we met in San Salvador. He was visiting there with a teaching organization. We were married and came back to the US, and I became a citizen. He traveled for his work, back and forth to Latin America," Estrella explained. "But on a trip to Nicaragua he contracted an illness. By the time he came home and had treatment in a good hospital here, it was too late. The infection overwhelmed his body."

"Oh dear, how awful for all of you." Ezra thought of her young children and how she had been left all alone in this strange country.

"We're managing, day by day," she said evenly. "My mother was able to move up here. She's a big help to me."

"What about your husband's family? Are they from New England?"

Estrella shook her head. "No. He grew up in Minnesota. His father is still there, but we don't hear from him much. My sister-in-law lives in Philadelphia. We see her from time to time."

Ezra nodded. It was a pity she didn't have any close family ties to help her. "You have a lot on your plate, young lady, a lot on your plate."

"It has been very difficult at times. But it gets better every day. I have my children, and they are a joy to me. No life is . . . smooth," she said finally, after searching for the word. "*Sí?*"

"That's right. There are always challenges, big and small. Is there any way we can help you?" he asked sincerely.

Estrella finally smiled again. A small smile, but to Ezra it shone like the sun peeking through clouds on a rainy day.

"You are kind to ask, Dr. Ezra. I am happy to have this job. That's plenty."

"We're happy to have you here," he assured her.

I am, at least, he added silently. Lillian would have to make the best of it, especially once she heard this young woman's story.

CHAPTER SIX

⌒⤙⤚

*T*HE SANCTUARY WAS THE PERFECT PLACE TO PRACTICE THE cello. The church was empty and quiet. Reverend Ben and Mrs. Honeyfield were gone for the day, and the nursery school had let out a few hours ago. Amanda knew she had several hours to practice before the choir arrived for the Thursday night rehearsal.

She had to make do for dinner, heating herself a can of soup in the church kitchen. But it was worth it. She would not be interrupted here, unlike in her room at home, which was theoretically private, but was not really sacrosanct, especially to her little sister, Betty. The sanctuary, with its domed ceiling and high stone walls, provided a much fuller sound and was much more like playing on a stage in a large concert hall. Much more like an audition would be . . . if she ever got a call.

Amanda sat with the instrument in the center of the altar, and the notes reverberated from every wall, up to the high arched ceiling and back.

She was practicing a piece by Vivaldi, the Cello Concerto in F Major.

The piece started with slow, sweeping notes, then built in intensity, with great tension and counterpoint. She came to a section marked *allegro*, and played fast and furiously, her strong fingers nimbly moving up and down the slim neck of the instrument, her bow working the strings to bring out just the right tone. She felt herself begin to perspire, beads of sweat on her hairline and forehead.

She didn't pause to wipe it away. She wouldn't be able to do that in a real audition. She wouldn't even be aware of her body—sweating with effort or trembling with fear—she would be so focused on the music flowing through her fingertips, flowing through the strings of her instrument.

While one part of her mind followed the intricate notes that she knew by heart, another reviewed again the email she had found on Monday morning. A note from the director of a symphony orchestra in Austin, Texas. One of her teachers, Professor Sloan, had recommended her for a seat that was about to become vacant. *Could she send her résumé and audition tape ASAP?* Amanda had left the church, run home, and brought everything to the post office and sent it by overnight delivery.

She had called Professor Sloan yesterday to thank her and, as politely as possible, ask what her chances were of getting the job. She knew there had to be other candidates.

"I don't want to get your hopes up, but I'd say your chances are very good. I know someone on the search committee. He said they listened to your tape as soon as it arrived, and it made a real impression. I put in a good word for you, too," Professor Sloan added.

Amanda felt so elated, she thought she was going to float away. When she told her parents about it at the dinner table last night, she had tried to be low-key and not get everyone's hopes up—including her own—but that was impossible.

"What great news, honey!" Molly said at once. "When will you hear?"

"Professor Sloan said they're going to pick two finalists and have them come in for a live audition."

"Oh, wow . . . dueling cellos," her mother quipped.

"That will be tough," her father agreed.

"I know they'll pick you, honey. I just have a feeling about this." Molly had gotten up from the table, carrying plates with one hand and giving Amanda's shoulder a reassuring squeeze with the other.

"It sounds like you have a very good chance," her father said, in a more reasonable tone. "We'll just have to wait and see, right?"

Don't count your chickens before they hatch was what he was really saying. Amanda knew that, but as she furiously tore through the remaining notes to the first section, putting all of her pent-up hopes and dreams into the rising and falling notes, she couldn't help but believe, down in her soul, that this was it. She was going to get this seat. It was meant to be, and very soon. Just after the New Year, she would be practicing like this up on a professional stage in a real concert hall.

She swept the bow across the strings one last time, drawing out the final chord, a hauntingly beautiful sound that echoed through the dark, empty sanctuary.

Then, nothing. Her bow hand dropped to her side. Her chin dropped to her chest. She sat in the silence, listening to the sound of her own deep breaths and feeling her heart pounding.

Then from up in the balcony, she heard the sound of someone clapping wildly. She was startled and frightened. She had thought she was alone in the building. Who was in here? Had one of the choir members come in early?

"That was awesome. You're a total genius!" Gabriel Bailey came to the edge of the balcony and looked down at her. "You should be in Carnegie Hall," he said.

"Gabriel, you nearly scared me to death." She was happy to see him, but he had practically given her a heart attack. She'd had no idea he was at the church today and had not caught sight of his truck or any of his equipment. In fact, despite their lovely outing on Sunday, she had only caught sight of him once this week, and they had barely said hello before Mrs. Honeyfield pulled her away for a phone call. She had been wondering if maybe he was avoiding her.

"I'm sorry. I didn't mean to scare you." He made a charming face. "I was going to say something, but I didn't want to interrupt you."

"Interrupt me next time. It's really okay." She really didn't like anyone listening when she was practicing. It was sort of unnerving. But as he came down the steps and walked toward her, her irritation dissolved.

He looked handsome as ever in a fisherman knit sweater, down vest, and his usual stained jeans. "I just stopped by to check one of the windows. I had to reshape a piece I used to repair it. I didn't mean to scare you, honestly."

She nodded, pushing her long hair to one side. She felt the moisture at the back of her neck and thought she must look a sweaty mess, as if she had just finished an aerobics class. "That's all right. I didn't mean to snap at you . . . Thanks for your good review."

"I rarely listen to classical music," he admitted. "But maybe I should start. That was beautiful. What was the name of it?"

"Vivaldi's Cello Concerto in F Major."

He nodded thoughtfully. "That's a mouthful. They really knew how to name them in the old days, didn't they?"

Amanda laughed. "The piece itself is actually quite long. I only played a section. I can burn a CD for you if you really like it."

She wondered then if he was just trying to be nice, saying he wanted to listen to classical music. She didn't want to force it on him.

"I'd like that a lot. I'd like to hear the whole thing. But it won't be you playing on the recording, I guess?"

"Oh, no . . . I meant a recording of someone famous. Yo-Yo Ma or maybe Pablo Casals," she said, naming two of the most towering artists in the world of classical music.

Gabriel shrugged. "I'm sure I'd enjoy that but, honestly, I'd rather hear you," he said, making her blush. "Are you going to play your cello in church Sunday, as special music?"

Amanda had been a soloist in church a few times when she was in high school. It hadn't even occurred to her to offer to perform with the cello here. She realized she had been keeping her church work and her "real" work in two separate compartments.

"I'm just practicing, to keep in shape for auditions," she told Gabriel.

"Like an athlete, right? You never know when you're going to be called up to the big leagues. And how's that going, any progress?"

"Some progress," she said cryptically, wondering if she should tell him that she was being considered for a seat in an orchestra in Austin.

"Really? That's good, then, right?"

"So far," she said tentatively. She decided she would wait to broadcast her news. If she didn't get called for the audition and get the seat, she would feel disappointed and embarrassed . . . and would be stuck making a lot of awkward explanations. She had been through that a few times and didn't want to go through it again.

"When did you hear about it?"

"Just a few days ago. One of my former teachers called me."

"Sorry I missed the news. I haven't been around much this week. I got pulled away by another job," he explained.

Amanda felt relieved to hear that. So he hadn't changed his mind about her after all. Before she could reply, he said, "Are you practicing all weekend?"

"Well, no, not every minute," she said vaguely.

"How about Saturday night? Maybe we can catch a movie or something."

Amanda's heart jumped. Then she realized she had promised her folks she would stay with her little sister so they could go out to dinner.

"I'd love to, but I have to take care of my little sister. I'd ask you to come over and hang out with us, but I have to take her to a birthday party that's at some place called 'Barbie Kingdom.'" She made a face. "Trust me, I wouldn't wish it on my worst enemy."

He laughed and seemed reassured she wasn't just putting him off. "I don't think I'd be much help to you there."

Amanda wondered if she should suggest a different time to get together. Maybe after church on Sunday? But before she could decide, someone called out from the back of the sanctuary.

"Amanda? Shall I turn some more lights on? It's so dark in here, I won't be able to read my music." One of the choir members, Vera Plante, walked into the sanctuary and clicked on all the light switches, turning on more overhead lights and entirely changing the atmosphere.

"That's better," Vera announced cheerfully. She stepped into a pew and shrugged off her puffy down coat and big knitted hat.

Amanda had been staring up at Gabriel, mesmerized by his brilliant blue eyes, for much longer than was good for her, and suddenly felt like she had been roused from a daydream.

He looked down and smiled, seeming to acknowledge that their private time was over.

"Are we going to sing 'Peace Like A River' on Sunday? I can't find my copy . . ." Vera sat down nearby, sifting through her black music binder.

"I have extras, Vera. I'll get one for you in a minute." Amanda stood up and rested the cello on its stand. Then she turned to Gabriel. "Choir is starting soon. I'd better get ready."

"I've got to run anyway. See you." He waved and turned away. She waved back, wishing they could have talked longer.

Well, they had almost figured out a date. At least he wanted to see her again. She certainly wanted to see him, which surprised her in a way, since he was the complete opposite of the type of men she usually dated—a long parade of musicians, some very moody and even competitive. They were, by and large, not easygoing guys, and her relationships with them were not easy either. But Gabriel always seemed so relaxed and even-tempered. So full of praise and encouragement. Sure, he drove around in a truck with ladders sticking out the back, and he hadn't finished college. But was he was definitely thoughtful, mature, and intelligent, and he had an artistic side, too.

Maybe she just wasn't used to things being so easy with someone she liked so much?

Amanda didn't know the answer to that and didn't have time to figure it out.

"Hello, Vera. There's a meeting of the Christmas Fair committee right after practice. Are you coming?" Sophie Potter's voice broke into Amanda's thoughts. Sophie marched up the center aisle and stepped into the pew behind Vera, where she dropped her coat and a tote bag full of craft items that Amanda guessed were headed for the annual church fund-raiser. Other choir members were coming in, too, greeting Amanda cheerfully.

It was time to focus on her duties here at church. And to forget about Gabriel and even the vacant orchestra seat in Austin.

"I CAN SEE YOU'RE GETTING VERY GOOD CARE, EZRA. THAT EASES MY mind considerably." Dr. Newton had not been able to stop by until Thursday evening. But it was good of him to make a house call at all, Ezra thought. He had done it in his day, of course, practically until he retired. But it was nearly unheard of these days, and Ezra appreciated the attention.

Dr. Newton had been listening to Ezra's heart and his breathing with a stethoscope and now put the instrument aside. "You know I was concerned when you decided to come home for your recovery. But it seems to be working out."

Ezra smiled. "Estrella keeps her eye on me . . . and Lillian, of course," he added quickly, glancing at his wife. "She keeps her eye on everything, don't you, dear?"

Lillian frowned. "Someone's got to do it," she said flatly.

Lillian sat in the armchair near the window, and Estrella stood at the foot of the bed, holding a chart of notes and the schedule of Ezra's medications. She was watching the doctor, and Lillian studied her.

Estrella's trial period was up tomorrow. Ezra was highly in favor of keeping her on. Lillian was not. She had many objections—significant issues, though Ezra dismissed them, claiming she found fault with everyone. She knew she could be critical, but she was only thinking of his welfare.

This Estrella was hardly the walking miracle Ezra seemed to think she was. Lillian couldn't figure out what Ezra found so impressive. She didn't do anything more than the other home health aides. She did a lot less, in fact.

Lillian had caught her a few times on the phone with her family. Ezra turned a blind eye. "If she's doing her job, she can talk to her children now and then," he'd said. "Mrs. Fallon was on the phone all the time with Holly."

Well, Mrs. Fallon was Mrs. Fallon. Lillian wouldn't dare compare the two.

"We were very lucky to find Estrella," Ezra was telling Dr. Newton. "She was a cardiac care nurse in El Salvador," he added.

Lillian pursed her lips. He was bragging about the girl as if she were his own daughter. Who even knew if that story was true? A cardiac care specialist, no less. Who could ever check such a claim?

I could learn as much about being a nurse from TV shows, and put on as good an act, Lillian told herself.

Dr. Newton seemed to buy it, though, Lillian noticed. "Just the person to watch over you. You won't let him eat any more bacon and eggs, will you? I know he loves them," Dr. Newton said to Estrella.

"Only the whites, Doctor. And no bacon . . . maybe turkey bacon," she added in her heavy accent. "Though recent studies show foods high in cholesterol may not be the reason patients develop high counts. It might be a product of the body."

"That's very true," Dr. Newton said. "It could be a genetic tendency in some individuals to produce cholesterol."

"Maybe someday scientists will remove that flaw from our genes," Estrella said.

"And we'll be able to eat bacon and eggs three times a day," Ezra chimed in.

"My, my . . . what a world that would be. Sounds like I walked into an episode of a show on the Discovery Channel," Lillian remarked.

Dr. Newton checked Ezra's broken arm and then his leg. "You'll have to come in next week for X-rays. I want to see how those bones are mending. Your heart sounds good, and so do your lungs. That's the main thing." He stood up and made a few notations in Ezra's chart. "Any adverse reactions to the medication?"

Ezra shrugged. "Not that I've noticed."

Estrella stepped forward. "Dr. Ezra had some high blood pressure this week. It spiked up two times. Here . . . and there," she noted, showing the doctor her chart. "And this morning, it was low," she added. She showed him her notation, looking concerned.

Dr. Newton took the chart and studied it a moment. Ezra looked at Lillian. She made a face. Tempest in a teapot. Estrella was just trying to act official, puff herself up. So they would keep her on after her trial period. That's what this was all about.

"Some fluctuations," Dr. Newton agreed, "but nothing too wild. I don't want to adjust your medication yet, Ezra. Let's just watch it."

"I'll keep my eye on that," Lillian promised firmly before anyone else could speak.

Dr. Newton glanced at her. "How are you holding up, Mrs. Elliot?"

"I'm holding up just fine. Fit as a fiddle," she snapped, irritated that now her health was being questioned.

Ezra glanced at her. "She's been a rock, Doctor. An absolute rock."

Lillian wasn't sure if she liked her husband's tone either. Was he being facetious? She decided to let it slide. For now.

After Dr. Newton left and Estrella had disappeared to prepare dinner, Lillian stood by the bed, watching Ezra. The bedclothes were pulled up nearly to his chin, and he seemed to be dozing off. The exam must have tired him out, she realized. But she wasn't ready for him to fall asleep, not when they had things to discuss.

"Ezra, are you falling asleep on me?" she said sharply.

"Hmm? I'm awake, Lily . . . What did you say?" He struggled to sit up, and Lillian leaned over to help him, though in truth, she was not much help at all in getting him higher in the bed. At best, she could rearrange his pillows, punching them into place.

"I want to ask what you think we should do about Estrella. Tomorrow is Friday, the end of her trial period. We agreed on a week, remember?"

"Of course I remember," he said calmly. "I thought it was all settled. I thought we were keeping her on."

Lillian stood back and smoothed out her sweater. "How could this be settled? I never discussed it with you. Are you losing your memory, too?"

"I know we didn't talk about it. But I thought it was understood. She's doing a good job, and she's here around the clock. What could possibly be the problem?"

"The problem is, I'm not nearly as confident of her nursing abilities as you are, for one thing. And I don't think she's a hard worker, for another. Every time I walk in on her in the kitchen, or wherever, she's on the phone with her mother or one of her children."

"Yes, yes, you keep saying that. But I've never seen it," he countered.

"Are you implying that I'm making this up? Of course you haven't seen it. You're stuck here in this bed, and she's not going to get on the phone when she's serving you breakfast or taking your temperature."

Ezra sighed and scratched his chin. She could see he had no answer for that.

"I don't see any reason to let her go, Lily. We've tried all those agency helpers, coming in and out every hour or so. You found fault with every one. We have no one lined up to take her place either," he reminded her.

He had a point. They couldn't go without help—heaven forbid they were left alone for a minute. Emily and Jessica forbid, she should say.

"I think we should keep looking. You promised you would respect my opinion on this. I think we ought to put her on notice, tell her it's not working out. I think that's the decent thing to do," Lillian insisted.

"If we tell her that, she'll just go."

"And?"

"I don't want her to go. I've found no faults with her work and, if I may remind you, I know a thing or two about medicine and competent nursing. Besides, she needs this job, Lily. You know why."

Lillian pursed her lips. Estrella was a widow, supporting two children and her mother. That was a sad story and a heavy burden to bear. At one time Lillian, too, had been a young widow with two children—and cut off from her entire family. But she had put her shoulder to the wheel and pushed on. No one gave her a helping hand out of pity. And she had not expected anyone to either.

"Yes, it's a sad situation. My heart goes out to her," she said. "But my first concern is you, not Estrella and her family."

Ezra glanced at her from hooded eyes. He was tired and she was tiring him even more. "I get your point, Lily," he said, before she could go on. "But I need to rest now. We agreed she would have a full week. We can decide all this tomorrow."

"Tomorrow?" Lillian was about to argue further when Ezra's eyelids dropped closed. He turned his head, breathing deeply, and then she heard him lightly snoring.

"Oh, bother . . . now he's fallen asleep on me," she grumbled. "That's one way to win an argument. Or, at least, table the discussion."

LILLIAN WANDERED INTO THE KITCHEN, LOOKING FOR ESTRELLA. THE enticing smells of dinner cooking met her on the way. The woman was a good cook, she had to hand her that. Though Lillian insisted that her meals be prepared in the plain, spice-free style she preferred, Ezra had a much more adventurous palate—salt- and cholesterol-restricted, but adventurous nonetheless. He did seem to enjoy the dishes that Estrella cooked, almost as much as he did Mrs. Fallon's cooking. He would miss that, no doubt, but it was a small price to pay when you looked at the larger picture.

Lillian didn't trust Estrella. Ezra may have fallen for her sad story, but Lillian was not taken in. Besides, if she was so wonderful, she would find another job easily, the way she had found this one.

I won't lose sleep over it, Lillian told herself.

As she approached the kitchen, her suspicions were justified. Estrella stood at the counter, pots bubbling on the stove and her hands chopping a carrot while her cell phone was wedged between her shoulder and cheek. "Jorge, you heard what *Abuela* said. No video games until you finish your homework. Yes, and the math sheet, too. When you come to that, you call me back and I'll help you."

It was bad enough she had to talk to them ten times a day. Now she had to give her son math tutoring? *And while I'm paying her.*

"Where is Marta? I need to talk to her . . . Oh, Mrs. Elliot . . ." Estrella glanced at her, then quickly said, "Good-bye, *mijo*. Mama has to go." She clicked off the phone and slipped it in her pocket. "I'm sorry. I didn't hear you come in. Can I help you with something?"

"You can stop making personal calls while you're on duty, for starters."

"I'm sorry. My mother called. She needed some help with my son. He can be stubborn. Smart in school, but doesn't like to do his homework. Dr. Ezra said it was all right. As long as I—"

"Spare me the details," Lillian said. "My husband is a very softhearted man, in a weakened condition. It will hardly be to your benefit to take advantage of him."

"Take advantage of him? How would that be, Mrs. Elliot?"

"Don't act so innocent with me. I have eyes in my head. Helping him with his Spanish, neck massages, cooking his favorite foods."

Estrella faced her squarely, her expression unreadable, though her dark eyes were intense. "A little kindness and positive interaction between the caregiver and the patient speeds recovery. Especially after a heart procedure, when patients are prone to depression. There are many studies."

"Yes, yes, I'm sure." Lillian cut her off, waving her hand dismissively. "You're very up on all these studies, aren't you? Well, I've said it before, but I'll say it again. You might fool my husband, but you don't fool me. Your trial period is over tomorrow," she reminded her. "If I have my way—"

"Estrella?" Lillian heard Ezra's voice calling on the monitor. Before she could react, Estrella ran over and answered him. "I'll be right there, Dr. Ezra. Are you all right?"

"I'm fine . . . just woke up," he mumbled. "May I have a glass of water, please?"

"Yes, of course. I'll bring it right in."

Estrella took a bottle of spring water from the refrigerator and poured it into a tall glass. "The medication he takes is dehydrating. He should drink at least eight glasses of water a day. I measure the intake, to be sure."

"Give me the water, please. I'll take it in to him." Lillian held out her hand, the other braced on her cane.

Estrella looked at her a moment, then handed her the glass.

"If he wants anything else, please let me know."

Lillian didn't answer. She turned slowly, the water in hand. It would be hard not to spill half of it during the trip from the kitchen to his room with this bum hip of hers. But she would try her best.

She wanted to deliver it personally and tell Ezra how she had found his perfect caregiver yammering away on the phone again and scheduling a homework help session with her son. *If I had allowed her to stay on that call, she might have never heard Ezra on the monitor. What if it had been an emergency? Then what?*

Didn't this just prove her point?

Meanwhile, taking care of Ezra wasn't exactly brain surgery. For goodness' sake, she could do it herself if Emily and Jessica would just let her.

CHAPTER SEVEN

*M*RS. ELLIOT? MRS. ELLIOT? CAN YOU HEAR ME?"
Lillian was awakened by the sound of Estrella's voice, on the monitor in her room. She sat up quickly and grabbed at the night table, knocking things over in the dark. She saw the glowing numbers on the digital clock: 2:32 a.m.

She couldn't work the monitor without her glasses and thrust it close to her face to find the right button. Finally she pressed it down.

"What's wrong down there? Is it Ezra?" She was shouting, she realized, though she didn't mean to.

"Dr. Ezra isn't well. I've called an ambulance. Please come down . . . and be careful. Do you want me to come up and help you?" Estrella offered.

"No, no. I'll be fine. I'll be right there. I'm coming . . ."

Lillian flung the monitor aside and grabbed for her cane and robe, which she kept at the side of the bed. She nearly lost her balance for a moment, but quickly righted herself, grabbing on to the bed's footboard.

Luckily, the night-light made it easy enough to find what she needed, and she flipped on lights as she scrambled along—first the lamp on the dressing table and then the switches in the hallway.

"Oh, God, please don't take him. Don't take him from me yet," she murmured in a desperate, angry sort of prayer.

She looked down from the top of the staircase. All the lights were on. She wanted to fly down the stairs and silently cursed the infirmities that limited her to such careful, crablike steps. She could have screamed with frustration as she worked her way down the long flight. But she knew it wouldn't help.

As she came to the bottom, she called to Estrella, "What it is? What's wrong with him? . . . Did he have another heart attack?"

Estrella came out of the room to meet her and gently took her arm. "His blood pressure, it's dropped very low. I called Dr. Newton and gave him something to stabilize it. But he has to go to the hospital right away."

Lillian nodded, trying to take it all in. Her legs felt so weak all of a sudden that she thought she would fall, but Estrella held her arm and led her to the chair by Ezra's bed. "Are you all right, Mrs. Elliot? Do you need anything?"

Lillian shook her head fiercely. "I'm fine. It's him. It's Ezra we have to worry about."

She stared down at her husband. He looked as if he were sleeping peacefully. Lillian leaned over and touched his hand. "Good Lord, he's cold as ice . . . Ezra, can you hear me?"

She leaned closer to him, waiting for some sign that he was aware of her presence. But he didn't move a muscle.

"Oh dear . . . oh dear . . ." She bent her head, trying to hide her distress. She felt a gentle touch on her shoulder.

"It will be all right, Mrs. Elliot. He's very strong . . . I called your daughter. She should be here soon."

Lillian lifted her head. She swallowed hard. "Thank you." She didn't know what else to say.

A hard knock sounded on the front door, and Estrella ran to answer it. Moments later the room was filled with bodies and medical equipment. A team of men and women in bright yellow jackets quickly surrounded Ezra's bed.

Lillian stepped aside, but not too far, while Estrella explained what had happened. She had been concerned about the fluctuations she had noticed in his blood pressure and was checking him every half hour. When she came in a short while ago, it had dipped dangerously low.

While she relayed the information to a woman with a clipboard, two young men were loading Ezra onto a stretcher.

Emily appeared in the bedroom doorway. "Mother, I'm here," she said. "How is he?"

"Ezra's blood pressure is too low. He's practically unconscious." Lillian tried hard not to sound hysterical.

"Yes, Estrella told me. Why don't you let Estrella go in the ambulance? We'll follow in my car," Emily suggested.

Estrella was standing nearby, holding her coat. "Mrs. Elliot should go with her husband. If it wouldn't be too difficult for her."

"I do want to go with him," Lillian agreed. "What about my clothes? I can't go like this . . . and there's no time to change."

Estrella held out her long down coat. "Take this for now. It will cover you. We'll follow in the car and bring your things to the hospital."

Lillian looked at the coat a moment. It would cover her from head to toe, no question. She had to be with Ezra right now even if it meant she had to jump into that ambulance dressed in a sack.

She took the coat without meeting Estrella's gaze. She put it on and zipped the thing to her chin. It felt as if she were wearing a big pillow, and she could smell Estrella's distinctive cologne on the lining. But there was no time to worry about such trivial matters. Ezra's stretcher had been rolled through the foyer and out the door. With Emily on one side of her and Estrella on the other, she was half-carried, half-dragged to the ambulance.

"You know where everything is up in my bedroom," she said to Emily as they hurried her out. "Make sure the insurance cards are in the handbag."

"I'll get everything, Mother. Don't worry. We'll be right behind you."

Lillian nodded. She was worried sick, but didn't want to admit it. A few moments later she was handed over like a sack of potatoes to the ambulance team and hoisted inside.

They set her on a tiny seat next to Ezra. She could barely balance, and she hunkered down to stay out of the way. He still had his eyes closed and was wrapped up tight as a mummy in thick blankets and strapped in. An oxygen mask covered most of his face, except his eyes. Some other medical equipment was already hooked up to his arm.

She reached out and patted his shoulder. As the rear doors slammed shut and the vehicle took off, the siren sounding and lights flashing, she couldn't stop herself from crying. As discreetly as possible, she thought. She didn't think the emergency techs in the back with her even noticed, they all seemed so busy, chattering on radios and adjusting equipment.

"Don't worry, ma'am. He's stable," one of the techs told her. "I think you caught him just in time."

I didn't catch him. Estrella did, she nearly answered. But, of course, no one here even knew who Estrella was, or why that admission would be so significant at this moment.

But she knew. And Ezra would, too. If he survived.

"Dear Lord in heaven . . . how I hope so," she said aloud.

AMANDA WAS TRYING TO WORK AT HER DESK IN THE CHOIR ROOM, going over the music scheduled for Sunday's service. But she could barely keep her mind on the order of the hymns, or when the special music—a very talented high school senior playing a flute solo—would occur in the service.

The search committee for the orchestra in Austin was due to contact her today, to let her know if she was a finalist for the chair. Amanda checked her email every few seconds, waiting to find the message. They would decide by five o'clock on Friday. That's what the last message had said. She could barely think of anything else and wondered if she would have to leave tonight for Texas. Professor Sloan made it sound very urgent. If not tonight, then maybe over the weekend, she guessed. She had even planned what she would pack.

She already knew what she would wear for the audition: a long black knit dress with a ballet neckline and a gored skirt that came down below her knee. A classic style that looked very sleek and dramatic onstage, with her long hair pulled back in a tight ponytail.

Lauren told her to wear big hoop earrings, or maybe something dangling. "That looks more arty than pearls," she pointed out.

But Amanda preferred pearls. "I need to go for elegant, not arty. Besides, they are going to hire me because they like the way I play the cello, not for my fashion sense."

"True, and I know you'll do great and get the job no matter what you wear," Lauren said. "I can't wait to hear. Text me the minute you know."

"You'll be the first, don't worry." Amanda meant that, too. Now if only she would see that email from the orchestra. She checked her mail again. Nothing.

She heard someone come into the choir room and looked up from the screen. It was Gabriel. She could never guess if he would be around unless she spotted his ladder. She hadn't seen any evidence of him today but was pleased to see him now.

"Am I interrupting you?" he asked politely.

She shook her head. "I was just going over some music for Sunday . . . and slacking off," she admitted with a guilty grin.

He smiled at her. "I know you're tied up with that Barbie party tomorrow night, but I wondered if you were free on Sunday evening. This is short notice, but there's a chamber music group playing in Newburyport. Would you like to see them and get a bite to eat? I promise I'll take you to a better place than the Clam Box," he added with a grin.

His invitation pleased her. It was just the sort of thing she had been hoping for when they were interrupted by Vera Plante the day before. But then her heart sank as she realized she had to decline again.

"I'd love to go . . . but there's something going on. Remember that job possibility I told you about? It's in an orchestra in Austin. I'm just waiting to hear whether I made the audition. If I did, I might not be here Sunday. I might have to leave for Texas tomorrow."

He seemed disappointed, but finally smiled. "Just what you've been waiting for. That's great," he said sincerely.

"Well, I haven't heard back from them. But one of my former teachers knows someone on the search committee, and she said they were very interested in me. I think I'll be called for the audition, at least . . . I'm sorry," she added sincerely. "The chamber music was a great idea. It would have been fun to go with you." She suddenly stopped herself. "I'm rattling on and on about this, aren't I?"

His smile widened and warmed her. "Not at all. It's great to see you so excited. I'll be starting a new project, too."

"Really? What sort of project?" she asked curiously.

"I entered a bid to design the entrance at a new community arts center in Essex. They liked my ideas and looked at my work, and it looks like I got the job. Tomorrow, I'm going in to take more measurements."

"Wow, that's great . . . You never even mentioned it." *Maybe because*

I'm always talking about myself, she realized with a wave of embarrassment.

But if he thought the same, his expression didn't show it. "I thought about telling you, but I wanted to be low-key about it. In case it didn't come through. It's the first time I'm installing an original design on such a large scale. I'm pretty excited."

"It sounds exciting. I'm happy for you," she said sincerely.

"Not quite as exciting as your opportunity," he added with a modest grin. "That really is big news."

"Thanks, but it's a little too early to celebrate. I'm also trying to be low-key about it." *Though I'm not doing a great job of that,* she thought.

"I hope you get good news. I'm sure you deserve it."

They stared at each other a moment. Amanda looked up at him, feeling awkward and forcing a smile she didn't feel. Then Gabriel leaned over and gave her a quick hug and a kiss on her cheek. "Good luck, Amanda. I know you'll knock 'em dead with that cello of yours."

"Good luck to you, too, Gabriel," she managed to reply.

A moment later, he was gone. The choir room was silent and empty again. Amanda sat staring at the screen saver on her laptop—colorful notes of music floating in a bright blue sky.

Had they really just said good-bye to each other? It felt that way, though even if she went to Austin and won that seat, she wouldn't be starting immediately. She would still come back to Cape Light and be here at least through Christmas. Perhaps she would see him at a Sunday service. But Gabriel wouldn't be working in the church, and she knew she wouldn't look forward to coming to work quite as much. Just the possibility of seeing Gabriel at work had added a spark to her days. She did like him. More than she had realized.

With Gabriel gone, it seemed even more important to know whether she was leaving, too. She checked her email again, for the ten thousandth time. But there was still no answer from the Austin orchestra.

* * *

AMANDA HEARD HER PARENTS IN THE KITCHEN. THE TV WAS ON, playing one of her little sister's shows; she could tell from the music. Her mother was cooking dinner, and she guessed that her father was sitting at the kitchen island, reading the paper, as he usually did this time of day. Her first impulse was to run straight up to her room. But they had heard her come in, and her father called out her name, then came out of the kitchen to look for her.

"How's it going? Any news?" he asked eagerly.

He stood in the doorway to the great room at the back of the house. Amanda remained in the foyer. She couldn't answer at first.

"I didn't get selected. They've picked other players to audition."

She tried to keep her voice steady, but it shook at the end. She felt her chin wobble and knew she was going to dissolve into tears again. She had hardly made it home in one piece, and had pulled over twice to calm herself between bouts of crying.

"Honey, I'm so sorry." Her father came toward her with his arms out.

Amanda froze in place, her chin tucked down to her chest. She was too old for this stuff. It was all right when she was in high school and hadn't made varsity soccer or had failed a chemistry test. But she was twenty-five, with a graduate degree. She should be beyond crying on her dad's shoulder, shouldn't she?

And her mom's? Molly clearly wasn't going to be left out of the comfort-fest and trotted out of the kitchen right behind him, wearing her white cooking apron and waving a wooden spoon. "I can't believe that! That is sooooo . . . not *right*!"

Moments later, they were both hugging her and patting her back. Betty appeared from somewhere and hugged Amanda's leg, even though she had no idea what was going on—just that Amanda had come home feeling blue. Very blue.

Amanda let herself be comforted, and after a little while, they all stepped back. Except for Betty, who looked up with a puzzled but adoring expression. Her mother had taken out some boxes of Christmas decorations, and Betty wore a pair of fuzzy brown antlers.

"Do you want my Barbie?" she asked quietly, offering a fashion doll in mismatched outfit with hair that had been half chopped off. The doll's remaining hair had been colored by a magic marker.

Amanda felt a small smile lifting the corners of her mouth. "Wow . . . she looks even worse than I feel. Poor thing."

Molly rubbed her shoulder. "I'm so sorry, sweetie. It sounded like it was a done deal. That teacher, Professor Sloan, she really got your hopes up."

"She did," Amanda agreed. "But it isn't her fault," she added quickly. "She only told me what she heard from her friend. I guess the committee was interested in other candidates, too."

"I'm sure you were competing against many highly qualified musicians," her father said. "I just wish they had called you in for an audition. Then they would have seen what a brilliant artist you are. You can't tell anything from a tape."

"And they liked the tape. That's what kills me. They would have loved the real thing," Molly added. "This is so unfair. You got so close. It's so frustrating."

Betty was watching and listening to the adults. Molly's excitement got her excited, too. "That is so terrible!" With her embattled Barbie doll in hand, Betty gritted her teeth, then made a growling sound. "I wish I was a tiger! I'd bite them for you."

She stared up at her older sister with a fierce expression, and suddenly, everyone had to laugh. Amanda rested her hand on Betty's beautiful curly hair. "You would be a wonderful tiger, Betty. Especially with those antlers. But you don't have to bite anybody for me. It's all right. I'll figure it out," she promised.

"That's right. You'll figure it out. There will be other jobs, you'll see," Molly promised her. "Something even better will come along. When you look back, you'll see this was a blessing in disguise."

Austin's wasn't the most renowned orchestra in the world. She might do better in the long run. But it was hard right now to think she would ever look back and view this as a lucky moment. She was so deeply disappointed.

"Your mother's right. This isn't the only orchestra in the country. You'll find an even better spot very soon. Just be patient. Keep looking and practicing," her father advised. "You can stay with us as long as you like."

She knew he was trying to comfort her, but his last phrase made her wince. Her mother must have noticed, because she jumped in very quickly. "Not that you'll have to stay very long. You might hear about more openings after the holidays," she suggested. "No one does much hiring right now. Even symphony orchestras," she guessed.

"That's probably true," Amanda agreed.

"Why don't you go upstairs and lie down? I'll call you when dinner is ready," her mother said. She patted Amanda's back again and kissed her cheek. "You'll feel better soon, I promise."

Amanda managed a small smile of thanks, then gratefully went to her room.

Molly heard Amanda climb the stairs and Betty return to the TV. "I thought this was it," she said to her husband. "I even checked the airfares to Austin, I was so sure we'd be going there to see her perform."

"I thought it was, too," Matt admitted, talking in a low tone. "I guess she got really close. That's a good sign, don't you think?"

Molly nodded. She was mixing a vinaigrette dressing with a whisk and held the bowl in the crook of her arm. "They're going to face disappointments, all four of them. That's life. That's what makes you grow and mature."

"I know. It's just so hard to watch her struggle. But Amanda's a fighter. She'll work through this and push on. She won't give up that easily."

Little Betty had been working the remote and clicked onto the local weather channel. Matt quickly turned to her. "Wait, honey. We need to see this." He glanced over at Molly. "They're talking about a big storm coming up the East Coast this week. I hope Lauren and Jill aren't stuck somewhere."

Molly was chopping vegetables and slid them from her board into a sauté pan. Jill was just finishing her finals for the semester. Today was Friday the thirteenth . . . well, she hoped her younger daughter was having better luck than Amanda. At least Jill wasn't planning to head home for the holidays until next weekend. Lauren was also heading home around that time; she was using some vacation days. There wasn't much activity at the art gallery where she was working, and the owner was off somewhere in Europe.

"I heard about that storm on the radio," Molly said. "Sometimes the forecasters get everyone in a panic, and it's nothing. A few flakes here and there."

Matt gave her doubtful look. "I don't think this one is just hype, honey. We ought to prepare. Better get some staples for the fridge, as well as some flashlights, batteries, and bottled water. I'll go downstairs later and look for the lantern and camp stove."

"The camp stove?"

"We needed it last time, remember?"

She did remember. The camp stove had come in handy when they lost their power in a big storm last fall. She hoped that didn't happen again; it was such an inconvenience.

"We still don't have a generator," he added. "I meant to get one but never got around to it."

"It's one of those things you don't think about until you need it. I bet a lot of people are saying the same thing right now. Let's hope it's not that bad."

"Maybe it won't be," he agreed.

"Just what I need on top of all the parties I have booked this week, plus trying to get ready for the holidays around here. I wanted to decorate and put up the tree this weekend, even if we wait for the girls to come home to trim it." She turned down the heat under the vegetables and checked a pan of red potatoes roasting in the oven. "The supermarket is going to be insane."

"Better safe than sorry," Matt said. "Don't worry. I'll get everything. I know you're busy."

"I know you're busy, too . . . but thanks. You seem to know what we need. I'll leave it all to you."

Molly had a feeling this weather forecast wouldn't amount to much. Matt always took these things more seriously than she did. He was the more sensible and cautious one in their partnership. But he was right. Better to brave the supermarket madness and have what they needed on hand than find themselves stuck in a cold, dark house without any creature comforts.

IT WAS AWFULLY DEPRESSING TO GET UP EARLY ON SUNDAY AND HEAD off to church. Amanda felt utterly hollow inside as she dressed and drove along the empty road to the village. She was glad now she hadn't told anyone about the Austin opportunity—except for Gabriel.

She knew it would be hard to see him again and admit that she hadn't even been called for the audition. He wasn't the type to make her feel worse about it. Still, she had sounded so sure of it. She had even turned down his date, thinking she would be en route to Austin. That seemed laughable now. Or it would be, if it didn't still sting so much to even think about it.

The service went smoothly. Amanda remembered all her cues, moving easily from the organ to the piano and back again, guiding the choir through their songs, and helping the flute soloist adjust her stand. The girl was quite poised and played very well.

Still, Amanda felt as if she were almost sleepwalking through the service. She looked out at the back rows a few times but didn't see Gabriel. She wasn't sure if she felt relieved or disappointed. She knew he wouldn't be back again to work on the windows, but she did expect to see him on a Sunday. Maybe he would show up for the Christmas service. She would feel better by then and be able to put a brave face on this Austin episode. She hoped so, anyway.

For one wild moment, she wondered if she should call him. Just to let him know that she hadn't left town, as she had expected. She didn't know his home phone number, but could easily find the number for his shop. Then what? Wait for him to ask her out again?

Or I could ask him.

Amanda sighed. She knew that worked for some women. But she just wasn't the type. She had tried it once or twice, and it always backfired somehow.

Maybe I'll run into him in town one of these days, she thought. He liked the Clam Box. She might even try eating lunch there sometime.

But I won't tell my mother. She'll never forgive me, she decided with a secret smile. Molly had a rather low opinion of the food served at the Clam Box.

Amanda sighed, thinking about Gabriel. One way or another, she would figure out how to cross his path again. Lauren was good at these guy problems and was coming home very soon. *She'll help me figure this out,* Amanda decided. *She's exactly the person to ask.*

"I CAN GO HOME TODAY? THANK GOODNESS." IT WAS SUNDAY AFTERnoon, and Ezra was sitting up in bed. His voice sounded strong and his color looked good, Lillian thought, despite the bleak hospital room.

"We needed to make sure your blood pressure was stable again," Dr. Newton explained. "But I don't see any reason to keep you here longer, Ezra. I've spoken to Estrella, and she'll be watching you very closely for the next few days."

"She watches me like a hawk, Doctor. If she hadn't come in to check my blood pressure in the middle of the night like that . . . Well, I hate to think of—"

"She saved your life," Dr. Newton said flatly. "No question."

"She did save him. Thank goodness," Emily said.

"I'll never be able to thank her enough. You know what I call her now? My star," he told the doctor. "That's what her name means in Spanish."

Dr. Newton smiled. He was leafing through a thick pile of forms and checking off boxes and signing his name here and there. "I'm not surprised," he said.

"She handled the emergency very well. She's a real professional," Emily noted.

"Now, now, let's not rehash all that again," Lillian said briskly. "It was just a minor setback. Nothing to worry about."

Lillian didn't want to be reminded again of that awful night.

How many times did they need to talk about it? She hated to remember how terrified she was, riding in the back of that ambulance, not knowing if Ezra would be alive or dead when they finally reached the hospital.

And she had no desire to be reminded again of how Estrella had saved him. Ezra would probably want to pin a medal on the woman when they got home. Or write her into his will. She wouldn't be the least bit surprised.

"The ship has been righted. Now full speed ahead," she urged all of them.

"Yes, full speed . . . as soon I sign all these papers," Ezra said. The doctor had been checking off boxes on forms and handing them down to Ezra to sign.

"I never realized that being sick involved so much paperwork. You might as well have a job at the Department of Motor Vehicles," Lillian said. "They have you filling out forms night and day."

Ezra looked at her fondly. "And that's hardly the worst of it. I'm sorry I put such a scare into everyone."

"We're just glad that it wasn't that serious and you can leave so quickly," Emily replied. "It's good that you're getting released today, before the bad weather moves in. They're talking up this storm like crazy. Tomorrow morning we're having a meeting of the village's Emergency Readiness Committee."

"Yes, I've heard the reports. Do you think it will be all that bad?" Lillian asked. "What should we do, get some flashlights? I can live without the phone and TV, that doesn't make much difference to me."

"I've already brought over what you need, Mother."

Emily was so efficient and organized. *Takes after me,* Lillian thought proudly, though she would never admit such a thing to Emily.

"I am looking forward to going home, no matter what the weather will be," Ezra said. "Will Estrella be there when we get back?"

Lillian felt herself bristle at the question, though she knew it was a perfectly logical one. On Thursday night, she had nearly fired the woman. Now here it was, Sunday afternoon, and Estrella was indispensable.

When she didn't answer right away, Emily replied, "I gave her some time off. She's with her family now, but she said to call when you're released and she'll come right over."

"Good. I want to thank her, face-to-face. Maybe we should give her a raise, Lily. What do you think of that?"

Lillian glanced over at him, wondering if he was joking. He was perfectly serious. "Let's just get home and settle in," she suggested.

But Ezra was obviously feeling better, because he wouldn't let it go. "She's passed her probation with flying colors, hasn't she?"

Lillian gave a reluctant shrug. "I suppose so."

Ezra just laughed at her.

She tried to answer with a scowl, but finally, couldn't help smiling. It was good to hear him laughing again . . . even if it was at her expense.

CHAPTER EIGHT

~~~

*L*ILLIAN HAD MADE LIGHT OF THE WEATHER REPORTS. THESE predictions were so often way off the mark. She didn't understand why these overpaid announcers called themselves weather forecasters at all. They should be called weather guessers, she thought. Or weather actors; they tended to get so dramatic over even a few raindrops.

But the rain did start Monday in the late afternoon, as predicted. She heard it falling, lightly at first, pattering against the living room windows. Ezra was taking a break from his room and a break from their usual gin rummy game. Instead, they decided to play Scrabble . . . and he was beating her.

"Rain is starting, just like they said," Ezra noted. He was lying across the sofa with his broken leg propped up and his good arm able to reach the game board, though he still needed help setting his letters down.

"Yes, I see. Are you going to put your word down any time soon? I've forgotten altogether what we're doing." She hadn't really; but just wanted to needle him.

"*P, E, C,* and *U,*" he said, handing her the tiles for his word. "Just tack those in front of *LIAR,* over there, and I'm in business."

"'Peculiar,' very good," she grumbled, adding up his points.

His lead was growing. She had to step up her game.

She would be glad when those casts came off and he was mobile again. The X-rays last week showed he was healing well. That was good news.

"Sounds icy," Ezra noticed, talking about the rain again.

"It does," she agreed, looking over her letters. The drops hit the glass with a sharp sound, like tiny stones. "Not a night to be out driving around. Everyone's made such a big deal of it, I imagine people will leave work early."

"I imagine so," Ezra agreed. "Maybe we should tell Estrella to go home to her family tonight. They might need her."

Lillian sat up straight, fussing with her tiles. "What about us? We need her, don't we? I realize it's only a little rain now, but what if the power goes out? Then we'll really need her. We can barely get around in the light."

She really needed a *Q.* She would have been able to put down the word "quark," and on a triple-point space, too. Otherwise, all she had going was "ark." Pathetic.

"All right, let's play it by ear," he suggested.

Which was what he always said when he didn't feel entirely settled about an idea and planned to debate it further.

"All I have is 'ark.' Here . . ." She set down the letters, then rose to fill her teacup.

Estrella had brought in a tray for them a short time ago with hot tea and a berry crumble with yogurt topping. No sugar in it, or butter. Just some cinnamon and granola stuff to make it crunchy on top. Hardly to her taste, but Ezra couldn't eat any sweets right now, so she had to make do.

"More tea?" she asked him.

"No, thank you." He was focused on his letters, and she dreaded to see what he would come up with.

She pulled the curtain aside to get a better look at the rain. It was coming down harder now, icy pellets coating the lawn and walk. The leaves on the holly bush near the window and the bare branches of trees were already coated, as if encased in glass.

The wind seemed stronger, too, branches swaying to and fro. A very large branch had landed on their lawn, torn and raw-looking where the fresh wood showed. It hadn't been some deadwood that would have fallen anyway. The wind had torn it right off. The realization alarmed her.

She watched a large town utility truck drive past the house, rocking from side to side. The she glanced up at the power lines. They were swaying a bit, too, she noticed. But don't they always?

The wind was fierce, no doubt about that. And the storm was building. How strong it would get was the question.

Estrella came in carrying a paper cup filled with pills and a glass of water. "Time for your medication, Dr. Ezra; and I need to check your signs."

"Perfect timing—I'm just about to put down the word of the game. Let's see if Mrs. Elliot can top this." Ezra glanced at Lillian with a glint in his eye, then back at Estrella.

Lillian sighed aloud. How he showed off for her, the old fool. It had gotten even worse after his hospital stay. Lillian could barely stand to hear them carry on. But what could she do? Estrella was his hero now, his *star*. And a person could just gag on these healthy recipes she was cooking.

"I'm shivering in my boots, Ezra. What have you got?"

"'Quixotic' . . . and I get a fifty-point bonus for using up all my tiles on one turn."

"Oh blast . . . You had the *Q*. I should have known," Lillian groused. Had he really just scored seventy-six points on one turn? Lillian quickly checked her math. Ezra was a sleeper. But he could surprise you. No wonder she had married him.

She was losing so badly now, she lost interest. While Estrella checked his pulse and blood pressure, Lillian looked for the remote. "Let's see what the weather watchers have to say. I guess we need to know how long this is going to last."

She switched on the set and found the weather station. A brightly colored map of the area appeared. There was some official-sounding talk about pressure systems and wind velocities. ". . . And because of the full moon tonight and the tide schedule, there are flood warnings all along the coastline. See those areas marked in red? Residents should evacuate and head to local shelters . . . "

"Evacuate? What are they talking about?" Lillian looked at her husband.

"Do they mean us, Lillian?" Ezra sounded alarmed as well; his good cheer from beating her at Scrabble had quickly evaporated.

"I don't think so . . . I've never heard of such a thing, and I've lived in this town for over fifty years." But Cape Light *was* on the weather map and was definitely in the red zone. She wasn't running to any drafty high school gymnasium tonight, that was for sure. She didn't want to believe the weather report . . . and yet, she didn't think she should ignore it entirely either.

"I'll call your daughter Emily, Mrs. Elliot," Estrella said. "She will have the best news about this area."

"Good idea, Estrella," Ezra said at once. "Call Emily. She'll know what to do."

Lillian begrudgingly nodded her assent.

Once again, Estrella was saving the day. *I should have expected that,* Lillian silently fumed.

"I JUST PICKED UP BETTY AT SCHOOL. I THINK YOU SHOULD COME home. I'll come and get you. I'm still in town." Amanda's mother was calling from her SUV and sounded in a dither about the weather. Amanda had just finished planning the next service with Reverend Ben and was in the sanctuary reviewing some hymns on the piano. She had heard the rain pattering against the church roof but didn't think much of it.

"Why do you have to pick me up? I can drive myself home." She glanced at her watch. It was only half past three on a Monday afternoon. The nursery school had let out, and Reverend Ben had left to visit someone in the hospital. Mrs. Honeyfield was still in the church office. She didn't seem worried.

"Not in that little car. You'll never make it. The roads are awful, Amanda. There are tree limbs down everywhere, and wires. Just listen to me, all right? Tell Reverend Ben you should all go home, right now."

"He's gone. He had to visit someone in the hospital. Only Mrs. Honeyfield is still here."

"She is?" Her mother sounded surprised and even more alarmed. "Tell her I'll bring her home, too. She shouldn't try to drive in this either."

Amanda was about to reply when Mrs. Honeyfield poked her head into the sanctuary. "I just spoke to the reverend. He said to close up the church and go. It's just awful out there. All of a sudden, too."

The secretary did sound frightened. She already wore her hat, gloves, and coat, buttoned to the chin. Before Amanda could reply, she heard a gust of wind whistling and then pound against a sanctuary window. There was the sound of cracking glass, and a few pieces of stained glass flew out and landed on the floor. From one of Amanda's favorite windows, too—the golden and blue one with the white dove.

Mrs. Honeyfield gasped. "Oh my heavens, look at that!"

"Manda? Are you still there? What's happening?" Molly was calling to her through the phone.

"Yes, I'm here, Mom . . . It's okay. A piece of the window in the sanctuary broke, but we're all right. Mrs. Honeyfield is with me. We're going to leave right away."

"Look for me in the parking lot, behind the church. Go to the door nearest the green," her mother instructed her.

Amanda agreed and ended the call. She looked up at Mrs. Honeyfield, who had retreated to the sanctuary doorway. Amanda walked quickly toward her and shut off the lights. "My mom says not to drive. She'll pick us up in her SUV. It's super big and great in bad weather."

"She will? What a blessing. My little car isn't very good in the rain, and it's worse with ice. I was about to call my husband, but I didn't want him out in this either. He'd get blown right off the road."

It was very dark outside for half past three, Amanda thought, even for a winter day. The wind off the water pressed them against the side of the building while icy pellets of rain stung her face. Amanda had to hold her hand up to shield her skin and could barely keep her eyes open. But she wanted to see. The storm was so awesome, so powerful. She had never seen anything like it.

The sound of the wind roared through the trees on the village green. The stately old oaks and elms, so tall and grand, hundreds of years old, were swaying back and forth, as if they were blades of tall grass. Broken bits of branches, leaves, and debris were scattered all over the green. At least one of the big trees had fallen, pulled up out of the ground. The pile of dirt and tree roots had to be at least ten feet high, Amanda thought, the broken tree extending at least fifty feet or more, breaking down benches and the playground fence in its toppled path.

But even more frightening was the sight of the harbor, the waves blowing wildly in all directions and the tide that was rising so fast and so high.

"Look . . . look at the water . . ." Mrs. Honeyfield pointed, practically crying out loud. Water had risen out of the harbor, up over the stones, over the grassy edge and walkway, past the benches and cement tables that were used for picnics and games of chess and checkers. Up over the grass on the village green and past the gazebo and bandstand where musicians performed all summer long.

"My car . . . the water is over the tires. I couldn't have gotten out anyway." Amanda pointed to her car, which was half submerged in the flooded parking lot.

"Oh dear, that's awful . . ."

Mrs. Honeyfield looked around for her car. "I parked closer to the church, on higher ground," she started to say, then gasped. "Oh, good heavens!"

They both watched as a huge chunk of tree flew through the air and smashed into a small green sedan, breaking the windshield and flattening the front end. The sound was horrific.

Mrs. Honeyfield gasped and grabbed Amanda's arm. "That's my car . . . I could have been sitting right there . . ." Her voice trembled as if she were about to cry.

Amanda took her hand. "It's all right, Mrs. Honeyfield. I'm sorry about your car, but . . . at least you're okay." Amanda heard her words of comfort sucked away on the wind.

The older woman clung to her a moment, then pulled herself together. "You're right, Amanda. Let's just be thankful I wasn't in it."

Amanda was having similar thoughts. What if Molly hadn't called her and she had come out to drive herself home?

"There's your mother." Mrs. Honeyfield pointed to Molly's SUV. "What a blessing to see her."

It did feel like a blessing. It felt like an emergency rescue from a sinking ship, Amanda thought as she splashed through puddles and climbed into the cavernous vehicle.

Betty was in the back, strapped into her car seat, looking terrified. "Manda, sit next to me," she pleaded.

Amanda jumped in the back and took a seat next to her little sister.

"Of course I will, honey." Amanda fastened her seat belt and took hold of Betty's hand.

Mrs. Honeyfield sat up front, next to Molly, and slammed the door shut. "Oh, thank you so much, Molly. You saved me."

"I haven't saved you yet. But I'm trying," her mother replied with her trademark grin.

"Mom, look at Mrs. Honeyfield's car. We were just standing here, waiting for you, and a huge branch flew out of nowhere and smashed into it."

"I saw it, honey. Let's just all say a silent prayer and buckle up . . . This is going to be bumpy ride," Molly warned in her Bette Davis voice.

Molly turned the SUV out of the lot, moving through the water slowly. Amanda felt as if she were in a small boat and wondered how high the water had to be before even her mother's vehicle would be trapped.

Her mom headed toward the first street that led away from the water, Scudder Lane, a steep hill that was hard to walk up but would probably not be flooded yet.

"Good Lord, look at that!" Mrs. Honeyfield gasped. They were just about to turn onto Scudder and had a clear view of the green and dock and the monument area near the harbor where the flagpole and veterans' monument stood. The water had come up over the dock and the monument garden. A capsized boat, pulled loose from its mooring, floated in the middle of a flooded Main Street.

"Oh, brother, let's get out of here," Amanda's mother said under her breath.

Amanda totally agreed and was relieved when they made the turn onto Scudder. But she hadn't really counted on the amount of water flowing down the street, like a river, pulled by gravity to the harbor.

"Can you make it, Mom?" she asked. "Maybe we should try another street?"

"They're all pretty bad until we get away from the village. If we can go a little farther on this one, I'll turn onto Highland, which runs parallel to the water. That should be better. It's my old rainstorm bus route," Molly confided without taking her eyes off the road.

Amanda nodded and swallowed back a lump of fear. What if a tree branch fell on them? One very well could, she realized. Or a wire. A lot of the power lines were loaded with ice, dipping dangerously low. Some had already fallen, along with at least one utility pole, she noticed, cracked like a toothpick.

Her mother turned onto Highland, a smaller road lined with trees, and with no houses visible from the street. Though it was slick with a layer of slushy ice, it wasn't full of water, Amanda saw with relief. They were no longer heading straight up, away from the harbor, but were making progress nevertheless.

"So far, so good," Molly murmured. Then suddenly Amanda heard her say, "Oh, no!"

The SUV jolted to a sudden stop. A huge fallen tree blocked their path. "Wow, that was big one," her mother said.

"Oh dear, I hope no one was hurt." Mrs. Honeyfield looked out her window. A car lay underneath the tree, even more thoroughly smashed than her own.

For a long moment, nobody spoke or even made a move. Amanda heard the steady beat of the wipers, whisking away the icy rain, and the sound of the car's blower, pumping hot air at them.

Suddenly Betty started to cry, her little face crumpled with fear. "Mommy, I'm scared!" she wailed.

"It's all right, honey. I'm just going to turn around. Don't worry." Her mother's tone was amazingly soothing. Amanda almost felt better herself . . . though she knew better. It wasn't all right. It wasn't all right at all.

Amanda leaned over and hugged her little sister, then kept her arm around Betty's thin shoulders. "It's just a bad storm, Betty. Don't be scared. We'll be home very soon," she promised.

Betty sniffled and seemed calmer, but didn't say anything.

Mrs. Honeyfield handed back a tissue. "Here, maybe this will help. Poor little thing."

Amanda wiped Betty's tears as their mother put the SUV in reverse. The big vehicle rolled back slowly toward a driveway where Amanda guessed her mother planned to turn and backtrack.

Then the SUV came to a sudden stop. "Oh, blast! We're stuck."

"Stuck? How did we get stuck?" Now Mrs. Honeyfield sounded frightened. She peered out of the side window, trying to see what had happened.

Molly sat back and put the vehicle in park. "I'll go out and see."

"No, Mom, don't get out of the car. I don't want you to." Amanda knew she sounded foolish—and a lot like Betty—but she was suddenly terrified that her mother might be hurt. Molly could get hit by a tree limb or step on a downed power line.

"Don't be silly, honey. I'll be fine. Just let me see."

Molly unhooked her seat belt and opened the driver's door.

"All right, I'm coming, too," Amanda said. Betty started crying when she unhooked her seat belt and grabbed at her jacket.

Amanda felt torn, but Mrs. Honeyfield turned and began to comfort the child. "It's all right, dear. Let's sing a song. Do you know 'The Farmer in the Dell'?" she asked cheerfully. "I bet you can name all the animals, can't you?"

Amanda couldn't quite believe it. It had to be some trick you learned when you were a grandmother. But it seemed to work.

Amanda pulled her hood up, jumped out of the car, and met her mother at the back of the vehicle. The wind was blowing so hard, she was pressed against the rear fender.

"It's a big branch, look." Molly pointed down. The back of the car had gotten stuck on a thick branch. Smaller branches shot off the main trunk and were poking up. "Think we can pull it out?"

"I don't know . . . what if it breaks the car or something?"

Her mother shrugged. "It might pull the muffler off . . . no big deal . . . Let me see what's going on down there . . ."

Her mother kneeled down in a mound of slush and looked under the SUV. How did she know about car mechanics, too? Amanda wasn't sure; she just did. She pulled at some parts of the branch and broke off a few pieces with her gloved hand.

Amanda held her arm so she wouldn't slip as she got up again. "You start it up, Amanda, and drive forward very slowly. I'll give a yank back here and try to get it loose."

"Mom, that's dangerous. You might get hurt. What if the car rolls backward or something? I think we should call Dad . . . or the police, even."

"If it doesn't work, we'll call for help. I don't feel like being stuck here all night, Amanda. Nobody is going to come for us in the blink of an eye. Let's just try."

Amanda gave her a look but finally turned and pulled open the driver's side door and got in. She already knew how stubborn Molly could be. She supposed they could have walked to a street with houses and knocked on some doors, asking for shelter, but that wouldn't be easy either, with Mrs. Honeyfield and Betty in tow.

Amanda took a breath, said a silent prayer, and started the engine. She glanced in the rearview mirror and saw her mother wave at her to go. Then very slowly, she pressed down on the gas pedal.

The wheels spun and spun, making a horrible sound. Betty had been singing quietly, then suddenly started crying again, making it even worse.

Amanda was about to give up when, suddenly, the big vehicle lurched forward—and drove smoothly down the street a few yards in the right direction. She quickly stopped and looked in the mirror to see what had happened to her mother.

But Molly was nowhere to be seen.

"Stay here. I'll be right back." She turned to Mrs. Honeyfield, who quickly nodded, then she jumped out of the SUV again.

She saw her mother on the ground, trying to sit up, then falling back again. "Mom . . . are you all right? Here, let me help you."

Amanda crouched down next to her mother. Her hood had fallen off, and her hair was plastered with icy rain. Her face and the front of her jacket were spattered with mud.

Amanda could tell from Molly's expression that she was in pain. "Hurt my back . . . a little," her mother grunted. "Help me up, my bottom is freezing off."

Amanda did so willingly, pulling Molly up with her arm around her waist. They hobbled back to the SUV, and Molly clung to the back door. "You have to drive, okay?"

Amanda's eyes widened. She had to drive? She rarely took this tank out, even in good weather. But she swallowed back her fear and nodded. "Okay, Mom, let me help you get in."

Molly nodded and Amanda pulled open the back door. "Hi, sweetie, Mommy's going to sit back here with you now." Molly forced a cheerful voice as she maneuvered into a seat next to Betty.

Betty stared at her, wide-eyed. "Mommy, what happened to you?"

"I fell in a puddle. It was really yucky."

Amanda was in the driver's seat, fastening her seat belt, and heard Betty give a little giggle at Molly's answer. *Thank You, God, for letting us get safely back into the truck,* Amanda silently prayed. *Now, if You could just help us get safely home . . .*

She started the engine, feeling strangely calm, though the wind still roared ferociously, rocking the heavy vehicle from side to side, and icy rain lashed at the windshield.

While Amanda drove at a snail's pace, Molly navigated from the backseat. They were not too far from Mrs. Honeyfield's house and dropped her off a few minutes later. Then they headed home.

More low power lines and broken tree limbs were scattered all along the way, and Beach Road was blocked at one point with a huge downed tree; the branches seemed at least two stories high. Somehow, they managed to get around it, driving on some side roads without too much trouble. Finally, the house came into view. Amanda felt so relieved, she practically started crying.

A trip that usually took twenty minutes had taken two hours, Amanda realized. But she was never so relieved to turn up the driveway.

Molly had called Amanda's father, who had told them their electricity was off, but he had somehow managed to get the garage open and they pulled in. He was waiting there, pacing back and forth. He eagerly helped Molly out of the vehicle, practically carrying her into the house.

Amanda took care of Betty. The garage was lit only by a camping lantern, and the house was dim as well. It wasn't completely dark outside, but soon would be. Her father had built a fire in the fireplace and lit some candles, which Amanda found a comforting sight.

"Get out of those wet clothes," her father told everyone. "Thank God you're all home safe and sound. I was nearly out of my mind worrying about you out there. How in the world did you hurt your back, Molly? Did you try to push that SUV out of a ditch or something? Are you totally crazy?"

Her father, the epitome of a reasonable person, rarely got angry or even raised his voice. But he was on the verge of losing it now.

"Calm down, Matt. We had a little trouble. With a tree trunk."

"Mom was very brave. She saved the day," Amanda cut in, defending her mother. "She was a total hero."

"Amanda helped, too. She had to drive us all the way from the village," her mother told him.

Her father sighed and put his hands up. "All right . . . you're all safe. That's all that matters. I'm going to get you some pain relievers and a salve for your back. I hope it's just a sprain."

Molly was already stretched out on a couch in the great room, her wet, muddy coat a heap on the floor, her face still covered with grime. "That was my secret plan. I just want to be waited on until the storm is over. How long is it going to last, did they say?"

"Last I heard, until tomorrow morning," Matt said, reappearing with the first-aid supplies. "I'll put the radio on again in a second. I didn't want to waste the batteries."

It was odd not being able to just turn on the TV, Amanda realized. She couldn't remember the last time they had to get their information from a radio. Her father turned it on, and the urgent tone of the all-news station filled the silence.

The reports were grim. The storm was enormous, sweeping up the East Coast and hitting all of New England. Hundreds of thousands of homes across three states were already without power. Cities and towns all along the coast were flooded, and it would get worse until the tide peaked later in the evening.

"We saw a boat in the street, Daddy," Betty said suddenly.

"You did?" Amanda could tell from his tone that he didn't quite believe her.

"Yeah, we did," Amanda assured him. "Right on Main Street. It had come loose from its mooring and floated up from the harbor."

"Holy cow . . . there was that much water on Main Street?"

Molly nodded, looking distressed. "A lot of stores on Main Street are going to have water damage. I just hope my shop isn't completely flooded."

"I hope so, too, honey. But we'll just have to deal with it." He shook his head and turned back to the radio.

Amanda had taken off Betty's wet jacket and boots and was about to fix her a cup of hot cocoa, using a flashlight to maneuver around the kitchen. Unfortunately their stove ran on electricity, but her father had set up the camp stove on a counter. She got it going and set up a pot of water to heat. Her father had already fixed them a supper of some soup and sandwiches and even had plates out. She guessed they would eat by the fireplace and maybe play some board games, the way they often did during a big snowstorm.

"Can I have a marshmallow?" Betty asked in a small, quiet voice.

It was a little close to dinner for sweets. Even the cocoa was pushing it. But, Amanda thought, all things considered, her sister really did deserve a marshmallow. They all did.

"Sure, pal. You go for it."

She smiled and turned back to the stove, pouring the boiling water into Betty's favorite cup.

She said a silent prayer of thanks that she was in this warm, safe house with her family, back safe and sound from their perilous journey. She knew that so many people tonight could not say the same. No matter what dissatisfactions she had with her life right now, she knew in her heart she was truly and deeply blessed.

THE POWER HAD GONE OFF SHORTLY AFTER LILLIAN AND EZRA HAD turned on the TV and watched a few minutes of news about the storm.

Lillian had almost been relieved when the screen suddenly went black and all the lights went out. The reports and pictures were very disturbing.

Emily had promised she would come as soon as she could. She was at the Village Hall and couldn't leave at a moment's notice to help them. She was the mayor, after all. She had to stay and do her job, tonight of all nights. People were evacuating their homes and going into emergency centers, and the police and fire departments were racing around, answering calls about power lines and fallen trees and other disasters.

Jessica had called and offered to send her husband Sam over to see what he could do for them. But Lillian had put her off. Emily, at least, would have use of the town's emergency vehicles. Lillian didn't want Sam driving around in that pickup truck of his. Pickups just weren't stable in weather like this.

"We're fine so far," Lillian had told her. "Don't make him drive around in this weather. It's not safe."

Now they were just sitting in the dark, in Ezra's room, the three of them—Estrella, Ezra, and herself. It wasn't dark entirely. Estrella had brought in the silver candlesticks, and there were flashlights. Jessica had brought them a battery-powered radio, but you could only hear the same news repeated over and over. Lillian was happy to have it shut off.

Ezra was dozing. Lillian was trying to do her cross-stitch, but it was almost impossible to see. Estrella was reading a book with the flashlight. Her cell phone rang and she jumped up to answer it, then walked into the hallway to talk. It had to be her family again. She talked to them in a torrent of rapid Spanish.

The phone had roused Ezra, and he looked over a Lillian. "Was that her family?"

Lillian shrugged. "I suppose so. She didn't say."

They had called before the lights went out. Estrella had made the conversation short, glancing from time to time at Lillian.

"Is everything all right?" Ezra asked with concern as Estrella ended the call.

"*Sí*, Dr. Ezra. The children are home from school. My mother just wanted me to know," she reported.

"You need to go home to them," Ezra said. Lillian looked at him. He had clearly paid her objections to that idea no mind.

But Estrella answered before she could jump into the conversation. "They are well, Dr. Ezra. I'm staying here, with you and Mrs. Elliot. I cannot leave you alone in the storm."

Lillian was relieved to hear that. Well, she was paid a nice sum to watch over them, and her job was fairly easy. She should stay here; there was no question in Lillian's mind. Estrella's mother could watch over her children. She did it all the time, didn't she?

If only the wind would let up. That was the worst part, Lillian thought. It was getting on her nerves and sounded even worse in the dark. Howling gusts beat against the old house like an old woman beating a rug with a broom. That's what she pictured—it was the way they cleaned in her day—and it felt as if the house might be beaten and blown right off its foundation. She knew that at least one wooden shutter had been pulled off and flung to the front lawn. And a few shingles. She imagined the house would have even more bare patches and tiles from the slate roof missing before it was all through.

Earlier, she watched the huge trees on the hill behind her property from the window in the kitchen. She saw a very tall one, at least three stories high, slowly tilt to one side and then come crashing down. Luckily, it had fallen in a woodsy spot, nowhere near the house. But it had still been frightening. When she came back to Ezra's room, she didn't tell him. No need to make him worry more in his condition.

There was a sound at the back door and they all looked up.

"Must be Emily, coming in with her key." Lillian put her handwork aside and started to get up.

"I'll go, Mrs. Elliot. You shouldn't walk around in the dark. It's not safe," Estrella said.

"She's right, sit tight, Lily. We don't want you taking a spill. Enough folks are lying around here with casts on right now," Ezra said.

Lillian hated to be ordered around but stayed in the room nonetheless, standing at the foot of Ezra's bed.

Emily appeared a few moments later, wearing a rain slicker that was a startling shade of yellow. Visible from a satellite in outer space, Lillian suspected. She carried a huge flashlight that was practically blinding.

Lillian had to raise her hand to her eyes. "My word. Do you need to keep that thing so bright?"

Emily turned the light to the floor and Lillian noticed that Dan had come, too, and was standing just behind her daughter.

"Sorry, Mother. It's standard-issue for village employees. It's all hands on deck tonight. Dan came out to help me, thank goodness. Janie is at Jessica's," she added, in case Lillian was wondering about her granddaughter.

Dan stepped forward, also wearing an impossibly bright yellow slicker. "Is everyone all right here? How are you doing?"

"We're holding up. Nothing much we can do. Some dinner would be nice. My stomach is growling," Lillian said honestly.

"Not served in the dining room tonight, on the good china," Ezra cut in.

"Of course not," Lillian huffed at him, though she knew what he was driving at. She did have a tendency to . . . overnormalize in an emergency. Was that such a bad thing, while everyone else was losing their minds? Cooler heads must prevail.

"I've brought you some soup and sandwiches. It's in the kitchen. Estrella is bringing it all in on a tray."

"On a tray? Why can't we eat in the kitchen?" Lillian was feeling claustrophobic, stuck in this room in the dark for the last few hours. The kitchen would be some change of scene.

"We can't get Ezra out of bed and into the kitchen tonight, Mother. Be reasonable."

Lillian glanced at her husband. "I'll sit with him here while he eats, and then have mine in the kitchen." She would eat her soup at a normal table, she added silently. Not slurp it all over herself like a second convalescent.

"Lily, let's get the big picture here. What does it matter where we eat our soup?" Ezra struggled to sit up straighter in bed, and Dan stepped over to help, giving him a firm lift. "Should we go to an evacuation center, Emily? Estrella needs to get back to her family. I won't keep her here. I really won't," he insisted.

"An evacuation center? Are you daft? I will not end up on a cot in some drafty gymnasium. We're perfectly fine right where we are. You go if you really want to," Lillian told him. She couldn't see how he could, if he couldn't even get to the kitchen safely.

"Now, now. Calm down, you two. Please." Emily took off her slicker and put it on a chair. It was dripping on the floor, but Lillian stopped herself from saying anything.

Before Emily could say more, Estrella came in with a tray. The food looked and smelled very good, and Lillian broke down, too hungry to wait to eat in the kitchen.

"I'll have mine over here, on this little lamp table," she told Estrella as she served Ezra on his bed tray. "Please," she added as an afterthought.

"And then you should go home, Estrella. Emily will take you. You can get her home in some truck or something, can't you?" Ezra asked Emily.

"The town vehicle that dropped us off will be back in a while. I just have to call."

Lillian knew Emily was very circumspect about using the town services for anything that had to with her personal needs or family. But Estrella was a village resident, virtually stranded here. So she supposed Emily had reasoned it out that way.

"I appreciate that, Ms. Warwick. But as I told your parents, I need to stay here with them tonight. It's not safe for them alone."

Her cell phone rang, and she answered it. Lillian squirmed at the note of worry in her tone. *"¿Mamá . . . ? ¿Qué pasa?"*

Lillian made a face and started eating. More drama.

The conversation was again brief and Estrella put the phone away. "My mother is taking the children to a neighbor a few doors down. They live on a higher floor. She was afraid our cottage would be flooded. Water was coming in on the porch."

"Oh my, that's awful. See, they need you." He glanced at Emily. "You need to take her to her family. I won't hear any more objections. We'll manage all right. Someone can come check on us in the morning."

"Yes, we'll survive . . . I hope," Lillian said quietly. She patted her mouth with a napkin. Scratchy paper; she hated that. But one needed to make do in an emergency. As everyone kept reminding her.

"I'll stay with you," Dan offered. "If you can spare me?" he asked his wife.

"Thank you, honey. That's a good idea. You stay for a while and I'll come back here later. I think there's only so much I can do out there until it stops raining." Emily turned to Estrella first. "I appreciate that you want to stay, Estrella, but Ezra is right. Your children and mother are most important. They need you. I'll take you to them right away."

"All right, Ms. Warwick. If you say. Thank you." Estrella looked at Lillian. "I'll get everything ready so Dr. Ezra will have his medications on time, and you can check his vital signs, Mrs. Elliot."

"Yes, yes, we can do that." Lillian brushed aside her concerns. "Dan here can help me, I'm sure."

"Yes, of course," Dan assured Estrella. "Just show me what I need to know."

Dan followed Estrella to the kitchen. It was some comfort that Dan was taking over for tonight.

This storm is a trial on many fronts, isn't it? Lillian hoped all the hullabaloo would soon be over.

CHAPTER NINE

~~

THE RAIN ENDED TUESDAY AROUND NOON, THOUGH STRONG winds and a light drizzle prevailed. Amanda followed her parents outside to look over the property. Tree branches littered the lawn and two trees had fallen, but they didn't hit anything, luckily. The house next door had not been so fortunate. A large tree had crashed into the roof, tearing a hole right through it.

"Oh, too bad for the Nelsons. We were so lucky," Molly said, turning to Matt.

"More than lucky, I'd say." Her father started gathering up the branches and putting them in a wheelbarrow. Amanda helped.

She heard her mother's phone ring and saw her answer it. It was her aunt Jessica calling again to see how they were. Her mother listened a few minutes, then said, "Of course we can help. Just tell me what time."

A few moments later, she finished the call and walked over to Amanda and her dad, who were heaping all the branches in a pile at the back of the property.

"Reverend Ben is setting up a comfort center at church. Jessica said a few of the deacons are going to hook up a generator there tonight and open up tomorrow. She said to bring any clothes we want to donate and food and things. I'm going to bring some food from the shop. I have to empty out the freezers anyway."

"That's a good idea. We should all go over and help. I can't open my office without electricity. Well, only for emergencies," Matt added. "And there's no school tomorrow. We already know that."

The school district had called and closed schools through Wednesday, and it could be even longer, Amanda thought.

"It will be good to do something productive," Amanda said. "All those photos on the news are getting to me."

They had learned from the news that the houses and businesses in Cape Light had gotten off lightly compared to many of the waterfront towns nearby. Cape Light's harbor was protected by land masses, but that was not the case in nearby Spoon Harbor, Hamilton, and Essex. Many beachfront houses had been washed right off their foundations or otherwise destroyed by the tide and winds. People had lost all their possessions, houses and cars, boats . . . everything was washed away in the monster storm.

Amanda realized again how lucky she really was. "I have a lot of old clothes I've been meaning to give to charity. I'll go upstairs and sort it out," she said.

"Me, too. I have a ton of stuff," her mother replied. "We should all clean out our closets and get everything together in bags. Jessica said they need shoes and coats . . . and blankets. Let's see what we can find."

Amanda was grateful for the assignment. She was starting to feel bored and cooped up. The first night of the storm had been exciting, and even fun, eating dinner by the fire and playing board games. But she didn't look forward to more of the same. Once it got dark out, it felt very cold and dismal in the house. It was hard to live without all the creature comforts and technology she took for granted. She could have used the time to practice, but had been forced to leave her cello at church.

She wondered if the church had been damaged. Her aunt hadn't mentioned that. Amanda knew at least a few panes of glass in the big windows had been broken . . . and she knew who would be called to fix them.

THERE WERE STILL A FEW LARGE PUDDLES IN THE CHURCH PARKING lot, but not enough to daunt the crowd that had come to help on Wednesday morning. Even Betty was eager to get inside and see what was going on. Outside, the nearby playground on the green was closed, with village workers all over the area, cleaning up debris. They were accompanied by a throng of gulls, who were pecking at the seaweed and shellfish that had ended up so far in from the harbor.

Amanda made her way inside with her family, tugging their big black trash bags full of donations. Long tables had been set up in Fellowship Hall, and many people were there, sorting clothes into neatly folded piles for women, men, and children. Blankets and other household goods were being sorted on the other side of the room, and in the hallway near the kitchen, more tables held nonperishable foods—soup, oatmeal, peanut butter, pasta, tuna fish—along with cases and huge bottles of water. So many towns didn't have any water supply right now.

Amanda had listened to the news on the radio that morning. It was hard to believe how many people were suffering and how much they had lost. Donations of clothes and food would not go very far toward replacing these losses, but it would be something, she reasoned.

Amanda soon lost sight of her parents. Everyone was going different ways. Her father left the church with her uncle Sam and a few other men to help some older congregants who were stuck in their homes. Her mother automatically gravitated toward the kitchen. Amanda followed as far as the door. It was filled with women, all much older and far better cooks than she.

"I've never seen such a thing, and I've lived here all my life." Sophie Potter was at the stove, where two huge pots gave off the pleasing aroma of fresh clam chowder.

"It was just as bad in sixty-three," Grace Hegman countered. "Don't you remember?"

"I don't recall nearly as many trees coming down," Sophie replied. "But that was a wicked one, no question."

Amanda watched her mother make her presence known and then slowly wheedle her way into the cooking. Amanda turned away with a smile. Before too long, Molly would have taken over the stove and Grace would be out in Fellowship Hall, sorting jars of peanut butter.

"Let's help in here, Betty," Amanda said to her little sister as they entered the hall. Betty clung to her hand, seeming daunted by the crowd. But once they were in the big room, she spotted a group of her little friends, helping their Sunday school teacher sort out children's clothing.

"I'm going to help Miss Pam," she told Amanda, then darted off.

Well, that was easy. Amanda had expected to have her little shadow around all day. Now she had to figure out where she could help.

Her aunt Jessica walked by, carrying a pail full of rags and two mops. "Can I help you clean something?" Amanda offered.

"There's water all over the sanctuary floor. Some windows are broken."

Amanda knew that already. She took a mop and followed Jessica to the sanctuary. A few of the deacons were there, along with Reverend Ben. They had pushed the pews to one side of the wooden floor and were cleaning up water and debris on the other.

"Amanda, good to see you," Reverend Ben greeted her. "I was so relieved to hear that you got home all right." Reverend Ben had called her house the night of the storm, just to make sure she was home safe.

"I saw the windows in here break that day," Amanda admitted. "I should have told you then."

"Don't let it trouble you," he replied. "I don't think anything could have been done until the storm was over anyway. And Gabriel has already patched them up with duct tape and plastic."

Gabriel was here. Amanda had to force herself not to look around for him. She hoped he hadn't already left.

"But I should never have left you and Mrs. Honeyfield here," Reverend Ben went on. "The weather report I was listening to said the heavy rain wouldn't start until the evening, and I believed them."

"That's all right, Reverend. The storm came in faster than anyone expected. I'm just glad I'm here to help clean up."

"So am I. What's that saying—'many hands make light work'?" said another voice.

Amanda turned to see Gabriel. He stood nearby, smiling at her, a large mop in hand. The minister was called away then by someone with a question, and Amanda found herself alone with Gabriel.

"I thought you would be in Texas by now. Did the storm delay your trip?"

Amanda shook her head. "I didn't get called for the audition."

"Oh . . . I'm sorry. That's too bad." He looked genuinely concerned for her. "You must be disappointed."

"Yeah, I am. Or, I was. Until the storm came. It's been a big distraction," she admitted. "And it put things in perspective. I mean, in the big picture—having a roof over your head and your loved ones safe and all your belongings and memories not floating away—missing out on a job isn't such a big deal, right?"

He nodded. "Right. Totally. I think the last few days have helped a lot of people count their blessings."

He started mopping the water and she did, too, working near him.

"How about your house? Was there any damage?" she asked.

"No, we got off easy. But a tree fell on the back of my shop and broke some glass, my own projects mostly. I should have stored them more carefully, I guess. But it's a small thing when you compare it to what other people have lost and are going through."

Amanda glanced at him, wondering if he was really all right about his artwork being ruined. It was hard to tell. She didn't know him all that well yet, she realized. "Well, it is a loss. It's your work, and it's irreplaceable. I'd like to see some of it sometime," she added.

He was squeezing out the mop, and the muscles in his arms showed through his long-sleeved cotton shirt. "Sure, anytime . . . Does that mean you're sticking around?"

She wasn't sure how to answer that. She didn't plan on staying here forever, but it seemed that God had a different plan for her right now. "Oh, I'll be here awhile, I guess. There's not much going on around the holidays."

"Good. Then maybe we can go out sometime, to the movies or something? When you don't have any practice sessions or Barbie parties planned," he teased her.

Amanda knew now there were few plans she would not cancel to go out on a date with him. "I'd like that," she said honestly.

"Good. We'll figure it out," he promised.

They worked together for the rest of the afternoon, first cleaning up the sanctuary and then working in Fellowship Hall sorting clothes.

Amanda found she was getting to know Gabriel in a different way. He was still charming and friendly but not always so glib and teasing. He was kind and patient with older people, like Digger Hegman, who came to their table to help sort and wound up telling stories about the "heavy weather" he had seen at sea.

"There was this one storm, the waves were higher than a house. Higher than the church steeple probably. We were three men on board and tied ourselves down in the cockpit. We was rocking and rolling.

Didn't know which side was up. Figured we were going to sink or that boat was going to get broke apart, like a hammer cracking a nut. We were praying and crying. Ain't no nonbelievers in a storm like that one," he added with a cackling laugh.

"I'll bet," Gabriel said, encouraging him to continue.

Digger pulled his ear and squinted, as if that helped him remember. "After a time of tossing around, some big wave picks us up like a giant hand, see, and we feel ourselves flying through the air . . . Maybe for a full five minutes. I ain't lying, son," he promised. "I was counting on my old watch, right here." He took out a round gold watch on a chain that was tucked in his vest pocket. "We were on the crest of that wave, just balanced there."

"Really? That's amazing," Gabriel replied in a totally serious tone. "What happened? How did the boat come down?"

"We come down right on the foamy brine and rolled into shore. Easy as pie. Boat come to a full stop, stuck there, in the sand. No one was hurt neither . . . and we never lost our catch," the old fisherman added, laughing softly. "Not one single clam."

"That's quite a story, Digger," Gabriel said, and Amanda heard admiration in his voice, though whether it was because he believed the story or appreciated a tall tale, she couldn't tell.

"It is, ain't it? Someone up there heard our prayers, I guess," Digger added with a note of awe.

Gabriel and Amanda exchanged a look. If even half that story was true, Amanda would have been surprised, but neither of them voiced a doubt to Digger. Sometimes the greatest wisdom was kindness, and Gabriel seemed to know that.

Grace Hegman, Digger's daughter, had come along and now stood beside her father. "Are you telling that story about the flying clam boat again, Dad?"

He answered with a deep nod. "I am, Grace. Folks wanted to hear it."

Grace glanced at the two young people. "Well, bless you both for listening . . . Time for us to go, Dad. I think you're tired."

Digger didn't argue, but he did take a moment to say good-bye. "See you two in church. Keep up the good work," he added.

"He's a real character," Gabriel said after the old fisherman left. "When I was little, I used to love his magic tricks."

"Me, too," Amanda said. She wondered now if she'd ever been standing beside Gabriel at some church picnic when Digger had taken out his cards and coins to entertain the children.

"Grace was very generous. She brought a heap of clothing from her store," Amanda added. Grace owned the Bramble Antiques Shop, which was in a pretty Victorian on Main Street. She and Digger had lived in the apartment above the store for as long as Amanda could remember.

"So many donations. People are really reaching out to help," Gabriel said.

Amanda nodded. "It's sad to know people are hurting, but nice to see how everyone is responding. The town is really pulling together."

"It is great. Too bad it can't be like this all time," he said. "Not the storm, of course. But the way everyone is so friendly, and how all the usual defenses seem to have melted away."

"I was thinking the same thing," Amanda said. "Why do we need a disaster to make us want to help other people? We should be like this all the time. I hope I can remember that."

"Me, too." He smiled and caught her gaze. "It's one good thing to come out of the storm, I guess."

She smiled back and nodded, feeling they were in sync today, working together and connecting in a deeper way than they had before. Much as she enjoyed his teasing mode, this was different, more meaningful. She felt good knowing that he cared about helping other people as much as she did. She was glad the storm had brought them back together, giving them a second chance to find out where their relationship could go.

It was the one good thing about not being called for the audition in Austin, she had to admit.

While they were working, a woman with thick auburn hair and bright blue eyes came over to their table. "Gabriel, do you want some soup? They're serving the volunteers now."

"No, thanks, Mom. I'm all right." He glanced at Amanda. "This is my friend, Amanda Harding. Amanda, this is my mother, Patricia."

Amanda put down the sweater she had been folding and smiled. "Nice to meet you."

Gabriel's mother had the same warm smile and deep dimples as her son. "I'm glad to meet you, Amanda. Isn't your father Dr. Harding?"

Amanda nodded. "The very same."

"He's a wonderful doctor. Please tell him I said hello."

"I'll do that," Amanda promised.

Everyone in town loved her father . . . though Molly inspired mixed emotions at times.

Gabriel's brother, Taylor, came up to the table. Amanda recognized him from the snowball fight. "Gabe, help us move the water," he said. "We need some muscle."

He disappeared into the crowd, and Patricia glanced at Gabriel. "Make sure he doesn't hurt himself. He's so macho now," she said, rolling her eyes.

"I'll go keep an eye on him. I can help move the water, too," Gabriel added. "Catch you later, Amanda." He touched her arm lightly.

"Right. See you." Amanda watched him go, then realized his mother was watching her. She felt herself blush a little and tried to focus on sorting the clothes.

Patricia smiled at her, that wide, warm smile that was becoming a familiar sight. "It was nice to meet you, Amanda. Maybe I'll see you in church sometime."

"Yes, I hope so," Amanda said, feeling suddenly shy.

She was glad that Gabriel's mother did not stay to make conversation. She felt a little tongue-tied. But it had been interesting to meet her.

Amanda stayed at church for the rest of the day, along with her family. They were all so tired by the time they headed home, they could hardly talk. But it was a good sort of tired, knowing they had worked hard to help others. Amanda knew she would do the same tomorrow. Reverend Ben was keeping the church open as a comfort center for as long as was needed, probably throughout the week.

As they headed up Main Street in her mother's SUV, Betty pointed out the window. "Look at the lights. Aren't they pretty?"

"What lights, honey? There aren't any . . ." Her mother turned, starting to correct Betty, then her eyes widened. "Betty's right! The power came on in the village. It must have just happened. I wonder if it's on at our house yet."

Amanda did a double take. It was true. The power had come back on in the village, and one strand of holiday lights that had been strung across the street a few weeks ago miraculously had not been blown down like the others.

It hung very low and on a crooked angle over the road, and the star in the center was missing half its tinsel. But the lights still glowed, cheering their way and reminding Amanda that Christmas would come, storm or no storm. Some things could not be stopped or delayed—not even by the fury of Mother Nature.

"WHAT WAS THAT . . . THAT THUD?" LILLIAN SAT UP SHARPLY. THE book she had been reading with her flashlight fell to the floor, as did the flashlight.

She realized she had drifted off for a moment and couldn't figure out where she was . . . or what was going on around her. Why was her grandson Tyler staring at her? Was she at Jessica's house?

"That was just the sound of the power coming back on," Tyler told her. He got up from his chair and bent to pick up her book and light. She realized finally that she was in her own house, and Tyler was just here to visit, along with his father, Sam. Everyone had been taking turns baby-sitting for them, which had been quite annoying. But necessary, she supposed. Not because of her. But for Ezra. *Just in case,* she reminded herself silently.

Sam walked in from the kitchen. "The power is on. Great, right?"

"Amen to that," she said quietly. Never underestimate Sam Morgan's talent for stating the obvious. Still, Sam had grown on her over the years. He was good man, a loving husband to Jessica, and a wonderful father to their three children.

"How is Ezra?" she asked. "Is he still napping?"

"He just woke up. He's asking for you. I'm going to make him some tea. Would you like some—or a bite to eat?" Sam asked.

"Tea will suffice, thank you." Lillian rose slowly, dreading her son-in-law's efforts in the kitchen. It wasn't that she questioned his abil-ity. Like his sister Molly, he was a good cook; all of Joe and Marie Mor-gan's children were. But Sam's culinary efforts favored burgers and chili and great big sandwiches, the sort of food that was just not appropriate for Ezra—or her. Even worse, his tea looked like a cup of water drawn from the harbor . . . and was about as tasty. He'd never made tea with loose leaves before, he had told her, and she didn't have the patience to teach him.

Leaning heavily on her cane, she slowly made her way to Ezra's room. Jessica would stop by with some dinner soon, she recalled. She hoped it wasn't one of her pasta dishes. They lay so heavily in her stom-ach. She would just as soon have some plain baked chicken and a boiled potato. Maybe now that the lights were back on, someone would take pity on her and accommodate this *extreme* request.

She finally reached Ezra's room and glanced at him from the doorway. "The lights are back on. We are coming to the end of this ordeal, I hope."

"'"Hope" is the thing with feathers—That perches in the soul—And sings the tune without the words—And never stops—at all,'" he countered. He had a good memory for poetic bits, her husband did.

"Bravo," she said flatly as she sat down in the armchair next to his bed. "I hope they'll leave us alone for a while now, give us a moment's peace."

She heard Sam coming and quickly sat back in her chair. He served Ezra a tuna sandwich first and then brought them both cups of tea. Hers sloshed a bit into the saucer. "Oh, sorry about that," he apologized.

"It's all right. It's fine."

Ezra glanced at her, then looked back at Sam. "Say, Sam, could you find my puzzle book? I think I left it in the living room."

Lillian knew very well it was right in the bedroom, but then guessed her husband had sensed her irritation and sent Sam out of the room to be helpful.

Sam disappeared, and she said, "I know he means well . . . but don't drink that tea. You'll regret it."

Ezra peeked into his mug and put it aside. "He certainly means well, but the meals have been a little catch as catch can," he conceded. "I'll be glad to see Estrella return. Maybe she'll come back tomorrow."

"I suppose that is possible," Lillian replied without meeting his eye. She would never admit it, not with her hand pressed to an open fire, but she was *almost* looking forward to Estrella returning as well. At least Estrella brought a sense of order here. Her cooking, though it was far from perfect, would be an improvement over what they had been surviving on the last two days.

"I think we should call her. After we have our tea," Ezra suggested. "See how she and her family are doing."

"Yes, let's," Lillian agreed. Her husband stared at her, looking quite surprised. "What? What did I say wrong now?" she asked sharply.

He shrugged. "Nothing, dear. Nothing at all."

She scowled at him. She knew that smug grin. As if he thought he had gotten one over on her. She just wanted all these meddlesome and chatty daughters and sons-in-law and grandchildren out of her house. How much could a person stand? It was wearing on her last nerve.

She wasn't dying to see Estrella, but her return would solve this problem. "Let's just say it's the lesser of two evils," she finally replied.

"If you say so, dear," Ezra agreed.

But he still wore that infernal smile. If he wasn't so ill, she would have pursued this point. Yes, she would have.

For the sake of his health, she took the high road, though she wasn't sure he appreciated it. Then she sat back and tried to sip the horrid tea Sam Morgan had served them.

CHAPTER TEN

⌒⌒

*E*STRELLA ARRIVED BRIGHT AND EARLY THURSDAY MORNING.
Lillian wasn't even downstairs yet, but she heard her coming in
the back door, then Ezra calling out, "*Hola*, Estrella!"

"*Hola*, Dr. Ezra," she replied cheerfully. Lillian heard her go into his
room, and then the Spanish lesson started, halting but earnest on her
husband's part and slow and patient on Estrella's.

She still hoped to heaven Estrella was not asking any critical health
questions in these tête-à-têtes. Ezra was liable to mix up the descriptions
of his symptoms and get the wrong medication.

But she worried far less about that now. She hated to admit it, but
she more or less trusted the woman. Estrella had proven so clear-headed
and decisive during Ezra's blood-pressure crisis. Was that only a week
ago? It seemed so much longer. The storm had distorted her sense of time
these past few days.

A week, or a year, she would never forget how terrified she had felt
touching Ezra's cold hand that night. Nor how Estrella had insisted that

she ride with Ezra and given her that coat, her own coat. Never said a word about it. Oh, maybe it was a small gesture. But at the time, it seemed like . . . something.

Lillian realized she had never really thanked her. Well, the moment had passed. She wasn't about to revisit all that again now. But she wasn't entirely displeased to see Estrella return. Absence did make the heart grow fonder. Well, not fonder, exactly. She wouldn't go that far. But she had grown accustomed to her. That much was true. She had gotten used to her ways, and Lillian supposed Estrella would stay—until Mrs. Fallon returned.

Finally, she reached the first floor and rested for a moment at the bottom of the staircase.

"Mrs. Elliot, I did not hear you coming down. How are you today?"

"I am well, Estrella. As well as can be expected." She paused, wondering how polite she needed to be to the help these days. "And how are you? How is your family faring?"

"We are safe. No one was hurt." Estrella answered decisively. "Our house, the cottage we are renting . . . it's full of water. Flooded."

"Oh, I'm sorry to hear that," Lillian said, caught off guard. Estrella's cheerful demeanor had given no hint at all of that. She took a few steps closer to Estrella, who was putting the living room back in order, since Lillian's grandchildren had left the place in shambles. "How much water was there? Did your furnishings and all get wet?"

Estrella glanced at her and nodded. "The cottage is one floor. No basement. Everything . . . all my children's clothes and books and toys, TV, beds . . . It's all ruin." She shook her head as if to shake loose the disturbing image. "I will make your breakfast. What would you like to eat?"

Lillian felt a little stunned and didn't know what to say.

It seemed that Estrella did not want to dwell on her misfortune. Just as well. Maybe later she would suggest that Estrella seek help at their church. Lillian had heard they had collected a lot of donations and were trying to help people in Estrella's situation.

"A poached egg on toast would be nice. Thank you," she replied. "I can eat in Dr. Ezra's room. I'll go check on him."

Lillian hobbled into Ezra's room. He was sitting up in bed. His gray beard had a few days' growth, and he scratched his chin.

Estrella always gave him a nice shave and washed and combed his hair properly, but during the storm they'd had to skip all that. Lillian would be pleased when he had his beauty treatments this morning.

He looked upset, and Lillian had a good idea of why. "Well . . . did she tell you? They've lost their house and everything in it. The family has been living in a shelter."

"She didn't tell me that part. What happened to the neighbor?"

Ezra shrugged. "You know how people are. Welcoming, to a point. Or maybe Estrella didn't want to impose. There may have not been much room in the neighbor's apartment."

Lillian nodded. It was hard for her sometimes to picture the way other people lived. As a doctor, Ezra had seen it all and could always empathize better than she could. But that was his nature, too. A shelter did sound grim. "How long can people stay in those evacuation places? Don't they shut down after the storm?"

"More or less. I think the places are open a few days. I don't know where they plan to go now. I haven't asked her yet."

"Maybe a motel somewhere. Maybe the government pays for that. We can ask Emily. She would know."

Ezra seemed distracted, lost in thought.

"Did you hear me? I said we should ask Emily. Maybe she could help them. And don't forget, Sam told us they've collected a lot of donations at church. Estrella ought to go there for some clothes and such."

"She could do that, I suppose." Ezra paused, then looked straight at her. "I think we should have them come here."

Lillian squinted at him. Had she heard him right? She hadn't even had her coffee yet. "Have them here? . . . Are you mad? Did you really say that?"

"I did," he countered in a deep voice, one she hadn't heard in weeks now. "We have plenty of room. They could have the entire third floor. It would be the right thing to do. The Christian thing," he said with emphasis.

Oh, bother. He was throwing the Good Book at her, wasn't he?

She was about to reply, then realized the door was open and Estrella, not too far away in the kitchen, could probably hear them. She stepped back to the door and closed it firmly, then turned to him.

"There are agencies and funds and plenty of services set up to help people like her. I know it's unfortunate," she added in a soft but emphatic tone. "But are we to invite in every family that's found themselves flooded out of their home? We have plenty of space, that's true. Should we give every stranger in town a bedroom?"

"Estrella is not a stranger," he said in a stubborn tone that got under her skin.

"No, of course not. She's your star. Isn't that right?" she chided him.

His pale cheeks took on some color, and Lillian suddenly feared for his blood pressure. "That's right. She is my star. She saved my life," he reminded her. "I, for one, believe I owe her this much. A small compensation in the larger scheme of things."

His rebuttal stung. Mainly because it was true, to some degree, she had to concede. But she still didn't want Estrella's mother and her two children living in this house. She couldn't imagine it . . . She couldn't bear the very idea of it.

"All right, compensation for her heroic moment. I get the point. We never gave her that raise you mentioned. I'm willing to give her a bonus of some kind, a nice gift, to help get her on her feet again. What do you think of that?"

Ezra's eyes narrowed. "I'm disappointed in you, Lily. This young woman has given us her all. Now she needs our help. Why is that so hard to understand?"

"I'm not disagreeing with you," she insisted. "I just think this problem could be solved differently."

They heard a knock on the door and both drew in short, quick breaths. "Come in, Estrella, the door isn't locked," Ezra called out, and Estrella entered the room. He gave Lillian a sharp look, then smiled warmly at his helper.

If Estrella had overheard any of their conversation, her expression did not reveal it. She set down Ezra's breakfast—a bowl of oatmeal with dried cranberries and cinnamon on top. "My, this looks good. I've missed your oatmeal, Estrella. And we've missed you," he added.

"Thank you, Dr. Ezra. I've missed you, too," she replied with a smile. She brought Lillian her dish, too. The egg was perfectly poached, sitting on a golden piece of toast. Not too runny in the middle, but not too hard either. It really did look good.

There was also a cup of berries and orange slices for each of them. And for Lillian, real coffee. She eagerly took a sip. Just right as well. What a great relief.

Once Estrella left the room, Lillian glanced over at Ezra. "We'll discuss this more later," she said quietly.

He nodded, chewing his oatmeal. "You can count on it," he replied with conviction.

Lillian kept a straight face but did waver a bit inside.

Ezra was not one to waste his powder. He chose his battles carefully. Once committed to the field, he did not retreat, or surrender. He was a lot like her in that way, as she knew only too well.

Lillian decided to call Emily while Ezra was napping before lunch. Even though her daughter would drop by at the end of the day, she needed to get a jump on this situation. She told Estrella she felt like a short nap and ambled up to her room, then shut the door to ensure complete privacy.

"Emily? It's me. I need some information," she began, hoping to keep the conversation low-key. She thought it best to speak in the most general terms. No need to get everyone up in arms about Estrella's family.

"Why are you whispering, Mother? You sound hoarse. Does your throat hurt?"

"My throat is perfectly fine," Lillian snapped in a slightly louder voice. "I know you're busy and don't have much time for me. Please just answer a few quick questions. Say a person's home has been rendered uninhabitable by the storm. Doesn't the town or the county—or somebody—provide some sort of temporary housing? Beyond those gymnasium centers, I mean."

"Yes, there are assistance programs, on the county, state, and federal levels. We're just starting to sort all that out now. I've been in meeting on top of meeting—"

"Yes, yes, I'm sure," Lillian hastily cut her off. She didn't need the play-by-play. She just wanted the bottom line. "What should a person do? Where do they apply? Can they get a little apartment somewhere, or maybe a motel room? Just until they get back on their feet."

"Mother, what is all this about? Why are you asking me all these questions?"

"No reason in particular," Lillian insisted. She paused, drumming up an excuse. "I've been watching the news and am just wondering about all these poor souls. It's quite distressing."

The news had disturbed her on a deep level, though no one she knew well had been so devastated. Her own family, thank heavens, had gotten through the storm with relatively few damages.

But now she did know someone firsthand. It wasn't just pictures of strangers in their washed-out homes, sifting through soggy possessions, everything ruined and washed away. It was someone she saw every day. Who lived under her own roof.

"Well, they have to apply for assistance, and we have counselors working to match them up with appropriate programs," Emily explained. "There is some temporary housing, but everything in Cape Light is pretty much filled by now. There are still some motel rooms available in Peabody, I think, and a little farther north."

Motels? Farther north? Lillian didn't like the sound of that. Estrella might not want her family so far from Cape Light, even though she wasn't with them much during the week. As long as they were in Cape Light, she did have proximity if an emergency arose with her children. Lillian knew that was important to her.

Lillian sighed. "I see. You've been very helpful. Thank you for your time."

"Mother? Are you all right? Maybe you should put the newspaper aside and not watch so much TV today."

"I hardly watch that idiot box at all. It rots your brain. I've always told you that," Lillian insisted.

"Yes, I know. But all this bad news can be . . . overwhelming. It does make some people depressed. Especially since it's almost the holidays."

"Well, I'm not one of them. So put your mind at rest," Lillian snapped back. "Can't a person be curious?"

"Yes, Mother, a person can be curious." Lillian could hear Emily shuffling papers and even talking sotto voce to someone nearby.

She hated to be double-tasked by her daughters. That really got under her skin. "I think you're busy. I'd better go. Have a good day."

"You, too, Mother. Oh . . . how is Estrella doing? I know she came back this morning. I didn't get to talk to her yet."

"She's doing fine. Ezra is over the moon at their reunion . . . and the Dish ran away with the Spoon," she finished tartly.

Emily laughed softly. "Thanks for the update. I'll see you later."

Shortly after the call, Lillian made her way down to the kitchen. Estrella was folding laundry and talking on the phone to her mother. She looked a bit wary when Lillian walked in and seemed about to cut the call short.

Lillian waved her hand indulgently. "You can talk. I just wanted a glass of water."

As Lillian took the water pitcher from the refrigerator, a glass magically appeared nearby. Estrella was somehow able to fold laundry, talk to her mother, and anticipate Lillian's needs. Some juggling act. One had to admire that, Lillian thought grudgingly.

Lillian sipped her water and looked over the mail, which Estrella had brought in earlier and left in the appropriate spot on the counter. Estrella was speaking in Spanish. Lillian could barely make out a word, but sensed that she was trying to calm her mother down. Lillian couldn't tell what the problem was exactly. Probably their housing situation. What else could it be?

Estrella finished her call, put the laundry aside, and smiled at Lillian. "Did you have a good rest, Mrs. Elliot? I was just about to check on Dr. Ezra and make the lunch."

"I looked in on him. Let him sleep a little more . . . I was wondering, Estrella, have you applied for any temporary housing? Or some sort of assistance? My daughter Emily might be able to help you . . . and we have a lot of extra furniture around here. I mean, when you get a new place. Our church, the one on the village green, is giving out clothes and all sort of things . . ."

Her voice trailed off. She didn't know what else to say. She was trying to help, wasn't she?

"Thank you, Mrs. Elliot. I have made some calls. I need to fill out papers. The offices are only open nine to five. I will have to take some time off to go there. My mother tried today, but she doesn't speak the language well enough to take care of these things. She's very upset, and I am just talking to her about all of this."

"Oh, I see. Yes, there would be paperwork." If Estrella was here all day and night, how could she apply for help with her housing situation? Lillian had not thought of that. "Well, you should look into it. I can give you some time off. Someone in the family can cover for you."

Estrella seemed surprised by the offer. "Thank you, Mrs. Elliot. I will make more calls and let you know what I find out."

"What are you talking about in there? I'm awake, you know, and I'd like to be part of the conversation."

The two women heard Ezra's voice, loud and clear, shouting at them over the monitor.

"Dr. Ezra, I will be right in with your medicine," Estrella said.

"Keep your shirt on, Ezra. No reason to make a fuss," Lillian added. She glanced at Estrella and shook her head. "I think he's very spoiled now, with all this attention you give him. Very spoiled."

Estrella had all the medications set out on a tray and was pouring a glass of water and marking her chart. "*Sí*, Mrs. Elliot. But he is a good man, your husband. I like to help him."

Lillian tried to maintain a disapproving face, but couldn't quite manage it. "You have helped him," she said finally. *Even more than I'm able to,* she added silently, though she would never admit that out loud.

A few minutes later, Estrella had given Ezra his midday pills and checked his vital signs. "How's my blood pressure?" he asked.

"Very good. One hundred twenty over seventy-five. That is good because, I think, the last few days, you have not been keeping so salt-free, Dr. Ezra?"

"I slipped up a little here and there." Lillian noticed a guilty look on Ezra's face.

"My family was cooking for us," Lillian explained, coming to his defense. "It wasn't his fault, really, but now he has to get back on the straight and narrow. We both do. Right, Ezra?"

Ezra glanced at her. "That's right."

He was still annoyed at her. Keeping his distance, at least. Lillian decided to just ignore it.

"I have prepared a nice lunch for you, all salt-free," Estrella reminded him playfully. "Do you want to eat in the dining room?"

"Oh, I don't care," Ezra waved his hand. "Listen, before you run off, what were you both talking about in the kitchen before? That monitor is on, you know," he reminded them.

Lillian blanched. Had that infernal monitor broadcast their conversation into Ezra's room? It was possible. More likely he had turned up his hearing aids to superhero level in order to eavesdrop on them.

Estrella glanced at her. Lillian could tell she was wary of replying.

"We were just talking about Estrella's situation," Lillian began. "I got some information from Emily. Estrella can apply for temporary housing for her family."

Though she might end up at some distance, she declined to add.

"I see." Ezra's eyes narrowed. Lillian could tell he was not pleased with her. He glanced at Estrella, his gaze softening. "Have you done that, dear? Filled out any forms and whatnot?"

Estrella shook her head. "Not yet, Dr. Ezra. Maybe tomorrow I can go in the morning. Mrs. Elliot said she would find someone to help you both here."

Ezra looked back at Lillian. "I see. We'll discuss that," he told her. Lillian answered with a shrug.

"I suppose we can eat lunch in the kitchen," Lillian said, hoping to change the subject. "Ezra, can you get up with your crutches or shall we get the chair?"

"I can use the crutches. I need the exercise," he insisted.

"Very good. I'll be back to help you. Don't try by yourself, Dr. Ezra," Estrella warned. She picked up her chart and medical equipment and left them alone.

Estrella had brought Ezra the newspaper, and he snapped it open, hiding himself behind it, as if it were a partition.

"Come out from behind there, Ezra. I know what you're doing."

"Reading the news . . . so much loss and grief. It's overwhelming. Makes a person want to help . . . in some small way . . . Most people do," he said pointedly, putting the paper down to look at her.

Lillian was so frustrated with him, she felt her teeth grind together and her hands clench into fists. She took a deep, steadying breath and exhaled. The way Dr. Newton had taught her once to calm herself.

It didn't help much.

"I know what you're thinking, Ezra Elliot. Now think about this: If they move in, there's going to be a racket around here, young children running around the house, the TV going night and day—"

"She only has two children, Lillian, and I suspect they are very well-behaved. When they watch TV, you can close your door."

"I can close my door? They can close their door," she countered. "We'll be stuck with them for Christmas. Did you consider that?"

"Of course I did. I think it would be great fun to have children in the house at Christmas. I think Estrella's little girl still believes in Santa. How can children have any sort of Christmas in a shelter or some cramped motel room? It seems heartless to let that happen, Lily, when we could prevent it. You and me. Not some faceless, anonymous government office somewhere."

She wanted to reply but felt her lips pinch together, anger welling up inside.

"This is a chance for us to extend ourselves, to be kind," he continued. "To take action on our Christian values . . . 'For I was hungry and you gave me food, I was thirsty and you gave me drink, I was a stranger and you took me in.' Matthew 25," he noted, tacking on one of his favorite Bible quotes.

Ezra and that relentless memory of his. Lillian swallowed hard.

"Yes, I know the Book of Matthew, thank you very much. You win the blue ribbon in Bible class."

He was letting loose the cannons on her today, wasn't he? Well, she had taken a few hits, but she wasn't going under yet.

"I'm very sorry for them, truly I am. And I do try to be a good Christian . . . which is not for you to say. 'Judge not, that ye be not judged,'" she fired back. "I just don't believe that means you must invite strangers into your home to prove it. I'm sure I'm not alone in this. You know how I feel about my privacy. I'm sure they can find some help. I'll see to it personally."

Ezra shook his head, looking disgusted. "You could see to it very personally. You just don't want to. And what is so sacrosanct about your privacy, may I ask? Is that so important to you? At this stage in my life, I want to be anything but private and alone. I want to be connected to people, even strangers, for as long as I'm able. That's what being alive is about. Don't you get it?"

Lillian stood up. She wasn't going to be lectured to like this, not even by her husband. "I have tried to meet you halfway, but this conversation is pointless, Ezra. You don't want to negotiate."

"There is nothing to negotiate here, Lillian. I'm right and you are wrong. Very wrong," he insisted.

Lillian was about to reply when Estrella appeared in the doorway with Ezra's crutches. "The lunch is served. I can help you out of bed, Dr. Ezra."

Ezra glanced at her, then at Lillian. "I don't feel very hungry, Estrella. Thank you. I think I'll just stay here and take another nap."

He rolled to his side, pulled the cover over his shoulder with his good hand, and shut his eyes.

Estrella looked surprised and stared at Lillian. Lillian shook her head and put her finger over her lips, signaling it wasn't worth trying to coax him.

How long was he going to carry on like this? She had never seen anything quite like it.

Lillian went into the kitchen and called Emily. "Emily? Do you have a minute?"

"What's wrong? Is Ezra all right?"

"It's not Ezra exactly. It's Estrella. Well, he's out of sorts, mad at me. But let's not get into that. Estrella's lost the cottage she rents. It flooded. Can you talk to her? Give her some pointers about where to find some help?"

"Oh dear, how awful for them. Yes, of course I'll help her. Is she there?"

"She's right here. I'll put her on."

Estrella had gone back to the pantry to bring out another bottle of spring water. She looked surprised when Lillian handed her the cell phone. "It's my daughter, Emily. She wants to help you."

"Hello? Mayor Warwick?" Estrella took the phone and began talking to Emily. She found a pad and started writing things down, standing at the counter. A good sign, Lillian thought. She felt encouraged and began eating her lunch. Maybe by the time Ezra gave up this pout, Estrella would know what to do and where to go. Everything would be settled.

She certainly hoped so. *Dear Lord above, with all I've been through lately, with Ezra being sick and Mrs. Fallon disappearing on us, please don't make me take these people in. I just couldn't bear it.* "The Lord doesn't give you a burden heavier than you can carry."

She had heard that motto many times. The thought gave Lillian some hope she would be exempt from taking on this one.

Lillian allowed Estrella to use the phone for the rest of the day, calling government offices and trying to make headway on her situation. Ezra was still in a dour mood and would not play gin rummy or Scrabble. He didn't want to leave his room and would barely speak to her when she went in.

Old grouchy pants. *Well, suit yourself,* she told him silently. Still, his silent reprobation stung. Was she really being so awful and heartless?

She still didn't think so.

"WELL . . . ANY PROGRESS?" LILLIAN WALKED INTO THE KITCHEN. IT was late afternoon, and Estrella was about to start dinner. "I mean with the housing offices. Did anyone call you back?"

Estrella shook her head, looking a bit worn out, Lillian thought. "Not yet, Mrs. Elliot. This takes time. I need to go in person tomorrow, to fill out forms. There's not much you can do over the phone . . . A relative called. My husband's cousin. She lives in Andover. She said we could go stay with her if we needed to."

"Andover? That's so far away. You'd be far from your children all week, working down here." Lillian caught herself. No need to point out the drawbacks. It was some solution, at any rate.

"Yes, I know. I am thinking if I have to go there, I would need to leave working for you and Dr. Ezra. It is too far. I would be worried if something happened. And it would be hard to leave my children during the week."

This was exactly what Emily had alluded to that morning. Estrella might be forced to move from the area—and leave this job.

Lillian felt caught between the proverbial rock and hard place. She heard a strange sound and looked up to see Ezra balanced on his crutches like a grizzled old flamingo, his bathrobe tied, but just barely. He had somehow gotten out of bed on his own and made his way to the kitchen—to confront her once again, she had no doubt.

"What's this I hear about Andover? Who's going way up there?"

"Estrella has an in-law, her late husband's cousin. She's offered her a place to stay."

Estrella was already at his side, looking concerned about his precarious balance on the crutches. "Come to the table, Dr. Ezra. Sit, please," she urged him.

Ezra sat and looked up at her, his gaze troubled. "Well, what do you think? I don't suppose you could move there and keep working here for us?"

Estrella shook her head, looking regretful. "No, sir. It would be too far away from the children—"

"I understand," he said before she could go on. "We would hate to lose you. But you need to do what's best for your family."

"She hasn't said she's going for sure, Ezra," Lillian pointed out. "It's just an invitation. Estrella has been finding out how to apply for some temporary housing around here. She's going to apply tomorrow."

Estrella glanced at her. "I will, Mrs. Elliot. But my relative in Andover, she has a large house with a nice yard. Very pleasant. It might be best for the children."

"Yes, a nice big house is much better for children," Ezra said, sounding as if the admission was painful. "Much more comfortable."

"Yes, sir, it would be. I would be sorry to leave here, though. I would be sorry to . . . disappoint you."

No one said anything for a long minute. Ezra seemed about to speak, then gazed down at the table. He almost looked as if he might cry.

Finally, Lillian couldn't stand it any longer. "All right, Ezra. I'm waving the white flag," she announced, picking up a dish towel from the drain board and giving it a limp wave.

Ezra made a face at her, and Estrella stared at her curiously.

"Estrella, would you like to bring your family to stay here with us? Until you can make some other arrangements," she added quickly.

Ezra seemed surprised but suspicious; he didn't entirely trust this sudden about-face.

Estrella looked surprised as well. "Mrs. Elliot, you are inviting us to stay here? With you and Dr. Ezra?"

"Yes, yes, that's right. Up on the third floor, there's plenty of room and a big bathroom. Very private," she said quickly.

"Really? . . . I would like this very much. Then I can stay and work for you, and the children can be at the same school."

"Yes, that's true. I didn't think of it," Lillian said honestly. It was hard to move a child in the middle of the school year. There would be that benefit for them, as well.

"You are sure this is all right? You have talked about it?" Estrella looked from Lillian to Ezra and back again.

"Oh, we have discussed it thoroughly," Ezra said. "We want to open our doors to you. To help you out, if we can."

"But this is too much trouble. Too much burden for you," Estrella insisted. "I'm not sure."

Lillian held her breath. She had some slim hope of reprieve and secretly crossed her fingers.

"Nonsense, nonsense. Don't even think of it." Ezra spoke with as much force as she had heard in weeks. "It's no trouble at all. We have this big empty house. We couldn't rest, thinking of your family in such dire straits. You'll be doing us favor, coming here."

Oh, brother, that part took the cake. Lillian bit her tongue to stop herself from calling a halt to the whole thing.

Estrella looked a bit shocked by her sudden turn of good fortune. She sat down at the table near Ezra. For a moment, Lillian thought she might cry, too. These worries about her family obviously weighed heavily on her, though she hid it well. Lillian could see that now and did feel a sudden pang of compassion, recalling how she had once shouldered such heavy burdens in her own life.

"Well, it's settled, then," Lillian said. "Why don't you take a look upstairs later and see if there's anything you'll need. Maybe Dan or Sam can come and move some furniture around for you. There are extra dressers in the guest room on the second floor," Lillian recalled. "You take what you need."

"Yes, you let us know whatever you need. We'll get it for you," Ezra promised.

"Thank you. Thank you both so much. *Muchas gracias,*" she added.

"De nada," Ezra replied with a smile.

Saints preserve me, Lillian silently prayed. *How will I stand this, Lord? Please show me the way.*

"When you do you think you'll move in?" Ezra asked cheerfully.

Estrella considered the question. "How about Saturday? That is usually my day off and will give me time to get the rooms ready."

Lillian answered with a tight smile. "If you think the rooms will be ready by then," she said. Saturday . . . it was so soon.

"Why not? There's not much to do," Ezra said. "You can come sooner if you like."

Estrella nodded, still looking glassy-eyed but smiling widely.

Ezra looked happy again, too. He sat up and smoothed his hand over his hair. "I'm feeling hungry. I shouldn't have skipped lunch. Any left-overs?"

Lillian watched Estrella fuss over him. She was glad the long siege was over, but she would have to set down some house rules. Especially for the children.

At least Ezra was happy. And things would get back to normal. He would play gin rummy with her later and not just stare at her with that pained, unhappy look.

A high price to pay, she thought. But she'd really had no choice in the matter, and "what cannot be cured, must be endured," she recalled.

CHAPTER ELEVEN

HOUGH AMANDA CAME TO THE CHURCH EVERY DAY IN THE week that followed the storm, Gabriel was only there that Tuesday, the day they had worked together to clean up the sanctuary. He had started another job in Essex right before the storm hit, and that was his first priority. But he and Amanda did agree that he would pick her up at church after work on Friday evening. Amanda had brought a sweater and jeans and what her sister Lauren called "fun" earrings and changed in the restroom at five o'clock.

It felt to her as if she'd known Gabriel much longer than three weeks, yet this was their first real date. The pancakes at the Clam Box somehow did not qualify, in her mind.

Their relationship was moving to a new level, and she felt a little nervous. But happy, too. The more she learned about Gabriel, the more she liked and even admired him.

She stood outside the church, near a bench on the green, waiting for him. He drove up right on time in his blue truck, then jumped out to open the door for her.

He quickly kissed her cheek before she climbed into the front seat. It felt like the most natural thing in the world—and surprised her at the same time.

As Amanda got settled in her seat, Gabriel headed out of the village. "I thought we could go up to Newburyport. There's another chamber music concert tonight, if you'd like to try it." He handed her a newspaper listing for baroque holiday music. It looked interesting to her, but she wondered if Gabriel would like it as well. It was touching how he was so eager to please her. Most of the men she had met lately were not like that at all.

"This looks good," she said, "but we could do something else. See a movie?"

He glanced at her. She could tell he knew why she was hesitating. "I don't mind," he told her. "It's good to try new things. Next time, we'll see some action movie with lots of car chases, okay?"

She smiled. "Okay, it's a deal." Somehow she doubted his taste ran to movies with car chases, but she was glad he already thought there would be a next time.

The concert was in an old theater with red velvet seats and matching drapes on the stage. The walls were coated with ornate gold moldings and lit by antique light fixtures that might have been gaslights in an earlier time. The theater and stage were decorated for the holidays, and the musicians wore old-fashioned dress as well. Amanda hadn't really gotten into a holiday mood yet; the storm seemed to have washed that away. But the beautiful atmosphere and music were just what she needed to get her moving in the right direction.

From time to time, she stole glances at Gabriel's expression as they listened to the different pieces. She could tell he was honestly enjoying the performance, and that made her enjoy it more. At one point, a cello player came out and played a remarkable solo, a movement from a famous piece by Bach. Gabriel squeezed her hand and leaned close to her. "That will be you someday, Amanda," he whispered. "Someday very soon."

I hope you're right, she thought, but couldn't quite say the words. If he was right, it could change everything between them.

After the concert they walked to a Japanese restaurant that Gabriel suggested. It was a chilly night but very clear. The streets and shops of Newburyport looked so pretty, the windows full of enticing displays. She hadn't done much shopping yet. Maybe she would come back here tomorrow or Sunday afternoon with her sisters. They were both due home by tomorrow night.

She did notice that the Christmas decorations were not quite as elaborate as they had been other years. Maybe they had started off elaborate, then been blown away by the storm, and this was the second try?

"I think the storm almost washed Christmas away this year," she said. "There are usually a lot more decorations up here."

"I noticed that, too. But it still looks pretty. Maybe this is the Christmas of less is more?" He glanced at her, and she replied with a questioning look. "I mean, maybe this year people will be less concerned about decorations and 'stuff,' and instead reach out to others who were hit by the storm. If we rush to get back to normal and act like it's business as usual—shop, shop, shop—we might forget. We might miss a really big message in all this."

"I know what you mean." Amanda had continued to work at the comfort center at church through the week, meeting many people whose lives had been devastated by the storm. "It's going to take a long time for people to rebuild and get back to normal, even though all the power is on again."

During dinner their conversation turned to lighter topics. Gabriel was back to his charming, teasing self as they talked about everything from books to movies to sibling silliness.

"So, any embarrassing nicknames I need to know about?" he asked.

"No, none at all." She was lying. Though not entirely. She did have a silly nickname, but it wasn't one he needed to know.

"Sorry, Amanda, but I can tell just by the way you're looking at me with those big baby blues that you're holding back. Come on . . . what is it?"

He'd caught her, but that didn't mean she had to admit it. "I do have a family nickname," she confessed. "But it's very silly . . . and I don't want to tell you."

"What's the big deal? I have one. It's worse than Pie Guy, too. I bet it's worse than yours," he challenged her. He took a big bite of sushi, then winced a little at the hot wasabi he'd put on top.

"Okay, tell me your nickname, and I'll let you know if mine is more embarrassing," she offered.

Which still didn't mean she would tell him the name.

He took a long drink of water and sat back. "My awful childhood nickname is . . . Gabby-gator. Yours cannot be half as bad as that."

Amanda laughed. "I get the 'gabby' part," she admitted. "Where does the 'gator' come in?"

He shrugged. "I don't know. We were on this long car drive to Florida, some family vacation. My brother kept saying I wouldn't shut up, and I guess he had alligators on the brain."

Amanda had to laugh at the story. "I hope you got him back for sticking you with that."

"Oh, I did, don't worry. But I'm sworn to secrecy, so don't ask me what the payback name is. Okay, your turn. I told you my darkest secret. You promised to tell me yours."

Her family nickname was hardly her darkest secret, but it probably was her most embarrassing. "I never promised that," she insisted. "But I'll tell you anyway." She took a breath and ignored his gaze, which was fixed on her in the most unnerving way. "My family nickame is . . . Manda Bear."

He burst out laughing. "Manda Bear? That's really cute. It suits you."

"I was hoping you wouldn't say that. It makes me feel so . . . unsophisticated or something."

"I think you are very sophisticated, Amanda. No question," he assured her. "But Manda Bear is sort of . . . cuddly. It's sweet."

She felt herself blushing and wished she could disappear under the table.

"So, how did you get stuck with such a creative nickname?"

"My little sister Betty couldn't pronounce Amanda when she was a toddler, but she had learned what a panda bear was. Or at least had learned the word. So she got it all mixed up in her head and then everyone in the family started calling me that. My sister Lauren still calls me that when she wants to tease me."

"I hope you figured out a good one for her."

"Oh, I did. But I'm sworn to secrecy, too."

"Did I see Lauren in church that first Sunday when you were leading the choir?"

"Probably. All three of my sisters were there that day. She's coming home tomorrow night for the holidays, and so is Jillian. Maybe you could meet them sometime."

She wondered if that was too much. Was she going to scare him off now, suggesting he meet her family? But he seemed pleased by the idea, his smile widening. "I'd like that. I'd like that very much."

They left the restaurant soon after and headed back to Cape Light. The drive took them along the coast, and the bright stars in the dark sky mingled with the lights out along the water.

"I love this part of New England. I love being near the water," Gabriel confided. "I couldn't imagine a nicer place to live."

"Yes, it's beautiful," Amanda agreed. "It hasn't changed much since I was a kid, and that's a good thing."

She did love this area, but knew she could leave it to pursue her career. In fact, it seemed as if she had to leave it in order to reach the goals she had set for herself.

Gabriel, however, seemed content to remain here, to run his business and make his own stained-glass creations when the spirit moved him. There was nothing wrong with that. He seemed happy, very much at peace, and she respected and admired that.

When they reached her house, Gabriel parked in the drive. "This was great," she told him. "I loved the dinner and the music. Thanks so much for taking me there."

"I had a great time, too. Maybe I'll turn into a baroque music buff—you never know."

"Yes, you never know." The light was dim in the truck, but she could see his brilliant blue eyes clearly. They were practically hypnotizing.

"Well, I'll see you soon, Amanda. Very soon, I hope," he said quietly. Then he cupped her face in his hands and kissed her. Softly at first, then slowly deepening, so that Amanda felt she might melt. She held on to his shoulders, which felt wide and strong. She didn't know how long the kiss lasted. Only that when they parted she felt dazed and . . . amazed. He was so sweet and strong and absolutely wonderful at the same time.

He drew away slowly, brushing back her hair with his hand. "Can I see you tomorrow?" he asked suddenly. "I know, very uncool, right?"

Amanda laughed at him. She liked him being uncool with her. She hated guys who were always playing some game, determined not to show they cared. "No, that was very cool. I'd love to see you . . . but tomorrow I have to hang out with my family. We've been waiting for my sisters to come home, so we could all decorate the tree together."

"Oh, that's all right. Just thought I'd ask."

"How about Sunday?" she said suddenly. "Is that too . . . uncool of me?"

He laughed lightly, seeming pleased by her eagerness to see him. "Not at all. I would love to see you Sunday. I'll wait for you after the service, okay?"

"Okay." Amanda's hand rested on the lever to open the door. She felt suddenly shy but totally elated—and daring. She gave him a quick, light kiss, then she dashed out of the car and ran to the front door.

Wow, what a date! She couldn't wait to tell Lauren all about it.

ESTRELLA AND HER FAMILY DID NOT ARRIVE UNTIL ELEVEN ON SATUR-day morning. Lillian had plenty of time to prepare herself, mentally and emotionally. But it was still too soon. She couldn't quite believe this nightmare, this desperate measure to appease Ezra, was really happening.

Luckily, Emily was there to help soften the blow and to help organize everything.

"Welcome, Estrella." Lillian heard Emily open the front door and greet the Salazars. Lillian remained in the living room with Ezra.

"Hand me my crutches, will you, Lily?" he asked.

"We can wait here. They know you have casts on."

"Lillian, these are our guests. We need to greet them at the door, not sit here like a king and queen in their court."

Lillian grumbled but got up and helped him. He was getting a bit stronger and more mobile. She would be glad when the casts came off, but they weren't there yet.

By the time they made it into the foyer, the whole family had come in. Dan had gone outside to help them with a few bags. They didn't have much, she noticed, reminded again of their unfortunate circumstances. She brushed the thought aside. Well, she was doing her part, wasn't she? No one could fault her now.

"Mrs. Elliot, Dr. Ezra, this is my mother, Bonita, and my daughter, Marta, and my son, Jorge."

Her mother and son politely extended their hands to say hello. The little girl was shy. She clung to her mother and peeked out at Ezra and

Lillian from behind Estrella's leg. She held a stuffed dog that looked a bit worse for the wear.

"¡Hola!" Ezra said brightly to Estrella's mother and son.

"How do you do?" Lillian followed up with a tight smile.

"Why don't we all go into the living room and chat a little?" Emily said. "We have some coffee and cookies for you."

The coffee break was Emily's idea, to make them feel welcome. Lillian thought it was overkill. For goodness' sake, how much more welcoming did she need to be? She was permitting these people—total strangers, really—to live under her roof. Did she have to give them coffee and cake, too?

But Lillian did think this would be a good opportunity to go over her house rules. She didn't want to be unwelcoming, but did think she should make her standards known at the outset. That way there would not be any misunderstandings.

The sweets were a hit with the children. They headed straight for a plate piled with bakery cookies, but much to their credit, held back, staring at it hungrily. "Mama, can I take a cookie?" the boy whispered.

"What do you say?" Estrella asked him.

"Please?"

She nodded and let him take one on a napkin, and the little girl did the same, though she took much longer deciding which one to choose.

While Emily served coffee and tea to the adults, Lillian watched the cookie crumbs raining down every which way. She held her tongue with fierce determination, until finally, she couldn't take it anymore.

"You there, young man, please eat that over the napkin. You're getting crumbs all over the rug. It's a real Persian rug," she added, then realized he had no idea what she was talking about.

The boy cowered and stared at his mother. Estrella gave him a firm look. "Be careful of the crumbs, Jorge. That's all."

Bonita sat in an armchair, watching Lillian. When Lillian looked at her, the older woman smiled. She began to say something in Spanish that Lillian did not understand, though she did catch the first word, *gracias*, which she knew meant "thank you."

Ezra understood her and started prattling along. His Spanish had improved since Estrella had arrived, and what he lacked in fluency he made up for in volume, as if speaking louder would somehow help him get his point across.

Estrella's family stared at him politely, but Lillian had a feeling they didn't understand him any better than she did. Which was not at all.

"Ezra, please. I told you that I don't want this house turning into the UN. It's not at all polite to speak a language that many of us present do not understand."

Emily and Dan did not understand it, she was almost positive. So she wasn't just speaking for herself.

"Yes, of course, Mrs. Elliot. That is correct," Estrella said, siding with her. "It is not polite, as you say. My mother needs to improve her English. It will be good for her to speak only English here." She turned to Bonita. "Try to speak English with the Elliots, *por favor, Mamá. Sí?*"

Bonita smiled and nodded. But she didn't say anything more.

Marta, who was cuddled on the couch next to her mother, tugged Estrella's sleeve, then whispered in her ear. "Later, Marta," Estrella answered. "We'll see."

"What's the matter? What does she want?" Ezra leaned forward, jumping at the chance to grant some wish of their new guests. He had suddenly turned into a genie popping out of a bottle, Lillian thought.

Estrella sighed. "She's just wondering if there's a TV here. The neighbor we stayed with gave her a movie. She's seen it about ten times, but it distracts her."

Emily gave the girl a sympathetic look. "Janie, our daughter, is just like that. She can see a movie she likes a million times. Remember *Stuart Little?*" she asked her husband.

Dan rolled his eyes. "Every word of it."

These children had been through a great ordeal, Lillian thought. Of course a movie would be comforting. But she didn't want them to watch TV in here, that was for certain. This room really needed to be off limits.

"There's a TV right in that antique cabinet," Ezra pointed out before she could say anything. "Mrs. Elliot likes to keep it hidden."

"And with good reason," she followed up smoothly. "This isn't really a TV-watching room. There are too many breakable items . . . and the furnishings are too fragile. I really don't want anyone watching TV in here," she said firmly. "Not without very strict supervision."

The children sat back, looking as if they'd been reprimanded but didn't know what they had done wrong. Estrella forced a smile. "I understand, Mrs. Elliot. This is a very lovely room with many fine things. I wouldn't want anything disturbed."

"There's no TV upstairs right now," Emily explained in a rush. "But my sister, Jessica, has one she can give us, and her husband will bring it over and hook it up for you. I'm not sure if he can come until after Christmas, though. He does a lot for our church and he's very busy over the next few days."

Lillian hadn't thought of that. Sam Morgan was the head deacon now. She had expected he would be able to come over with the television for them sooner. This was going to be a problem.

"We have plenty of books," Lillian said. "It's much better to read a book than watch TV," she told the children. "Look at my daughter. I never allowed her to watch much television, and now she's the mayor," she added, pointing at Emily. "You can borrow any of the books we have . . . Well, most of them," she amended, thinking of some rare editions she didn't want them to touch. She should actually put those away, she realized. "If you'd like to borrow a book, just show me and I'll tell you if it's all right," she added.

The children stared at her, then looked at their mother. "Reading is the best thing," Estrella agreed. "You use your imagination. Now that I'm with them every night again, I can read a story before bedtime." She smiled at Lillian. "That is one good thing about us being all together again. Thank you for that, Mrs. Elliot."

Lillian nodded. Well, at least Estrella understood what she was trying to say.

"There's a TV in my room," Ezra said suddenly. "It has a movie player and all that stuff," he added, talking to Marta. "You can come in and watch your movie with me."

"Dr. Ezra, that's very nice," Estrella said quickly. "But the story is about a pink unicorn who has to break a magic spell and find his family. It might bore you."

"Would you really like that, Ezra?" Lillian asked innocently. "The last time you watched a film about unicorns, it was a documentary about the restoration of medieval French tapestries, as I recall."

Ezra ignored her comment and gave Marta a friendly smile. "I would like to watch your movie. Any time," he insisted.

Children always liked him, she reflected. He'd had a real way with them as a doctor.

"Well, it's been lovely meeting all of you, and I'm happy that you're here. But I'm a little tired," Ezra confided. "I think I'll go back to my room. If you'd like to see your movie, or just say hello, stop by anytime. I'm right down that hallway." He pointed to his room.

Marta stared at him. She didn't smile, but Lillian could tell she was considering the offer.

"Why don't we help you get settled upstairs?" Emily suggested, getting to her feet.

"I'll bring your things up," Dan offered.

The family only had two small suitcases and some big plastic bags of belongings.

"I'll help you, Mr. Forbes," Estrella said. "Jorge, you help, too."

Jorge obediently rose from the couch and followed his mother. Bonita took Marta's hand, and they left as well. Marta paused in the doorway and glanced back at Ezra. He winked at her and she ran away.

He laughed. "She's adorable. And the boy is very polite," he added.

"Yes, model children. For now, anyway," Lillian said drily. She had a feeling their mother had warned them to be on their very best behavior today. "Let's see how it goes once they get warmed up."

"It's nice to have children around the house. Gives the place a sense of life." Ezra leaned forward on his crutches and rose slowly, then swung himself back to his room.

He was whistling, she noticed. He never did that unless he was quite happy. *Well, let's just see how he feels when these full-of-life children are running around making a racket when he wants to take a nap or watch one of his history shows.*

And just how long will these good folks be living with us? she wondered. So far, nobody had said a word about that.

ON SATURDAY EVENING, JUST BEFORE HER FAMILY SAT DOWN FOR DIN-ner, Amanda got a call from Reverend Ben. "I'm sorry to call so late," he began, "but I've been visiting parishioners all day, and I wanted to discuss some changes I'd like to make in tomorrow morning's service.

"I know it's only four days until Christmas," he went on, "but there's no ignoring the storm and its consequences. I've decided to preach on that, and I think the choir should set the tone with some familiar hymn of comfort. Something that sends the message that we've all been through a mighty test but must hold fast now to our faith."

Amanda felt the same. It would be the fourth Sunday of Advent, but the effects of the storm still hung over the town, and she knew that it had washed away the holidays for many in its wake. It wouldn't be right to just paper over those feelings with the usual holiday cheer.

"I was thinking about that, too, Reverend. I'm not sure what we could sing, though . . ." Amanda gave the question some thought. If Sunday hymns were a category on *Jeopardy!*, she would never win the round. But she had sung in the choir for a few years, and a familiar standard came to mind, one she had always loved that was written by William Cowper. "How about 'God Moves in a Mysterious Way'?" she suggested. "Is that the sort of hymn you mean?"

"That would be perfect." Reverend Ben sounded pleased by her suggestion. "I can even work some information about Cowper into the sermon. He faced many challenges and dark hours, but still expressed such steadfast faith in his hymns and poems. The choir can sing it for the introit. And I was thinking we might close with something upbeat and faith-affirming, like 'This Little Light of Mine.' It will be an intergenerational service, and the children always enjoy that one."

Amanda agreed, glad of the changes. For the first time since she stepped into this job, she understood what it meant to work at a place of worship and to try to help people find peace and comfort, hope and connection, and how those things could all come through the music. "Oh, and Frank Borge called me yesterday. He won't be in church," Reverend Ben added. "He has to go down to Marblehead to help his mother."

Amanda expected quite a few members of the choir would be absent on Sunday, their lives still unsettled by the storm. But their starring tenor was scheduled to sing a piece of holy music by Verdi.

Maybe they would just skip the special music, Amanda thought. Frank could sing the piece in a few weeks. But before she could respond, Reverend Ben said, "I wonder if you could play something for us on your cello instead—if it's not too much trouble. I've heard you practice in the sanctuary. You play remarkably well."

Amanda was surprised. She hated to refuse the reverend this favor, but it was very short notice. "I would like to step in, Reverend, but I feel unprepared," she said honestly.

"Oh, play anything that comes to mind. It will be a real treat, a wonderful distraction for people from their worries right now."

Amanda knew that was true. She decided to play part of the Vivaldi concerto, the one she'd been practicing for possible auditions; the one that Gabriel liked so much.

WHEN AMANDA ARRIVED ON SUNDAY MORNING, THERE SEEMED TO be a different feeling at church, just something in the atmosphere. The few choir members who were able to get there arrived early, as she had asked, and they held a short rehearsal, going over the Cowper hymn.

As members of the congregation drifted in, they greeted each other warmly. It was normally a very friendly group, but everyone seemed even warmer and more caring today.

The pews slowly filled, and she noticed that there were almost as many in attendance as there would be on Christmas Day. Less than a week ago, their world had been shaken like a snow globe, and they had come seeking some solace and guidance, she realized.

Her family soon arrived, taking seats in the middle section, not up close, thankfully. It was distracting enough having them here.

She smiled at her sisters. Lauren gave her a thumbs-up while Jill and little Betty waved.

The choir was gathering in the narthex with Reverend Ben, getting ready to come in. Amanda was about to turn back to the piano when she spotted Gabriel. He had slipped into a pew at the very back. He looked at her a long moment and slowly smiled. Even at that distance, she felt their deep connection.

Amanda played the prelude as the congregation gathered. When the choir was ready to enter, she struck the first chords of the opening hymn, feeling a deep sense of purpose.

"God moves in a mysterious way . . . His wonders to perform . . ." The

choir was reduced in number by almost half, but sang with double the spirit and energy, she noticed. *"He plants His footsteps in the sea . . . And rides upon the storm . . ."*

As their voices rose and filled the sanctuary, Amanda felt her spirit rise, too. She wasn't sure why or when it had happened. She just felt different, very present. She wasn't just sitting here playing in a competent and dutiful way, as she had on Sundays past. She was doing something more. She put her heart and soul into each note.

She could tell from the expressions on the faces in the choir that they noticed, too. She felt them pushing themselves to reach higher with their voices, lift their notes to heaven in sonorous harmonies. When the hymn ended, Amanda blinked back tears.

Reverend Ben then began his sermon about the storm, about the bewilderment and anger people experience facing such great losses.

"It's only normal for us to question, and even to doubt. To say, 'Why God? Why me? Why did You do this?' Life doesn't seem fair or just. God doesn't seem fair. Or even loving.

"But I ask you to look back on the words of the poet William Cowper, the stirring lyrics of his most famous hymn, which the choir sang so beautifully for our introit today. As some of you might know, Cowper was a brilliant poet, whose work set English literature in a new direction. But he was also plagued by mental instability and great emotional anguish. Had he lived in our time, he might have been diagnosed and treated, and gone on to live a relatively normal life. But back in the late eighteenth century, this brilliant and sensitive artist endured a long confinement in a mental institution, called an insane asylum in his day. One can only imagine the primitive, brutal treatment of the patients. Cowper somehow survived and returned to normal life, and was taken in by the famous minister John Newton and his wife. He lived in relative peace and comfort for a time, but again faced a dark hour and attempted suicide.

"But rising out of those painful depths, he wrote this hymn, 'God

Moves in a Mysterious Way,' acknowledging God's power and superior intelligence and wisdom, which are so often beyond our frail, human understanding."

Reverend Ben paused and picked up the hymnal. "'Ye fearful saints, fresh courage take, the clouds ye so much dread . . . Are big with mercy and shall break in blessings on your head.'" He paused. "These lyrics strike me as particularly relevant to our feelings about the storm. 'Where is the mercy? Where are the blessings of this disaster?' you may be asking." He paused, giving the congregation time to consider the question.

"I see God not in the senseless, random destruction," Reverend Ben said, "but in the many stories of survival and the many lives spared. We have all heard those stories and even experienced some of those events ourselves."

Amanda thought about her own ordeal, stuck on the road with her mother, Betty, and Mrs. Honeyfield. It seemed almost miraculous that they had made it home that night unharmed.

"I see it in the amazing way people have prevailed during this trying hour," Reverend Ben continued. "And while full recovery will take months or even longer in some cases, so many are already starting to repair and rebuild. What courage that takes. What energy! Surely God's hand and breath must be at work in these efforts.

"Mainly, I see it in the opportunity God has given us to be the living instruments of His love and mercy. Of His charity and goodness. To be the channel of His undiscriminating love for all, by reaching out and lending our hands to others, to anyone who's hurting and in need of help right now. By being love in action, that's how I see God in all of this. The storm is a disaster. But the aftermath is an opportunity, truly a gift and a blessing.

"We've seen it in the news and right in our neighborhoods. We've seen it here, in our church. As Cowper reminds us, we may not comprehend God's mysterious purpose in this event. But it is unfolding, petal by petal, hour by hour. 'The bud may have a bitter taste, but sweet will be the flower.'"

He paused again and looked out at the congregation. "This morning, I encourage you to trust that some good comes of even the darkest hour and most dire event. Like William Cowper, I encourage you to carry on in faith and prayer."

The church was silent a moment. Then Amanda played the anthem. She was very moved and had to force herself to focus on the music. The reverend's wise words had helped her, and she felt sure they would help many others who had come to church this morning. She felt quietly proud that she and the choir had helped bring some comfort and a sense of renewed faith to those attending, too.

When it came time to play her cello, right before the offertory, Amanda put forward her best, and her audience listened intently. Maybe they were not music connoisseurs who had paid a hundred dollars or more for their seats. But Amanda played one of her favorite Vivaldi pieces for them as if they were the most important audience in the world.

This was what the reverend meant about giving service with her talent, the gift God had given her. She had thought she had understood. Now she realized that she had only understood intellectually, but had never truly experienced it in her heart.

It was finally time for the closing hymn, "This Little Light of Mine." Amanda was already seated at the piano and gave the choir the signal to start. The choir and congregation all stood and sang with her. Reverend Ben was right; the hymn was a crowd-pleaser, and they all sang with full, joyous voices.

Her family rushed up to her as soon as the service ended. Her mother looked like she had been crying and gave her a kiss on her cheek. "You were magnificent! Absolutely fabulous. I was so proud, I could bust!"

"You played beautifully, Amanda, every note," her father said.

Her sisters chimed in with rave reviews as well. She was so busy accepting everyone's praise that she didn't notice Gabriel standing nearby, just outside the family circle.

She caught his eye and beckoned him closer. "Mom, Dad, this is a friend of mine, Gabriel Bailey," she said.

"Hey, I remember you . . . Didn't you come to the shop on Thanksgiving Day?" Molly asked.

Gabriel grinned. "Guilty as charged. And you gave me a pumpkin pie."

"I did, didn't I?" Molly laughed, remembering. "Well, stop by the shop on Christmas. Maybe I'll give you another one."

Amanda cringed. Her mom could be so embarrassing at times.

She glanced at Gabriel, wondering if he felt awkward, too, but he just laughed. "That would be too generous. But I do love that hazelnut cheesecake you make. I'll definitely order one of those."

"Good choice. That's my favorite, too. I invented it," Molly said proudly.

Amanda was relieved that Gabriel had artfully turned the exchange into a compliment to her mother's culinary skills. But she also knew that this subject held its own danger; Molly could talk for hours about her cooking. They could be here all afternoon.

Her father, sensing her distress, said, "Let's go say hello to Reverend Ben, honey. The line is very short now." He glanced at Gabriel and smiled. "Very nice to meet you, Gabriel." Then he took her mother's arm and ushered her away.

Jill and Betty followed, but Lauren lingered. "I've heard so much about you, Gabriel," she said in a teasing tone. She glanced at Amanda, and they exchanged a look. "Hope to see you soon."

Amanda wanted to choke her but knew that would be very inappropriate in a church. Why were families so embarrassing? Wasn't she too old for this?

Once they were gone, Amanda was too tongue-tied to speak. Gabriel must think she had been talking about him with Lauren nonstop. Well, she had a little. But not that much.

Gabriel helped her put the cello in its case. Then he carried the instrument back to the choir room for her.

"Your family is very nice," he said finally.

Amanda busied herself straightening up her desk and checking the choir robes. She still felt too embarrassed to speak.

"Your mother is a real character," he added.

"She has a very memorable personality," Amanda agreed.

He smiled and finally managed to catch her gaze. "Well, I'd say that runs in the family."

She finally relaxed and smiled back at him. "Memorable in a good way, I hope you mean?"

He laughed. "Of course . . . most of the time."

HIS TRUCK WAS PARKED ACROSS THE GREEN, AND AMANDA APPRECI-ated the first blast of fresh air as she stepped out of the church and began walking. The town maintenance crews had done a good job of cleaning up after the storm, but there were still piles of tree trunks and branches everywhere, and even big raw holes in the dirt where trees had been totally uprooted.

They stood side by side for a moment and gazed out at the water. The harbor was calm today, reflecting the clear blue sky and drifting white clouds. The serene scene contrasted sharply with the long wooden dock, which was ravaged—a piece at one end torn from its wooden pillars and half-sunk in the harbor.

"Look at the dock. It snapped right off, like a stick," Amanda said.

"I know. It's sort of sad looking . . . But this will all be rebuilt even stronger. Just like Reverend Ben said, storms come and go. But the human spirit prevails. That's just the way we're made," he said simply.

Amanda glanced at him. When they had first met, she never suspected that he had such strong faith. But he did, and she had come to like that about him. She was even beginning to share that same faith.

Gabriel took her hand as they continued to walk. Then he said, "I forgot to tell you, the music was great at the service today."

She glanced at him shyly. "Thanks. I wanted to do a good job, to have it be more meaningful. I felt sort of . . . different as I was playing and the choir was singing. I hope the congregation felt lifted by it, at least a little."

"It *was* different. I think everyone felt it." He thought a moment. "When you're all worried and stressed, beautiful music like that is like going on a mini-vacation. I'm serious," he added, and she could see he was not trying to make a joke, just struggling to express himself. "It sort of takes you out of yourself and refreshes you. It shows you something beautiful and makes you forget your problems. For a little while at least. It gives you hope," he added. "I've always taken the music in church for granted. But since I met you, I think of it differently."

Amanda nodded. "I think of it differently, too. Since I took this job, I mean. I didn't realize what I was getting into," she admitted. "I really just took the job because it seemed better than working in my mom's shop. I didn't think it would be anything more than a weekly choir rehearsal and sitting up there every Sunday playing the hymns. No big deal musically—or spiritually. But this week I understood what that music can do. Now I really get it."

"Well, it showed. Maybe I have no right to say this, but I felt very proud of you."

Amanda smiled, surprised at his admission and unsure of how to respond. "Thanks," she said finally. She twined her fingers in his as they walked across the rest of the park.

Once they were in his truck, Gabriel headed for Main Street.

"What's the plan?" she asked as the Clam Box came into view. "More cinnamon pancakes?"

"I was thinking of something different. How about driving over to Angel Island?"

"Oh, I haven't been there in ages," she said, loving the idea. "But how did it do in the storm? Will we even be able to get across the land bridge?"

The island was connected to Cape Light by a narrow two-lane land bridge that was often submerged during a high tide or storm.

Amanda wondered if the bridge and roadways on the island were even passable.

"The bridge has got to be open," Gabriel said. "Claire North lives on the island, and she was there this morning in the choir."

"True," Amanda agreed. "But you know Claire. She's classic Yankee stock. She would have made it to church today if she had to swim across the harbor."

Gabriel laughed. "She would, too. But I called the General Store this morning, and they said the roads are all open. Overall, the island fared better than the mainland. They don't have nearly as many trees."

"Well, let's go, then," Amanda said. "I'd love to ride around there. My folks used to take us to the island for long bike rides. Then we would go swimming and have a picnic."

"It's a little cold for a picnic today, not that I didn't consider it. There's a café I know of on the north side called the Peregrine. It's only open on the weekends in the winter, but they serve Sunday brunch."

"The north side, right . . . I heard they improved the beach there and built it up."

"There's a real boardwalk now, and bathhouses. There's even a ferry from Newburyport. But it's not too built up."

"It sounds like you go there a lot." Amanda glanced at him. Was he taking her to his favorite spot?

"As often as I can. I like to just walk the beach or sketch sometimes. I get ideas for my glass pieces. There are some spectacular views."

Amanda guessed that Angel Island was an ideal place for artists. With few year-round residents, it still remained beautiful and wild.

They had reached the outskirts of Cape Light. Gabriel slowed down on a side street and pointed out his shop, an old wood-frame building, with worn cedar shake shingles and green shutters.

"It's not a very big shop, but it's all I really need," he said.

Amanda saw a sign in the window, made from a large piece of stained glass with beautiful lettering in the middle, surrounded by a bold design. "Bailey Stained-Glass Workshop," she read. It was a real work of art and a perfect advertisement for his expertise. "The sign is beautiful. Did you make that?"

"I made it for my father, as a gift. It was one of the first projects I did on my own. But I never thought it would be my sign someday. I never expected to be in this business . . . or carry on by myself. It's all right for now," he added. "But sometime soon I'll be free to go back to school or try something else. Once my mother has settled into a teaching job, I can get back to my own life."

"I'm sure you'll know what to do when the time comes," Amanda said. She believed that, too. Gabriel had shown great character and loyalty to his family, leaving college to support his mother and brother. She was more impressed by that decision than if he had ten college degrees to brag about.

They soon came to the land bridge that led to Angel Island. The gate was up, and the narrow road was covered with thick bunches of seaweed and ridges of sand, obviously having been submerged by the storm's high tides, but they crossed easily.

AMANDA HAD FORGOTTEN HOW BEAUTIFUL THE ISLAND WAS AND wondered why she didn't come here more often when she visited home. The rolling open meadows were lovely, even in the wintertime. They passed quaint white cottages and the Inn at Angel Island, where Claire

North was the cook and housekeeper. Her mother sometimes catered weddings and other big parties there, and she would want to know how the inn had fared in the storm. The beautiful Queen Anne looked a bit battered, missing a shutter or two, Amanda noticed, like a grand dame who had taken a fall, a bit disheveled, but was back on her feet.

They did see a lot of sand on the road and a few trees down, pushed to the shoulder, but nothing blocked their path. They soon made their way to the island's north side and the dock and boardwalk.

They were among a handful of diners at the small café. It was decorated for Christmas and very pretty, Amanda thought, as she ordered the house French toast.

At the end of a thoroughly delicious meal, Gabriel persuaded her to share a dessert. "They say you can't come here without having the Chocolate Barge. It's their specialty."

"Chocolate Barge? Oh, that sounds very slimming."

"Hey, it's Christmas. Calories don't stick from Thanksgiving to January second. Besides, you look perfect. I don't know what you're worrying about," he added, making her feel very perfect . . . or almost.

"One Chocolate Barge please, and two spoons," he told the waitress. Amanda groaned when she saw it but didn't hesitate to dig in. After she enjoyed a good share, she sat back, sipping an espresso and watching Gabriel polish off the rest. He seemed to be one of those lucky people who could eat anything they liked and never show it.

"You're so quiet. Anything wrong?" he asked when he finally put down his spoon.

Amanda shook her head. "I'm just unwinding, I guess. It's been a pretty intense week. I can't believe Tuesday night is Christmas Eve. We're just three days away from Christmas."

"I can't believe it either. It totally snuck up on me this year. The storm threw everything off. I've hardly bought any presents. I'm one of those last-minute types," he admitted.

"I'm almost set with gifts." *Including one for you,* she nearly said aloud. "But I haven't wrapped anything." Amanda knew she should probably be finishing her shopping and wrapping today, but she could not remember when she had last felt so relaxed and happy. "It will all get done," she added with uncharacteristic ease.

"Yes, it will," he agreed. "Sometimes the best gifts you give aren't bought at the mall, right?"

Amanda agreed with that. She had two small gifts for him. One was store-bought. Well, bought online, actually. And the other was more or less homemade. She hoped he liked them.

Gabriel took a different route back to the land bridge than the way they had come. The island only had two main roads, and Gabriel pointed out that you couldn't come here and not use both of them. That seemed a waste.

The sun was moving toward the horizon, and the long curving shoreline darted in and out of view between the trees and brush, cast in a clear afternoon light. Gabriel pulled up to the side of the road and parked the truck. "I want to show you something," he said.

He reached behind the driver's seat to a storage space and pulled out something flat and wrapped in flannel. "This isn't quite done yet," he said, removing the cloth to reveal a piece of stained glass that was about twelve inches square. "But the design is based on a sketch I made up here, from this view."

It was very impressionistic; she had to hold it at arm's length to see the scene, which at first just seemed to be abstract, colored shapes. But then the image came through, the pure, bright colors blending into a bold design, perfectly capturing the essence of the sky and cliffs, and the ocean below.

"This is so beautiful, Gabriel. I think it's amazing," she said honestly. She looked up at him. "It's a real work of art. A painting in glass. You should spend more time on your own work. You're incredibly talented."

He shrugged and smiled. "I don't have too much time for my own work right now, though the windows at the art center in Essex will be a start," he added, mentioning the new project he had begun before the storm. "But it's hard to make a living from commissions of original designs. I think about the future, too. I'd like to have a family someday," he confided.

Amanda nodded. She did, too, but a long way off from now. All she was thinking about now was her musical career. She couldn't even imagine her life that far into the future. But she could easily see Gabriel with a family. He was so warm and caring.

He wrapped up the piece again and stowed it carefully behind the seat. Then he brushed her hair from her cheek with his hand. "Maybe I'll do a portrait of you in glass someday, Amanda. You have such a beautiful profile and such luminous eyes. I have the perfect color glass to use for those."

Amanda turned to him, feeling self-conscious. "Oh, I don't think I'd be a very good model," she said.

"I disagree. You're very inspiring to me," he said quietly. Before she could answer, his arm slipped around her shoulders and he pulled her close. Then their lips met in a soft, sweet kiss that slowly deepened. It felt so wonderful to be in his arms, Amanda wished the kiss would never end. As the sun slipped toward the sea, she felt herself melting into Gabriel's embrace.

Finally, it was time to go. Gabriel started the truck again and pulled away from the view. They rode the rest of the way with his arm around her, Amanda's head resting on his shoulder. They reached her house too soon, she thought, and exchanged another kiss.

"Shall I walk you to the door?" he offered.

"No! I mean, thanks, but my sisters will stampede you and probably drag you inside and force you to eat Christmas cookies all night," she warned.

"That doesn't sound so bad. But if you think I should go, I'll just skip the stampede and cookies this time."

"Trust me," she replied. He laughed and quickly kissed her one more time. Then Amanda hopped down from the truck and ran to the front door. She had just a moment to wave good-bye to Gabriel before the door swung open. They were all standing there staring at her—Lauren, Jill, and even little Betty.

Lauren stepped outside and looked around. "Bummer. I thought you would bring him in for a little while."

"He had to get going," Amanda replied. Not quite a fib, she decided. He did have to get going, in her opinion.

"So how was your date?" Lauren followed her through the door and into the foyer.

"He's really cute," Jill said. "Where did you go?"

"We went to Angel Island."

"I love the island. It's so romantic . . .Was that his idea?" Lauren asked.

Amanda nodded. "It seems to be one of his favorite places. He does a lot of artwork out there."

Lauren practically sighed. "Wait a second. I'm the art history major. I should be going out with him."

Amanda gave her sister a look. "Back off, Snorie. I saw him first."

Lauren just laughed. "Wow, you really must like this guy. I never heard you growl like that, Manda Bear. Tell me more. We're making cookies."

Amanda happily let herself be dragged along by her sisters. Their towering Christmas tree, set up in the living room, was decorated and lit with tiny lights, piles of presents growing underneath. Jill had gone into the great room to wrap boxes with their father. There was a Christmas video on the kitchen TV, one of Betty's favorites, about a little beagle named Spot who helps Santa find his lost reindeer.

Betty was only partly watching as she sat perched at the counter, working hard. There was as much icing on her face, and even in her hair, as she got on the gingerbread people on the cookie tray. But no one had the heart to stop her. Since Molly was out working all day today and into the evening, Amanda knew that she and Lauren would have to wash the icing out of Betty's hair.

Amanda slipped on an apron and stepped up to help. She suddenly felt so thankful to be right where she was, home with her family, enjoying so many blessings that she used to take for granted. Weeks ago, she had looked forward to this time with dread—feeling so defeated and even ashamed of herself. That attitude seemed crazy now. What had she been thinking? Her family loved her and thought the world of her. No matter if she ever won a seat in an orchestra, she loved them, too.

It was really a rare gift to have a place like this to come home to. She wanted to enjoy every minute of it.

LILLIAN AND EZRA USUALLY PUT UP THEIR TREE THE WEEKEND AFTER Thanksgiving, but Ezra's accident and the storm had thrown them off schedule. Lillian had asked Emily to find the usual small, tabletop model she preferred. Unfortunately, they had discussed this in Ezra's room right after the Salazar family arrived.

"Let's get a big tree this year," he said. "It will be fun for the children to decorate it. It will give them some distraction, some cheering up. They can certainly use it."

Lillian could only think of her living room, overwhelmed by a huge, messy tree, shedding pine needles that would be ground into her beautiful rug. And even if that problem could somehow be avoided, a big Christmas tree would definitely present yet another temptation for the children, drawing them into that room, where they could break things. Ezra, of course, gave none of this the slightest consideration.

"I thought the Salazars would have their own tree, upstairs," she said honestly. "Why do they have to share ours?"

"Oh, Lillian . . ." He waved his good hand at her. "Sometimes I don't know why I even bother."

"Just tell me now, Ezra. Will everything I do from now on be dictated by the needs of these visitors? Whom I didn't even want here in the first place?" she asked in a low tone.

His face took on that pinched look again, and he turned away, crossing his good arm over his chest.

Emily glanced at both of them. "I can find one that isn't too big, Mother. It might cheer up everyone to have a real tree this year."

"Exactly," Ezra agreed.

Lillian knew it was time to give in. "All right. Get a reasonably sized tree, if you must. But get some plastic Christmas ornaments. I don't think I'll bring my good things down from the attic this year," she added wistfully. She did love to see her holiday decorations. Most had been purchased when Emily and Jessica were small, when her husband was still alive and they lived in the huge house on his family's estate, Lilac Hall. Some were even from his family, though most of those antiques had been left as part of the trust. The mansion and estate had been sold to the county to satisfy her husband's creditors and turned into a historical center. She still sat on the board of trustees. They decorated every year very nicely, in the Victorian tradition.

A few ornaments in her collection had been in her own family, the Merchants of Beacon Hill. Those pieces had been sent to her by her brother after her parents died, even though she had been cut off from her family after her marriage to Oliver Warwick. But there were some happy memories of her childhood in the big house on Beacon Hill. And good memories of the times when her own girls were young, too. They loved to trim the tree and got so excited, Lillian could hardly direct them to do it at a reasonable pace.

But why think of all that now? Christmas made one feel such nostalgia. It really wasn't good for old people like herself. Or Ezra.

"Yes, get lots of brand-new ornaments, preferably the kind they can't break. Maybe they'll want to take them when they leave," she added. She glanced at her husband. "Well, are you happy now?" she asked. "I'm trying to be nice."

He nodded but didn't quite smile. "Yes, I see. A regular Mrs. Santa Claus."

Lillian sighed. There was just no pleasing him, no matter how she tried. It was all this inactivity, being stuck in that bed. It was making him very moody. Everyone thought she was the difficult one, but she needed the patience of a saint with him at times like this. And she never got any credit for it.

EMILY AND DAN WEREN'T ABLE TO BRING THE TREE UNTIL LATE Sunday afternoon, just three days from Christmas. The children had been told it was coming and had been waiting all day. They were in Ezra's room, the little girl watching her unicorn movie for the umpteenth time. Even the music from the film drove Lillian crazy. She didn't know how Ezra could stand it. He had probably turned off his hearing aids.

The boy was in there, too. Ezra had played checkers with him on Saturday night and on Sunday morning, he started to teach him chess, praising his every move.

She had tried to sit in there, too, to do her cross-stitch in her usual spot. But she had felt pushed out. The room was too small for that many visitors. Besides, Ezra didn't want to play gin rummy with her or do the crossword puzzle. He had new playmates. She was old hat, too boring for him now.

Emily and Dan came in through the kitchen. "We have the tree. It's a very nice one," Emily called out, full of holiday spirit. "And we brought some pizza . . . Is anybody hungry?"

The children ran out of Ezra's room a split second later. Ezra came along on his crutches. "Pizza . . . My, that smells good. The tree smells wonderful, too. That pine smell just fills up the house, makes it really feel like Christmas. Right, Lily?"

Lillian nodded. Dan had left the tree in the mudroom while he set up the stand. Emily served the pizza. She had thoughtfully brought along paper plates and napkins. But Lillian still feared it would end up all over the house.

"Sit down and eat it right here, children," Lillian urged them. "Make sure your hands are clean before you walk around the house," she warned.

Ezra took a seat between the children and happily helped himself to a slice, which was undoubtedly full of salt and not good for his heart. Lillian had been looking forward to some soup and salad for dinner. Pizza was so greasy and rich, but once it was set before her, she couldn't resist it, though she ate standing, as if to signal that she wasn't fully giving in to this decadence.

Estrella and Bonita came down the back staircase, into the kitchen. Estrella helped Marta cut her pizza and served herself and her mother.

"Mmm, *bueno*," Bonita said with a smile as she took a big bite. "*Gracias*, Emily. Thank you," she managed. She glanced at Lillian and moved her chair over to make room. "*Señora*, sit," she urged her, looking puzzled at Lillian's hesitation.

Lillian shook her head. "I'm quite all right, thank you."

Finally, the pizza was done. Estrella lingered in the kitchen to clean up while Emily herded everyone into the living room. Dan had set up the tree near the big bay window that faced the street, at the far side of the room.

The tree had not seemed that tall in the mudroom, leaning against the wall. But when it was set in the stand, Lillian found herself tilting her head back to take it all in. The top branch grazed the ceiling, and she had high ceilings. She had not seen such a tall tree in this house in years.

Dan had already strung some lights and now plugged them in.

The children sighed with awe. Especially the little girl, Lillian noticed.

"Here are the ornaments." Emily came in with a pile of boxes and opened them, putting some on the coffee table.

Ezra hobbled in on his crutches just in time to see the children attack the boxes. Bonita slowed them down, scolding them in Spanish. She had apparently forgotten Estrella's "only English" rule. But for a good cause, Lillian thought.

Marta was too small to get her ornaments very high. Ezra leaned on one crutch to help her. "On this branch?" he asked patiently. "Is that where you want it to go?"

Lillian was alarmed as he balanced so precariously. "Ezra, please. Sit down. You'll wind up in the hospital again. Here, let me." She took the ornament and stuck it on a nearby branch. "There, that looks pretty," she insisted, though even she could see that ornament was hanging at an awkward angle. Oh, bother. She simply didn't have the patience for this.

Jorge dropped his ornament. When he tried to pick it up, he kicked it by accident and it bounced across the rug. He looked up, laughing, then chased after it. Marta laughed, too.

Lillian swallowed hard. If that her been one of her blown-glass ornaments from the early 1900s, she would be having a stroke by now.

It was stressful enough watching them run back and forth to the boxes, liable to bump into so many of her good things en route. She had put her very fine pieces out of harm's way, up on the mantel and in the china cupboard. But there had to be a few things decorating the room. She hated taking her entire house apart. Why should she? Children need to learn to be careful and respectful of other people's property.

She had to admit that these children weren't that rowdy, not like her grandsons had been when they were little. But she still had to keep an eye on them.

Finally, the boxes of ornaments were empty. The children searched them a second time, looking sad.

"Wait, I almost forgot. I found a little crèche," Emily said. She pulled another box from a shopping bag and handed it to the children. "You can set this under the tree. You know how it goes, right?"

Jorge nodded eagerly. "We need to save the baby for midnight."

"Save the baby? What is he talking about?" Lillian looked about for some explanation.

Estrella laughed. "When we set up the manger scene, we have a custom. We leave the cradle empty and put the figure of baby Jesus in on Christmas Eve, at midnight."

"I see," Lillian said quietly. The two children were having a fine time arranging the animals and the wise men.

Marta rose and ran over to her. "Here, you keep this, Mrs. Elliot. He's yours." She dropped the little plastic figure of the Savior in her lap.

Lillian held it in the palm of her hand. "All right, I'll keep the baby in a safe place." She would put it in the secretary, she decided. Such an important role to play. Well, at least they'd included her in some way.

But Emily had another surprise and produced bags of candy canes to top things off, which the children were happy to add to the tree.

"My, my, that looks perfect," Ezra said. "The only thing we need is a shiny star for the top."

"I can make one, Doctor Ezra," Jorge offered. "I can make it at school tomorrow."

"That would be great, Jorge. I'm sure the one you'll make will be perfect," Ezra encouraged him.

At least they had one more full day of school tomorrow, Lillian thought. Then they would have vacation for more than a week. How she was dreading that. Maybe, with Emily's help, they could be well on their way before the New Year. Lillian certainly hoped so.

Finally, the project was done. Lillian felt exhausted, even though she had only hung one ornament. Emily and Estrella were clearing up the boxes. Lillian thought they would all head to their rooms now. Wasn't it late enough? Hadn't they shared enough holiday cheer? And there was school tomorrow, she wanted to remind everyone.

"How about singing some Christmas carols?" Ezra looked around to see what the others thought. "That's what we always did in my family, when I was a boy. We would decorate the tree and sing Christmas songs. What's your favorite?" he asked the children.

"'Jingle Bells'!" Marta jumped up, very excited.

"Good choice." Ezra turned to Emily. "Would you play for us, Emily? I remember you used to."

"Oh, Ezra, I hardly remember a thing about the piano," Emily admitted with a laugh.

"That piano is very out of tune. Nobody's touched it in years. I don't know why I still keep it here," Lillian said, relieved they wouldn't have off-key music along with the off-key carolers.

"I can play a little." Estrella looked at Lillian and then Ezra but didn't approach the old upright piano.

"Go ahead, go ahead. Please do. Who cares if we're out of tune? It's the spirit that counts," Ezra insisted.

Estrella sat down at the piano and opened the cover. Then her hands ran over the keys in a quick, fluid scale.

She can *play,* Lillian thought, *and more than a little.*

"Okay, let me see. I'm not sure if I remember how it goes . . ." Estrella began very haltingly, picking out the melody.

"Oh, my word." Lillian let out sigh. "There's a music book in the bench, red cover. Christmas carols. All you want." She waved her hand impatiently. The woman might as well have the music. The sooner this got rolling, the sooner it would be done.

They started with "Jingle Bells" and slowly worked their way through the book. Lillian left as they began "Feliz Navidad" for the second time.

She went into the kitchen, where Emily was making the children hot cocoa, at Ezra's request.

"Well, the tree was a big hit," Emily said.

"Yes, wasn't it." Lillian sat down heavily at the table.

"Would you like some hot chocolate, Mother?"

"Are you daft? That will keep me up all night . . . I'll take some soup, if you can warm it up for me. Soup and crackers, that's all I want."

Emily soon brought her the soup. The cocoa was ready, too, and Emily began to set up a tray with mugs and cookies.

"Don't you dare serve that in my living room," Lillian said sharply. "They can have it in here, after I'm done eating. I'm tired and I have an awful headache. I'm going up to bed."

Emily gave her a sympathetic look. "All right. You have had a busy day."

Lillian finished her soup and headed upstairs to her room, using the back staircase, which was perilously narrow for her to climb with her cane. But she didn't want to see any of them and be forced to make more pleasantries.

She needed to be alone. Too much noise and agitation, just as she had expected. It wasn't good for her health. Ezra wasn't the only one around here who needed consideration. But nobody worried about her. *No one down there would miss me, not if I keeled over right now and croaked on these stairs,* she reasoned. *Not even Ezra.*

Feeling very low and sorry for herself, Lillian made it slowly up the stairs and down the hall to her room. She could still hear them singing downstairs when she firmly shut her door.

CHAPTER TWELVE

~~*~~

*L*ILLIAN USUALLY DREADED THE CHRISTMAS EVE GATHERING at her daughter Jessica's house. So many people and such casual dress, a big help-yourself buffet instead of a decent, sit-down dinner served in the dining room and not all over the house. It was not at all the way she had entertained on the holidays.

But as she hung her dress on the bedroom door to shake out the wrinkles and laid out her jewelry, she was actually looking forward to the change of scene. It would be good to get out of her own house tonight, which had been taken over in the past few days by Estrella and her family.

Jessica had politely invited the Salazars to the party, but Estrella had declined. Lillian didn't blame her. She would have felt odd with the family, who were all strangers to her, except for Jessica and Emily. It was just as well.

The Salazars were having their own little holiday party right here. Estrella had gone shopping to special stores yesterday, and Bonita had already started cooking. Lillian had considered allowing them to eat in the dining room but did worry about the furniture and her china cabinet. What if the children got rowdy and ran into it? She had already caught them running in the house once or twice, chasing each other down the long hallways. Granted, the house was large, but it wasn't a gymnasium.

No, the kitchen would be fine for their dinner. There would only be four at the table. They would be more comfortable there, she reasoned.

She found her way downstairs and headed for Ezra's room. It was going to take a long time to get him ready. Estrella had given him a close shave this morning, as well as a haircut. He had needed that. He looked much better now, even in his bathrobe.

She found him in the living room watching the television. That was a good sign. Jorge was there playing with a truck on the floor, rolling it on the carpet. Ezra looked up at her.

"Oh, Lily. I was just going to call you down. They're predicting some bad weather for tonight. Did you see? Snow and ice. I'm starting to worry about going out."

Lillian was stunned. "But Ezra . . . it's Christmas Eve. You love that party at Jessica's."

"I do love it, Lily. But they've posted all kinds of warnings about the roads. There's going to be ice everywhere. What if I slip and fall? I can't chance it . . . and I'm feeling tired. I can't bear the idea of dressing up— and cutting up a perfectly good shirt and pair of suit pants."

"We don't have to cut the pants, Ezra. We'll just split open the seam. Estrella said she could sew it right back up for you when the cast comes off."

Of course, by then, Estrella would probably be gone. Ezra was only partway through his recovery and due to keep the cast on his leg for another four weeks. By then Mrs. Fallon would be back, Lillian felt sure of it.

"Lily, I don't think it's a good idea."

Estrella came in, carrying the phone. "Dr. Ezra, it's Dr. Newton. He wants to check in with you." Estrella handed Ezra the phone and waited, in case Dr. Newton had any questions for her.

It was not unusual for Dr. Newton to call. Estrella spoke to him frequently, reporting Ezra's progress. Lillian was glad he had checked in with them tonight. Perhaps he would back her up.

"Ask him if you can go out tonight, Ezra. I bet he says it will be good for you," Lillian encouraged him.

Ezra nodded, and when he got the chance to speak he said, "I noticed a forecast for bad weather tonight. Do you think I should go out to a family party, Doctor?"

He listened a moment and nodded. "Yes, just what I thought. My wife is eager to go, though. I feel badly for her."

Lillian's heart fell. That silly Newton. What was he thinking?

Ezra ended the call and gave Estrella the phone. "I'm sorry, Lily. He said not to take the chance. You can go without me, I don't mind. I won't be alone. I'll eat here. Maybe I'll go to bed early," he added.

Lillian stared at him in disbelief, then sat down in an armchair, wondering what to do. Try again to persuade him? Use some other tactic? He did have a cast on one arm, and on a leg, too. And he was recovering from a heart attack. Maybe he did need to remain housebound a little longer. Lillian wasn't sure she should push him.

But she couldn't face the party without Ezra. Then she would really feel shunted off to a corner.

"Mrs. Elliot, why don't you both have Christmas Eve dinner with us? My mother is cooking a wonderful meal. There's plenty," Estrella said. "It will be a small way for us to say thank you."

Lillian was surprised by the invitation. She hadn't even thought of it. Ezra looked surprised, too . . . and pleased. He sat up, suddenly finding a burst of energy.

"There's an idea. What a lovely invitation." He looked over at Lillian. "What do you say, Lily? Why don't we stay here and celebrate with the Salazars?"

Because that's the last thing in the world I wanted to do when I got up this morning, she nearly snapped at him. But she counted to five and held her tongue.

"I don't want to go to Jessica's house without you," she said at last. "So I suppose that's what we'll have to do."

She knew she sounded ungracious, but there was no sense in putting a false face on it.

"We'd be delighted to join you, Estrella. Thank you so much for including us," Ezra said, quickly smoothing over her rudeness.

Estrella seemed pleased. "Very good, Dr. Ezra. I'll go tell my mother. She'll be so happy to cook for you."

Estrella headed for the kitchen, and Lillian released a sigh.

"I wonder what she's making. It sure smells good," Ezra said happily.

Lillian had to admit it did smell flavorful. But foreign foods did not agree with her digestion. She was sure she wouldn't be able to eat a bite. Maybe a little rice. If that wasn't spiced to high heaven, too.

My, my. What a Christmas this is shaping up to be.

LILLIAN WAS AWAKENED BY A SHRIEK. IT SOUNDED AS IF A BIRD HAD gotten into the house, but she knew it was probably just the little girl, Marta. The shrill note was soon followed by the sound of footsteps galloping down two flights of stairs from the third floor.

She rolled over and checked the clock. Barely seven a.m., which was much earlier than she wanted to get up this morning. Last night's Salvadorean Christmas festival had knocked her out. The food had been quite heavy and, as she could have predicted, she had indigestion. Turkey tamales turned out to be meat pies, steamed in a doughy corn pastry, wrapped in banana leaves, of all things, then smothered by some sort of tomato sauce. She had picked through the dough to find some turkey meat, olives, chickpeas, and other ingredients, none to her liking. There had also been a passable shrimp dish and even roast pork, plus vegetables and salad and lots of rice, cooked in a big casserole.

Ezra had been in his glory. She hoped he wasn't sick today, he'd eaten so well—sampling a portion of every dish and both desserts. She would have preferred it if the desserts had been served promptly, but first they had to play their music. The children danced quite wildly. Estrella and Bonita danced, too. Ezra wanted to dance, but with his casts on, he could only stand on his crutches and tap a rhythm on the table. Luckily all that wildness took place in the kitchen, where they couldn't break anything.

Finally the sweets were served, and she was able to get some nourishment. A decent rice pudding appeared, and something Bonita called *ayote en miel*: pumpkin cooked with honey and brown sugar.

After that Lillian headed for bed. The rest were staying up until midnight to put the infant Jesus figure in his cradle in the crèche scene. She told them where she had saved it but didn't feel the need to do the honors herself.

The children were going to open one present each, knowing there would be more in the morning.

Well, morning had come, and they were obviously stampeding downstairs to see what Santa had delivered. Lillian rolled over and closed her eyes. She was just drifting off again when she heard Estrella and Bonita heading downstairs as well, speaking in Spanish. Quietly, she had to grant, but she could still hear them.

She pulled the quilt up over her shoulder. Let them have their Christmas morning mayhem. She didn't need to be drowned in wrapping paper. She hadn't thought to buy them anything either, she realized, feeling a little pang of guilt.

She closed her eyes and allowed sleep to overtake her once more. She had nearly drifted off, too, when Ezra's voice over the infernal intercom roused her. "Lily? Aren't you coming down? Everyone is waiting for you."

She sat up and grabbed the monitor, practically shouting back into it. "Waiting for me? Why in heaven's name are you doing that? You don't need me to open the presents."

"Yes, we do," Ezra insisted. "The children are being very patient. I hate to see them wait so long, Lily. Please come down. Right away."

Lily wanted to refuse, then felt her stomach rumbling with heartburn. She needed some antacids anyway. She may as well go down, she reasoned.

It took her a few minutes to get her robe and slippers on and make her way down with her cane. She didn't rush herself. If they wanted her so badly, they could wait. When she finally entered the living room, the children cheered. Well, that was a surprise.

"I'm here," she snapped. "What's all the fuss?"

"It's Christmas, Lily. We all want to see what Santa brought. I'm sure there're a few things for you under there," Ezra teased her.

She gave him a look. "I need something for my stomach. You can all go at it if you like."

"Is your stomach bothering you, Mrs. Elliot? I will get you some antacid pills and some water," Estrella offered.

"All right, if you wish," Lillian grumbled, and sat in an armchair near Ezra.

"Mama, can we open our gifts now?" Jorge asked her.

Estrella glanced at him as she left the room. "Yes, one each until I come back," she said.

The children dashed to the tree and looked over the boxes.

Marta picked up a big box and shook it. The contents made a muffled sound. Lillian guessed there was clothing inside. The little girl must have guessed the same and put down the box. Next, she picked up an oddly shaped package and when she shook it, there was a rattling sound. Probably a toy inside there, Lillian thought.

Once again, Marta's gift radar was working and she quickly tore at the wrapping paper just as her mother returned to the room.

She had barely gotten half the paper off when she emitted her trademark shriek of glee. "Mama! Look . . . look what Santa brought me! Serena Rock Star!"

She ran to Estrella with the half-wrapped package. It seemed to be a large doll that came with a plastic electric guitar and all sorts of accessories.

Lillian chewed her heartburn pills, hoping that the plastic guitar didn't actually play music.

"Oh my goodness . . . just what you wanted. How did Santa know?" Estrella helped her daughter take off the rest of the paper. The doll had a shock of bright pink hair and an outfit to match. Marta hugged it tightly. "I love her."

Ezra laughed. "Oh, she's quite something," he agreed.

Jorge had opened his gift. A soccer ball and a sports jersey, which he unfolded and held up for all to see. "Wow, this is so cool! Brazil, my favorite team."

"I'm glad you like it, son. That one is from Mrs. Elliot and myself," Ezra said.

Lillian glanced at him. She suspected that many other boxes under there were from Ezra as well. She knew how he loved to play Santa Claus.

The rock star doll and soccer ball were just the beginning. There were several other toys, books, and board games. Sweaters, hats, and warm jackets. Many of these gifts had been purchased by Estrella, of course. But there were gifts for Estrella and Bonita, too. The tags were signed from Lillian and Ezra, though Lillian knew she'd had nothing to do with it. There were also bottles of a very good perfume and gift certificates to a nearby department store. Lillian thought that was a good solution. All Ezra's doing, obviously.

"Thank you so much, Mrs. Elliot! And Dr. Ezra," Estrella added, glancing at each of them. "So generous of you."

Bonita looked very pleased after opening her gift, too. *"¡Muchas gracias!"* she said.

"You're very welcome. Enjoy," Ezra said happily. "It was nothing, really."

"You're quite welcome," Lillian replied. She could just imagine the size of the gift certificates Ezra had chosen. Enough for them to each buy a new wardrobe, probably. He loved to give presents. Well, they did need new things due to the flood, the adults as much as the children.

The Salazars had put gifts for herself and Ezra under the tree, as well. Lillian found a beautiful pair of leather gloves in her package. Very good quality, too, she noticed.

"These are very nice. How thoughtful of you," she told Estrella. "I was only saying the other day that I must have lost one of my gloves at the doctor's office. The receptionist said she didn't find it."

"Yes, I know, Mrs. Elliot. I heard you telling Dr. Ezra. That's how I knew you needed them."

Lillian met her glance. "Well, it was very thoughtful. Thank you."

Ezra received a book he wanted—Estrella had noticed a review he'd cut out from the *Globe*—and the children gave him a new pair of slippers.

All the while that gifts were being unwrapped and admired, Bonita had been in and out of the living room. As the children picked up the bits of wrapping paper and stuffed them in a plastic trash bag, Estrella announced that breakfast was ready in the kitchen. Bonita had been cooking it.

Ezra glanced at Lillian. "Ready for some breakfast, Lily? I could do with a bit more of that rice pudding we had last night." He patted his stomach, making the children laugh. *"¡Mucho bueno!"*

"For breakfast, Ezra? You must be kidding."

"But it's Christmas, Lily. Didn't you notice?"

"Believe me, I noticed. It's been impossible to avoid it around here this year."

Ezra laughed at her. "Yes, I must agree; and just as it should be, too."

Lillian did not agree with that assertion. She still maintained that she should be able to observe the holidays the way she preferred, in a quiet, decorous, dignified manner. Not with all this fuss and noise and rich food.

Well, that wasn't to be this year. All she could do now was wait it out. It had to be over soon, didn't it?

THE FAMILY CHRISTMAS EVE PARTY AT AUNT JESSICA AND UNCLE Sam's house went on until after midnight, as usual. Amanda was sure she would be too tired to get up for church the next day, but knew that she had no choice. Luckily, Betty—known around the house as the human alarm clock—was up even earlier than usual, with enough Christmas spirit for the entire family.

She stood by Amanda's bed and shook her shoulder. "Manda, Santa came. Wake up! We have to go open our presents."

Amanda opened her eyes to see Betty's adorable face glowing with excitement. She realized that even at the ripe old age of twenty-five, Christmas morning was still a thrill.

"Okay, Squirt, lead the way. I'm right behind you," she promised her little sister in a sleepy voice.

Betty had already alerted the rest of the family, and Amanda joined them around the Christmas tree. Her father was giving out the gifts while her mother brought in a tray with coffee and croissants. Amanda managed to open most of her gifts and enjoy the Christmas morning family rituals before it was time for her to shower and dress for church. She had to get there before her family for a quick rehearsal with the choir.

"I hope we'll be singing 'O Come, All Ye Faithful' today," her mother said just as she left the house. "You know it's my favorite."

"I've asked Reverend Ben to include it just for you, Mom," Amanda replied as she flipped a bright new striped scarf around her neck, a gift from Jill.

"Thank you, dear. I'll be singing it loud and clear."

Amanda didn't doubt that for a moment. Her mother had a very strong voice when she really liked a song. Amanda had thought of encouraging her to join the choir, then thought better of it. Molly would not be easy to manage.

Amanda soon found that the exciting feeling of Christmas Day was in the air at church as well. The sanctuary was decorated with rows and rows of red and white poinsettias, garlands of fresh pine branches, and glowing candles on the altar. It was a beautiful scene, made even lovelier by the stained-glass windows. Set back by the storm, Gabriel had not quite completed the job, but for the most part, the windows sparkled again with jewel-like colors, filtering the light of Christmas morning. Amanda knew she had to tell him what a wonderful job he had done. Her gaze was drawn to the Nativity scene, the window now whole again, showing the Christ child in the manger.

The beautifully crafted scene had a new meaning for her this morning. Just like the window, she, too, had been restored these last few weeks. Her innate sparkle and colors were shining through again.

Coming back home, she had somehow turned a page in her life; she had been renewed by this job and by living at home with her family again. It had not been a defeat after all, but a blessing to come back here.

She once again believed that the world held infinite possibilities for her and knew it had been wrong to give in to despair. It was wrong to lose faith in herself . . . and in God's plan for her.

Maybe that's what Christmas was about in a way—the blessed Christ child, symbolic of the new start that was possible for everyone, at any moment, if you held fast to faith and believed it could be.

"Amanda, there you are. Merry Christmas!" Amanda turned to see Reverend Ben bustling toward her down the center aisle of the sanctuary. He was already dressed in his white cassock.

"Merry Christmas, Reverend Ben," Amanda replied.

"I believe most of the choir is here already, donning their robes. Right on time, too," he said, checking his watch.

"We'll have a quick rehearsal," Amanda replied. "But we worked very hard this week. I think everyone knows their parts."

"I'm sure they do. It is Christmas. The music is so familiar, everyone just sits back and enjoys it."

Amanda knew that was true. She felt surprisingly relaxed, as if nothing could go wrong, despite her considerable responsibility. It was one of the most important days in the church calendar, and definitely the most important musically. But she felt very sure in her heart that the service would go well and the choir would sound wonderful—as if some greater power were helping her.

The time for despair had passed. It was a bright new day, time to herald the newborn King.

CHAPTER THIRTEEN

THE CHOIR MARCHED INTO THE SANCTUARY AT A STATELY
pace, singing "Joy to the World" with a solid, full sound. Reverend Ben followed, wearing his beautiful gold-and-white mantle, which was reserved for Christmas. Amanda accompanied on the organ, playing with all her might. It was a dramatic and uplifting start, she thought, and one of her very favorite hymns.

Their well-rehearsed voices rose clear and pure as the organ notes rippled and echoed. *"Joy to the world, the Lord is come! Let earth its praises bring."*

After the first verse, the basses and altos split from the sopranos and tenors, and the two groups sang the chorus in rounds.

". . . and heaven and nature sing . . . and heaven and nature sing . . .

". . . and heaven, and heaven and na—ture . . . sing!"

Amanda glanced at the choir members as they finished the carol with spirit, striking every note perfectly. Their eyes and faces were glowing. They had put their hearts and spirits into the carol, and she felt moved by their energy. She knew the congregation felt it, too.

Reverend Ben beamed as he stood before the altar and greeted the congregation. It was, predictably, a very full house today, with every seat occupied, and even a few rows of folding chairs at the back of the sanctuary.

"Merry Christmas, everyone, and welcome! Let us gather in prayer this glorious morning to celebrate the humble birth of our Savior, Jesus Christ.

"God of light, we thank You for giving us the gift of Jesus Christ. We come before You with wonder and delight that You come to us in the child born in a manger. Be with us on this day of birth and rebirth. Come, honor us with the presence of Your gracious, joyful Spirit. Fill our weary hearts with renewed hope and joy. Rekindle in our souls the light of Christ. Glory to You in the highest, O God, glory in the highest! Amen."

A scripture reading from the Book of Hebrews followed Reverend Ben's opening prayer. It was soon time to sing her mother's favorite, "O Come, All Ye Faithful." Luckily, this was a hymn for everyone to sing. Amanda knew her mother would have sung it anyway, sitting out there in the second or third pew back from the front, beaming at her like a miniature Christmas tree.

Everyone rose with their hymnals as Amanda struck the opening chords on the piano, and the choir led the congregation along.

"O Come, all ye faithful, joyful and triumphant. Come ye, O come ye, to Bethlehem . . . Come and behold Him, born the King of angels . . ."

Everyone sang with full voices and great spirit and if a few in the pews were off-key, or not quite in rhythm, they blended in perfectly as the great wave of voices rose higher and higher. It was all about the feeling of joy this morning, Amanda realized, not the technical excellence.

And the feelings were strong and true, overflowing with the spirit of Christmas.

"O come, let us adore Him, O come, let us adore Him . . . Christ the Lord . . ."

It was soon time for the second reading, from the Gospel of John. "The Word became flesh and made his dwelling among us. We have seen His glory, the glory of the one and only Son, who came from the Father, full of grace and truth."

Reverend Ben chose the many lights of Christmas as the theme for his sermon—lights on trees and decorations. The candles glowing in windows and up on the altar this morning. He recalled the star that guided the shepherds and wise men to the baby born in the manger.

"Each time we see these Christmas candles flickering, even these small votives," he noted, pointing to the display that covered the altar, "we are reminded of God's gift to us this day, His only son, and His steadfast presence in our lives. Every day of the year, let us always remember Christ is the light of the world, sent here to earth to guide our way.

"And let us all be deeply thankful for this gift today, of the Good News we have received. The Light of God shines in the World. Shout and sing with joy, and celebrate the hope and promise of this day."

At the close of the service, the choir and congregation sang together again, this time "Hark, the Herald Angels Sing."

"Hark the herald angels sing, 'Glory to the newborn King! Peace on Earth and mercy mild. God and sinners reconciled . . ."

The carol was definitely another crowd-pleaser, and the entire church was bursting with joyful voices. Amanda knew that Charles Wesley, brother of the famous Methodist minister John Wesley, had written the lyrics, but the tune was based on a piece by Mendelssohn and sounded magnificent—even celestial—played on the organ.

". . . Join the triumph of the skies . . . With the angelic host proclaim:

'Christ is born in Bethlehem.' Hark the herald angels sing . . . Glory to the newborn King . . ."

Reverend Ben stood at the back of the sanctuary now, his hand raised as he gave a final blessing for Christmas Day. "And now may the glory and love of God surround you. May the peace and grace of Christ dwell deep within you. May the power and presence of the Holy Spirit uphold you. Amen."

Amanda played some peaceful incidental music after that as the congregation filed out of the sanctuary. When she finally rose from the organ, she felt a bit dazed, as if the last hour had passed in the blink of an eye. Still, she felt very good inside, her heart and spirit light.

"Great job, Amanda."

"Well done."

Members of the choir congratulated and thanked her as they stepped down from the risers. She thanked them all, too, downplaying her part. "You guys did all the heavy lifting. What are you thanking me for? You were all fantastic," she said sincerely.

"We couldn't have done it without you," Sophie insisted. "You've been a wonderful inspiration to us these last few weeks."

"No question," Claire agreed.

"Bravo. *Bravissimo!*" Frank Borge said as he fixed her with his dark gaze and clapped his hands, which started the rest of the choir clapping, too.

Amanda thanked them again and wished them all a happy Christmas as they walked back to the choir room. She felt gratified by their praise. Maybe being the music director at a church was not her true calling, but she had learned so much here in such a short time. It had been a very valuable experience, one that she would remember for the rest of her life.

"Hey, Merry Christmas, Music Girl. The choir was awesome today. Even I sounded good singing with them."

Amanda looked up. Gabriel stood by her desk, gazing down at her with his bright blue eyes.

"Was that you croaking in the background out there? I had to play a little louder to drown it out. I think I managed it."

He laughed at her teasing. "Hey, I'm not that bad . . . Maybe you shouldn't get a Christmas present after all. Just coal for you this year, Music Girl."

He had been hiding a box covered in wrapping paper behind his back but now held it out for her to see.

"Suit yourself," she said. She stood up and reached into the leather tote on her desk. "But if you don't give me my present . . . maybe I shouldn't give you yours."

She pulled out the gifts she had wrapped for him, hoping she would see him here this morning.

"You have a present for me? That's so sweet." He seemed surprised and pleased she had thought of him, even though he had come prepared with her gift.

"It's not much, but I hope you like it."

"I hope you like yours. Only one way to find out. You go first," he said. He handed her the box and watched as she unwrapped it.

It was fairly big box but felt too heavy for clothing, which was a relief. Amanda rarely liked any clothing picked out for her, and it was hard to pretend otherwise.

There was some tissue cushioning inside, which seemed to eliminate a book. Then she pulled the tissue back and quickly realized what the gift was: the beautiful stained-glass beach scene he had shown her when they drove to Angel Island.

"Gabriel . . . you're giving me this? It's so beautiful," she said, holding up the glass creation. "But you shouldn't have," she said suddenly. "I mean, this is your artwork. You must need it. To put in an art show or something."

He shrugged. "It's not quite that wonderful. But I'm glad you think so. I finished it just in time. I put this chain on the top so you can hang it in a window if you like."

"Of course I'll hang it up. I can't wait." She set it down carefully and looked up at him. "I love it. I truly do. Thank you so much." She knew that wasn't a very articulate response, but she couldn't quite find the words—or the courage—to convey her feelings, to tell him how precious this gift was to her. She reached up and put her arms around him and hugged him a moment. "Thank you," she whispered.

"You are so welcome. I'm so glad now I didn't get you something safe, like a book or a calendar," he admitted with a laugh.

"I am, too . . . but my present isn't half as interesting or original," she said as she handed him the box.

"Somehow I doubt that." He quickly tore off the paper to reveal the large-format art book she had found online for him. It was about stained glass, the history of it and the most famous examples from churches and buildings around the world, featuring major artists who worked in the medium, like Louis Tiffany, Marc Chagall, and Frank Lloyd Wright.

Gabriel paged through it, looking so interested she wasn't sure he was going to get around to opening his second gift. "Wow, this is perfect. Talk about inspiration . . ."

"I wasn't sure if you already had something like that. The gift receipt is in there if you want to return it."

"Return it? I love it. I don't have anything quite like this. I'm going to read it cover to cover. It will give me a lot of references and ideas."

Amanda found herself smiling once again.

"And what is this?" he asked, holding up a much smaller package.

She shrugged. "Just a little something else." She watched him unwrap it and explained, "I bought a CD for you and burned one, too, from my audition recording. It's that classical cello piece you liked. You have your choice between Yo-Yo Ma . . . and me."

He looked at the two CDs and laughed. "Let's see . . . who do you think I'd pick from those choices?"

Before she could answer, he leaned over and kissed her. A quick, hard kiss on her lips. "Thanks, Amanda. This is a great gift. Whenever I play it, I'll feel as if you're right there with me."

Amanda hadn't even thought of that, but loved it that he had.

"Amanda, are you still here?" Amanda heard her mother's voice, then saw Molly peering into the choir room. "Oh, hello, Gabriel. Merry Christmas."

"Merry Christmas, Mrs. Harding," he answered with a smile.

"I was just coming, Mom. I have my own car, remember?"

"I remember, honey. I was just wondering if you'd left yet." Her mother glanced at Gabriel again. "I guess I'll see you back there."

Great timing, Mom, Amanda thought, fighting down a flush of embarrassment. "Well, I'd better go," she told Gabriel. "There's a family party at our house today." She stood up and slung her new scarf around her neck, then slipped on her coat.

"Same here. Let's get together next week. I'll call you."

"Great. The church is closed for a few days. I have the whole week free."

"Sounds good to me. You worked so hard to get ready for Christmas, you deserve a few days off."

Amanda didn't think she had worked all that hard, but it had been stressful, and now she was looking forward to being able to hang out with her sisters.

Gabriel walked her out to her car and gave her another quick Merry Christmas kiss. "Have fun today. I'll talk to you soon."

She smiled and waved as she drove away. His gift was on the front seat right next to her, and she rested her hand on the box. It was such a wonderful present, one of the best Christmas gifts anyone had ever given her. She couldn't wait to hang it up in her room. It would make her feel as if Gabriel was never very far away. And that, she realized, was starting to seem very important to her.

*   *   *

AMANDA THOUGHT SHE WOULD SLEEP LATE ON HER FIRST DAY OFF BUT woke to the buzzing sound of her phone, signaling that an email had arrived. She was about to roll over and go back to sleep but decided to check to see who had sent the message. Was Gabriel getting in touch this early, the day after Christmas? Well, that would be worth waking up early for.

But it wasn't Gabriel. It was even better, if that was possible. She clicked open the note and sat up quickly to read it.

An orchestra in Portland, Maine, wanted to see her for an audition and an interview. A seat for a cello had just become vacant, and they needed to fill the spot promptly. She had sent them a package with her résumé and a recording months ago, when she was still in New York, but the only response had been a form letter, acknowledging receipt and noting that there were no openings at the time.

The message of this email, however, was just the opposite:

Please call us at your earliest convenience if you are interested in making an appointment for an audition and an interview.

Amanda jumped out of bed and ran downstairs. She was so excited she didn't even need coffee to wake up, but she was still happy to see someone had already made a pot.

"Hey, early bird. I thought you were sleeping in." Her father sat at the kitchen table and put down his newspaper to greet her. Dressed in a crisp white shirt and tie, he was ready for his workday. Germs didn't take holidays, he often reminded them.

Her mother was there, too, wearing her Christmas pajamas: bright red flannel covered with polar bears wearing Santa hats. She looked very tired, sipping her coffee and staring into space. "Happy day-after-Christmas, honey," she mumbled.

"It is a happy one for me. I just got an email from an orchestra in Maine. They want to see me for an audition."

Her parents both smiled, looking pleased. But her mother didn't jump out of her seat and do a jig around the kitchen again, Amanda noticed. She could tell what they were thinking. They didn't want her to get her hopes up and be disappointed if she didn't get the job. Maybe they didn't want to get their hopes up either. Amanda understood, but she couldn't help being hopeful.

"That's great, honey. Where in Maine?" her mother asked.

"Portland. It's a very good orchestra. They just hired a new artistic director last year, and he's made a lot of changes."

Her parents didn't know much about the music world, and it was too hard to explain it all to them. Her father stood up from his chair and slipped on his suit jacket.

"Portland's a lot closer than Austin. We can come and see you play there much more easily."

"We'll buy a season subscription," her mother promised. Her father gave her mother a look. "I mean, when you get the job. Which you will," she added in a very positive tone.

"I hope so," Amanda replied. All she could do was hope—and maybe say a prayer or two. She was excited but also scared, especially after losing out on her last opportunity. But she also felt differently than she had about the job in Austin. It didn't feel as if this one was the last opportunity she would ever get—or that she would be a failure if she didn't get the job. Maybe the storm had helped her see the bigger picture. She knew she had a lot to be thankful for in her life, with or without a job in a symphony. She felt differently about her job at the church, too. Her work there felt so meaningful, and had even strengthened her faith. She was excited about this opportunity and planned to do all she could to prepare, but she also trusted that God had a plan for her, too, and only He knew if Portland was part of it.

RIGHT AFTER BREAKFAST, AMANDA CALLED THE NUMBER ON THE email and arranged an appointment in Portland for Monday, December 30. She wished she could go up sooner and get it over with. If they had asked, "Can you come today?" she would have jumped in the car with her cello, barely pausing to change out of her pajamas. But some members of the search committee were out of town until then. The wait did give her four full days to practice, counting today.

She was showered, dressed, and carrying her cello out to the garage by the time her sisters were stumbling around the kitchen, just out of bed.

Jill stared at her. "Hey, where are you going with that thing? I thought we were all going to the mall today."

"I have to go over to the church and practice awhile. I'll be back in time to mall crawl with you," Amanda promised. "I have an audition for a job in Portland in a few days. I got an email this morning."

Lauren was eating a bowl of Greek yogurt and granola. Now her spoon hung in midair. "An audition? Awesome! I can shop for you, don't worry. I know what you like."

Amanda laughed. No telling what her fashion-forward sister would come home with. "That's all right. I can meet up with you. Just text me later and let me know what you're up to."

THE CHURCH WAS LOCKED, BUT AMANDA HAD A KEY. SHE CARRIED her cello into the sanctuary. Every step echoed. The church was so empty, dark, and cold. She wasn't sure how to turn up the heat in the sanctuary and didn't know if she was even allowed to fool with the thermostat. She uncovered the cello and set it on its stand near the altar, just to one side of the piano and choir risers, where she knew there were good acoustics. She took off her coat but kept her sweater on. She needed to prepare a few pieces, to show her range as a performer. She had standard pieces she played for auditions but had not performed them in a while, except for the section of the Vivaldi concerto she had played at church. She supposed that counted as practice in front of a real audience, but it was not quite the real thing.

She started with some Mozart and was soon focused, working on a few tricky bars, playing it over and over again to get the phrasing just right. Expression and precision were so important at this level. Anyone could read the notes and play. Well, almost anyone. Interpretation was key, but without taking liberties with the music. It was a fine line, she knew. She also knew that the people she would be playing for would not want to see too much ego. They wanted someone who was brilliant but not a diva.

She was just finishing off the last few notes of the Mozart when she suddenly heard a metal rattling sound. She looked up and saw Gabriel at the back of the sanctuary, carrying an extension ladder.

"I would have clapped, but I know you don't like to be startled."

"You're right, and I don't think that was quite applause-worthy anyway." She couldn't get over how glad she was to see him.

"Sure it was." He propped the ladder up near one of the windows and walked back for his toolbox. "I thought you had the week off."

"Oh, I'm not here for work. I got an email this morning about an audition. For an orchestra up in Portland. So I came here to practice. It's quieter than our house, and there's better sound in here, too. I wish I could go up to Maine tomorrow and get it over with . . . but at least I have a few days to brush up."

"That's great. Will it bother you to have me working here? I promised Reverend Ben I would have these windows fixed by the new year, but I can come back later. I'm sure he'll understand."

Normally, she preferred to be totally alone when she rehearsed, but she didn't want to chase Gabriel out of the space when he was supposed to work . . . and she did love the sound of her cello in here.

And it might even be a good thing to have him here. It was nice to hear some random applause from time to time.

"Let's see how it goes," she said finally. "If you're distracting me, I'll just go."

"You always distract me, Amanda. But I'll try to ignore you. I'd rather not chase you away."

His teasing smile and the way he caught her gaze and held it made Amanda forget why she had even come. Then she remembered and picked up her bow again. "All right, enough chitchat. We both have work to do."

Gabriel looked back over his shoulder. "I bet I'm the only guy in town today working with live music. Sure beats the radio."

Amanda started playing again but couldn't help smiling.

At first, she did notice the random sounds of Gabriel working, the sounds of his tools and the small torch he used to melt the lead tape that held the pieces of glass together. But as usual, Amanda soon lost herself in the music and lost all sense of time passing.

When she was finally ready to take a break, she noticed she was alone again. Gabriel had left his ladder. Maybe he went out for supplies. Sometime later, she wasn't even sure how long, he came back in. He sat in a pew in the back of the sanctuary and listened to her play, waiting until she was ready to stop.

She leaned her head back and took a deep breath. She was playing so hard now, she felt as if she were working out in a gym.

"I brought you some lunch. Aren't you hungry?"

He stood up from his seat. He still had his coat on and held up a brown paper bag. It smelled good, whatever it was, and she did feel very hungry all of a sudden.

"Thanks. I'd love some lunch. Why don't we eat in Fellowship Hall?" She stood up and put her cello on the stand. "What time is it?"

"It's almost two."

"Oh wow . . . I have to text my sisters. They're waiting for me at the mall." Amanda grabbed her sweater—she had taken it off during an intense bout of playing—and followed Gabriel out of the sanctuary.

There were a few folding tables and chairs set up in Fellowship Hall, and Gabriel chose one near the window and set out their lunch. She was glad it was hot soup, because the hall was even colder than the sanctuary had been.

"This looks good," she said, dipping her plastic spoon in the soup.

"At least it's hot," he said, taking a sip of his. He glanced at her. "You look cold. Want my jacket?"

Amanda shook her head. "No, that's okay," she said, but couldn't fight off a shiver. Her passionate playing had worked up a sweat, and now she was covered with goose bumps.

Gabriel ignored her answer and gallantly took off his leather jacket and slung it around her shoulders.

"Thanks," she said, glancing up at him.

"No problem. I never get cold," he said. She thought he was just being nice but saw that he was wearing a hooded fleece pullover and did look warm. "What about your sisters? Are they still waiting for you?"

"I'm not sure. I forgot to text." It was easy to forget about things when she was with Gabriel, she noticed. When they were together, she felt as if they were in a world of their own.

Amanda pulled out her phone and sent Lauren a quick note, saying she couldn't make it to the mall, after all. "I'm sure she's fine. She loves shopping. I can barely keep up with her."

Lauren answered Amanda's text right away. No problem with not meeting her. She had met up with some old college friends and had decided to give Amanda a makeover tonight. Gabriel watched her as he ate his lunch.

"Uh-oh," Amanda said, laughing, when she read the message.

"Something wrong?"

"Not really. Lauren is shopping for me. She wants to give me a makeover."

Gabriel shook his head. "No way. Tell her I said you're perfect just the way you are."

Amanda felt quietly thrilled by his compliment. She stared into her soup and swished the last few noodles around with her spoon. "Well, thanks. That's sweet. But if I tell Lauren you said that, she'll just say you don't know anything about clothes."

He shrugged. "I do like the way you dress, but I wasn't just talking about that." When Amanda didn't answer, he said, "Your playing was pretty intense today. I've heard you practice before, but I've never seen you like that."

Amanda laughed. "Yeah, sometimes I can really go into the zone. Did I scare you?"

"A little," he said with a grin. "I mean, the roof could have caved in, and I don't think you would have noticed."

"I probably would have . . . after a few minutes. But that's good. I need to be intense for this one."

He nodded. "You were. And you were fabulous," he added.

He was always so full of praise and encouragement. She didn't allow herself to believe half of it, but it still helped her tremendously, warming her right now as much as the soup.

"Feeling nervous?" he asked.

"Yeah, I am, but I'm trying to be more low-key than the last time. If I get it, that will be great. But if I don't, it's not the end of the world, right?"

He smiled and tilted his head to one side. "Well, you never know. If you'd gotten that job in Austin, you wouldn't be sitting here with me now, shivering in a drafty church social hall, eating soup and crackers."

"That's right. I would have missed out on all this glamour," she agreed in a very serious tone.

He started laughing, and she did, too. A little while later, she said, "I was just thinking of something you said about your artwork. That there was a plan for you. Maybe there's one for me, too. So I don't have to worry so much."

"I know there is, and I know you don't have to worry," he promised her. The jacket had slipped from her shoulders and he fixed it, resting his hand on her shoulder. Then he leaned forward and kissed her softly on the forehead.

He was so sweet to her and she cared for him so much. If she got this job in Portland, she would be leaving Cape Light. Leaving Gabriel, just as they were getting to know each other. Amanda couldn't even let herself think about that right now.

He leaned back and smiled, then started gathering up the trash. "Well, time to get back to work."

"Me, too." She helped him clear off the table and returned to the sanctuary. Amanda practiced for another hour, then packed up her cello. Gabriel was still working, high on a ladder, as she walked up the side aisle to the exit.

"Will you be here tomorrow?" he asked.

She nodded. "I think so. I got a lot done today."

"Good, I'm glad I didn't bother you. I'll be here, too. If that's all right."

"It's fine. No problem." *Better than fine,* she wanted to say. *I can hardly think of a better reason to come back to a cold, empty church to rehearse all day.* "My turn to get lunch tomororrow?"

He laughed. "That's a deal. See you then."

She waved to him. "See you," she called back.

As the days passed, Amanda and Gabriel developed a routine. She played while he worked on the windows. He would occasionally offer encouragement or even an opinion when she asked if he liked the sound of a few notes played one way or another.

They took a break for lunch together and sat and talked. Not just about her audition and his work, but about all kinds of things—their favorite foods and movies, their best and worst teachers, countries they wanted to see. As the audition loomed closer, she felt they were getting closer, too. She had never imagined she could tolerate anyone hanging around as she prepared for this important day. But Gabriel was different. His presence somehow drowned out the doubting voices that sometimes took up residence in her head. They were hard to hear over his words of encouragement and praise and the laughter she and Gabriel often shared. And even when the voices rose up after she had put her cello aside for the day, all she had to do was think of him. Picturing his warm smile and blue eyes gazing into her own was enough to silence the doubting voices completely.

Would she win this seat up in Portland? Amanda knew it was impossible to say. But she felt more confident and centered than she ever had before, and she believed that whatever happened, she would be at peace with it.

Lillian was sure she had never given permission for anyone to watch the television in the living room, but somehow that rule went by the wayside. The television upstairs was not yet connected to the cable, so, of course, the children weren't very interested in staying upstairs.

They didn't seem very interested in doing anything constructive. Not even playing outside and getting some fresh air, which she thought might tire them out.

When she came downstairs on Saturday morning, even though it was quite late, there they were, still in their pajamas, watching cartoons—and eating bowls of cereal in the living room.

The Christmas tree was surrounded by gifts covered in torn wrapping paper, falling out of their boxes, and brightly colored toys were underfoot everywhere. She had nearly slipped on a miniature race car the day before.

Lillian felt her blood pressure rising.

"No cereal in here. I've told you that before," she said sternly. She tapped her cane on the wooden floor to get their attention. "And pick up all these toys! They should all be upstairs. There's plenty of space up there. Do you want me to end up in the hospital—or worse?"

The children scurried. Jorge shut off the TV set, and Marta put the bowls and spoons on the coffee table, which made Lillian shudder with even greater horror. Milky spots on her genuine Duncan Phyfe burl pedestal . . . Oh, there was no mercy in this world. No mercy. She leaned over and snatched them up.

Bonita ran in from the kitchen to see what the commotion was about. Jorge spoke to her in rapid Spanish as he ran past with two glasses half full of juice.

They had juice in here, too? Lillian had to sit down when she saw that. She held the bowls in her lap.

Marta walked over and shyly patted her hand, then put a stuffed animal on the arm of her chair. Lillian could hardly tell what it was. A small white rabbit, perhaps, or maybe a polar bear.

"*¿Señora* Lillian? *¿Estás bien?*" Bonita leaned toward her and gently took the bowls away.

Lillian stared at her. "Speak English, please. I can't understand a word."

"She wants to know if you're okay." Jorge had returned and looked up at her. He had his mother's serious expression and fine dark eyes. "Should I call my mother? She's a nurse."

"Yes, I know your mother is a nurse," she snapped back. "I would be fine if anyone around here would pay me any mind. I have asked that you heed a few simple requests, and this is what I get." She looked around and tossed her hands in the air. "It's a complete disaster area in here, utter and complete."

Bonita put her arms around the children's shoulders, then ushered them from the room. Estrella came in just as they were walking out.

"Mrs. Elliot, I'm so sorry. I was taking care of Dr. Ezra, and I didn't realize the children were in here. I told them to go upstairs and get ready to go out with their *abuela*."

"Well, they did not obey you, obviously . . . and there's no eating in here. Or watching TV. I thought I'd made that perfectly clear." She pointed to the table with her cane. "Look at that . . . stains on the wood. How will I get that out? It has to be refinished."

Estrella took a closer look at the table. "I'll try with some lemon oil. If that doesn't work, I'll pay for the repair. Please don't worry."

Lillian stared straight ahead, breathing in and out heavily, trying to get her temper under control. "It's just the idea. No one is listening to me. It's fine that you're all here. But there has to be some order, some respect for my rules."

"I understand," Estrella said calmly. "It's hard with the children on vacation. I'll try to keep them upstairs," she promised.

Lillian felt uneasy about that, too. Stuck in those stuffy upstairs rooms, what sort of mischief would they concoct? One day they did stay upstairs to play. They made a big tent with sheets and flashlights. That would have been fine, but they had some sort of music player blasting so loud you could hear it all over the house.

"They should go outside, get some air. Walk to the library," she suggested. "Have they ever seen the exhibit in the historical center? That might keep them occupied for a while."

Estrella nodded. "Good idea. My mother will take them there today. They won't be underfoot, I promise."

Lillian let out a long sigh and heaved herself up. "I'd like some breakfast when you get a chance," she added over her shoulder. "A poached egg on toast would be nice. I'll be in Dr. Ezra's room. Please call me when it's ready."

"Yes, Mrs. Elliot. I will call you," Estrella said politely.

Estrella had started picking up the toys and other items scattered around the living room. Lillian wished she would simply throw it all out. Including that infernal tree. Christmas was over as far as she was concerned.

GABRIEL ASKED AMANDA IF SHE WANTED TO GO OUT ON SATURDAY night, but Amanda was busy with her family. It was Lauren's last night at home, and they were all going out to dinner.

Molly had told Amanda she could invite Gabriel to join them for the family dinner, but Amanda decided not to. As her audition drew closer, the reality that she might be hired and might soon move to Maine cast a shadow on their relationship. Well, it did in her mind. It was hard to tell what he was thinking.

They had gone out to the movies one night after her practice session at church. She had been a bit distracted, feeling nervous about the audition. But Gabriel seemed to understand. When they said good night, he asked her out for New Year's Eve. She had been secretly hoping he would and had been glad to accept. Then she realized that it might be difficult to spend that evening together if she knew she was moving away. New Year's Eve was supposed to be the start of things, not an ending.

It felt as if their relationship was just getting started, and if she did win the seat in Portland, it might be too fragile to survive such a big change.

Luckily, Lauren was still up, watching a movie and willing to talk things over. "It's not as if you'd be moving to California," she pointed out. "Portland is only two hours away. Besides, with texting and Skype, it's almost like a person is in the next room. We stay in touch pretty well, don't we?"

She and Lauren were in touch constantly. They had video chats and sent photos and texts over the phone, night and day.

Amanda sometimes even knew what Lauren was eating. But messaging like that with her sister seemed different somehow.

"You're not a guy. You're my sister."

"Duh."

"It's just different. And people usually do the long-distance thing when they've been going out a long time. Gabriel and I have only known each other a few weeks."

"You know him well enough to walk into walls every time you get back from a date. Don't deny it," Lauren added with a laugh. "That's what counts."

Lauren knew her too well. Amanda couldn't remember when she had felt this way about anyone. But it was all so . . . new, and she might be starting a new life in Portland. One that was very different from his life down here. She wasn't even sure if he would want to keep up their relationship if she moved. And she wasn't sure she could bear to ask.

THE CHOIR HAD THE SUNDAY AFTER CHRISTMAS OFF, BUT AMANDA had to attend the service; she played the piano and organ as the congregation sang hymns. The sanctuary was nearly empty, but Reverend Ben put the same spirit and heart into a service even if there was only one person in the pews. Gabriel was among the handful and waited for her afterward.

"You had to make do without the choir today. How come you don't get a day off, too?" he asked.

"I did have the day off. That was recorded music," she teased him. "I just sat up there to make it look good."

He grinned, surprised to be getting some of his own medicine. "Well . . . the big day approaches. Tomorrow, right? How do you feel?"

"Pretty good, though I do want to get in some more practicing today."

"Does that mean you can't go out for dinner tonight?" Before she could answer, he added, "No, I don't want to tempt you. You probably have to get up really early."

"I do," she said, though she really did want to spend time with him. "How about lunch? My treat," she offered. She glanced across the village green at the Main Street. "How do pancakes sound? With lots of cinnamon, of course."

"I'm always up for pancakes on Sunday morning. And there is a certain symmetry to it," he added. "That was our first date," he reminded her.

Of course she remembered. How could she ever forget? She had been thinking that, too.

As they headed toward the diner, he took her hand. "You seem so quiet. Are you worried?"

She shrugged. "A little. I did read that a certain amount of stress is good when you have to do something like this."

"Probably true," he said with a grin. "What time do you have to be there?"

"At eleven. But I'm planning to get up there by nine or nine thirty, so I have some time to unwind and warm up."

"Good idea. How long will they keep you?"

"It's hard to say. Probably about a half hour. It's not the length of time—it's the intensity . . ."

"That sounds tough."

"It will be. But worth it, I hope," she added. She suddenly wished he could come with her. No one besides the search committee could sit in on the audition. But she would feel better just knowing he was nearby.

He would probably come if she asked him, but she knew she couldn't do it.

"Don't worry. You'll do fine," he comforted her, misreading her silence. "By this time tomorrow, it will be all over," he reminded her. "Will they tell you right there?"

"I wish, but it's not likely. There are probably other candidates. But I don't think they'll wait too long. I have a feeling they need to fill the seat right away."

"Maybe we can get together when you get back," he said.

She turned to him, feeling the wind off the water pull at her hair. "I'm going to stay over with an old friend from college that night. She lives up there, and it will be fun to see her . . . but I'll call you and let you know how it goes."

"Good, call me right away. We're still on for New Year's Eve, right?" He glanced at her as if he wondered if she had forgotten his invitation.

"Of course. I'm looking forward to it."

"I am, too. I made reservations for dinner in Spoon Harbor. Just making sure." He smiled and put her hand to his lips a second. "Maybe you'll know by then, one way or the other," he added quietly.

"Maybe."

Though neither of them dared say it, Amanda felt she knew what he was thinking. That very soon, not only would she know about her own future, but about the future of their relationship, too.

Chapter Fourteen

On the day of her audition, Amanda woke at six, well before her alarm sounded. The trip to Portland usually took about two hours, but it was a Monday morning, and there might be traffic on the interstate, even at this time of year. She had to get on the road by seven if she wanted to leave herself a comfortable cushion of time. She hated to rush before an interview, especially if she had to perform.

When she came downstairs, her parents were already in the kitchen, drinking coffee. "I can drive you if you want," Molly offered. "That way you can relax and you won't be stressed from driving and trying to find the address and all that."

This was her umpteenth offer to chauffeur, and while Amanda was tempted, she really wanted to do this on her own.

"I'll be fine, Mom. Besides, I'm staying over at Melissa's tonight, remember?"

"Oh, right. I forgot. Well, make sure you call or text when you get there."

"And again when you're done," her father added. "We want to hear what happened right away."

"I'll call you as soon as I finish," she promised.

Amanda grabbed a travel mug of coffee and a muffin and yogurt for the car. She kissed them both good-bye and grabbed her portfolio of music.

"Here, let me help you with the cello," her father said.

She could have handled it on her own, but knew it made him feel better to do something for her.

Her parents looked cute, she thought, standing in the doorway, waving good-bye. They wore long bathrobes that matched. They matched, too, she thought. It was so nice to see how much they loved each other, even after all these years. Amanda hoped she could have a marriage like that someday. That would be as fine an accomplishment as any.

A few minutes later, she was driving along Beach Road, heading for the highway. Her iPod was plugged into the car stereo, playing some of the pieces she planned to perform, recorded by the real stars of classical music.

The traffic on the highway was very light for a Monday morning, due to the holidays, Amanda guessed. She arrived at the concert hall with time to spare, just as she had hoped. After letting a receptionist know she was there, she was given a key to a practice room where she could warm up. As she made her way to the practice room, she passed another musician, also carrying a cello, but on his way to the performance area. *My competition,* she realized. She forced a small smile, and the young man barely smiled back. He looked pale and distracted.

That's what I'm going to look like about an hour from now, she realized. She checked the time on her cell phone and found a text message from Lauren.

Break a leg. Or should I tell you a finger? Wait, don't break anything. But good luck. Hope you get it. Let me know ASAP. XO.

Lauren's message cheered her, and she sent a short note back. No message from Gabriel, she noticed. She suddenly wished she could hear his voice. Just for a second.

She played for a while, reviewing the toughest sections of her pieces. When she felt sufficiently loose and focused, she checked her phone again. Still no message from him. Then just as she was about to put the phone away, she saw a message and opened it.

A photo of a bare foot?

Good luck, Amanda. I know you don't need it. I know you'll knock their socks off.

She laughed and wrote him back quickly. Thanks for the laugh. I do feel a little nervous.

She was about to erase the admission, then left it. She could always be honest with him; he never judged her. P.S. Was that your foot?

He wrote back quickly. I know you must be nervous. It's only natural. Just pretend all the judges aren't there, and you're playing in the sanctuary. Yes, that was my foot. What's wrong with it?

She knew that he meant, pretend you're alone and no one is listening. But she suddenly realized she could do her best if she pretended that only Gabriel was listening. The insight immediately calmed her, and she felt a surprising burst of confidence. As if she suddenly had a secret weapon.

Good advice, thx, she wrote without telling him her real plan. Nothing wrong with the foot. Thought it might be a photo from a supermarket tabloid. Proof of Sasquatch?

Good one, he wrote back. Tell some jokes. It will get them in a good mood. Then he signed with a smiley face and a big XO.

Finally Amanda put the phone away. A second later, a sharp knock on the door told her it was showtime. She took a few deep, steadying breaths and headed for her audition.

*   *   *

SHE KNEW IT HAD TAKEN A HALF HOUR, OR MAYBE LONGER. BUT THE time went by in a blur. All she could remember was walking onstage with her instrument and sitting down. She had to enter through a stage door and had not seen the inside of the hall. It was quite stunning, with brand-new blond wood everywhere she looked and sleek black seating. The stage curtains were so high, she was embarrassed to tip her head back that far to see the top of them. Beautiful modular chandeliers dropped down from the ceiling, providing light over the rows of seats. The stage lights were on and the seating area dark. It took her eyes a few moments to adjust.

She saw three people seated in a row about midway back, one woman and two men. They introduced themselves. One was the orchestra's artistic director, but Amanda immediately forgot the names and titles of the others. They each had a copy of her résumé and asked questions about her studies and her different jobs.

Finally, she was asked to play. She announced the pieces she had chosen, and they selected two and told her the order they wanted to hear them in. As requested, she had brought along copies of the pieces so they could follow along—and see where she missed notes and made mistakes.

But she tried not to think of that. She started off the first piece with less conviction and expression than she had planned, and that threw her off a bit. But very soon she remembered to pretend that she was not in the huge, intimidating concert hall at all but back in the cozy sanctuary of the stone church on the green. Back in Cape Light, playing her heart out with only Gabriel listening, smiling warmly as she played, the music making his eyes even brighter. Looking at her sometimes as if she were the most amazing person in the entire world.

Finally it was over. Amanda felt as if she were coming out of a trance. The interview panel thanked her. She couldn't really tell if they had liked her performance or not. She knew she had tried her best and done a good job. And she tried to remember that beyond that, it was truly out of her control.

There's a plan for me, she reminded herself, *and if this job is meant to be, it's meant to be.*

AMANDA WAS BARRELING DOWN THE HIGHWAY, JUST THREE EXITS from Cape Light, when her cell phone rang. Lost in thoughts about her date tonight with Gabriel, she glanced at the screen quickly, hoping it was him. She felt a flicker of irritation as she saw the name Stephan Guillet. Who was Stephan Guillet? She didn't know anyone by that name.

And then she realized she did. That was the name of the artistic director of the Portland Orchestra!

Amanda's heart raced as she signaled and pulled off onto the shoulder of the highway. Because she knew that she couldn't possibly drive safely while taking this call, no matter which way the decision went.

"This is Amanda," she said, her voice shaking.

"Hello, Amanda. This is Stephan Guillet." The tone of his voice was cool, giving nothing away. "We were wondering if you would be willing to be our fourth-chair cello."

"Oh my God." Amanda breathed the words, a prayer of astonishment and gratitude.

"Is that a yes or a no?" he asked, sounding perplexed.

"It's a yes," Amanda told him, trying to keep from shouting with joy. "It is most definitely a yes!"

A SHORT TIME LATER, SHE STOOD IN FRONT OF HER MIRROR, GETTING ready for her New Year's Eve date with Gabriel. She glanced at the shimmery top Lauren had made her keep, then put on a pair of sparkling rhinestone earrings. But her mind wasn't on her outfit. All she could think about was that she would soon be telling Gabriel her good news. She had almost called him the second she hung up with Mr. Guillet, but she decided to wait and tell him in person. She had never been so happy and excited about anything in her life, and she just knew he would feel the exact same way. This would be a New Year's Eve to celebrate!

Gabriel came to the door, looking too handsome for words in a deep blue dress shirt, tweed jacket, and brand-new jeans.

He came in just a minute to wish her parents a happy New Year, and then they were off. They were going to a restaurant in Spoon Harbor that had a live band and a dance floor. Amanda was looking forward to dancing. She still had a lot of nervous energy to work out.

"You look pretty spectacular for a girl who just went through the wringer," he said.

"I feel pretty spectacular," she replied. She paused, not knowing if she should tell him her news yet. She had thought she might wait until dinner but she wasn't sure she could hold back that long.

He glanced at her, sensing something was up. "Did you hear anything yet?" he asked.

She nodded quickly. "I did . . . when I was driving back. The artistic director called and offered me the job. I was so excited when he called, I could barely see the road. I had to pull over. And then I just sat there in my car for, like, five minutes, yelling, 'Yes! I did it! I won a chair in a symphony orchestra!'"

"Amanda, that's fantastic! I knew you could do it," he said happily. "Why didn't you tell me sooner?"

"I was going to call you, right after he called me," she admitted. "But I wanted to tell you in person."

"So which pieces did you play for them?"

"They only wanted to hear two. That scared me. So I played the Mozart and the Vivaldi, the one you like."

He nodded. "I had a feeling. What did your parents say?"

"They're really happy for me—and so glad they didn't have to deal with another wailing and groaning scene."

"I bet they would have put up with you, but this news is much better. When do you start?"

That was the question she didn't want to answer. Her mood suddenly swung from high to low.

"I have to go back right away. They want me at rehearsals on Thursday."

"This Thursday? That's the day after tomorrow."

"Yeah." It did sound awfully soon when he said it that way. "I'm going to pack tomorrow morning and drive back up in the afternoon."

There would probably be no time to see him again before she left either, she realized.

"That sounds like professional baseball. When they call you out of Triple-A to the majors, you have to drop everything and go."

"I guess it is a lot like that." Amanda didn't know anything about baseball, but trusted his analogy.

"Will you stay in a hotel or something until you find an apartment?"

"My friend Melissa has an extra bedroom. She's been thinking of looking for a roommate to help with the rent but didn't want to deal with a stranger. So she offered me a place for as long as I need it."

"That's lucky. One less thing to worry about."

She nodded. That was true. There were a few things to figure out before Thursday, but the thing that worried her most was her relationship with Gabriel. Would they be able to keep things going long distance? Or should they just let it go? They had never really talked about their relationship—what it meant to them, or where they saw it going. It had been too soon for one of those conversations, Amanda realized. But now it seemed important to clarify things. Important but so hard to do. She had never been good at that sort of thing.

"It's nice that you have a good friend there, someone who can introduce you to people," Gabriel went on, his voice even. "It's hard to move to a new place not knowing anyone."

"I guess that is a plus. I didn't really think about it. I'll be working so hard to catch up—there will be reams of music to learn—I doubt I'll have much time for a social life."

"Well, sure, but you're definitely going to make some new friends up there. You'll get to know the people you work with and all that. It's going to be a whole new world for you, Amanda." He turned and smiled, but the expression didn't seem to reach his eyes.

Amanda felt her heart catch. She could sense that he was trying to tell her something, something that was hard for him to say.

They had reached the restaurant, and Gabriel found a parking space near the waterfront. They sat together in the truck's quiet cab, looking out at the dark water and night sky, dotted with tiny white points of light.

"Listen," he said, "I'm going to miss you like crazy. But I'm also glad you've got this amazing opportunity. I guess . . . I just wasn't expecting everything to change this fast."

"Neither was I," she admitted.

"But it is," he said quietly, "and that means we're going to change, too."

Amanda felt something like fear stirring inside her. She wanted to go to Portland and play in an orchestra, but she wasn't ready to lose what she had with Gabriel. That was never her plan.

He took her hand, his thumb stroking hers, as if to comfort her. "What I'm trying to say is, even though you won't be that far away in terms of distance, it's going to be a world away from this place. You lived in New York—you know what I mean."

Amanda nodded, struggling to find her voice. "I know. My life will be way different from the way it is here." When he called to offer her the job, Mr. Guillet had mentioned touring in Europe in the summer.

"That's what I mean. I think you're fantastic . . . and I care for you. I really do," Gabriel said quietly.

Amanda tensed. She could feel a "but" coming up.

"But I don't want to hold you back. You're going to meet new people—other musicians and artists. You're going to travel, have adventures. You have to get out there . . . and go for it. I don't want you to have any regrets, you know what I mean?"

Amanda pulled back and looked at him. She nodded "yes," but, in fact, she didn't understand this at all. He said he cared for her, but now it seemed he was trying to push her away. Maybe he didn't feel as much for her as she did for him.

Despite all his sweet gestures and encouragement, she realized Gabriel hadn't stepped up and told her he wanted to find a way to stay together. That's what suddenly hurt and made it so hard to admit that that was what she wanted to hear.

She swallowed hard, trying to dissolve the lump in her throat. "I appreciate you saying all this, Gabriel. You're right. Life will be different for me up there . . . But we'll still be in touch, won't we? And maybe you can come see me play sometime?"

Don't you want to be together? That's what she really meant.

She had pictured him sitting in one of the seats, in the beautiful big hall, his face among a sea of faces that would all fade away when she looked out at him. She had wanted to tell him how much his encouragement and support had helped her, how she had imagined playing for him at the audition, rather than the panel of three who sat judging her. And how she really believed that was why she won the seat she had so wanted.

"Absolutely. I'd love that." He reached for her hand again. "I want to be in touch, hear how you like Portland and how you're doing," he assured her. "I just don't want you to feel . . . obligated or something. I would never want to pressure you or make you unhappy, Amanda."

She wasn't sure what to say. It was suddenly all so confusing. A tiny part of her wondered if she would still feel the same way once she had been in Portland for a while. Was it possible that in separate places with very different lives, they would outgrow each other, lose all the things that made them feel so close now? But a larger part of her—her heart—honestly did want to be committed to him, even though it seemed much too early in their relationship for that.

But what she wanted wasn't the issue. It was what he didn't want. He would be down here on his own, and he clearly wanted to be free, maybe to date other women. That thought hurt, but she tried to be mature about it.

"Yes, I understand," she said as unemotionally as she could. He reached over and touched her cheek but didn't lean over and kiss her.

And she couldn't move toward him. It felt as if this conversation had put them at a great distance and was sending them on different paths.

"Okay, so we got all this heavy stuff out of the way." He turned and faced forward again. She could actually hear him sigh with relief. Then he smiled at her, a real smile this time. "Let's get out there and ring in the new. You have a lot to celebrate, Amanda. I'm going to do my best to help you."

He was back to his charming, playful, teasing self, and Amanda tried to lighten her own mood. Okay, so he wasn't into the big commitment. It was hardly the end of the world. He was still an incredibly cute guy, and she knew they could have a good time together.

She reached over and squeezed his hand. "I'm glad you're here, too," she said honestly.

They walked into the restaurant hand in hand. But she couldn't help wondering why it had to be like this. She was finally on her way, starting a job she had dreamed about and worked so hard for. But did she have to lose Gabriel in order to do that?

NEW YEAR'S DAY . . . ANOTHER FAUX HOLIDAY IN LILLIAN'S BOOK— more forced gaiety. She could not recall ever enjoying herself on this day. It was just a day to get through, a good day to take down the Christmas tree and put the holidays away. She yearned for January second, when life could officially get back to normal.

She had mentioned taking down the decorations to Estrella that morning and was glad to see she had started the task. Ezra had complained it was too soon. He liked to wait for what he called "Little Christmas," January sixth.

Little Christmas, Big Christmas. She'd had enough holidays of any proportion. Having these children underfoot had worn away what little patience she had.

She wandered into Ezra's room to see if he had woken from his nap. Emily was coming by later to wish them a happy New Year—and to take back a few presents she had bought for them that were not right. She found Ezra reading a book about President Lincoln that Dan and Emily had given him. He glanced up at her over his reading glasses.

"Oh, you're awake. Good. Emily is dropping by. To wish us a happy New Year."

"That's thoughtful . . . Where is everyone? It's so quiet out there. Jorge promised me a chess match," he added.

Ezra had proven a good teacher of chess, and Jorge an apt pupil. Ezra had created himself a new partner. Lillian knew how to play, but didn't really enjoy it. Now it was all her husband wanted to do in his spare time. No interest in Scrabble or gin rummy or even finishing a cross-word with her lately.

Well, she wasn't going to chase him. He would be begging to pass the time with her as soon as Estrella's children returned to school. Then they would see if she had any free time to amuse him.

"Jorge's gone out. Bonita took both children to town right after lunch. To the playground near the harbor."

That had been Lillian's suggestion. It took them about an hour to get ready, with much searching for gloves and hats and deciding which toys to bring. Lillian gritted her teeth just watching. But it was well worth the fuss. The boy had brought his new soccer ball, and the girl was rolling a toy stroller with a stuffed bear covered in dish towels, which she pretended were blankets. No harm in that, Lillian thought. As long as she brought them all back and they were bleached in the laundry.

"The playground? It must be ten below out there today. They'll freeze into ice statues. I hope they were well dressed," he added with concern.

"Don't be so dramatic. You've often told me how you skated across the harbor in this kind of weather when you were a boy. One would think you would appreciate a little peace and quiet. You were able to have a nice long nap, weren't you?"

"They never disturb my nap," he insisted.

"Well, they disturb mine," she snapped, then tried to compose herself. "Cold, fresh air is good for children, clears the lungs. They'll sleep well tonight, too. They go back to school tomorrow," she added in a cheerful tone. "Their vacation is over."

She could have danced a jig at that news, though the children had been walking around all morning with long faces.

"Yes, I know. It went so fast."

"Not for me." She picked up her cross-stitch piece and picked at the loose threads on the back.

"Yes. We know, Lillian. I appreciate your many sacrifices. Indeed I do."

She felt gratified for a moment . . . then eyed him narrowly.

Was he being sarcastic, after all she'd done for these strangers? Before she could get into it, the blessed silence in the house was shattered by a crashing sound, glass breaking . . . and a woman's cry.

"*¡Dulce María, madre de Dios!*" she heard Bonita shout.

The ruckus seemed to be coming from the entrance hall. Lillian stared at Ezra. He stared back.

"Go see what happened, Lily!" he urged her. "See if anyone is hurt. You know I can't run in there."

Pale with concern, he scuttled like a crab to the edge of his bed and grabbed for his crutches. Lillian turned on her cane and started toward the foyer as fast as she could.

"Bonita? What in heaven's name happened? I heard something fall . . ."

She saw the three of them not far from the front door, Bonita and her two grandchildren. Still wearing coats, gloves, and wool hats, the children's cheeks red from the cold weather. The boy and girl looked shocked and frightened, their eyes wide. Jorge stared at the white and black tiles on the floor, holding his soccer ball.

Bonita stood behind them. She murmured something, but Lillian didn't understand her. Then she covered her mouth with her hand.

On the tiles near the coat tree, Lillian found the casualty—her beautiful Tiffany-style lamp, the stained-glass shade shattered to colorful bits. It normally sat on the mail table, not far from the front door.

"Who did this?" Lillian asked, looking from one child to the other. She had her suspicions but wanted the guilty party to confess.

Bonita started talking in Spanish. Lillian could tell from her tone she was trying to explain and apologize.

Lillian put out her hand to silence her, then stared down at the children.

Marta blinked and started to cry. She turned her face into her grand-mother's jacket.

"Oh, it was you?" Lillian moved closer to the little girl.

Jorge stepped between them, still holding his ball. "No, I did it, Mrs. Elliot. It was an accident. We were playing. Marta tried to take my ball and I pulled it away from her . . . I don't know . . . we just bumped into the table. I bumped into it, I mean," he added quickly.

"So you're taking the blame? How noble. Sounds to me like it was a partnership." Lillian's voice rose on a sharp note. "How many times have I asked you not to play in here? Not to play in this house—except upstairs. How many times?" she practically screamed at him, leaning down, so that they were face-to-face. "See what you've done? It's broken, ruined . . . Are you happy now?"

"Lillian, please! Just stop. Leave the boy alone. You've made your point." Ezra had finally made his way to the front hall and hobbled closer on his crutches. "For goodness' sake, it's just a lamp. As long as no one's hurt, that's all that matters."

Before she could tell him that he had no right to dismiss her feelings this way, quick footsteps sounded on the stairs. Lillian saw Estrella coming down, her face an angry mask.

"Mrs. Elliot, you've said enough." Estrella stepped between Lillian and her son and put her arm around his shoulders, gently leading him to one side. "I am sorry this happened. But I'm sure the children didn't mean it to—"

"They didn't listen either when they had the chance," Lillian cut her off. "They don't listen to a word I say. You don't either. You're their mother. You have to control them. That boy should be punished, not coddled."

"It was an accident. They are only children," Estrella repeated tersely. "I'm very sorry. I take full blame. I will replace the lamp for you."

Lillian practically laughed. "You can't replace that lamp. It's an antique. An heirloom from my late husband's estate, Lilac Hall."

"Oh, Lily, come now. It's not nearly so valuable," Ezra argued.

"It certainly isn't now," Lillian retorted. "It's a pile of broken glass. It *was* quite valuable, museum quality," she told Estrella.

Estrella blinked and took a deep breath. "Well, it should have been in a museum, then. Not in a busy house, right next to the front door."

Lillian felt a thud in her chest as if someone had punched her. She had to stop and catch her breath.

"You see here, young lady. Don't you speak to me like that." There were spots before her eyes. She could hardly see straight.

"Lily, please. Let it go. The lamp is broken. There's nothing we can do," Ezra said.

Lillian turned to him. "I can think of something. Your guests have to go," she said simply. "I want them out. Tonight. I don't care where. I'll pay for a night in a motel if I have to. I have twisted myself in a knot to accommodate everyone. Everyone but myself. Now I want some say. I want my house back. Before any more damage is done."

Estrella said nothing, but her large brown eyes grew darker.

"Oh, Lillian, don't do that. It's not right. Where will they go tonight?" Ezra's voice was so weak and plaintive, it turned Lillian's stomach. She answered with a cold look, and he turned to Estrella. "Please, don't go. Not tonight. She doesn't mean it. Lillian, apologize . . . For my sake, please."

"Have you gone completely mad?" Lillian stared at him. "What do I have to apologize for? My house . . . torn, shredded, stained . . . shattered. I meant every word of what I said. Every word," she repeated emphatically.

Estrella met her glance, her lips sealed in a tight line. Lillian thought she was going to fire back some smart remark again, but instead she turned to Ezra, her expression softening.

"I'm sorry, Dr. Ezra. I, too, think it is time for us to go. Mrs. Elliot is right. This is not working out. We cannot stay where we're not welcome."

Her son was hugging her around the waist, his face hidden in her dress. "Mama, I'm so sorry. I didn't mean it."

"*Mijo*, don't cry. It's not your fault. Mama is not angry with you. Go upstairs now. It will be fine. You'll see," she promised in a soothing tone.

Jorge ran up the stairs as if a ghost were chasing him. Estrella turned to her mother, who stood nearby with Marta huddled against her side. Estrella said something in Spanish. The older woman nodded, then took the girl's hand and headed for the stairs as well. As she passed Lillian, Bonita looked up with a sad, sorry expression, shaking her head from side to side.

It was not a look of remorse or even sorrow at being chased out, Lillian realized. Instead, her glance had been pitying.

That old woman, homeless, with barely the clothes on her back, feels sorry for me? Has everyone gone mad? She stood in shock, watching Bonita slowly climb the staircase.

Estrella had disappeared a moment ago but now returned wearing rubber gloves. She carried a broom and dustpan and started picking up the shards of glass, one by one.

"No . . . no. Don't trouble yourself." Ezra took a few shaky steps toward her on his crutches. "Someone else will do that."

Lillian gave him a scalding look. *Who would that someone be? Does he possibly mean me?*

But before she could argue the point, the front door opened and Emily appeared. Everyone stared at her wordlessly.

Emily took in the broken lamp and the expression on her mother's face. "Oh, my. The Tiffany lamp . . . How did that happen?"

CHAPTER FIFTEEN

AMANDA HAD BEEN IN PORTLAND FOR THREE WEEKS BEFORE she had a weekend off and time enough to relax and forget about music for a while. She was starting to feel as if her cello had become attached to her body and often felt herself playing it in her sleep.

She had expected a real seat in a real orchestra to be demanding, but had never quite imagined the intensity and commitment required. She had been working 24/7 since she joined the orchestra, rehearsing with the string section and on her own and learning new music every spare minute.

So far, she was doing well, holding her own in the string section with far more experienced musicians, which was gratifying. But she also deeply appreciated the chance to get away from Portland for a few days—and away from her instrument.

She had been invited to go skiing this weekend with her roommate, Melissa, and a group of Melissa's friends. Amanda was tempted, but finally declined. She knew what she had to do and decided to go home instead.

She had told Melissa she needed to pick up a few more things at her parents' house. But there was another reason she had decided to return to Cape Light. One far more important than the white rocking chair in her bedroom or a few more sweaters. She wanted to see Gabriel. Face-to-face. Even if the conversation hurt her deeply, as she expected it would.

She had tried to keep their connection going with emails and clever texts. But his calls always seemed to find her at some inconvenient moment: rehearsing late, or dragged along by Melissa to meet friends for dinner or drinks at some noisy café.

"You sound busy. I'll catch you later," seemed to be Gabriel's favorite way of cutting their conversations short.

I'm not busy! I miss you. I really want to talk to you, Amanda wanted to shout back. But the moment never seemed right.

It had only been three weeks, she kept reminding herself. Maybe they would get better at this. But it just wasn't the same as it had been back in Cape Light. A certain spark was gone.

He had been trying to let her down easy on New Year's Eve, she realized now. He must have been hoping that her new job and new social scene would make her forget him. Or that she would just plain give up.

Had she only imagined the intense feelings that had seemed to be building between them just before she left? She really thought he felt the same. But maybe it had all been on her side. Maybe she had mistaken his natural charm and warmth for something more personal. Maybe she had just been a fling for him and now it was out of sight, out of mind. She had talked it over with Lauren, wondering what she should do.

"Maybe he's just not comfortable on the phone, or texting and all that," Lauren suggested.

"I don't know. I think it's something more than that," Amanda worried aloud.

"Well, there's no way to know unless you ask him. I know it's hard. But it's better to find out than to drive yourself crazy guessing. Because that's what you're doing now."

"And driving you crazy, too, right?"

"A little," Lauren admitted. "But it will be my turn soon to be nutty about something, and do the same to you."

Was she really nutty about Gabriel? *Well, yeah. I am,* Amanda realized.

"All right, I'll ask him," she promised. "But not over the phone. That would be horrible. I have time to go home this weekend. I'll do it then."

Lauren approved the plan, then made Amanda practice exactly what she would say. Then made her promise to call if she got cold feet once she got there.

Amanda appreciated the pep talk and support. Now her mind was set. She couldn't go on believing that there was something there if there wasn't. She was starting to feel like she was chasing him. And that was humiliating.

She still believed Gabriel was a good person. He wouldn't want to hurt her. He would tell her the truth—if she had the courage to ask him.

As she drove into the village and headed down Main Street, she passed the Clam Box and couldn't help but recall their first date—the snowball fight with his brother and pancakes for lunch. A bittersweet feeling overwhelmed her. She parked by the diner and tried his cell. It rang several times, and she finally left a message, forcing her voice into a calm, breezy tone that she didn't feel.

"Hey, Gabriel. Guess what? I came back for a visit this weekend. I don't have to go back to Portland until Monday. Would you like to get together for lunch? I'm right on Main Street," she added, looking around for his truck. She caught herself; that was so silly. No telling where he might be working right now.

She put her phone aside and started up her car again. She would just go home and wait for him to call back. He would call, wouldn't he? Amanda hated to feel so worried and insecure. At least her parents and little Betty would be happy she was home. That was some consolation.

She turned up a road that led out of the village toward her parents' house and found herself passing Gabriel's shop. She pulled up in front and looked around. The shop was dark and she didn't see his truck. The beautiful stained-glass sign was gone from the window, and instead a small paper sign read, FOR RENT, with a number listed below to call.

Amanda sat back in her seat, stunned. He had closed his shop? Why didn't he tell her? Had he moved out of town, too?

She wasn't sure what to do next. She didn't even know where he lived, she realized, or the names of any of his friends. She sat for a moment, then turned her car around and headed back to town. She would go to the church and ask Reverend Ben. He might know. And he would understand.

AMANDA WAS SOON PARKED IN FRONT OF THE CHURCH ON THE GREEN. She went through the front doors and headed for Reverend Ben's office. Then she heard the sound of someone in the sanctuary. She walked in and looked around. The lights were off and the space was cast in the amber, rose, and blue light diffused through the stained-glass windows.

Amanda heard sounds coming from the sacristy. "Reverend Ben?" she called. "It's me, Amanda."

Someone came out of the small room and stood by the door. She squinted, making sure her eyes weren't playing tricks on her. It wasn't Reverend Ben. It was Gabriel. He stared at her, then dropped one of the tools that he held in his hand.

"Amanda. What are you doing here?"

She felt so relieved to see him, but suddenly nervous, too. His truck must be parked behind the church, she realized. That's why she hadn't seen it.

"I came back for the weekend. I just called your cell. Didn't you get the message?"

"I heard it ring but couldn't check the number. I had my hands full." He walked toward her quickly, looking concerned. "Is everything okay? Is everything all right with the orchestra?"

"Everything's fine. I'm doing well. The director and conductor seem to like me."

"Good." He nodded but still wore a serious look.

"Are you still fixing these windows? What else can happen to them?" she tried to joke.

"Just taking care of one last little job. A piece I replaced came loose and a bird flew in last Sunday. The bird caused quite a stir," he added. "Digger Hegman jumped out of his seat, saying it was a sign from above. You should have been there."

"That does sound exciting," she said with a smile. "Sorry I missed it."

They fell back into their easy bantering so quickly. And he was looking at her with so much warmth in his eyes. Why couldn't he be like this over the phone and in emails? Was he just not an emailing or phoning sort of guy?

"I went by your shop," she said. "Are you closing down or something?"

"Not exactly." He glanced at her as he put a few tools back in his big canvas bag. "It's funny that you came home this weekend. I was planning to come up to Portland. To surprise you," he admitted.

"You were?" The news gave her some hope. Then she pulled back, thinking that maybe he just wanted to break it off with her face-to-face. That would be the decent thing to do.

He put his hand on her shoulder and led her out of the sanctuary. "Let's go outside and talk."

"All right."

Now that he was here, right beside her, she felt a flood of feelings. She was afraid of what he was thinking, and she wanted to say what was on her mind first. Maybe he thought she didn't care enough about him. She missed him terribly—but she was mad at him, too. She had to tell him everything. And do it before he started acting distant again or gave her some other reason to lose her courage.

They walked out onto the green and sat on a bench that faced the harbor. Gabriel turned to her, a serious expression on his handsome face. "I want to tell you why the shop is closed . . . I've decided to make some changes. Big changes. I'm moving my business, for one thing."

Big changes? She didn't like the sound of that. No wonder he had been so distant. He had been distracted by his new plans and hadn't confided in her. That didn't bode well.

"That is news," she cut in before he could go further. "And I want to hear all about it. But there's something I need to tell you first."

Now it was his turn to look surprised, and even worried. "Really? What is it? You met someone you like?"

She shook her head, hardly able to believe how wrong he could be. "There's no one in Portland, Gabriel. How could there be? I miss you so much, I can barely read my music. And when I do have free time, I'm thinking about you."

"That, I doubt—I've seen you in the zone, Amanda. Remember?"

Amanda didn't understand at first, then realized he was talking about her practice sessions in the sanctuary, how he had seen her block out everything but her music, playing so intensely and with so much focus.

"Don't interrupt me," she replied, taking a breath. "I need to say everything . . . I was stupid on New Year's Eve. I was upset, because it felt like you were pushing me away, but I tried to pretend it was okay, so you wouldn't know I was hurt. Maybe you thought I wanted my freedom. But what I really wanted was to know that going to Portland wouldn't mean losing you."

He seemed about to interrupt again and she gave him a look.

"I have made some new friends . . . and met some attractive men," she said honestly. "But I can't even remember what they look like. I don't want to start dating anyone new in Portland . . . or anywhere. I want to be with you. But you've been acting so cool and distant on the phone. I'm just so confused . . . What happened? Everything was so great between us . . . Can't it just be like it was?" she asked. "Even if you're making changes, maybe even moving away from here. It would be no distance at all if I knew . . . if I knew you loved me. The way I love you," she admitted.

Then she sat perfectly still, stunned by her own words. *What had she just said?* Amanda had practiced this encounter with Lauren. That last part was definitely *not* in the script. She had ruined everything . . . Now he would really feel as if she was desperate and totally chasing him.

Gabriel's eyes were wide and bright, suddenly brimming. Amanda thought he was about to cry. But she couldn't tell for sure what that meant. Until he suddenly slid right across the bench and pulled her close in a tight embrace.

"I love you, too, Music Girl," he whispered, pressing his face into her hair. "You're the best thing that's ever happened to me."

He hugged her close for a long moment and gave her a long, deep kiss. Then he leaned back and smiled at her.

"I never meant to hurt your feelings, Amanda. Or act all cool and distant," he added, echoing her words. "I just didn't want to hold you back from all the things you want to do. Whenever I called, you sounded busy, like you were getting on with your life. You told me your plans when we met. I just wanted to give you some space, to give you a chance to find your way up there. It wasn't the distance in miles. But it is a whole new world, and I didn't want you to feel held back because of me."

She had to be sure. "So you really weren't trying to push me away?"

"That's the last thing I ever wanted to do."

"And"—she hesitated, still uncertain—"you love me?"

"I love you," he said. "But what kind of love would it be if I didn't want you to be happy?"

"I am happy . . . now," she said, realizing that she was so happy she was actually crying. She wiped away the tears. "So, tell me about these big changes. I want to hear everything."

He smiled, his blue eyes looking even brighter. "Right after you left, Mayor Warwick brought me her mother's lamp to repair. Tiffany-style, a real antique. The shade was smashed to bits, and her mother was very upset. I started piecing it together, following some traditional designs I researched with that book you gave me for Christmas. I couldn't replicate the design exactly, but I did a pretty good job, and they were happy," he reported. "It gave me an idea about starting a new business, producing lamps and windows that were my own designs. And pitching more of my original work for public works and churches. Like those door panels I'm making for the community center in Essex."

"That's fantastic!" she said. "I treasure the piece you gave me. It's incredible. You have so much talent, Gabriel."

"I hope so," he said. "In any case, I should be able to get projects that are more challenging and creative. I spoke to a friend in Peabody, who has a bigger shop, set up for that sort of thing. I'm going to rent some space there and use some of his equipment. I probably won't make much money at first. But I have to take this chance. That's why I'm giving up the small shop, the one that was my father's. That part is hard," he admitted. "It really marks the end of something for me. But it marks a new beginning, too. And eventually, I'll go back to school to finish my degree."

"Wow. That is a lot of change. You're launching off in a whole new direction."

He shrugged and smiled. "I think it started with you, Amanda. You changed my life. Watching you pursue your goals, no matter what got in your way . . . Falling in love with you . . . Well, it made me look at my own life and my own plans. All the things I've put on hold, or maybe started to think I would never get to do."

"What about your family? Don't they still need your help?"

"I won't be around as much, but Peabody's only a half hour away. So they're all for it. My mother says it's time I stopped worrying about them and do what I need to do. She's found a teaching job, so it's perfect timing." His tone was quiet and sure. "It's been perfect timing meeting you. I can see that now. It's like the pieces of a window, a large design that you can't see when all the fragments are scattered. But little by little, it fits together perfectly."

Amanda had to smile. "All part of a plan, you mean?"

He nodded and smiled at her. "Exactly." Then his expression became more serious. "I'm not sure exactly how we'll work it out. The logistics, I mean. I know you perform most weekends, but maybe I can drive up and visit you anyway or you could come down this way on your days off. And eventually," he went on, smiling again, "we'll find a way to live in the same town." He kissed her again. "Hopefully, in the same house, as husband and wife."

"We'll find a way to make it work," Amanda promised, her arms wrapped tight around him. Gabriel had been right. God had a plan for both of them, one that had brought them together, and would keep them together, always. His design was better than any she could ever have imagined for herself.

IT WAS PRACTICALLY EIGHT WEEKS TO THE DAY; EZRA'S CASTS ON HIS arm and leg were finally removed. Dr. Newton gave him a clean bill of health and a prescription for physical therapy. It should have been a time for celebration around Lillian and Ezra's house or, at least, a sip of sherry. It was Friday afternoon, the start of the weekend, after all. But Ezra was still in a blue mood, still angry with her about the way she had dismissed Estrella and her family.

Lillian thought he would have gotten over it by now. For goodness' sake, the family had left on New Year's Day and here it was, more than three weeks later, and he was still walking around with his chin dragging on the ground. Lillian was losing her patience but, of course, couldn't say a thing. She was the villain in this piece. Never mind that those children had ripped her house apart. It was really so unfair. He couldn't see it that way. And no one would take her side in this, especially not Emily, who had tried to play the peacemaker but finally gave up and drove the Salazars to a motel.

Emily had saved the pieces of the lamp and brought it all to a young man in town, a glass artisan. Lillian didn't even know such people still existed. The beautiful glass shade would never be the same, but he had done some careful, creative work, following the original design. The lamp had lost all its worth, no question, but it sat once again in its post by the front door, like a wounded soldier of some unnamed war.

If only the rest of her life could fall back in order so easily. Mrs. Fallon was still needed by Holly and her grandchildren. No salvation from that front. The aides from some agency had been coming and going since Estrella had left. Ezra required less and less help, which was fortunate, considering that they were a parade of simpletons. But she held her tongue. Ezra didn't need any more commotion to slow down his recovery.

Though his body had healed, his spirit seemed depleted. Nothing she did or said would distract him or shake him from this low mood.

ON SATURDAY NIGHT, LILLIAN AND EZRA WENT OUT FOR A BITE TO eat at the Spoon Harbor Inn. The place had a somewhat formal atmosphere, which she preferred. She had held Jessica's wedding here. It was a place that still took dining and service seriously.

"How is your bisque?" she asked Ezra, hoping to spark some conversation.

He looked up from his soup and nodded. "Passable," he said. Then he added, "I'd like to go to church tomorrow, now that I can walk in on my own two feet again."

A good sign, she thought. *He's finally coming around.*

"Good idea," she said. "It's been a while. Reverend Ben might not recognize us."

"No chance of that. I've been attending for almost ninety years," he said, dismissing her small attempt at humor.

True enough. She had been a member over fifty years herself, and Ezra had attended since he was a boy. "Who do you think holds the record as longest-running member of the congregation? It's either you or Sophie Potter . . . or maybe Digger Hegman."

Ezra started to take another spoonful of soup then pushed the bowl away. "I don't know. What difference does it make?"

Lillian sat back. He used to enjoy working out these little queries with her. What difference did anything make? One could stamp that attitude universally. It would make for quite a boring existence.

Maybe the church service would snap him out of this, get him back to his good-natured self. They had not been to church since his calamitous fall, not even on Christmas. The weather was too cold and the walkways much too icy to chance it. Although Estrella and her family had attended the church on the green, on Ezra's suggestion. Lillian thought Estrella might have even sought some assistance there after the storm.

Lillian had a sudden, anxious moment, wondering if she and Ezra would run into the Salazars on Sunday. But she brushed that aside. Most likely, they had left the area. Maybe they had gone to that relative in Andover or been set up in some emergency housing somewhere. Emily might be able to find out, though Lillian quickly decided not to ask her. Best not to stir up this pot again. It had hardly settled.

Estrella was an able and resilient person, no question about that. But she wouldn't start attending our church, Lillian decided. She was much too proud . . . *A little like me,* she realized.

EMILY PICKED UP LILLIAN AND EZRA RIGHT ON TIME ON SUNDAY morning. Lillian fussed over Ezra as they headed out. "It's quite cold, please wear your muffler," she said, holding it out to him.

"I'm fine, Lillian. That one irritates my skin."

"It's silk on this side. How can that scratch?"

"Let's just go, please. I hate to be late."

At least there was one thing they still agreed on.

The ride to church was blessedly brief. Lillian was glad of that. Dan dropped them off in the front of the church. and they proceeded slowly but surely to the big wooden doors.

Everyone made a fuss over Ezra from the moment he hobbled into the sanctuary. Their son-in-law Sam found them seats, front and center, in the pew she preferred. The new music director was playing the prelude, and many people came up to them to welcome Ezra back. Later in the service, during "Joys and Concerns," Reverend Ben put Ezra in the spotlight again. "I'm sure that we're all very pleased to see Dr. Elliot back with us, after his long recuperation."

Ezra stood up in his seat and waved while everyone applauded. She had not received such a warm ovation after her illnesses, she realized. But still, this was a good thing for both of them. He did glow under all the attention. She hoped this spurt of good cheer would carry through at home and wasn't just for the cameras.

There was a moment when Ezra's expression turned dark again. Tucker Tulley asked for prayers for families displaced from the flood and storm damage. He was a police officer and saw all sorts of unpleasantness.

"It's a little over a month now since the storm, and families are still hurting. It's going to take a long time for many people to come back from this. I hope that we continue to keep the storm victims in our prayers and continue to reach out to help them."

Of course, all Lillian could think of was Estrella's family. She glanced at Ezra and knew he was thinking of them, too. What could they do about it now? God didn't expect you to work miracles. That was His bailiwick.

The chorus led them in a hymn, distracting Lillian from thoughts of Estrella. She liked being among people, she realized, for a limited period of time. As long as she didn't really have to speak to them. A church service was just right, she thought.

When the service ended, they followed Emily down the crowded center aisle and waited their turn to greet the minister.

"Ezra, Lillian, how good to see you both." The reverend gave Ezra a hearty handshake. "It's great to have you back. When did you get your casts off?"

"On Friday. My leg is a little weak," Ezra admitted. "I have to use this cane awhile and have some physical therapy, but I should be tip-top by the spring."

"Oh, much sooner than that, I expect," Lillian said encouragingly.

"Well, it must have been hard to be housebound so long. I'm sorry I didn't get to visit more often." Reverend Ben had come to see them once or twice. It had been a respectful, though not overwhelming, amount of concern, she thought.

"That's all right, Reverend. I appreciate the thought," Ezra said. "I had plenty of attention and good care," he added. Lillian lifted her chin, expecting her husband was about to praise her. "We hired a nurse, live-in. A lovely young woman," Ezra continued. "Estrella was her name.

I think she's come here to church a few times over the holidays, with her children. Maybe you met her?"

"Estrella? . . . No, I don't think so. So many families have visited since the storm and come for services during the holidays. We welcome them all, of course. But it's hard to get everyone's name."

"Yes, of course. How could you possibly remember everyone?"

Lillian gave her husband a sharp look and tugged on his arm. "We are thankfully free of nurses and aides in our house right now. And very grateful for Ezra's recovery."

Ezra seemed about to say more, but instead quickly bid Reverend Ben a good day and allowed himself to be led out of the church and back to Emily's car.

He sat in the back on their way home, staring out the window and barely saying a word. Once they were home and alone again, his dismal mood continued.

Emily had brought them lunch, and Lillian served it. "Would you like some salad dressing? I think it's French," she said, peering into the container.

"Oh, I don't care," he answered.

She sat at the table across from him and finally couldn't hold her tongue any longer. "Ezra, enough of this moping. I thought getting out to church would snap you out of this infernal blue mood. It did seem to, for a few minutes there," she reminded him. "But here we are, and you're more miserable looking than ever. Life is short. Is there any sense in fretting over things we can't control?"

"That's just the trouble, Lillian. We did have control. You did. And you did the wrong thing. I've tried to let this go, but I just can't. Especially when you can't even admit that you made such a gross error in judgment."

Lillian sat back as if slapped across the face. "Is that really what you think?"

He nodded slowly. "I'm sorry. It is. I have loved you truly, through all your missteps and battles, real and imagined. I have always done my utmost to understand you. But this is something I just can't accept."

Did he really mean that? Or was he just talking out of anger? Lillian feared it was the former, his voice was so cold and even. "Ezra . . . please. Everyone has their faults. Nobody is perfect."

"I've never expected perfection, Lillian. You know that. But other times when you've lost your way, you always seem to come back. This time, you've . . . disappointed me," he said sadly.

Lillian sat silently. That was the most hurtful thing Ezra had ever said to her. And she couldn't think of any way to argue it.

Ezra stood up. "I think I'll take a rest. In my room."

"What about lunch? You haven't even touched your salad. Aren't you hungry?"

He shook his head. "Not at all. I'm just tired. I'm not used to being out and about, I guess."

"Yes, I suppose that's it. Have a nap. You'll feel better."

As he stalked off, she truly doubted he would wake up feeling any differently than he did now. This was a penance she had not expected. Ezra, so disappointed in her. Her ever-accepting helpmate, her closest friend and ally, who had loved her from afar for decades and was, by his own admission, the happiest man on earth the day they finally married.

Ezra, who had always forgiven and ignored her many flaws and idiosyncrasies. Enjoyed them, even, at times, it seemed. Ezra was disappointed in her. He was disaffected from her. A breach had opened between them that she could not negotiate.

This was serious. Very, very serious indeed. Her first thought was to call Reverend Ben and ask if he could perhaps speak to Ezra. Wasn't it divine to forgive? Wouldn't the minister remind him of that?

But she quickly pulled back from that idea. Airing their dirty laundry, even to the minister, was a last resort in her book. Perhaps if she was able to find out what had happened to the Salazars and Ezra was reassured that they were settled someplace and happy, it would help him see that—however the situation had come about—it was finally the best outcome for everyone.

And if they were not happily settled . . . well, she wouldn't tell him what she had found out. But she would find some way to send them assistance. She did feel a twinge of conscience now. Maybe it had started with that prayer request from Tucker Tulley in church. Or maybe a little sooner than that. However it had happened, it seemed to be growing by the hour.

Estrella had received her pay in full, of course, and even extra, which was Emily's doing. But Lillian hadn't argued. That should have helped some, Lillian reasoned. But it cost a lot to house and feed four people . . . and perhaps Estrella had not found a new job yet.

It could be a very bleak situation, Lillian realized, once she allowed herself to really think about it. Now she knew she really must find out what had happened to them.

As she considered the question, it seemed obvious that Emily was the one for this assignment, though her daughter might argue that this was not the best use of her time and authority. But perhaps she would do it for Ezra's sake.

Sometimes I think my own children like him better than they like me, she thought as she carefully cleared away the lunch dishes. *In fact, I know they do.*

As Lillian had expected, Emily argued at first. "Mother, it's really not right for me to go hunting through public records. I'm not even sure I can find them."

"You won't know unless you try. With all the computers and things these days, I'm sure it won't take that long if you ask the right person.

You're the mayor. Doesn't that count for anything? You certainly act as if it does when you're around me."

Emily didn't answer. Lillian heard papers shuffling and someone asking her a question, and then another phone rang. "All right. I'll see what I can do. But if they've left the county, I'll have no way of knowing. This is Village Hall, not the FBI."

"Believe me, I've noticed."

Lillian hung up the phone, satisfied to get the ball rolling. Well, she had done what she could do. It was in God's hands now. But it never hurt to remind Him.

Alone in her room, she shut the door and said a brief prayer. "God, if you have any interest in this situation, it would be very helpful if you could help bring this information to light . . . I suppose that losing my temper and telling that family to go was not my shining hour," she admitted. "I am trying to make some amends. Not just so that Ezra is nice to me again. For the right reasons . . . I think. But I could use some help. Please?" She sighed and added, "Amen."

Her daughter did not report back until Tuesday, despite Lillian's many prods and reminders. And it was difficult to call her without Ezra overhearing. Lillian had to wait until he took a nap or was in the shower.

"So, have you found out anything at all about them yet? I don't see why it should take this long."

"I did find out something, Mother. I was just about to call." Lillian sat down, taking in the news. Estrella and her family were living in a motel room provided by a storm assistance program. Estrella had taken a job there, cleaning. Bonita was working, too.

Bonita was cleaning rooms at a motel? She had to be in her late sixties. That was no work for a woman her age. And Estrella, a highly trained nurse . . .

". . . At least the children are still in the same schools," Emily continued. "That's probably why she didn't go farther. Or maybe they didn't find anything else yet. She's probably waiting to find a better job so she can afford a real apartment. There's no cooking in those rooms. It's rather basic."

Lillian's mouth felt dry. She forced herself to say, "I'd like the address if you have it."

"Why is that?"

"I want to send her something. Anonymously," she added hastily.

"Really? Are you having second thoughts about what you did?"

Lillian bristled but couldn't deny it. But she wouldn't admit it either. It was quite rude of Emily to ask so bluntly, Lillian thought. She had taught her better manners than that.

"I am not obliged to explain myself to you. 'Judge not, that ye be not judged.'"

"I wasn't judging you, Mother. Just wondering."

Lillian didn't believe that. "The address, please. You must have it."

Emily read it off, and Lillian wrote it down quickly. She heard Ezra coming and had to hurry. "Thank you for your help. I have to go. Ezra needs me."

Before Emily could reply, she hung up the phone.

IT TOOK HER ALL DAY AND NIGHT TO DECIDE WHAT TO DO. EVEN EZRA noticed she was distracted. "Didn't you hear me, Lillian? I asked if you would hand me the remote."

They were watching TV after dinner, a news show. Lillian had no idea what it was about, though several well-spoken experts were engaged in a heated debate.

"Here you are," she said, giving him the remote. "I must have dozed off."

"Do you feel all right? You don't seem yourself," he noted.

My, my, now the pot is calling the kettle black, is it? she nearly replied. But she held back, seeing her opening. "I do feel a bit off . . . I might be coming down with a little something. I was thinking of seeing Dr. Harding tomorrow morning."

"Tomorrow morning? The physical therapist is coming. I won't be able to go with you."

"That's all right. I can manage. Maybe Emily will take me."

Ezra glanced at her. "Well, all right. If you think you'll be okay on your own."

He went back to his program. That was easy. She could be robbing a bank for all he'd notice, or care.

LILLIAN LEFT THE HOUSE THE NEXT DAY JUST AS EZRA'S THERAPIST arrived. She had called a taxi, claiming Emily was busy in a meeting. "Don't wait for me to have lunch. I may need to stop at the bank as well," she told Ezra.

"All right. Be careful walking," he reminded her.

They were so infrequently parted that even though he was angry with her, she could tell he still felt a certain loss. As if part of himself was going off in a different direction for the day. She felt the same as she walked slowly to the taxi that waited near the back door. But this had to be done if they were ever to be reunited as before.

The motel complex was not far, just outside of town, near the highway, and as worn and depressing looking as Lillian had expected. Maybe even more so. It was a cloudy day, and that made the place look even worse. The taxi pulled up in front of a sign that read, OFFICE. Lillian told the driver to wait.

She got out and peered through a glass door. There was a desk but no one behind it. How would she ever find Estrella? Knock on every door?

Well, I will if I have to, she decided. She suddenly felt as if her life depended on this. Her life with Ezra did.

She wasn't quite sure when she heard the rattling sound coming toward her. Then she saw a cleaning cart being pulled out of a nearby door. Estrella was pulling it, and Bonita, pulling an identical cart, was not far behind.

What luck, she thought. *Maybe God heard my prayer after all.*

Lillian stepped toward them. "Estrella, I've come to see you."

Estrella looked up, her expression shocked. "Mrs. Elliot? What is it? Is Dr. Ezra all right?"

"He's fine. Fit as a fiddle . . . well, physically at least. He's not himself, though. Not really."

He's very unhappy. Still mad at me for the way I treated you, she could have said. But she was not prone to baring her heart that way.

"I know I have no right to ask, all things considered. But is there someplace we can talk? It won't take long."

Bonita had been silent but now spoke to her daughter. She looked quite upset, Lillian thought, and was probably telling Estrella she shouldn't give Lillian the time of day.

Estrella reached out and calmed her mother, then turned back to Lillian. "We can go into our room for a few minutes. My mother will take a break in the office."

Bonita headed for the office, glancing back over her shoulder and shaking her head, muttering something Lillian was glad she didn't understand.

Estrella took a key from her back pocket and opened a nearby door.

The room was narrow and dark with two large beds, neatly made up, and two long, low dressers against a wall. There hardly seemed any space to walk. A small closet near the doorway was bursting with clothing. One corner of the room was piled high with suitcases and big black trash bags—full of their belongings, Lillian suspected. She glanced into the bathroom as she walked by. Clean and neat as a pin, but with cardboard cartons in the bathtub, some of the Christmas toys sticking out of the top. It was clearly a challenge to keep all their belongings in such a small space, but she could see that they tried to keep it orderly.

Lillian took a seat on the edge of the first bed and leaned on her cane. Estrella remained standing, staring down at her.

"What is it, Mrs. Elliot? I don't have much time. If you've come to offer us money, please don't bother. I won't take anything from you."

Lillian was shocked by that response. She felt the wind blow out of her sails. She had, in fact, stopped at the bank and had a sum to offer Estrella.

"Well, I did want to offer my assistance," she admitted. "But more than that, I've come to"—apologize was not a word she could say easily—"to make amends. For my behavior. Perhaps I shouldn't have reacted as I did when your son broke the lamp."

"*Perhaps* not," Estrella replied. She folded her arms over her chest, her dark eyes narrow. Lillian couldn't quite tell if she was being sarcastic. Well, probably. *But perhaps I deserve it.* "Is that it? Is that what you came to say?" Estrella's expression was questioning, and Lillian could tell she was quickly losing her patience.

"I . . . I have no explanation, really," Lillian faltered. "Except that I'm an old woman, set in my ways. I've had to fight much of my life for my own sense of . . . security in this world. You may not think that," she added, seeing Estrella's doubtful look. "But it is true. And with Ezra sick . . . well, it's hard to get old. And to feel your life is . . . out of your control."

"We all feel afraid at times," Estrella said quietly.

Lillian felt relieved at this small sign of understanding.

"Well, I used to be braver when I was young. Like you," she added in a matter-of-fact tone. "But I'm not that strong anymore. I am weak and somewhat . . . rigid, and I give in to those traits far too easily. I did that night, and I lashed out at your family. Maybe someone else . . . like my husband . . . would have been more forbearing and patient. But those virtues have never been my strong suit. I can see now that my outburst has caused your family much more distress and discomfort than I ever expected. Living here, all cramped together in one small room . . ." Lillian couldn't but help glance around, acknowledging the bleak situation.

"It's been hard. But at least we have this space. And we are due to get a good apartment at the end of the month. We had to wait so that the children could stay in their schools. With so many other changes, it's important for them to keep their teachers and friends."

"That's what my daughter Emily thought. That's how I found you. I asked her . . . You see, the thing is, I . . . I really can't rest easy with this on my mind. Ezra is very unhappy. But he doesn't even know I've come here," she admitted. "It doesn't always come easily to me, but I do try to do the right thing. Finally."

What she did not tell Estrella was that she feared Ezra would never forgive her, that this estrangement would never be repaired. She knew Ezra would never leave her. Only death would part them. But she truly feared the rest of their days would pass in this malaise of disaffection. Only one thing could redeem her. And it all depended on what the young woman in front of her would say.

Estrella leaned back, her lips pursed. "Dr. Elliot, he's very kind. I thought he sent you."

"No, it's all my doing. He doesn't know what I'm up to . . . but if he were here with me now, I know what he would do."

Estrella looked at her curiously. "And what is that?"

"He would ask that you and your family come back and stay with us again. For as long as you need to. He would not just ask—he would insist on it. Will you please at least consider it?" she said quickly, sensing the young woman was about to refuse. "Now that I've come . . . I don't know that I can face him, knowing you remain here."

Estrella sighed and sat on the other bed. Facing Lillian, she leaned closer. "Mrs. Elliot, is that what you want, too? Truly? Because my children cannot go through another scene like the last one."

Lillian nodded. She felt her throat tighten as she realized how awful she must have seemed to them. "They're probably terrified of me now . . . But I will be better, I promise. I can be nice, if I put my mind to it. You'd be surprised."

She had stated that in all seriousness, but noticed that Estrella was trying hard to hide a smile. There was hope, then.

"I'll send a taxi here for you anytime you like," Lillian offered. "Two taxis might be necessary, with all your belongings . . . Think it over," she suggested, hoping time would help her case. "You don't have to tell me now."

Estrella sat quietly for a long moment. Then she lightly touched Lillian's hand. "All right, Mrs. Elliot . . . We will come. We'll come tonight, after the children return from school."

Lillian felt so happy she wanted to do a cartwheel.

She stood up and tapped her cane on the floor. Then she turned to Estrella and bowed her head. "Thank you. From the bottom of my heart."

WHEN LILLIAN ARRIVED HOME, SHE FOUND EZRA IN THE KITCHEN eating a sandwich and reading the newspaper. He barely glanced up at her. "Oh, there you are. I didn't know when you'd be back, so I made myself lunch."

"That's all right. I'll fix myself something later. I'm not very hungry right now. How was your physical therapy?"

Ezra shrugged and turned a page of the paper. "Not much to report. The usual drill. Some exercises and whatnot . . . How was the doctor?"

"The doctor is fine," she quipped. "But he thinks I have a little virus or something. I'm going upstairs to lie down awhile. My adventure seems to have tired me out." She meant that part sincerely.

Ezra glanced at her again and nodded. He didn't suspect anything was amiss, she realized. Which was just as well. She had considered confessing all when she came in but now was glad that she had held back. It would be very hard for her to admit how she had sought out Estrella and apologized. No, she had done her part and was too tired for any more soul-baring today.

Cloistered in her room, Lillian made some phone calls to complete her plans. Her daughter Jessica was only too happy to offer the assistance of Sam and their sons to help the family move. Sam would take all their belongings in his truck, and the family would come back in a taxi. Jessica said she would call Estrella to iron out the details.

Nothing left to do after that but wait. Lillian decided to take a nap. She had not been sleeping well lately and had chalked it up to any number of reasons, mostly the holidays upsetting her routine and digestion. But it was the situation with the Salazars; she knew that now.

She put her head down on the pillow and closed her eyes and, for the first time in weeks, fell into a deep, sweet sleep, imagining the look on Ezra's face when his "star" arrived.

"LILLIAN, ARE YOU ALL RIGHT UP THERE?" EZRA WAS CALLING ON THE monitor, waking her up. The room was dark. She had no idea how long she had been sleeping and picked up her clock in a panic.

Four o'clock already? They would be here soon. She had to go downstairs. "I'm fine, Ezra. I'll be right down," she told him through the monitor. While she partly despised the contraption, it did come in handy. She flicked on the lamp and went to her dressing table, tidying up her hair and putting her cardigan back on. A dash of lipstick would not hurt either, she decided.

Then she headed to the stairs, where she found Ezra waiting for her in the foyer. He stared up the staircase at her as she carefully made her way down. "Are you sick? Do you have a fever?" he asked.

More puzzled than concerned, she thought. But it was something.

"I must have been overtired. I'm much better now," she promised, hardly able to hide a note of mirth in her voice.

He stared at her, looking even more puzzled, and was about to say something, she thought, when a knock sounded on the door.

He looked at the door. "Are you expecting anyone?"

She shrugged. "It could be Emily, I suppose. But she usually uses her key . . . You could answer it and find out who's there," she suggested.

"Yes, I suppose I could," he replied tartly.

The knock sounded again, and his expression turned impatient. "I'm coming. Hold your horses." He moved quickly to the door and pulled it open.

Lillian remained at the bottom of the stairs, her breath catching in her throat. She could not see Ezra's face, but the set of his shoulders and the way he stepped back telegraphed his complete astonishment.

"Dr. Ezra, *hola*!" Estrella stood in the doorway, a child on each side and Bonita peering over her shoulder.

"Estrella . . . *hola*." Ezra's voice quickly faded. He looked back at Lillian. "Look who's here," he said weakly.

"Yes, I know, Ezra. Let our guests inside, will you please? It's quite rude to keep them standing out there. Come in, come in . . ." Lillian walked forward, trying to welcome them. "Did Sam get all your things?"

Estrella nodded. "Yes. He and his boys took care of everything for us. They will be here soon."

"Sam took your things . . . back here?" Ezra stared at Estrella and then at Lillian.

She knew the jig was up. She had to explain to him, but it was so hard to do. Though she should get some credit for this.

"Dr. Ezra, Mrs. Elliot has been kind enough to invite us back. To stay with you until we can move into our new apartment."

"Mrs. Elliot invited you? Oh . . . I see." He looked over at Lillian. "So those long naps, you were making phone calls?"

"Not all the time. I did need some extra sleep." Lillian shrugged.

Bonita and the children had come in, and she was helping them take their coats off. They had knapsacks and two small suitcases, and Jorge had his soccer ball. Lillian practically winced at the sight, but restrained herself.

As if reading her mind, Estrella said, "Mama, please bring the children upstairs. They can start their homework. Mr. Morgan will be here soon, and we'll unpack."

"Thank you, Estrella. Good idea," Lillian agreed.

"Well, I'm delighted to see you all, no question," Ezra said to Estrella. "But I'd still like to understand how this all came about."

Lillian felt it was her place to answer. "Emily helped me find them. I visited this morning and . . . we talked things over."

"You apologized, you mean?" Ezra said, catching her eye.

"In a manner of speaking, I suppose I did," she finally admitted. "Estrella was . . . very gracious," she added, glancing at the younger woman. Lillian folded her arms over her chest. If he thought he was going to get any more mealymouthed admissions from her, he was mistaken.

They heard another knock, and Lillian saw Sam's truck parked in front of the house. "Here's Sam with your things," she announced, opening the door and glad of the chance to change the subject.

"Well, hello, everyone." Sam was cheerful, as ever. "Shall we bring this all upstairs?"

"That's right. Please wipe your feet," Lillian added to Sam and her two grandsons, who traipsed in carrying boxes and big black plastic bags.

"I will go up and help them," Estrella said. She smiled at Lillian and then Ezra. "Then I will help you with dinner, Mrs. Elliot."

"Oh, you take your time. We can manage." Ezra smiled back, practically beaming. When he looked back at Lillian, they were alone in the foyer. He took a deep breath and shook his head. "Lillian . . . my head is spinning. I don't know what to say."

Lillian shrugged. "What is there to say? They've come back. You should be happy."

"I am happy. But you tricked me."

"I know. But it seemed necessary. I didn't want you to be disappointed if they wouldn't return."

"I see. But why did you do it? For me? Because I was angry with you?"

Lillian considered his question. "I thought that was why I was doing it. At first. But when I saw her, I knew that wasn't the entire reason. And the place they were living . . . all four of them in a dreadful little motel room. Well, I am not perfect, Ezra, God knows, but I do know when I take a misstep. This one was . . . well, a doozy, as they say. I suppose I needed to do the right thing. Or, at least, to know I tried."

Ezra listened, his head bowed a bit. He slowly nodded, then reached for her hand. Lillian was so moved by the small gesture, she felt as if she might cry. "You did well, Lily." He had not called her that for weeks now, she realized. "I must say, I'm proud of you. You've reminded me why I love you."

Lillian lifted her chin, her vision blurred by sudden tears.

"I will admit, that's what I hoped you would say." She squeezed his hand a moment. "And now I don't believe we need to speak of this dismal chapter anymore," she added quickly. "Let's carry on, as we do. Another year together, God willing."

Ezra agreed with a nod of his head and a familiar light in his eyes. All things considered, that was enough for her.